Where Liberty Lies

Nathaniel M Wrey

Published in 2023 by Waterman Books

ISBN Paperback: 978-1-9163705-6-2

Ebook: 978-1-9163705-7-9

A CIP catalogue copy of this book can be found in the British Library.

Cover designed by MiblArt.

Map illustration by Juliet Percival Copyright. © Juliet Percival 2023.

WHERE LIBERTY LIES

The truth is everyone lies

Acknowledgements

This book could not have been written without the support and input of the following people, to whom I extend my sincere gratitude: Mary Whinder, Jessica Hollands, Dominic O'Donnell, Delphine Gatehouse (Daniel Goldsmith Associates), Lee Dickinson (line editor at bookediting.co.uk), map artist Juliet Percival and, of course, my family.

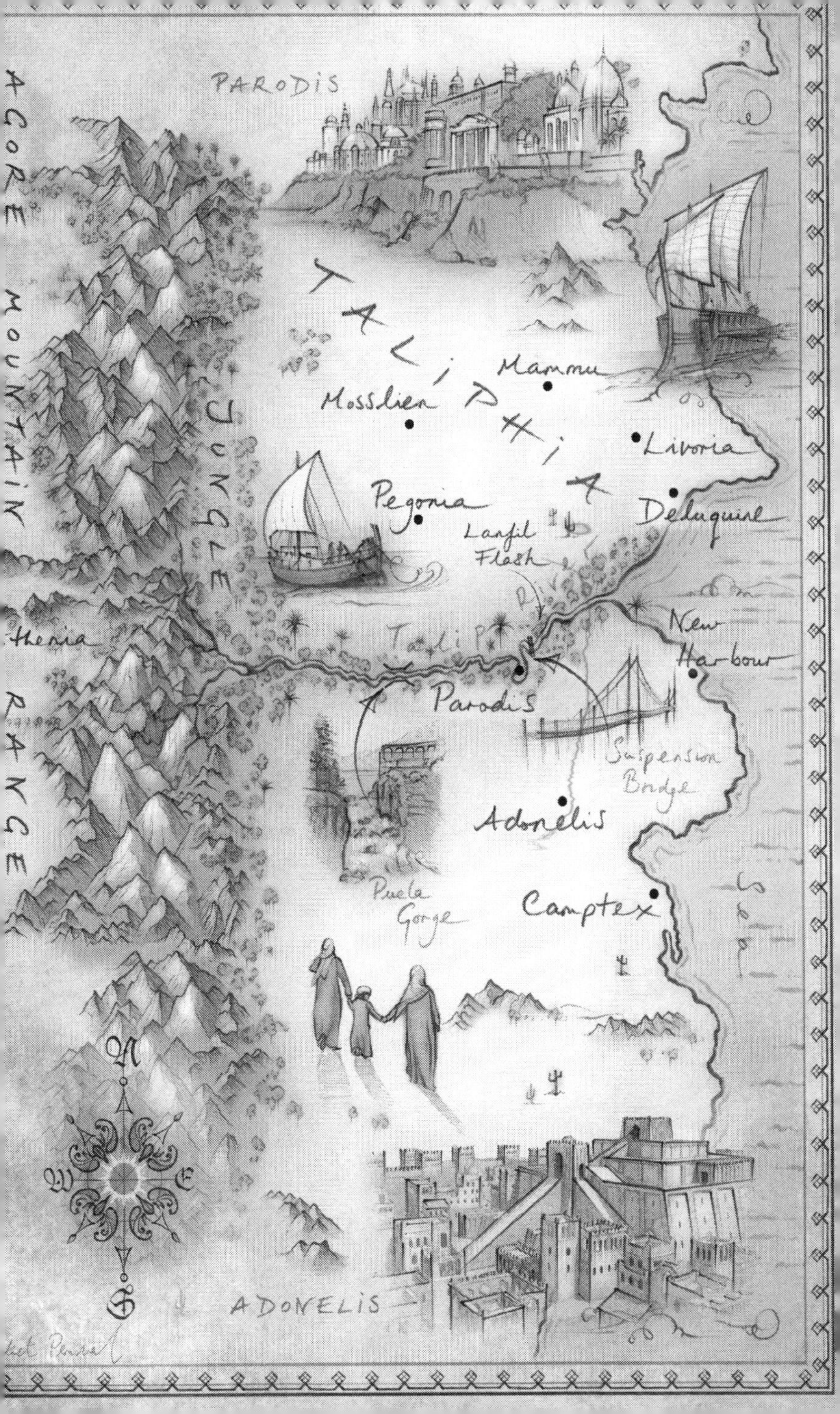
PARODIS
AGORE MOUNTAIN RANGE
JUNGLE
TALIPAXIA
Mammu
Mosslien
Livoria
Pegonia
Deluquine
Lanfil
Flash
thenia
Tali P
New
Harbour
Parodis
Suspension
Bridge
Adonelis
Puela
Gorge
Camptex
Sea
N
W
E
S
ADONELIS

Prelude

A new world stretched out under a rich blue sky, then vanished behind descending clouds. Three figures, deprived of the sun's pitiful warmth, staggered on. A freezing fire filled their lungs, replacing precious, thin mountain air, hard fought for with each breath. The lead, Finbarl, called out, his words lost to the roaring wind.

As Aminatra and Karlmon faded in the fog, Finbarl reached back to clasp each by the hand. He held without feeling, his rag-bound, frozen fingers bringing their bodies towards his own. Huddled together, unmoving, bombarding snow reduced their visibility to zero. Fatigue muddled thought; sleep beckoned with a promise of peace and warmth. Finbarl fought the urge, aware death lay on the other side.

Where had luck, their fourth companion across the roof of the world, gone? Each complacent step risked death, every mountain a test of strength and will. Yet there they were, so close to their final descent, the benign-looking foothills below. Benevolent weather had deserted them. Luck's wick burnt down, snuffing out light and hope.

Cocooned within this torturous white world, Finbarl wondered if death offered the freedom they sought. He had never known such pain. Every nerve screamed, invaded by the unrelenting cold. Finbarl tightened a blanket around Karlmon, his tiny body already suffering withdrawal from the drug Jumblar. The layers of clothes and material covering their bodies seemed pitiful. How could the cold burn so or the white maelstrom appear so dark?

And then it was over as quickly as it had started. The pain remained, but the sun tickled on dry, burning cheeks. Finbarl sniffed at a fragrance of air, pushing out his chest, drawing it in. To his side Aminatra stirred, her head buried within his beard.

"Are you all right?" Finbarl asked, rubbing his hands up and down Aminatra's and Karlmon's backs, brushing off snow, trying to warm them.

Aminatra turned her head upwards, slow and deliberate. With the same strenuous effort, she forced a smile.

"We had better keep moving," urged Finbarl. "We won't survive another storm, nor staying still."

"I'm not sure I can move," whispered Aminatra, reaching out to squeeze her family closer together.

Finbarl nodded, ruffling his face into the warmth of her hair. "We must. Come on! You help me up and I'll help you. Use your staff."

"I never thought ... I would miss ... the heat of Athenia," Aminatra said between ragged breaths, pushing against Finbarl as he creaked to his feet.

"The quicker we climb down, the sooner we'll be warm. Come on, Karlmon! Grab your staff. Help your mother up. Karlmon?"

Silence.

"He's not moving!" A mother's scream morphed to a croak in the thin air. "Finbarl! He's not moving."

PART ONE

Chapter One

A curling flame leapt in the darkness, escaping the campfire chorus line. Above, a skinned, spit-tied rodent dripped fat, hissing, whipping the flames into their dancing frenzy. Elsewhere, serenity pervaded. Sounds of nature escaped from the surrounding forest, adding a soothing, rhythmic soundtrack. Around the fire four huddled figures bathed in its warmth and faint glow. At the prompting of the excitable blaze, Finbarl shuffled forward, flicking a forefinger, rotating their dinner. Aminatra, readjusting her legs, angled a book to capture the light. Snug between the two adults, Karlmon opened his eyes to discover why his mother paused her reading. To the other side of the fire another pair of eyes struggled to stay open.

"A few more minutes," said Finbarl, licking his finger for a tantalising sample of the meal to come. He glanced towards their new companion, who'd lost the battle to keep his eyelids from closing. "He's asleep."

"His mumbling didn't help my reading," remarked Aminatra, examining the great mane of hair circling the man's face.

"That's what going without Jumblar does to you," said Finbarl, grateful his mother's wisdom aided in their own safe withdrawal off the drug. "And being alone all this time. He retained wit enough to make it over the mountains and survive this long."

"I wonder how long he's been here," mused Aminatra. "From the state of his thawb and hair, I would say a long time. He looks old. I don't recognise him from Athenia."

"Could just be worn down." Finbarl rotated the spit once more. "Hard to get info out of him. Seems to have lucid moments but most of the time ..." He shook his head. "Having company will help. It's a miracle our paths crossed. Almost feels like he was waiting for someone else to cross the mountains before going further."

"I don't like him," said Karlmon, blushing at the confession.

"We hardly know him." Aminatra checked the man still slept. "Two weeks is no time at all to form an opinion of a person. He is strange but so was Johansson."

Finbarl acknowledged mention of their old friend from the prison with a smile.

"You didn't get to know him, but you would have liked each other," continued Aminatra. "No, give our new friend time."

"Introducing himself by rushing at us with a machete shouting 'Ferral' wasn't an endearing start," said Finbarl. "Lucky I didn't shoot him."

"No, knocking him out was far more welcoming," quipped Aminatra. "What's wrong with a simple 'hello'."

"Sorry I saved you." Finbarl winked at Karlmon.

"Why won't he tell us his name?" asked the boy.

Finbarl shrugged, while prodding the rodent with the tip of his knife. "Not right in the head."

"Oh, Finbarl!" chastised his wife.

"Hang on. I was going to add, but it's good to have another pair of eyes and hands in this place. From his mumbling, sounds like the Ferrals have spread across the mountains too."

"I've seen no sign of them or anyone else," said Aminatra, reopening the book, trying to ignore the shiver flushing through her. She had no desire to think about the wild humans known as Ferrals: the plagued of Athenia. Their life in that unforgiving land was now a hundred miles behind; a soaring range of conquered mountains separating them. "No more talk of our guest. It's not polite. I want to find out what happens next to Snowy and Napoleon."

Karlmon giggled, aware his mother knew the full plot to *Animal Farm*, having practised her new reading skills on it several times.

With her deliberate, plodding style, Aminatra worked her tongue round a less familiar word, continuing the ancient fable rescued from Athenia's library as the flames approached.

Karlmon closed his eyes again, content to listen to his favourite book as he recovered his strength, unaware how close *Animal Farm* and the other two books Finbarl rescued from the rubble of Athenia had come to being sacrificed to the mountains. As Karlmon lay lifeless, sucked dry by the blizzard, what did the heavy books matter? With a mother's crazed devotion, Aminatra carried Karlmon down the mountain at a reckless pace, feet slipping and stumbling, death beckoning an inch either way. But she never let go or fell. Aghast at his wife's nerveless descent, Finbarl followed, ready to forego his load to keep pace. He hung on, Karlmon came to in the thicker air and warming embrace, and Aminatra sobbed in relief. They all cried when the rocks transformed to grass, the land levelled out and a lush, strange world welcomed all three and their precious cargo.

With the mountains behind them, Mandelaton, the place of hope and security they sought, felt closer. The city's precise location, and what awaited them if found, remained a mystery. A simple letter seeking friendship, discovered in Athenia's archives, written by unseen ambassadors from Mandelaton, was their only breadcrumb. Its words gave little away, its existence offered so much. Against the insular, corrupt and paranoid qualities of Athenia, a city reaching out appealed to Finbarl and Aminatra. So, ignorance and optimism fuelled their journey, with the wish to be anywhere other than Athenia. They hadn't expected to bump into a fellow Athenian, but such was the nature of adventure.

Recognising a favourite line, Aminatra looked up, quoting the book from memory, joined by Finbarl and Karlmon on the last sentence "Long live *Animal Farm*!" Aminatra closed the book. "A suitable place to stop."

The chorus woke the stranger. "Ferrals!" His hand grabbed at his machete's hilt, eyes wide in terror before a calming wave brought him back to reality. "Is that rat ready yet? Penela, don't forget the Jumblar. I can't feel my toes. Do you want a toku?"

Karlmon shrank, moving closer to his mother.

"The meat is ready," confirmed Finbarl, wondering if anything else within the man's odd rambling was aimed at him.

"Can you read some more after we've eaten?" Karlmon's imploring eyes pressed his mother.

"No, it'll be too dark."

Karlmon straightened up, fighting off his fatigue. "But I like you reading." He smiled. It was his way to encourage his mother in her lessons. That brief period of education as an Athenian cadet cultivated a liking as both tutor and superior to his parent.

"Well, if you don't behave, I'll read you *Hamner's Definitive Medical Guide* tomorrow!"

As expected, the threat elicited a giggle from Karlmon.

A turgid book with unfathomable words, Aminatra often wondered why Dul-biblex, Athenia's wise old librarian, gifted it as one of his essential three books. Sometimes Aminatra read it alone as the others slept, stretching her newfound literacy skills, equally confused and in wonder at the authors and their past world. It stirred memories of Maddy, Finbarl's deceased mother. As a doctor, she would have understood the medical guide. Aminatra missed her.

"Here, pull off a leg each!" Finbarl removed the rodent from the fire, motioning the steaming carcass towards Aminatra and Karlmon.

The man scurried round, eager to claim his piece. "Thank you, Wardyn. Yes, sir. I promise. Not more than you can spare." He retreated to his spot, continuing a one-sided conversation.

"It's hot!" cautioned Aminatra, as her son ripped off his portion.

Karlmon passed the leg from one hand to the other as fingers reached their pain threshold. He blew, then took a satisfying bite out of the thigh. "I prefer deer," he mumbled through a full mouth.

Aminatra clipped his ear, angry and disappointed. "Be grateful for what we can find!"

"He meant nothing by it," said Finbarl. "I prefer your stewed Yucca." His reference to their days in the prison prompted the sought-after reaction, as Aminatra's scowl turned to a smile.

Karlmon appeared unaffected, intent on teasing the meat from the bone.

"I suppose cheekiness is a good sign," sighed Aminatra. "Proves you're back to normal."

Karlmon nodded his bulging cheeks, his brush with death forgotten.

A private smile stole on to Finbarl's lips. His dreams, scarred for months by Karlmon's terrified face, now found a new image of a happy family. That guilt, from the moment he'd ripped the boy from his mother's clasp at her arrest, dissipated when the boy's life hung in the balance and Finbarl felt a father's love for him. He reached across and ruffled Karlmon's hair.

With appetites sated, sleep beckoned as the only choice. Karlmon and the stranger dropped off in no time, exhausted and ready to dream. Aminatra followed not long after. Despite worries, a tired body dragged her into a deep slumber. For Finbarl, trained as an Athenian guard, he remained vigilant, alert to every nocturnal sound. He sat awake, thinking, his mind alive with this new world, their new home and strange companion.

On descending to the foothills, the fertility of the land announced itself. Rain fell more often, and the countryside, though still hostage to a ferocious sun, looked luscious under its green blanket. Why so different this side of the mountains? The clouds appeared to queue at the mountains' summits, lacking the nerve to go beyond and drop their rain on Athenia. It felt cruel but ordained.

And an absence of people confused Finbarl. The early encounter with their fellow Athenian exile lulled him into believing more would follow. Not travellers from Athenia, such as themselves and the stranger, but indigenous folk. If humanity hung on in the barren wasteland around Athenia, why was this fertile and pleasant land so devoid of humanity? Their companion's ravings fuelled his insomnia. Soon, he expected to encounter a Ferral.

These humans, once a noble and civilised people but now primitive and crazed, tormented Athenia's citizens. They lived among the foothills on the Athenian side of the mountains, roaming the plain for food, attacking any fool caught out there. It took no stretch of the imagination to think their territory extended here. Would freezing summits perturb these naked beasts who showed no fear? Finbarl's body wanted to believe they might, and the stranger's warnings stemmed from Jumblar damage, not experience. Then he might drift off to sleep, but his mind hung on to every possibility, until, after a few more hours, exhaustion overtook him.

Time passed, as it does during the fitful domain of sleep: the mind flitting awake, lamenting the burden of time, until, without awareness, sleep reclaimed. During one such semi-conscious flirt, Finbarl sensed a vague notion of movement. He pondered the motions in a dream-like context. Faces from the past appeared in this newfound world of forests, brushing through the verdant leaves, appearing, then disappearing. Gauret, his lamented friend in the guards, hovered and vanished; Crixus, a traitorous prisoner, materialised in his final, deathly state. Governor Elbar, the epitome of power in Finbarl's old life, lurched towards him as an ogre, before morphing into a camel.

A timid yelp pierced the subconscious, dragging Finbarl from his fanciful world. He sprang upright to find Karlmon awake, staring through the darkness into the trees, his body rigid with fear. Sleep and memories of abstract thoughts clung to Finbarl as he tried to understand the information his brain absorbed. Finally, his eyes adapted to the sparse moonlight. Aminatra groaned to his right, still deep asleep. He gently shook her, while focussing his attention on where Karlmon stared. The stranger snored across the clearing, too far away to awake in silence. Finbarl's first attempt to stir Aminatra elicited a contented moan. He shook harder. She fidgeted, one eye opening, assessing her disturber.

"What?" she mumbled.

"Wake up!" whispered Finbarl. "There's something out there."

Aminatra sat upright in a flash, looking around for her son. "Karlmon!"

"Quiet!" hissed Finbarl. "We're being watched." His hand searched for the pistol on the ground. In the first weeks of their journey, with food scarce, he used it to kill prey. On discovering only three bullets remained, they rationed those for emergencies. This seemed like one. The trio stared into the dark forest, a waft of smoke blowing up from the burnt-out fire, smudging the view. Silence compounded their fear. Framed in a cluster of shimmering leaves, the moonlight caught the stationary features of a face staring back. Piercing eyes, wild hair and snarling mouth identified their watcher: a female Ferral.

Chapter Two

F inbarl's hand trembled as he aimed the pistol in the interloper's direction. It had been a while since he last fired a gun in anger, and a while since he'd seen a Ferral. The familiar odour of cordite filled his nostrils as he pulled the trigger.

BANG!

Aminatra screamed, while Karlmon burst into tears, clinging to his mother. The stranger bolted upright, flapping in the dark for his weapon. Finbarl leapt to his feet, darting towards the trees, his gun poised to fire a second shot.

The Ferral had vanished. Leaves, where her face once appeared, shook, echoing the commotion. Finbarl examined them for signs of blood. He brushed past, into the consuming foliage, the branches snagging on his thawb.

"Ferrals!" cried the stranger, dashing forward, sweeping his machete from side to side. "Monsters! Devils!"

"Silence!" hissed Finbarl, turning to glare at the man. "And watch where you're swinging that thing!"

"Don't go too far!" pleaded Aminatra.

Finbarl hesitated, the following silence extenuating his blindness. Did a pack of Ferrals await them?

"Get the fire started again!" he ordered, retreating to the opening, leaving the stranger to hack at the unoccupied trees. Flames offered the best defence against the pyrophobic Ferrals.

"Kill the Ferrals," muttered the old Athenian, attacking every shadow with a thrust of his sword. "We must destroy and cleanse. Save pretty Penela."

A hint of dawn coloured the sky. The faint glow from a sunrise, followed by a radiant blue, crept over the black blanket of night. Aminatra grasped Karlmon by the shoulders. "There's no time for tears. We must get the fire alight. Quick, add the kindling to the smoking wood. There may be heat enough to reignite it."

The boy complied. Time as an Athenian cadet instilled the discipline suited to emergencies, even if vulnerability lay beneath the surface.

Aminatra reached into her bag, gathering dried moss, while Karlmon laid scraps of wood on the near dormant fire. Pushing the tinder in the gaps, she bent forward to blow. A plume of ash blew up in Karlmon's face, making him splutter, but, without complaint, he continued positioning the kindling. Soon the rising smoke thickened. A flame burst forth, engulfing the moss. Karlmon held shaved strips of wood to the flame, allowing the miracle to spread.

Meanwhile, Finbarl paced around the perimeter of the opening, roaring into the darkness. If the gun's report failed to scare the Ferral away, what hope his shouting, but it consumed some adrenaline.

The stranger ceased his attack on the harmless vegetation, returning to the clearing with tears in his eyes. "Penela is gone!" he wailed repeatedly, adding to the dawn uproar.

All around the forest creatures stirred, each voicing annoyance at their early awakening. Despite it still being too dark to see, Finbarl's gut told him they were again alone. He turned back to find the campfire roaring and Aminatra and Karlmon looking with anxious eyes in his direction.

"I knew there would be Ferrals!" he cursed. "Things were too good to be true."

"Did you hit it?" asked Karlmon.

Finbarl shook his head. "No, it escaped."

"She," said Aminatra.

"Sorry?"

"She was most definitely a 'she', not an 'it'."

"Does it matter? It's a Ferral!"

"We shouldn't dehumanise them, just because we fear them." Aminatra stoked the fire as she lectured Finbarl. "We might as well have stayed in Athenia if we're going to behave like Athenians."

"They will eat us all!" declared the stranger. "We must kill them."

"Don't be silly!" chastised Aminatra. "They are more like us than you realise."

The man looked aghast, and Aminatra wondered if she had spoken out of turn.

"What do you mean?" A lucid focus shaped his face. His eyes locked on Aminatra's, awaiting an answer.

Sensing the tension, Finbarl stepped forward. "We discovered things back in Athenia: things the Wardyns kept secret. The Ferrals' ancestors once occupied the town. We're all descendants of the bandits who stole it from them, laced them with Jumblar and left them to survive in the wild."

"I see," said the man, scratching his thatched beard. "Interesting. I still wish them all dead."

"They're dangerous but not unsavable," said Aminatra.

"Why do you want to save them?"

Aminatra struggled to comprehend this change in persona, his articulate tone at odds with the previous erratic nonsense. "Because they've never had an opportunity at a better way of life. Our ancestors robbed them of that."

"Interesting," repeated the stranger.

"She was pretty for a Ferral," Karlmon remarked.

"Yes, she was," concurred Aminatra, trying not to laugh at her son's innocence, but failing when Finbarl chortled. Karlmon joined in despite having no sense of what was so funny.

"Not the best time to be laughing," said Finbarl, spotting their companion's sombre features and reverting to the vigilant protector. "We're safe for the time being, but best not take that for granted."

"You're right," said Aminatra, climbing to her feet. "At first light, we'll be on our way. Let's get our things together ready to go. Karlmon, you keep the fire burning bright!"

"What's your name?" asked Finbarl of the stranger, exploiting his lucidity.

"Have I not introduced myself? How rude. I'm Bokanda-gula."

"When did you cross the mountains? Were you alone?"

"I ... I don't remember."

An hour later, they traipsed through the tangled forest, Bokanda leading with his machete, cutting away at the clawing branches, the others beating down the lower foliage with their staffs. Finbarl carried a flaming stick to deter watching Ferrals, but it soon burnt itself out. Occasionally, they stumbled across an animal track, making their going easier, but for the main, they weaved around obstacles on a slow, tortuous route.

The cool air of dawn became humid as the sun warmed the forest. Water shortage no longer concerned them, but they drank often to replace the copious sweat. Finbarl missed the dry heat of Athenia. He didn't understand why, in the forest's shelter, it felt more uncomfortable. Whenever they stopped to rest, he checked the perimeter for signs of anyone on their trail. The forest appeared empty, yet the feeling someone watched them remained.

"It's strange we've seen just one Ferral since arriving in this land," commented Aminatra, wiping the sweat from her eyes.

"With the thickness of this forest, we're lucky we can see each other," replied Finbarl.

"Perhaps she was alone." Their chat often turned to the mysterious Ferral girl.

"That's unlikely. How do you reckon that?"

"Well," pondered Aminatra. "The odds of a Ferral getting across the mountain range seem slim. Adapting to an unfamiliar environment brings no end of difficulties. Think how hard it's been for us or Bokanda. New plants and animals, the forest. We have knives and a gun too."

"Perhaps they evolved on this side of the range from another community of humans," suggested Finbarl.

"Impossible," said Aminatra. "We know how the Ferrals came about. Very specific circumstances: madness from Jumblar withdrawal, then surviving in the wilderness against the odds. Perhaps she wasn't a Ferral."

"No, she was a Ferral. I'd recognise that stink anywhere."

"You don't smell so good yourself," said Aminatra with a wry smile. "Perhaps she thought you were her mate!"

Finbarl stooped, mimicking a Ferral, snarling with teeth bared. Karlmon exploded with laughter and joined in, circling Aminatra as their prey.

"Stop it! Stop it!" implored Bokanda, tapping his forehead with a vigorous knuckle.

"Eh? Oh, sorry," said Finbarl. "Have you lost someone to the Ferrals?"

The question hung unanswered. Consumed again in his private contretemps, Bokanda pressed fingers to his skull as though holding down an invisible tormentor.

"You were both a bit too good at that," whispered Aminatra to her family. "He thought you were the real thing. How about dried camel to sate your bloodlust?" Aminatra rummaged within her bag, seeking the last of their supplies carried from Athenia. "That's strange?"

"What?"

"I can't find it. I never unpacked it when we stopped last night."

"You're sure it's not in another of the bags?" asked Finbarl.

"It's not impossible, but I'm sure it was in here. We'll have a better search tonight."

At day's end, aching muscles swore they had covered fifty miles, but Finbarl sensed their meandering steps may have led them but a third of that distance. An ill-defined destination left them with no sense of disappointment, only tired feet and bodies, and grumbling stomachs.

The further they progressed into the forest, the harder it became to find food. Life flourished around them, but all of it was unfamiliar. In the arid foothills they gathered berries, cacti and other edible vegetation recognisable from Athenia and easily found with the knowledge of Bokanda. In this lush terrain of plenty, where all looked appetising, they had no way of discerning healthy from poisonous. The wildlife made itself known with its continual chorus of sound but deigned not to show itself. That night, snake filled the menu, after making the mistake of pouncing on a vole as they passed. However, they craved a flavour of home.

The tree canopy snuffed out the remaining daylight, signalling an end to their day's trek. On finding a clearing, they stacked their bags by a tree and, while Finbarl undertook his tour of the surrounding land, Aminatra and Karlmon collected wood to prepare the evening's campfire. Bokanda, complaining of tiredness, reclined against a tree.

"All clear?" enquired Aminatra, as Finbarl returned to the small opening.

Finbarl shrugged. "I couldn't see anyone, but ... I don't know."

"What?" pressed Aminatra with concern.

"Well, our own presence either causes a raucous outburst among the wildlife or absolute silence."

Aminatra nodded.

"I stopped and hid in the undergrowth for five minutes. While I could hear the background chatter of the forest to the east, it remained silent from the direction we came."

"You think we're being followed? What should we do?" asked Aminatra. "Keep going through the night?"

Finbarl grimaced. "No, that's just as dangerous. I'll stay up all night, keep the fire alight. Sleep with your staffs close to hand. We may need to defend ourselves."

"You can't do that! You need your sleep. We'll take it in turns."

Finbarl looked at Bokanda, now fast asleep. "I see our friend has taken the first shift."

"I don't think he's well. Did you hear him struggling for breath?"

"It's hard work battling through this forest. If he let me use his machete, I'd be able to help. But not one for sharing."

"Now," announced Aminatra. "I'll find that dried meat. You can cook the snake, as Bokanda did the dangerous part in capturing it ... and biting its head off."

"It's the Ferral in him," quipped Finbarl, sitting down, beckoning Karlmon over. "I'll show you how to prepare our slippery friend. You can use the knife." Karlmon leapt across, excited to use their one and only short blade. Finbarl dangled the lifeless reptile between his fingers, pointing to its underside. "Okay, start by making a half-inch slit here. Be careful with your fingers ... and mine!"

As Karlmon learnt to peel the skin, Aminatra rummaged through their bags. Things worked their way to the bottom. They were hard to find, but usually found. This time, the dried meat remained missing. "That's strange," she said to herself. "Perhaps we left it behind." She squeezed the corners of each bag and looked for unnoticed holes, shaking her head in perplexed thought. They could not afford such carelessness with precious cargo. She turned to confirm the loss but, seeing them laughing, decided not to spoil their mood.

"It feels a little cooler this evening," she commented, sitting down at Finbarl's side. "I wonder if we can expect more rain?"

"Nothing's impossible in this land," replied Finbarl, as he watched Karlmon cut the snake into chunks. "Who'd have thought life could survive with so much water?"

"Perhaps the miracle is life survived with so little in Athenia," Aminatra remarked.

Finbarl sniffed an acknowledgement but paid minimal attention. "Bend your index finger or you'll chop it off!" he cautioned Karlmon.

Aminatra smiled, pleased to see them interacting. "When you've finished, I'll read *Animal Farm*," she offered, generating an enthused cheer from Karlmon.

"Focus!" exclaimed Finbarl. "Any lost fingers go on the fire for supper." The comment elicited the opposite effect. Karlmon rocked with laughter, even less conscious of the dangers from the knife. Finbarl shrugged, whispering to Aminatra, "Perhaps an accident is the best way to learn."

Aminatra glared back.

"Only a minor nick!" added Finbarl, trying to extricate himself.

"You're worse than Napoleon!" she retorted.

Finbarl snorted in reply.

"Oh, get on with your work!"

How nice to lose ourselves in meaningless conversations, thought Aminatra, forgetting for a moment the real perils they faced. As strangers in a strange land, what else awaited in the darkness? What dangers hid around the next corner? Now they knew Ferrals lived amid this forest, there would be little chance to relax.

The sweet smell of the roasting snake mixed with the smoke of the fire. It stirred Bokanda, who sauntered over and held his hands over the flames.

"We escaped Athenia because I believed anywhere else was better," he said, staring into the fire. "I was wrong."

"You sound refreshed," observed Aminatra, closing the book. "Did you escape with others?"

Bokanda's head turned, eyes directed at Aminatra but looking through her. "My wife, Penela. Sweet Penela."

"Ahh." Aminatra nodded, understanding part of his tortured ruminations. "Is she dead?"

"We should never have left Athenia. A life together is better than one apart."

An unfamiliar bird called in the distance. Aminatra eased herself to her feet, as Bokanda's gaze returned to the fire. "I think it looks ready," she opined of their dinner. "I need to relieve myself. Get it off the spit for when I'm back!"

As she vanished into the trees behind, Finbarl prodded the meat with his knife. "Your mother's right," he commented to Karlmon. "Make a bed of leaves for me to lay it on!"

Karlmon had witnessed the adults do this a hundred times and arranged several rubbery leaves in a square.

"Good," praised Finbarl. "Because this meat is light, we just," his tongue pressed into his inner cheek as he concentrated on manoeuvring the hot spit off the fire, "need to do this." Flashing the knife down the row of snake meat chunks, Finbarl pushed them off the charred stick onto the leaves. Karlmon nodded his head, absorbing another lesson in survival. "Let it cool a while," cautioned Finbarl, "or Aminatra will have words."

The youngster smiled, familiar with his mother's default reaction to endangering himself.

A strange, muffled yelp sounded before them. Bokanda whipped his machete from his belt, as Finbarl jumped up, pistol in hand. "Aminatra! Get back here, whatever you're doing!" He held the pistol forward, aiming into the darkness, an expectant finger on the trigger. A simple nod towards the fire instructed Karlmon to pull out a large stick, one end ablaze, as agreed during the day. The boy pressed into Finbarl's side, holding the torch out. "Aminatra!" Their plan for further Ferral incursions involved Aminatra being present.

Loud, rustling leaves announced the approach of something large. Karlmon emitted an uncontrollable whine, and Finbarl squeezed his shoulder in reassurance. "Aminatra!" he yelled again, concerned at her continuing silence. Perhaps Ferrals already surrounded them? Perhaps they had Aminatra?

"I'm here!" It was Aminatra. Her voice emerged from a contrary direction, accompanied by a peculiar, stifled drone.

Finbarl shared a perplexed frown with Karlmon, his finger easing off the trigger. Into the light of the fire Aminatra appeared, struggling with another figure: the source of the odd noise. It was the Ferral girl. Her legs thrashed as Aminatra held her torso in a firm grip, one hand covering her mouth.

"Cronax!" cursed Finbarl. "What are you doing?"

As the words left Finbarl's mouth, Bokanda screamed, raised his sword and dashed forward.

"Finbarl!" Aminatra swung round, shielding the girl with her own body as the crazed Athenian approached.

"Oof!" Bokanda collapsed to the floor, Finbarl's arms round his ankles, the machete bouncing away.

"Stay there," growled Finbarl, brushing the dirt off his elbows and placing a firm boot on the sobbing Bokanda's back. "Karlmon, pass me my gun and take that machete away!"

"You've got some explaining to do!" Finbarl waved his gun towards Aminatra's captive, uncertain what to do next. Should he shoot the Ferral, knock her out or ...?

"Hold her!" cried Aminatra.

"Stay there!" repeated Finbarl to Bokanda, as he removed his boot. He slid the gun in his belt, then wrapped his arms around the girl's waist, as Aminatra released her grip. With her mouth now free, the girl let out a piercing scream and tried to bite Finbarl's neck. He pushed her away, keeping a tight grip on her shoulders. She twisted and kicked, surprising Finbarl with her strength. When her foot caught his shin, he released her shoulders and grabbed her leg. With a sharp yank, he tipped the Ferral onto her back. As a further scream left her lips, Finbarl flipped her over, collapsing his weight on her light frame. He heard the wind knocked out of her and she remained still and silent. Using a technique perfected as an Athenian guard, Finbarl pinned her arms down with his own.

"It's the end!" sobbed Bokanda, now rolled onto his back, head tilted back to watch the drama. "May Cronax forgive us. Penela, will you forgive me?"

Karlmon stood before his mother, emboldened by the machete and a flaming torch in either hand. With a jab of his torch, he caused the prostrate Ferral to whimper like a wounded animal.

"Come away!" ordered Aminatra. "Finbarl's got her under control."

Karlmon edged back without complaint, his display of courage complete.

"Are you going to explain?" asked Finbarl, one eye ensuring Bokanda offered no threat.

Aminatra brushed the tangled vegetation from her clothes and hair and looked down at her husband, comfortable in his position atop the Ferral. "It was the missing food."

"What missing food?"

"The dried meat we couldn't find the other day," continued Aminatra. "I knew I'd packed it away and so couldn't understand where it could be. You or Karlmon wouldn't steal, and, while it wasn't beyond reason an animal raided our bags, it was unlikely. They would have caused damage. I couldn't rule out Bokanda but ..."

"You surmised it was our Ferral friend?"

"Yes," said Aminatra, pleased Finbarl caught on.

"And you decided not to tell us, capturing her on your own! Getting Bokanda all riled. What if she were in a pack?"

"Sorry. I knew if she watched us, it was important you and Karlmon behaved naturally. I didn't consider how Bokanda might react ..." She let her voice trail off. "And I was confident she was alone."

"How?" asked Finbarl.

"If part of a pack and they wanted our food, then we would have been dead long ago. No, she's an outcast, or her pack is dead. Just a hungry, lonely girl looking for a meal."

"Hmm, you could be right." Finbarl considered the body beneath him. The girl needed a nutritious meal. "Perhaps someone killed her family." He tilted his head in the direction of Bokanda.

"He certainly has a pathological hatred of Ferrals, but so did we, once."

"How did you know she was there?"

Aminatra grinned, wallowing in her success and guile. "If she were our thief, she'd be looking for more food. Those birds alerted me: their warning calls. Suspected they might be in response to our friend approaching, I crept out in the opposite direction and circled round. Found her crouching ten yards from you."

"Well, aren't we the clever one," said Finbarl. "Now, what do we do with her? I'm okay with the snake, but more than happy to give roast Ferral a try."

"I don't think there's much meat on her," quipped Aminatra. "You can start by tying her up to that tree. I do need to relieve myself now!"

"And him?" Finbarl's eyes fell on Bokanda, still prostrate and whimpering.

"Stop him from doing anything stupid for a few minutes. My needs are more pressing!"

A few minutes later, Aminatra returned to find Finbarl finishing his task. He bound the Ferral's hands with torn rags, then her feet and, as she squirmed and gnashed, sat her at the base of a tree. With some vines collected on their travels, Finbarl secured the interloper to the trunk. Bokanda now sat beneath his own tree, consumed with a dirge of abstract words he seemed unable to stop. Transformed by custody of the machete, Karlmon battled imaginary enemies around the fire.

"Oh, you've not brought me another Ferral," said Finbarl, as Aminatra examined his work. The girl watched them both, her fear masked by a threatening snarl.

"You're only allowed one a day," replied Aminatra. "More and you'll get spoiled. Any problems with our other companion?"

"No, he's fighting his own internal demons. I'll tell you what, I'll take her back into the woods. Finish her with my knife. No noise. Problem solved!"

Aminatra looked aghast and whispered, "You'll do no such thing!"

"Why not? And why are you whispering?"

"Because," continued Aminatra, leading Finbarl away from the girl, "we shouldn't talk about killing her in front of her. You stopped Bokanda doing the deed, why so keen now?"

"She doesn't understand a word we're saying," said Finbarl. "I stopped Bokanda killing you, not the Ferral. I've killed dozens in my time. Why is this one different?"

"She may sense what we're talking about and she's a girl, only just a teenager."

"A teenager who'll rip your throat out if given the chance!"

Aminatra sighed, sharing Finbarl's fears but recognising the innocent child in the frightened eyes. "I don't think Karlmon should have to witness such an act. I want him to grow up free of violence. And remember what Maddy said?"

"What's my mother got to do with it?"

"She believed Athenians and Ferrals could reintegrate, with time."

"You want us to keep her as a pet?"

"No!" exclaimed Aminatra, punching Finbarl on the shoulder for his petulance. "I suggest, when we leave tomorrow, we loosen her bindings just a little so she can escape by the time we're far away. It will be an act of kindness she may remember: a tiny step towards integration."

"That's an enormous risk. Who's to say she won't follow our tracks and murder us in our sleep?"

"It's a risk I'm willing to take," said Aminatra, determination clear in her eyes. "Let's see what Karlmon thinks. Karl …" As Aminatra turned to call to Karlmon, she gasped in horror. Through the shimmering air above the fire, she looked upon her boy crouching in front of the Ferral, a piece of snake meat held before the girl's face. "Karlmon!" screamed Aminatra. He rocked back, stumbling onto his backside. In a second, Finbarl and Aminatra raced over and dragged his slight frame away. "What in Cronax do you think you're doing?" shouted Aminatra.

The tears flowed; his voice wavered. "She looked hungry, so I was feeding her."

"She's dangerous," added Finbarl in a calmer tone. "Even when tied up."

"She could have bitten your hand!" Still Aminatra shook.

"But she was just interested in the snake," offered a hesitant Karlmon. "She sniffed the first piece for a while but ate without trying to bite my fingers."

"The first piece!" echoed Aminatra in despair. "How many pieces have you fed her?"

"Just the one. She enjoyed it."

"I suspect she's never had cooked meat," suggested Finbarl, getting a frosty look from Aminatra for his efforts.

"You're to stay away from her!" Aminatra bent down, glowering into her son's eyes. "Do you understand?"

With bottom lip protruding, Karlmon nodded.

"Now," began Aminatra, her tone calmer and caring, "come and sit with me. We'll eat our meal and read some more."

Finbarl ran a hand through his hair, puffed out his cheeks and released a deep breath. He examined the wiry creature. The fire glinted in her frightened eyes. Every time a crack escaped, she flinched, struggling against her bindings. They had always been central to his life, yet Finbarl had never studied a live Ferral before. It was an anticlimax: two arms, two legs, ears, a nose. All normal. Her skin, unwashed and dirty, lacked the paint or decorative mud seen on those attacking Athenia. Despite her age, a tough life etched itself on her naked form, exposing scars and scratches. The eyes moved with an unnerving intensity but stared from a face like any Finbarl had seen walking the streets of Athenia.

Noticing the snake meat dropped by Karlmon lying among a patch of moss, Finbarl picked it up, blowing on it to remove the dirt. Thoughts whirled as he grasped it between forefinger and thumb. He presented it to the girl. Her eyes softened; her nose twitched. Bestial, but not without charm. Finbarl recalled camels showing less decorum at the offer of food. Her eyes studied his as her lips opened. Instead of placing the meat in her mouth, Finbarl withdrew it. A deep disappointment presented through her face, but no anger or ferocity. He offered the meat again and this time, as the mouth opened, he released it, whipping away his hand. Glancing behind to ensure his show of fear went unnoticed, Finbarl's attention returned to the girl who chewed on the morsel. A soft hum of contentment emanated from her throat. He shook his head in disbelief.

"You're right," he said, walking over to Aminatra. "We'll let her go in the morning."

"Good," replied Aminatra, squeezing Karlmon. "We're agreed then. I suggest you speak to Bokanda. Make it clear we don't treat Ferrals like animals any more."

"You think he'll understand?" asked Finbarl, glancing across to the Athenian rocking under his tree.

"You were a guard, trained in persuading people."

Finbarl sighed.

Chapter Three

While night's darkness hinted at isolation, dawn unmasked the illusion with its chorus of birdsong, insect signals and other strange sounds. For Finbarl, the noise brought relief from another sleep-deprived night. He and Aminatra agreed to take shifts guarding their prisoner, watching for other dangers, resting in between. Finbarl's healthy paranoia made napping impossible.

He studied the Ferral throughout the hours of darkness. She struggled in her bindings, humming strange, repetitive noises, as though an animal calling out. After a while, he considered gagging her or knocking her out, but the rhythmic beauty of her warbling grew on him. It lacked the cutting power of an alarm, appearing more a coping mechanism. Karlmon also hummed when scared.

When sleep overcame the girl, he continued to watch. She lost her ferocity under the placid comfort of unconsciousness, her face that of a normal teenager.

"Is she awake?" Aminatra rubbed her eyes, her body still deciding whether to rise for the day.

Finbarl's mind had wandered; his vigilance wavered. "I ..." He looked across to find the girl's piercing glare and stern mouth set in their direction. "Looks like she is."

"And we still plan to release her?"

Finbarl understood the unspoken meaning. The cold light of morning always offered a fresh perspective on old problems. "We release her," confirmed Finbarl. "I'll slacken her bindings and, if we leave a little food, she'll not need to follow us."

"It may attract animals, some not so friendly."

"That's a risk I'm willing to take," said Finbarl, his newfound sympathy reaching its limit. "Wake up Karlmon and start packing our things! How anyone can sleep through this racket is beyond me."

Aminatra looked across to her boy, his face a picture of contentment. "Your snoring has trained him well."

"Ouch. I may have to leave you behind with our Ferral," retorted Finbarl.

"Oh, to have intelligent company again!" exclaimed Aminatra, hiding under her blanket with a laugh.

"And what about our other problem?"

"You mean Bokanda?" Aminatra peered over the edge of her blanket. "We need him. It's safer with the four of us." She exposed a foot, prodding Karlmon awake.

"I dreamt of Ferrals," said the boy with a yawn.

"You sure it was a dream?" joked Finbarl, enjoying the tingling relief of a morning stretch.

"They learnt to use guns," added Karlmon.

"Cronax! Then they really would be just like us." Aminatra folded her blanket and looked across to the still sleeping Bokanda. "Why do I get the impression he didn't get much sleep before we arrived?"

"Couldn't have been easy for him. He's certainly making up for it now. Do you think I'll look like that in a few years?" Finbarl twiddled his beard.

"Not if I have a say," said Aminatra. "I'll wake him. You sort out the girl. Karlmon, you start packing the bags."

The girl stiffened at Finbarl's approach, hissing through exposed teeth. He scratched his chin, wondering at the delicate job before him. Dealing with Ferrals was so much easier through the barrel of a gun, he considered, as her mouth snapped at his probing fingers. The wrists he left bound with the freedom to twist and turn. She would soon cut herself loose on a branch or stone. As Finbarl went to grab her ankles, she whipped her legs in. "It's okay," he said, hoping the tone conveyed his intent. He reached in again. This time she kicked out, but with no leverage to generate power. Finbarl caught her limbs, squeezing them under one arm against his torso, the fettered legs to the fore.

"Eeehhkkk!" The Ferral yelped, pain creasing her face.

Finbarl loosened his grip, wondering what he had done to elicit such a reaction. On her left leg, below the ankle, he found a small, circular wound. His finger pushed down, causing a wince to spasm through the girl's features.

"Aminatra," called Finbarl. "Come and see this!"

The call attracted all. Aminatra wandered over, Bokanda and Karlmon in tow. "What?"

"Look!" Finbarl lifted the Ferral's ankles higher into the air, disregarding her discomfort. "Is there something in the wound?"

Aminatra squinted, examining what appeared to be an innocuous spot of blood. "I think it's a thorn. She's tried to get it out, but without luck."

"Abomination," muttered Bokanda, reacting to the captive's hissing. "Evil child of Dezamden."

"Back off!" ordered Finbarl. "Are we going to have a problem? Remember what I said last night?"

Bokanda continued his mumbling but walked away, circling the fire with a nervous automation.

"And what did you say?" asked Aminatra.

"A few empty threats," admitted Finbarl. "And a promise to keep his machete if he misbehaves."

"Well, let's hope once we're Ferral-free, we don't have to worry about his behaviour again. On that subject: the thorn!"

"Painful to walk on, I imagine. If we leave it in, it will be harder for her to follow us."

"If you leave it in, you can go on your own!" snapped Aminatra. "Give Karlmon your knife!"

"Why?"

"Just do it!" commanded Aminatra, before turning to her son. "Karlmon, hold the tip of the blade in the flames for a few minutes."

"You're cutting it out," said Finbarl, stating the obvious. "You think our friend here will thank you?"

"I don't need her thanks when I know I'm doing the right thing."

"Go ahead then." Finbarl tightened his grip on the girl's legs. "I'll bear the pain from her kicking."

Aminatra ignored Finbarl's facetiousness. "Karlmon, it should be ready. Pass it here." The boy ran the few steps, his eyes locked on the red-hot tip. "Now fetch the water bladder." He dashed away, returning holding the half-empty container. Aminatra gripped the bladder's plug between her teeth, pulled it out and poured a little liquid over the knife. A hiss accompanied a release of steam, causing the Ferral to whimper. "Right, hold her still!" she instructed Finbarl.

"I am holding her still!"

Aminatra leaned forward, pinching the blade between her fingers so only the tip protruded. As soon as the metal touched the flesh, the girl writhed. Her upper body arched within the confines of the bindings, causing Finbarl to push down on her thighs, limiting the movement in her lower legs. A long, high-pitched scream made Aminatra pause in concern and Karlmon cry.

"Get on with it!" cried Finbarl. "Just get it over with."

With thumb and forefinger, Aminatra stretched the skin on either side of the wound. A black core oozed blood, and Aminatra pushed the tip of the knife in a fraction. The Ferral's frenzy increased still further. "The knife's too big!" cursed Aminatra. "I'll cause more damage than the thorn."

"Loosen the thorn as best you can, then suck!"

"Suck?" exclaimed Aminatra.

"Yes, suck!" repeated Finbarl. "It's what you would do if you had a small splinter in your finger."

"That's not a small splinter; it's a bloody big thorn. And what about hygiene?"

"Really?" Finbarl looked at the sky. "For the sake of Cronax, stop arguing and try it!"

Aminatra paused, considering a riposte, but, with Finbarl struggling to restrain the girl, she dismissed the idea. If the Ferral broke her bindings now, things could get bad. "Okay!" Aminatra winced and pushed the knife tip against the rim of the barb, moving it from one side to the other. She bent forward, put her lips round the sore and sucked hard.

As Aminatra pulled away, gasping for an intake of air, Finbarl peered at the wound. "Did it work?"

Aminatra's tongue toured her mouth, seeking a wayward thorn, but an inspection of the Ferral's ankle revealed it remained, jutting out. "Karlmon, we need your delicate fingers." The boy edged forward, his eyes fixated on the struggling Ferral. "Now," continued Aminatra, "put a thumb either side of the head, nails inwards. That's right. Squeeze it gently!"

Karlmon followed the instructions, and as his digits came together, the thorn eased out. He held the barb up for everyone to see, his fear of the Ferral forgotten.

"It was a big one," commented Finbarl, his grip relaxing as the girl calmed.

"Well done, Karlmon," said Aminatra. "I wonder how long it's been stuck in there?"

"Who cares," answered Finbarl. "I only came over to loosen her bindings! May have to leave them a little tighter than planned. She'll be wanting revenge."

"I don't think so," said Aminatra, focussed on the Ferral.

The girl looked with intense interest at the thorn grasped between Karlmon's fingers, her features placid. As Finbarl released her legs, she pulled them in, concentrating her attention on the trickle of blood from the wound.

Finbarl climbed to his feet. "Do you think she understands what we did for her?"

"I don't know," answered Aminatra. "If it's been causing her grief for a while, she must notice the difference."

"Can I keep this?" asked Karlmon, holding the simple thorn towards his mother.

"Err ... of course," shrugged Aminatra. "Mind you, don't get it stuck in your skin!"

"I'd better finish what I started," said Finbarl. "With all that screaming, every Ferral will have heard." While the girl sat still, exploring the novel throbbing sensation in her ankle, Finbarl untied the knot holding her feet, retying it as a granny knot. He repeated for the binding around the tree. Escape now only required time and determination. Finbarl stood back, a layer of nervous sweat covering his palms.

Even with little food to spare, Aminatra offered the girl a cold chunk of last night's snake meat. Finbarl broke a flake off, presenting it to the Ferral. Her teeth plucked it from his fingers, and she chewed with noisy satisfaction. Then, wrapping what remained in a leaf, Finbarl held it up, catching her attention. He placed it on the ground next to the smoking embers of the fire. It was a location to deter other animals and delay the Ferral's own compulsion to approach the gift too quickly. They needed as much time as possible to distance themselves from their stalker.

"We're ready!" called out Aminatra.

Finbarl inspected the girl one last time. "Good luck!"

She tilted her head, inquisitive, no longer showing fear.

With bags draped over shoulders, the travellers vanished into the thick foliage of the forest, the Ferral out of sight, never to be seen again, they hoped.

Chapter Four

The sun tracked across the sky with eternal grace, vanishing below the western horizon, reappearing in the east. They walked many miles, but how far Finbarl could not say. He spent half the day checking over his shoulder for signs of a pursuer, a habit shared with the lagging Bokanda. In spite of his persisting fear, Finbarl wished her free and back to her normal life. After an intense night in her company, he felt a strange affinity. Like a wolf rescued from a mud pit, they had determined her future, taking responsibility for it.

Karlmon, braver in her absence, adopted the girl as an object of fascination. "Where is her mother?" he asked, among a dozen other questions.

Aminatra, reluctant to share a realistic hypothesis, answered, "She'll be looking after her other children."

"Why didn't she remove my thorn?"

"They don't have knives or clever children like you," responded Aminatra, smiling at her son's possessive nature towards the thorn.

"Why don't they have knives?"

Aminatra rolled her eyes. Was her son special or did all children ask endless questions? "Ferrals can't make metal."

"They're not as smart as us," added Finbarl.

"How do you make metal?"

Finbarl opened his mouth but, realising his own ignorance, looked to Aminatra for help.

"No idea," answered Aminatra, unwilling to lie.

This caused Karlmon to pause his interrogation, considering the facts. "Then why are we smarter?"

"No more questions!" pleaded Finbarl.

"Perhaps we're not," said Aminatra, before adding, "Now, no more questions!"

"Is everything okay?" Finbarl called back to Bokanda, now thirty yards behind. No answer came. "He looks pale. Perhaps we should let him catch up."

A sour expression answered for Karlmon.

"You're right," said Aminatra. "Time to give him his machete back?"

"He only has to ask." Finbarl struck the sword against a tree, lodging it within the bark. "We'll see if he wants it back."

Aminatra passed round a water vessel, and they drank, awaiting Bokanda.

The straggler caught up, gripped the hilt of his machete and yanked it free, then continued past, with no word spoken to his companions, just his meandering gibberish.

"I guess he wants it back," said Finbarl, shaking his head. "A 'hello' would have been nice."

"Leave him be," said Aminatra, watching Bokanda pull ahead. "He's ..."

"Cronax!"

A creature, blurred by speed, shot from the dense vegetation, leaping on Bokanda. A stunted shriek escaped from the man before he and his attacker disappeared in another mass of green.

"Help him, Finbarl!" cried Aminatra, sprinting forward herself. "Shoot it!"

"The gun's not loaded." Finbarl, a couple of yards ahead of his wife, grasped his staff, ready to launch it as a spear. A cry left his mouth, designed to scare.

A large cat bared its teeth, hackles raised behind a possessive stare. The limp body of Bokanda lay between it and the advancing Finbarl.

"Away! G'away!" He jabbed the staff into the air before him, unwilling to launch and squander the weapon.

"Keep back!" urged Aminatra to her son as she arrived at Finbarl's side, threatening with her own staff. "Is he alive?"

"Let's worry about the lion first," said Finbarl, creeping forward, eyes focussed on the beast.

The animal, hunched and unmoving, watched the humans with equal intensity. Jaws parted wide, it declared ownership of its prize with a hiss.

"Pass me your staff!" instructed Finbarl, waving his free hand backwards towards Karlmon. He felt the wood in his grip and swapped the smaller staff to his preferred hand. "Got to make this count." With a grunt he released the spear, watching it hurtle towards the lion.

"Missed!" cursed Aminatra, as the staff landed a yard wide of the cat, skidding in the dirt.

Alarmed, the feline retreated a little, weighing up the threat from these perceived rivals. A stone smacked a nearby tree and then another forced the creature back still further.

Karlmon stepped forward, one hand full of small stones, the other projecting them forward.

"Great idea," cried Aminatra. "Pass them round and find some more."

A bombardment started. The humans edged forward with confidence, the lion retreating in anguish at every direct hit. With one last bitter glare, it accepted defeat and vanished into the undergrowth with a snarl.

"Well done, Karlmon," cheered Finbarl, dashing to the side of Bokanda.

"Is he alive?" asked Aminatra again.

Finbarl blew out a long breath. "Yes. Looks like he knocked himself out with the fall. Just a few gashes from claws. Lucky we weren't too far behind."

"Lucky you weren't still leading," said Aminatra. "And what do you mean the gun's not loaded?"

Finbarl dribbled a little water on to Bokanda's forehead, stirring him to consciousness. "I didn't want you-know-who stealing it and shooting the other you-know-who. A bit ironic it almost got him killed."

"What's ironic?" Bokanda sat up, rubbing his head.

"Ah, we have coherent Bokanda," whispered Aminatra to Karlmon.

"Sit still," urged Finbarl, ignoring the question. "Let's wrap those cuts up. You've had a lucky escape."

"The Ferral?" pressed Bokanda, scanning his surroundings for danger.

"A big cat," corrected Finbarl, rolling the man's torn sleeve up. "Karlmon here saved you."

"The Ferrals change into lions. They haunt all wild souls."

"Not so coherent," said Aminatra, as Karlmon pursed his lips in disappointment at the lack of recognition.

With strips of cloth bandaging the wounds, Finbarl helped Bokanda to his feet. "You good to walk?"

"I seek utopia and am pulled towards it. Penela awaits me."

Finbarl shook his head in bewilderment. "You almost got to see her. One more minute with that cat ... Let's try a more scenic route."

***

The absence of food played on Finbarl's and Aminatra's minds more and more. In their haste to distance themselves from the Ferral they neglected hunting and, now they had the time, their prey became illusive or was scared away by the incessant gabbling of Bokanda.

"Cronax!" swore Finbarl as his target scampered into the under-growth, his whittled staff lying useless in the mud.

"Not sure I fancied eating whatever it was. Too many spines," commented Aminatra.

"Give it one more day without food," said Finbarl, "and you'll eat anything we can find. Maybe it's time to part ways with Bokanda? One less mouth to feed, and he's not pulling his weight."

"We can't. Not yet anyway. He's not well." Aminatra looked back to the solitary figure of Bokanda, labouring in the heat. "What about those berries I picked?"

"They look delicious," replied Finbarl. "But death's a heck of a way to discover something's poisonous."

"We may have to try one and find out," suggested Aminatra.

"No!" responded Finbarl. "Well, not before we've exhausted all other options. Give me more time to spear one of these minolax."

The minolax remained elusive all that day. Each hour stretched in the mind, sapping hope.

"What have you got there?"

The voice startled Karlmon. Bokanda appeared at his shoulder, somehow finding the strength to catch up. "It's a rock. I'm practising throwing for hunting."

"That's quartz," remarked the man. "Have you considered a sling?"

"A sling?"

"A strip of material. Here, best I show you." Bokanda untied one of his blood-soaked bandages, dangling it beneath gripped fingers. "Place your stone in the cradle."

A suspicious Karlmon hesitated.

"I once killed a boar with one stone. That's it. Drop it in." With Karlmon persuaded, Bokanda swung the weapon above his head, building up speed and angling it to forty-five degrees. He released one end of the bandage.

As his rock shot into the forest, ripping leaves on route, Karlmon clapped his hands to the accompaniment of a squeal.

"What do you think of that?" asked Bokanda.

"Can I try?"

"Would you look at that," said Aminatra, glancing behind to observe the interaction. "They appear to be bonding."

"Maybe Karlmon's managed to translate nonsense," remarked Finbarl. "Can you believe that man? Left us to do the hunting but knows how to use a sling!"

"He's a different man when coherent. Don't get bitter. How much further do you think before we reach Mandelaton?" asked Aminatra.

"I don't know," answered Finbarl. "The letter didn't mention distance, just it lay this side of the mountains. We might arrive tomorrow; we might take another year. Are we too far south or north?"

"What do you imagine it's like?" Ruins of an illustrious past littered the landscape, stirring hope and fear within Aminatra. The stone outlines of once substantial buildings lay buried beneath the consuming forest, only discovered as they climbed over the obstacles. Was this the fate of Mandelaton? Hope sprang only as fuel to keep moving.

Finbarl's own fears lay hidden beneath his dreams. "It is a place of freedom. People go where they like, talk about whatever, read and write about all and nothing. Food's plentiful. There's no fear of starvation, disease or Ferral."

"Where you do what you want," added Aminatra, appreciating the flight into fancy. "People can learn, invent and advance; be safe and loved."

"Who's loved?" Karlmon ran up from behind. "Look what Bokanda gave me!"

"A bloody rag. How lovely."

"A sling!" announced Karlmon, adding a stone and whirling it. Instead of hurtling afar, the rock escaped in a disappointing trajectory to hit Finbarl's boot.

"Ouch," uttered Finbarl with sardonic restraint.

"I have thrown a good one," declared Karlmon, examining the rag as though faulty.

"Practice, practice," said Aminatra.

Finbarl's stomach grumbled, prompting Karlmon to declare, "I'm hungry!"

"I know you are," said Aminatra. It was the first time Karlmon had complained. "We'll find you something this evening. Be brave and keep alert for anything edible."

"You get that sling working properly and we'll be able to bag plenty of food," encouraged Finbarl, his voice raised. "You too, Bokanda."

No reply came from behind.

"Everything looks like we can eat it," Karlmon observed as he made his way through the lush vegetation.

"I know what you mean, but nature is not beyond deceit," said Aminatra. "Have another go with that sling."

"Here, let me show you," offered Finbarl. "Don't want my toes walloped again."

With Finbarl and Karlmon distracted, Aminatra swallowed a few red berries gathered earlier, motivated by neither greed nor sacrifice. Someone had to prove their edibility or die proving otherwise. Her stomach welcomed the meagre donation with a cry for more. Already weak and tired from exertion and lack of food, her mind loitered upon a pessimistic fate, but as minutes passed into hours, anxiety melted into relief. She would keep her promise to Karlmon.

After their toughest day's walk since the mountains and snow, a perfect overnight camp clearing beckoned.

"There's a dead tree over there," observed Finbarl, his unenthused tone reflecting the mood of all. "Should make excellent firewood."

"Are you okay?" Aminatra asked Bokanda as he shuffled the last stretch and collapsed to his knees. "You're pale."

"Ah, Penela, don't be afraid. I'll protect you. They'll not take our souls."

Finbarl stomped over. "Enough of that! Get up! A bit of a coincidence you go crazy when there's work to be done. We're all collecting wood tonight." Gripping under Bokanda's armpits, Finbarl raised him to his feet.

Under a sweat-glazed brow, Bokanda stared out. "I'll kill us before they have a chance, my dear Penela."

With a gentle shove, Finbarl encouraged Bokanda on his way. "Karlmon, make sure he comes back with an armful."

"That was harsh," confided Aminatra. "I don't think he's faking. He looks ill."

"Don't care," answered Finbarl. "We can't afford to carry anyone. Same laws as the prison."

They traipsed into the trees, no further words spoken, their actions automated.

As Aminatra returned to the opening, loaded with kindling, she slid one hand into her pocket, hunting for the berries. Once the fire was alight, she planned to offer them around, taking the expected flak for her reckless tasting. Karlmon made it back before her, his own bundle of wood still in his arms, his face a picture of confusion.

"What is it?" asked Aminatra.

"That!"

Aminatra stood by her son, examining the ground in front. On a neat platter of leaves lay a dead lizard the length of an arm. Three sizeable pieces of unfamiliar fruit lay at its side. "Where ...? They weren't here a moment ago!"

"Finbarl caught us something," declared Karlmon.

"Finbarl!" called out Aminatra.

He dashed from the trees, his gun drawn, alert for trouble.

"You found us food?"

Finbarl frowned. "Err, no. What do you mean?"

"Look!" said Aminatra and Karlmon in unison.

"Cronax!" exclaimed Finbarl. "Where did that come from?"

"So, you didn't capture it?" asked Aminatra, her eyes scanning the surrounding woods.

"No," replied a confused Finbarl, gripping the gun tighter. "Where's Bokanda? We're not alone!"

"I left him collecting wood," said Karlmon. "He was very slow."

Aminatra continued scanning their surroundings. "But it's a friendly gift? If someone's out there, they wish us no harm."

"Or it's bait," countered Finbarl. "It's what I'd do to attract prey. Bokanda! Where is that lazy ferralax?"

"We're not some unthinking animal. There are easier ways to capture us. I'm willing to take the risk to satisfy my hunger. Are you joining me?" Aminatra knelt, picking the lizard up by its tail.

"If a gift, what do they want in return?" challenged Finbarl, prowling the perimeter, seeking signs of their benefactor and their absent companion. "Perhaps they took Bokanda? An exchange for the food. Not a bad swap."

"Shut up and go and find him!"

Karlmon sniffed at the fruit Aminatra held up, then nodded with enthusiasm.

"Perhaps they want nothing," suggested Aminatra. "Perhaps it isn't a gift. But I'm eating it and will thank or apologise to whoever later."

"Well, you'd better get the fire going. Throw me a fruit," requested Finbarl. "I'll try it first: ensure it's not poisonous."

"You still here?" Aminatra threw one of the green-orange fruits to Finbarl, then picked up another, took a big bite and smiled with bulging cheeks at the delicious flavour.

"Or you could try it first." With a shake of his head, Finbarl disappeared back among the trees. "Bokanda!"

Under the tree canopy, the dropping sun cast little light. Finbarl held his pistol forward, inspecting floor and shadows for signs of the missing and the mysterious. A diffused ray of light fell on an exposed sleeve, a hand flat on the ground.

"Bokanda! If you're sleeping, you go without food." A knot in his stomach cautioned Finbarl. He edged forward. "Cronax! Bokanda, are you all right?"

The Athenian's body lay still, head turned, exposing a flaccid, grey face, with the stain of vomit covering chin and floor. His chest slowly rose then descended, accompanied by a rasp.

"Why didn't you call for help?" asked Finbarl, kneeling to Bokanda's side, fingers feeling for his pulse. "Your heart's racing. What's wrong?"

An incomprehensible mumble left Bokanda's open mouth, his eyes flickering in helpless bewilderment.

"Aminatra! I need your help," cried Finbarl, hoping the tone was measured.

"Finbarl?"

"Over here. It's Bokanda. He's collapsed."

"I told you he was ill!" Aminatra arrived with Karlmon, both carrying their staffs in readiness for danger. "Oh, you poor thing."

"Help me get him back to the clearing. It's not safe here. Do you think it's something he ate?"

Aminatra shook her head. "He's eaten what we've eaten and that's hardly anything."

"He might have tried some of those berries."

"They're not poisonous." Aminatra spared Finbarl a sheepish glance. "Look at his arm, around the wound."

The sparsity of light stifled colour, but around the weeping wounds left by the lion's claw, the skin darkened. "Infected. The same as Maddy," Finbarl sighed, a nauseous flush reminding him of his mother's fate.

"Let's get him next to the fire. The chill of night won't help."

"We have to move you." Finbarl lifted Bokanda's torso until he sat upright, his head listless. "You're going to have to help. Let's get you up." He locked his arms around Bokanda's waist, lifting him onto wobbly legs. "Take one arm, Aminatra!"

"You got the staffs?" she asked Karlmon, wrapping Bokanda's limp arm around her shoulder.

"I'll protect you," announced the boy. "Shall I take the gun too?"

Struggling under the near-dead weight of their load, both Aminatra and Finbarl answered with a parent's glower.

The movement stirred Bokanda. "There were no Ferrals. I thought there were."

"You're back with the living," said Finbarl. "Good to have you mumbling again. Thought we'd lost you for a minute."

"No Ferrals. Why? Poor Penela. You didn't have to die. I thought I was saving your soul."

Finbarl and Aminatra exchanged a confused expression.

"Come on, let's get you warm," urged Finbarl, leading them back to the opening.

"At least our food's still here," remarked Aminatra, as they lowered Bokanda to the floor in range of the fire's warmth.

"He can have my blanket tonight," said Finbarl.

"If only Maddy were here. She'd know how to help him."

"She'd know how to help us," added Finbarl. "He can't travel. Our options are we stay a while to nurse him or go on without him."

"What about Hamner's?" piped in Karlmon.

Finbarl shrugged. "We can see what it has to say, but ... Well, I can't fathom out half the words."

"We need food inside us first," declared Aminatra. "That will help us think more clearly."

They chatted as the sweet aroma of the cooking lizard tickled under-used taste buds, their mood reversed. Bokanda slept soundly, the glow from the fire adding a little more colour to his cheeks. Speculation filled their excitable conversation. Who was their mysterious angel with gifts of food? Even Finbarl lowered his defences, content to relax.

Hamner's Definitive Medical Guide lay open, its pages flicking in the wind. "I've heard of antibiotics," said Finbarl, "but there's nothing here saying how to make it."

"Sleep's the best medicine," said Aminatra. "And it's time for my dose."

They allowed exhaustion and a sated stomach to lead them to a peaceful slumber. That night, if someone spied on them, they didn't care.

Finbarl awoke early, his complacent attitude discarded. The fire, long gone out, threw ash into the blustery air. Cursing his behaviour, Finbarl slapped his cheeks, stirring his senses, punishing his negligence.

A strand of Aminatra's long black hair crossed her face, fluttering to the rhythm of her breath. Finbarl brushed it away with a delicate finger, watching his sleeping wife for a moment, reminding him of his good fortune in these challenging times.

He climbed to his feet, arching his back, and surveyed the peaceful surroundings.

"How's the patient?" Aminatra smiled up at him.

"Hope I didn't wake you?" Finbarl smiled back and wandered over to inspect Bokanda.

"Na, who wants to sleep on a morning like this."

"Bokanda for one." Finbarl frowned. Something wasn't right. He crouched and shook the man by his shoulder. "Wake up. We'll get some broth on for you."

No response.

Finbarl pressed the back of his hand to Bokanda's face. Stone cold. "Cronax! I think he's dead."

"Dead?" Aminatra threw off her blanket and leapt across the ashes.

"Well, that solves one problem."

"Finbarl! You can be a heartless guard sometimes." Aminatra shook her head as she looked down at the body. "There's no doubt about it. Poor Bokanda!"

The dead man's face showed no anguish, just the placid finality of death.

"I'll dig a hole, you tell Karlmon," suggested Finbarl.

"To think, he waited all that time for someone else to arrive over the mountains and, having found us, he's gone."

"He was lost a long time ago," said Finbarl, scraping at the soil with Bokanda's machete. "Probably when Penela died."

"You may be right. Something bad happened there. I hate to think what."

Chapter Five

I t came as a relief as the landscape changed from tiresome forest to open, rugged terrain. When under the dense tangle of trees and vegetation, it seemed endless. To see the open sky again, feel the breeze, have a horizon to aim towards, felt good. Someone on their trail had nowhere to hide.

A cluster of bright yellow flowers glowed in the sunlight, delighting Aminatra and Karlmon. They stopped to pick some, sampling the fragrant, drifting aroma, then placed the blooms in each other's hair. Finbarl moved ahead, standing upon a raised crag, inspecting the land ahead. Air shimmered over the sandy stone vista, reminding him of home. For all its faults, he missed Athenia. All his memories dwelt there. But with bridges burnt, returning seemed impossible. Perhaps one day, when they found Mandelaton, he could bring the two civilisations together. If they ever located the fabled land.

"You look nice," said Finbarl, as Aminatra joined him on his vantage point.

"It's in memory of Bokanda," answered Aminatra, adjusting a flower in her hair.

"I miss him, and I don't," said Finbarl.

"I know what you mean. Not someone I would have chosen to travel with and yet we shared this journey. Who else has crossed the mountains and explored this land?"

"I didn't expect Karlmon to take it so badly."

"He's bitter you're the new custodian of Bokanda's machete," said Finbarl. "No, seriously, he's not seen as much death as you or I."

"I envy him."

"What direction should we go?" asked Aminatra, her arm sliding through Finbarl's.

"What evidence of life in any direction?" questioned Finbarl with a sigh. "That low ridge of hills limits our view. I suggest we head for them. Once on top, we'll have a better idea."

"And food? I've been looking for last night's fruits, but no luck."

Finbarl shrugged. "Any prey can see us coming now. Can't use the gun with Ferrals around. Unless we find a fresh-killed carcass, I'm not confident."

"Perhaps our benefactor will provide for us again?"

"Mmm, I'd rather they didn't. Or at least have the nerve to offer it in person."

"I was just grateful to have a meal," said Aminatra. "I don't think I could've managed another day's walking without it."

"We managed in the prison," observed Finbarl, refusing to acknowledge gratitude where owed.

Aminatra rested her head on his shoulder. "Ah, but there we relied on others to find food. Here, it's just three of us."

***

With the ridge of hills their target, they made excellent time, the open sky affording more daylight, their path a straight one. Twilight fell as they climbed the ridge. At the summit, a warm, pastel-pink sky stretched in the distance, seeping away as the sun disappeared behind the horizon.

"Looks like we won't see what lies ahead until the morning," said Finbarl, dropping his bag to the floor.

"I'm hopeful," said Aminatra, for no other reason than it was important to end each day with positive thoughts.

As they collected wood, each wondered what might await their return. Finbarl considered hiding in wait for their mysterious benefactor, but his needy stomach persuaded him not to scare off a meal.

"The wood's drier out of the forest," he called out to Aminatra.

"Reminds me of the land south of Bluebeckers," replied Aminatra, referring to their past life in the prison. Tall, gnarled bracken scrub dominated the heights, their broken twigs littering the floor. "Mind the thorns!" warned Aminatra towards Karlmon, who rummaged at the limits of her sight. He ignored her, deciding, when the inevitable mishap occurred, to ask Finbarl to remove the thorn from his throbbing finger.

"This should get going quick," declared Finbarl, returning to the campsite with arms full of wood. "I ..." He juddered to a halt, dropping his load, reaching for his pistol. As on the previous night, presented amid the clearing, a plate of leaves hosted a dead mammal amid a fruit selection. A significant difference also awaited.

On the far edge of the clearing, in the fading light, squatted the Ferral, her eyes locked on Finbarl. She balanced on her tiptoes in an undecided poise; escape or staying were both an option. Aminatra and Karlmon crept up behind Finbarl.

"She's back!" stated Karlmon, a little too loud for Finbarl's liking.

The girl flinched at the sound.

"So, she's our saviour," whispered Aminatra. "Why?"

"How did she follow us?" The muttered words escaping from the side of Finbarl's mouth. He held the gun at a forty-five-degree angle to the ground. Something prevented him aiming at the girl. "What does she want?"

Aminatra removed the machete from her belt, placed it on the ground and stepped forward one stride. The girl watched, nervous but stationary. With grace, Aminatra bent down, reaching for a piece of fruit.

"What are you doing?" hissed Finbarl.

"Shush!" Aminatra gripped the fruit, lifted it and displayed a smile to the girl. "Thank you," she said, her tone hushed. The ritual complete, she stepped back.

"What are you doing?" repeated Finbarl, his brow expressing exasperation.

"I'm accepting her gift," answered Aminatra. "Now, do the same!"

"Why?"

"Because! Join Finbarl, Karlmon!"

The boy shuffled next to Finbarl, any thoughts of the thorn in his finger forgotten. There, he awaited his elder's lead.

Finbarl, his eyes fixed on the Ferral, eased forward, stretching out his free hand. Karlmon copied.

"Don't make any sudden movements!" urged Aminatra from behind.

"Of course," whispered Finbarl, rolling his eyes for Karlmon's benefit, "because that would be crazy." With fruit in hand, they retreated. Karlmon mimicked his mother, smiling at the girl. Finbarl offered his finest surly acknowledgement.

"Now," instructed Aminatra, "take a bite and look like you're enjoying it, no matter what it tastes like."

Finbarl looked to the sky.

"Mmmmm." Aminatra led by melodramatic example, a crisp crack and slurp accompanying her bite.

The others followed. Finbarl, wishing to loathe in protest, savoured the refreshing, sweet juices flooding his mouth, emitting an uncontrollable, satisfied sigh.

The girl, still statuesque, somehow lost the sense of imminent flight. They were communicating at the most basic level, but they were communicating.

"I'll now offer her a piece," explained Aminatra, taking a step forward.

Finbarl tensed but refrained from commenting. He still didn't understand, but it was working.

Aminatra crouched down, imitating the Ferral. One piece of fruit remained. She picked it up, offering it forward. Only the girl's eyes reacted, growing by a fraction, as though boosted by hope. Aminatra nodded. "For you."

After an age for Aminatra, the girl pushed a leg forward. Finbarl's hand tightened on his gun. Aminatra remained motionless. Cramp invaded her legs, but she resisted the urge to move, desperate not to frighten the girl. Another step forward. Aminatra smiled: it hid fear but conveyed her sincerity. Karlmon positioned himself behind Finbarl, scrutinising round his legs.

The girl's progress reminded Finbarl of a scrub rat he once observed building its courage to take food from a prisoner's hand. That had provided a tasty meal. Was that Aminatra's intention now, to capture the girl again?

Ever closer she edged until within touch of Aminatra's hand. The Ferral's willowy arm stretched forward with equal patience. Aminatra studied her: the callused hands, half-formed breasts, protruding ribs and those penetrating eyes. She possessed a vulnerability, as though she might break in the wind. But this was the same girl who tracked them for days on end, finding food where they failed. Aminatra suspected her appearance belied an inner strength.

The Ferral's hand whipped across the last few inches, plucking the fruit from Aminatra's palm. A scuttled retreat followed, but closer than before.

Aminatra backed away, rising to her feet in a slow, unthreatening manner.

"What was all that about?" whispered Finbarl.

"She wants to join our pack," replied Aminatra.

"Our what?"

"Our pack," repeated Aminatra, as the girl bit into the fruit, offering the closest expression to a smile Aminatra had seen on a Ferral. "I think she's alone and sees us as a family to join." Aminatra bit into her own fruit again, smiling back. "She needs our protection. No one likes to be on their own."

"Can't she find her own kind or a pack of wolves?" said Finbarl, gurning in objection.

"Perhaps there aren't any more or they've rejected her," opined Aminatra.

"Great, a Ferral reject wants to join us!"

Aminatra gave her 'look'. "Eat your fruit and smile!"

Finbarl obeyed.

The cloudless sky fast sucked the heat from the evening and, while other things dominated thoughts, goosebumps and shivers prioritised the construction of a fire. Their earlier harvest of sticks lay scattered where dropped. Finbarl bent down under the inquisitive gaze of their guest, gathering the wood into a pile. "Karlmon, get the tinder kit from the bag," he instructed. "It seems rude not to cook the rodent our friend has brought us."

"I'll skin it," offered Aminatra. "We should offer some to her too. Do you think she wants it cooked?"

"Well, I'm not eating it raw!" protested Finbarl.

"I'm not suggesting we do," said Aminatra. "There's not much to go around, but we could give her a leg before we cook it."

Finbarl shrugged. "A happy, fed Ferral is better than an unfed, testy one ... if she must stay. Lucky Bokanda is no longer with us. Not sure they would have got on."

As Karlmon returned with the small tinderbox, Aminatra answered. "I'm not sure we have a choice. Unless you want to force her to go?"

Finbarl considered his previous struggle in tying up the girl and tutted in vague defeat.

The girl looked pleased as Aminatra lifted the rodent, watching with curiosity as the knife cut away the hide. Finbarl laid out a flat stone, building a small nest of dried fur, grass, fungus and wood shavings. His eyes flickered between his task and the girl. Placing a small-ringed metal pole in the middle of his kindling, he flicked a piece of flint down the metal. With practised technique, the sparks flew. Their fleeting existence appeared in vain as they disappeared into the nest, only for a faint ribbon of smoke to escape in triumph. The smoke built in density and then, as if by magic, a ball of flames materialised. Finbarl lifted the base-stone, laying the burning nest into the wigwam of twigs. When the twigs caught alight, they added larger sticks until the fire raged.

The Ferral, her attention consumed by Aminatra's use of tools, reeled back in alarm.

"Should have considered your fear of fire before joining us," crowed Finbarl.

"How do they keep warm?" asked Karlmon, putting his finger in his mouth to suck at his irritating thorn.

"Good question," replied Aminatra, as she moved towards the girl with reassuring gestures. "It's okay. It's safe as long as you don't touch it."

"I don't think she's mastered our language yet," chuckled Finbarl.

Aminatra ignored him, holding her palms up to the fire, rubbing her shoulders to show warmth. The fire, leaping high into the sky, lit up the Ferral's fear-etched face. Aminatra beckoned her forward, but without success.

"Leave her be!" said Finbarl. "You'll not convince her of anything. She's a Ferral."

"A smart Ferral, brave enough to reach out to us." Aminatra tried coaxing the girl one last time but conceded she had reached the limit of tonight's successes.

"Can I take the leg to her?" asked Karlmon, as his mother tore the limb off the carcass.

Aminatra smiled, pleased to see her son more accepting than her husband. "No, let Finbarl do it. We still don't know how she'll react to us." The boy screwed his face up in disappointment. "Finbarl!" Aminatra held the leg towards her reluctant husband.

The girl relaxed under the hypnotic, dancing flames. She flinched at the loud cracks, but the proximity of her new 'family' to the fire reassured her. As Finbarl approached, her eyes flicked to the leg of raw meat. She straightened, and with surprising confidence, accepted the offering, ripping the flesh from the bone with her teeth.

She was a problem they didn't need, pondered Finbarl, as he hovered, surveying their guest. How could they sleep knowing a Ferral lived among them? And yet ... He scratched his unkempt hair in contemplation. And yet she was familiar with this land, she found food, and better her an ally than an enemy. The thought of food coincided with the aroma of their supper cooking in the flames. What a strange form of freedom we've found, he said to himself, wandering back to the others: reliant on a Ferral to survive!

With a meal in their stomachs and the hard day's walk behind them, sleep came easily to the Athenians. Finbarl tried to stay awake, his eye focussed on the girl as she examined each section of her own body, but his mind soon drifted until sleep consumed him. His next conscious thought was not of the chilled morning air on his face but the warm body of Aminatra pressing against his back. He stretched out an arm, enjoying the pleasure of stimulating muscles after a night of stagnation, and he turned with a smile to greet his wife.

"Cronax!" Finbarl leapt to his feet, looking down at the naked body of the Ferral, her lithe figure moulded to his vacated shape and Aminatra's on the other side. The cry awoke Karlmon, who leapt up to join Finbarl, while the Ferral, eyes wide open, pulled herself into a ball.

Aminatra creaked an eyelid ajar but remained under the comfort of her blanket. "What is it?" she mumbled.

"The Ferral!" answered Finbarl, his voice higher by a degree. "She slept between us!"

"We wondered how they keep warm," said Aminatra, accompanied by a yawn. "Now we know."

"But ..." Finbarl sensed something in Aminatra's tone. "You knew she was there all night?"

Aminatra turned over, adjusting her body to find the warmth of her blanket. "If you will let the fire go out, then I'm not turning down additional warmth."

"Cronax!" cursed Finbarl again, this time more controlled. "You didn't think she might attack us?"

"Too exhausted to care. Now, if you don't mind, I was having a pleasant dream before you so rudely woke me."

"Pardon me!" Finbarl threw his hands in the air for the benefit of Karlmon, who giggled.

With Aminatra's sedentary response, the Ferral girl sensed the danger amounted to nothing. She found the married couple's exchange more interesting. Her fingers explored the blanket, intrigued by the fabric's smooth, warm texture against her naked skin.

"It's no good," announced Aminatra, sitting up. "I'm wide awake and cold."

"I'll get the fire started again," offered Karlmon.

"Thank you, but make it a small one," instructed his mother as she rolled up her blanket. "We'll just warm up the broth for breakfast, then get going."

"What about her?" sniffed Finbarl, nodding at the girl.

"Well, for starters, I'm not happy with a naked girl in the company of my son or snuggling up to my husband. Let's clothe her."

"I meant, what do we do with her when we head off?"

"I knew what you meant," said Aminatra. "We'll not shake her off. The only alternative is she comes with us. That's why I want her dressed and decent."

Finbarl had already come to the same conclusion but was neither willing to own the decision nor show support. He huffed, walking off into the undergrowth to urinate.

"Don't worry about him," said Aminatra to the girl. "He's a big softy."

The girl frowned and, at the sight of the smoke Karlmon generated from his twigs, retreated to her spot from last evening to suck the marrow from a bone.

Finbarl re-emerged, his finger scratching at an earlobe. "She can come with us," he declared, as though his own decision. "But she's not having any of my clothes!"

Aminatra sighed. "You only have one thawb and two undergarments. I don't think any would fit her."

"Mine are too small," added Karlmon. "Can she really come with us?"

"Yes."

"What do we call her?" asked Karlmon, excited at the prospect of a new friend, despite his continued nervousness around the Ferral.

"No idea. She won't have a name, so I guess we must think of one."

"How about 'Ugh'?" suggested Finbarl with a wry smile.

"Don't be cruel," chided Aminatra. "I was thinking perhaps 'Maddy', in memory of your mother."

"Maddy!" cried Finbarl with wide-eyed disbelief. "You want to keep my mother's memory alive through the form of this pitiful beast?"

"She's not a beast!" corrected Aminatra. "And you well know your mother's beliefs about the Ferrals. She recognised they were just like us and could be ...," she hunted for the right word, "... civilised."

Finbarl sniffed in derision. "What about Goya? Like the sewage master's wife. They share a certain aroma."

"I like 'Maddy'," opined Karlmon, as Aminatra opened her mouth to castigate Finbarl.

"Ganging up, eh?" said Finbarl, his tone a little more amenable for the boy.

"Let's see what she wants," said Aminatra, turning to face the young Ferral, who sucked and slurped on her bone. "MAD ... DY. MAD ... DY."

"GO ... YA. GO ... YA" Finbarl couldn't help but join in, talking in the same slow, loud manner adopted by Aminatra. "AUD ... E ... LECH."

The girl stopped chewing her bone, bemused at the odd behaviour of her pack.

"MAD ... DY," repeated Aminatra and then spoke without theatrics as the girl's eyes rested on her. "Maddy."

"Mmm ..." The Ferral made the noise but failed to enunciate beyond.

Aminatra willed her on, mimicking the sound, trying to guide her towards the next tonal change, her hands wafting encouragement.

"She likes the name 'Maddy'," declared Karlmon with a jig of delight, as the Ferral repeated her first effort.

"She can't even say it," huffed Finbarl. "For all we know, she just likes the taste of the marrow."

"Maddy it is," announced Aminatra, ignoring her husband, bringing an end to the discussion.

Chapter Six

"Where's Maddy?" asked Karlmon, as they strolled across a flat, open valley.

Finbarl ignored the question, still unwilling to accept the name.

"I don't know," answered Aminatra. "She seems to come and go as she pleases."

"Looks like rain's on its way," observed Finbarl, pointing to the black clouds above the distant hills, hoping to change the conversation.

"That'll be a relief. It's stifling today and we need to refill our water carriers." Aminatra adjusted her restless hair. A touch of rain would be most welcome, she contemplated, trying to recall the last time she had washed it.

The parched land showed evidence of recent rain with clumps of khaki grass. A gopher emerged from its hole, bobbing back down at the sight of the strange bipeds. Above, a vulture hovered on the thermals, surveying the landscape for carcasses, its shadow flitting across them. Finbarl suspected it also regarded the living, hopeful of some mishap.

From out of the dancing heat haze, the Ferral girl ran in from their flank, her new blouse contrasting with her rich, naked, red skin.

She glided, skipping obstacles, sweeping left and right, showing no concern for the rough terrain on her bare soles.

"Maddy!" exclaimed Karlmon on spotting her.

"Mmm." Maddy replied with her stock sound. She eased down to the pace of her companions with no after-effects from the recent exertion.

"Can you imagine if there had been more of them?" said Finbarl. "They'd have been on us in a flash. We wouldn't have stood a chance."

"By 'them', I presume you mean Ferrals?" replied Aminatra. "I wouldn't worry too much. They wouldn't eat you; you're too bitter."

"Ha, ha," responded Finbarl.

Maddy halted, crouching down, focussing on a distant object. The others stared into the shimmering air, seeing nothing.

"What is it?" asked Karlmon, a quiver of nervousness in his voice.

"Something's caught her attention," said Finbarl.

The girl dashed forward, gliding across the valley toward whatever piqued her interest.

"Come on," said Aminatra, "let's follow her! See what she's up to."

With less grace, their bags bouncing off their backs, Aminatra and Karlmon set off in pursuit. Finbarl stood for a moment in defiance, then followed with reluctant obedience. They made no impact on closing the gap but kept Maddy in sight. Every now and again she stopped, crouched, assessed the situation, then took off again.

"It's too bloody hot for this," yelled Finbarl, trailing behind Aminatra and Karlmon. Running in the day's heat was madness.

Aminatra swung her head, a finger to her lips. She waited for Finbarl to catch up, then whispered, "Our Maddy's on the hunt. Watch!"

In the distance, Finbarl made out tiny white dots moving across an isolated rock outcrop. "Cronax!" he gasped, struggling to gain control of his breath. "How on earth could she see back where we started?"

"No idea, but I'm keen to see what she does next."

With a deep breath, they continued their pursuit. After another 200 yards, they slowed to a sedate walk. Maddy, still far ahead, took her familiar, squatted stance, one leg stretched out as though ready to pounce.

"They're goats," said Aminatra between desperate attempts to fill her lungs.

Sweat glistened on Maddy's body, but she showed no other side effects from her mile run under the sweltering sun.

"We'd better not ... get any closer," urged Finbarl, his hand pressed against his burning chest. "The amount of ... noise we're making ... will scare them off."

The goats hopped between rocks, burying snouts into nooks, ripping out meagre morsels of growth. Finbarl counted a dozen but, just when he had accounted for all, another appeared, while others vanished amid the shade and rocks.

"Do you ... think you could get one ... with your spear?"

Finbarl inferred Aminatra's question as a challenge. He eyed his staff with its sharpened end. "Let me ... get my breath back first," he wheezed. The idea of another sprint and hopeful lob of his spear languished behind death on his list of preferences at that moment.

"How does Maddy ... intend to kill ... one?"

"With her smell?" Finbarl tried smiling at his own joke but found the fight for breath more pressing. He reached for the water bladder, pouring a generous splash over his face.

"Don't be so wasteful!" chided Aminatra, her breathing stabilising.

Finbarl let out a satisfied puff. "Those clouds are coming our way with rain." With a flick of his wrist, he splashed Aminatra. She flinched in surprise but smiled at the pleasing relief of trickling water running from her chin to her chest. A blurred movement in the corner of their eyes curtailed their urge to laugh. Maddy was on the move again. She remained low to the ground, her legs swinging in wide, long arcs, one arm trailing behind. The goats turned their curious heads, jaws still gyrating.

"By the time she's close enough to do anything, they'll escape," declared Finbarl, with Maddy still forty yards from her prey. Before the words left his mouth, the flailing arm of the Ferral ripped forward with ferocious speed, propelling an object at a low trajectory. The herd scattered in fright. Finbarl, overcome with surprise at the speed of it all, opened his mouth to remark on a miss, when he spotted a single, unmoving white mass. "Cronax! She got one!"

"I didn't see her pick up a stone," commented Aminatra. "Incredible!"

"Do you think she'll show me how to throw?" asked Karlmon, searching the ground for a suitable stone.

Finbarl climbed to his feet. "The stone will have stunned it from that distance. I'll finish it with my knife."

"You must run again," said Aminatra through a grin. "Maddy's got a head start."

The girl, already at the base of the outcrop, took two leaps up the rocks until level with her downed prey.

"I'll leave it to the Ferral," conceded Finbarl. "As long as she doesn't ... Oh, Cronax!"

In a single movement, Maddy snapped the spine of the unconscious goat and tore at its neck with her teeth. Blood squirted out, soaking her skin until she angled the flow into her mouth.

"Ouuh!" squirmed Karlmon.

"Once a Ferral, always a Ferral," remarked Finbarl.

"I'm with Karlmon," said Aminatra. "Ouuh!"

Maddy turned, searching for her companions. "Nnnarloooon!" She released a throbbing, triumphant cry from the depth of her throat. The dead goat, its flow of blood exhausted, lay across her shoulder as she descended to the valley floor.

"Maybe the blood was her treat for capturing the prey?" suggested Aminatra, as they walked towards her.

"Cronax! What sort of punishments do they have?" said Finbarl.

"Be thankful. We'll have plenty of meat for the next few days."

"Don't worry," said Finbarl. "She can take over all hunting duties. I still don't trust her, though."

Aminatra sniffed with contempt.

"What was that for?" asked Finbarl.

"You've spent most of your life trusting the wrong people," answered Aminatra. "The irony is, I suspect Maddy has no capacity to betray us. She just wants to belong, and now she's joined our pack, that's where her loyalty lies."

"I trust you," said Finbarl.

"And see where that got you!" Aminatra found relief in laughter, steering the conversation to less sensitive ground. "She wants you to have it."

Maddy held the lifeless goat by the nape of its neck, offering it to Finbarl.

"Why me?" he asked, a little self-conscious.

"Why?" said Aminatra. "Because you're the alpha male and in charge of this pack."

Finbarl laughed, accepting the goat. "If only she knew!"

Their journey continued, exhaustion forgotten at the thought of the goat for dinner. As the rain clouds approached, the heat dropped, bringing a comfortable temperature to the valley.

"I don't like the look of those clouds," commented Finbarl, as the sky darkened. "Have you ever seen anything so black?" A distant rumble added to the foreboding.

"Thunder," stated Aminatra.

"I'm scared," said Karlmon, his concerns accompanied by a faint whine from Maddy.

"There's nothing to worry about," comforted Aminatra. "It's only rain on its way. When we lived in the prison, we always danced and celebrated when it rained."

"Really?"

"Oh, yes. Rain brought life and was so rare; it was special whenever it fell. Maddy's scared, so it's important we show her there's nothing to be afraid of."

"Don't worry," Karlmon said, looking across to Maddy, distracted from his own concerns, as planned. "I'll look after you."

The Ferral, ignorant of words or language, continued her strange noises, reluctant to go towards the darkness.

A few weighted raindrops fell, speckling the ground.

"We're about to get wet," said Finbarl, as the rain increased. After a few seconds, the skies opened, delivering a torrential downpour.

"Shall we dance?" asked Aminatra, lifting her face into the rain.

Finbarl obliged, holding his wife by the waist. They twirled and floated upon laughter, their clothes drenched and clinging. Karlmon squealed in delight, jumping up and down in the lying water. Maddy looked on bemused before the excitement infected her.

A flash of lightning tore the sky apart, followed by an immediate retort of thunder, making the youngsters freeze. Aminatra and Finbarl continued unperturbed, their confidence inspiring Karlmon and Maddy to return to their antics. Soon they mimicked the adults, with Maddy leading in her own unique, unpractised manner. With a tilt of her eyes and a smile, Aminatra brought their imitators to Finbarl's attention. The sight of Karlmon clutched in the arms of a Ferral felt wrong, yet the laughter said otherwise.

The dancing lasted five minutes before the turning and pirouetting brought on a wave of dizziness. Finbarl released his wife with a formal bow. She clapped and twirled one last time. Karlmon copied, leaving Maddy confused and lost. She hadn't understood this experience, though enjoyed it.

The ferocious rain continued for another twenty minutes before subsiding to a gentle drizzle. Finally, it ceased. The ground, once golden, turned a darker hue as it absorbed the water. Deep footprints appeared on the soil, where once just vague impressions of their steps disintegrated in the sand. An old, dry channel now contained a trickle of water. Karlmon, still seeking fun, skipped through the water, splashing along its path.

"It's good to see there's still something of the child in him," commented Aminatra.

Finbarl nodded, conscious he had lost his own childhood by Karlmon's age.

"I'll top up the water pouches," suggested Finbarl.

"Excellent idea." Aminatra reached into her bag, retrieving the goat bladders.

Maddy joined Karlmon, her attention distracted over her shoulder.

"What's wrong with her?" asked Finbarl, returning with bulging water pouches.

"Perhaps it's the thunder," surmised Aminatra. "Listen, you can still hear it."

Finbarl shrugged, shoving the full bladders back into the bags. "Your hair looks nice."

Aminatra stroked her swept-back hair. "Thanks, it needed that rain. Your beard looks ... bedraggled."

"Thanks. I'd shave it off, but the knife's lost its sharpness."

Aminatra tugged on his sodden strands. "I think it looks nice too and makes Maddy feel she's with her own kind."

Finbarl reached forward to wrestle with his teasing wife.

"Eeiikk!"

Finbarl turned to see Karlmon and Maddy leap on the bank as a tangled nest of logs and debris led a torrent of water along the channel. "Cronax! Where did that come from? Don't stand too ..."

Before Finbarl finished his warning, the sandy bank collapsed, throwing Karlmon and Maddy into the ravenous waters.

"Karlmon!" cried Aminatra.

"Karlmon!" echoed Finbarl, as he ran towards the channel. The water churned, fighting its way down the valley, but the youngsters had vanished. Finbarl looked back in despair at Aminatra, who pressed her palms to either side of a gaping mouth.

"I heard a rumble, but assumed it was thunder. They ..."

"It happened too fast for us to do anything," said Finbarl.

"I don't understand where it came from," exclaimed Aminatra, staggering to the water's edge, scanning all directions for a sign of Karlmon. "I've never seen so much water."

"Come back from there!" cried Finbarl. "I don't want you swept away too."

"But he can't swim!"

"Nor can you. Get back! Our best bet's following the channel from the side. With this water's flow, they're some way ahead of us by now."

"Do you think he's all right?" Aminatra heeded Finbarl's advice, retreating from the danger.

"Sure, he is," answered Finbarl, his confident words hiding his own doubts. Like Aminatra, he failed to understand how a channel, dry one minute, turned into a river the next. The rain had ceased a while before, vanishing into the soil. This was more akin to a serpent attacking, winding across the landscape, devouring the children. So much of this world remained beyond his understanding.

They ran, calling out Karlmon's name but receiving no answer. A branch floated past, its vague shape lulling a moment's hope before an eddy exposed the truth.

"Maddy!" cried Aminatra.

"She doesn't know we've called her Maddy," shouted Finbarl, ten yards ahead of his wife. "She doesn't understand a word we say and can't answer either."

"Maddy!" Aminatra ignored Finbarl's insensitive pedantry. "Karlm ... Look!"

Away in the distance, amid the landscape's shades and colours, two black shapes nestled within the canvas. "It could be them," yelled Finbarl. "Come on!"

Aminatra found a reserve of energy, catching up with Finbarl. "It is them. I know it!"

After a further fifty yards, the figures sharpened, disclosing their human identity. Two individuals sat in silence, their feet dangling in the rushing water.

"Karlmon!"

The cry stirred movement. One figure turned its head, then they rose to their feet. Each yard closer exposed more. One yard confirming the slim, fragile frame of a child, the next proof they had found Karlmon.

"Karlmon!" screamed Aminatra, anguish replaced by joy. The boy expressed bemusement as his mother rushed towards him, arms open wide. Aminatra gathered him in a loving embrace until his squirming and complaints forced her to release him. "I thought we'd lost you!"

"I'm fine," replied Karlmon, as if nothing had happened. "It was fun."

"Fun!" exclaimed Finbarl, hands on knees, gasping for breath.

"Maddy can swim," Karlmon announced with admiration. "When we hit the water she held me, and it carried us along. I was scared to begin with, but soon it was fun. After a while, the river wasn't as ...," he sought the correct word, "... angry, and Maddy swam to land. I want to learn to swim."

Aminatra and Finbarl looked at Maddy, splashing the water with her feet like any other child. "Thank you," said Aminatra, bending down to hug her. The Ferral flinched, before recognising affection in the gesture, and nuzzling her head against Aminatra's neck.

"Thank you, Maddy," said Finbarl, uttering her adopted name for the first time, unnoticed by the others.

Chapter Seven

"It's not the first time she's saved a life," commented Aminatra, the traumatic day of the flood providing a regular source of conversation. "We were starving, remember? Her gifts fed us and gave us hope."

Finbarl nodded. "Not as dramatic, but you're right. I don't know what we'd have done without her." He stopped to nibble another meal provided by Maddy's lethal arm. "Look at the pair of them! They could be brother and sister."

Aminatra glanced across to where Karlmon and Maddy played, the former sharing his budding skill with a sling, launching stones at a target. Somehow, they communicated, a bond of trust developing in the wake of her heroics. "I don't think Karlmon's won yet, but he's enjoying himself. Maddy looks better now she's dressed and cared for. I feared she wouldn't keep them on, but I think she's keen to be like us."

Finbarl chortled as Maddy dashed off, pursued by Karlmon. "He follows her everywhere. He's learning a lot."

"I wonder if there's a danger he might pick up some of Maddy's less pleasant habits?" asked Aminatra. "He's obsessed with her. I've had to stop him eating raw meat."

Finbarl refrained from replying, aware of his redundant role in this one-person conversation.

"Oh, the truth is she can teach us so much. It's fitting we named her Maddy. Both kept us alive. Your mother would have liked her."

Nodding, Finbarl recalled fond memories of his mother. She was someone who made a difference in the brief time they knew each other.

"She's the only human we've discovered so far – not counting Bokanda," observed Aminatra. "She tracks, hunts and thrives in a land we don't understand. If Karlmon learns something from her, then it can only help. And I think she's learning from us too. She no longer fears fire, the clothes, and she's fascinated when we read the books."

"Have you spotted she sometimes tries repeating words?" remarked Finbarl, feeling it time to join the conversation.

"I have. She wants to speak. I wonder if she can, physically?"

"How would we teach her if she could? Perhaps we should try." Finbarl's relationship with the girl had undergone a revolution. He still worried, but now like a father. In the months since joining their pack, Maddy made their lives easier and more enjoyable. For the first time, Finbarl felt free. He had a family, happiness and contentment. Each morning, he awoke with the warm body of Aminatra pressing against his, Maddy now repositioned to sleep between Aminatra and Karlmon, looking forward to the day. Life's challenges persisted, but they possessed a belief that, together, they could overcome them. Karlmon matured at an astonishing rate, Aminatra and Finbarl bickered less, and the land seemed to be abundant with food – it had always been there but was now in view to their re-educated minds. Although they journeyed to a destination, a part of Finbarl hoped the journey would never end.

***

After another hard but satisfying morning walking, with the sun at its zenith and the heat almost unbearable, they stopped to rest. Maddy vanished to hunt with her shadow, Karlmon, in her wake. Aminatra sat under the shade of a tree, repairing clothes, while Finbarl, pleased hunting no longer concerned him, found a quiet spot atop a ridge of hills to inspect the magnificent vista.

"Where to next?" he asked aloud. At those quiet moments of introspection, he often talked with the spirit of his mother. She never replied, but somehow it helped him find the right question and often the right answer. "What's needed from the landscape to survive?" These were questions he knew his mother would have answered. She was the most intelligent, inspirational woman he had ever met. If they survived, there was hope they'd find other life, other civilisations, even Mandelaton. The wide, open plain below, which was an appealing, dappled mix of green among the broad strokes of sandy colours, was their next destination. They needed to find water. Despite more frequent rain compared with Athenia, they had limited capacity to collect and carry it. After three days, they exhausted their supplies. The occasional, juicy fruit helped sate their thirst, but not for long.

A hawk soared high above, riding the thermals. Finbarl watched, admiring its calm, languid circles as it climbed higher and higher. "Are you trying to tell me something?" The bird drifted across the bright blue background, now too high and too small to distinguish detail or discern how close it was. As Finbarl struggled to keep it in sight, the hawk plummeted, swooping at astonishing speed. Halfway down, as it broke the line of the horizon, it stopped, its wings caressing the air as it hovered. A moment later it plunged again, but Finbarl's eyes remained fixed on its previous location. In the far distance, smudged by the heat haze, a distinct line of vibrant green stood out. It lacked the disruptive, sandy patches seen elsewhere below, weaving left and then right. Finbarl thought back to the time they began their trek, high in the mountains, looking back at his old home of Athenia. From their vantage point, he had recognised the familiar route of the solitary river carving its way down from the glaciers to the town. In the arid landscape, a guard of verdant green marked its course. Could this landmark signify a river too? It was hard to tell how far away it was: twenty or thirty miles? "Thank you, mother." Their direction for travel had been determined.

Maddy and Karlmon's hunt proved unsuccessful, but they returned in high spirits. "I've taught Maddy to use a sling," Karlmon declared. "She's better than me already. Although I did hit a tree."

"Poor tree," said Aminatra.

"I almost hit a rabbit."

"Then we'll just have to eat tree tonight," quipped Finbarl. A crestfallen Karlmon prompted Finbarl to add, "But don't worry, you'll soon get your eye in."

"I'm nearly finished here," said Aminatra, threading a needle through a stocking. "I don't suppose there's a wonderful city down there?"

Finbarl shook his head. "No, but maybe a river."

"Water," sighed Aminatra.

"Swimming!" cried Karlmon, motioning towards Maddy.

She responded with a simple smile, her understanding still in question.

"I said 'maybe a river'," stressed Finbarl. "It gives us somewhere to aim towards."

"You're not to go anywhere near the water unless I say so!" ordered Aminatra of Karlmon, ignoring Finbarl's attempt to manage expectations.

"When I've learnt to swim, I can teach you, Mother. Just like I'm doing with your reading."

"Am I talking to myself?" muttered Finbarl, lifting his bag over his shoulder. "Come on, let's get moving. The river may vanish if we waste any more time."

Aminatra and Karlmon shared a perplexed expression and shrugged.

They walked another three days until the trees grew in density and the distant sound of babbling water caught their attention. A fox, accompanied by two pups, eyed them with suspicion before vanishing into the undergrowth.

"Where there are hunters, there is prey," commented Finbarl. "And all rely on a water source."

"The sound's coming from down there," said Aminatra, as the land sloped away before them. A thick line of trees obscured their view of the other side of the valley. They scrambled down the slope, holding on to the trunks to maintain balance. Maddy led, her poise unaffected by the challenge.

"I can see water!" cried Karlmon, pointing through a gap in the trees. The gradient steepened as they descended but, sure enough, the glistening melody of flowing water announced the river.

"Yee-haw!" shouted Finbarl, causing Maddy to turn in alarm. "Sorry, just pleased to find water." The smile on Finbarl's face put the girl at ease.

"It doesn't look deep," said Karlmon, with a hint of disappointment, as they slid down the last few feet to a pebbled bank.

"It isn't deep," confirmed Aminatra with a sense of relief. She could now enjoy her son paddling without worrying he might drown.

Crystal clear water flowed over rounded boulders, about twenty yards wide but only half a foot deep. The sunlight projected silver and gold dapples through the overhanging trees with long, stringy weeds dancing in the current.

Finbarl discarded his bag and crashed to his knees in the water, splashing the cool liquid on his face, letting it dribble into his mouth. "It tastes good!" He fell forward, face down, arms stretched out, causing a loud slap as he hit the water, before rolling onto his back and laughing aloud. Karlmon followed him in, sparing a quick glance upstream for unsuspecting torrents. Maddy remained with Aminatra on the bank, inspecting the surface and the strange behaviour of her companions.

"It's what boys do," explained Aminatra. "Even the grown-up ones."

Something in Maddy's eyes said, 'I don't understand your words, but I know what you mean.'

"Aren't you coming in?" cried Finbarl, now sitting upright, his drenched thawb clinging to his torso.

"I can swim!" declared Karlmon, happy to overlook the fact his knees walked along the riverbed.

"Well done," praised Aminatra, removing her shoes. "I'm going to cool my feet, but I've no desire to walk in wet clothes." A splash of water caught Aminatra across her face. Finbarl's sheepish grin exposed guilt, his hand poised to splash again. "Don't you dare!" challenged Aminatra, feigning anger.

"Have you ever seen such an enormous river?" asked Karlmon.

"No," answered Finbarl, "but I understand they can get much bigger. Huckal ... Hucko ... Huckle ... I'm trying to remember a book I read when your age …" He pondered for a moment. "Nope, it's gone. A river so wide you couldn't see the other side."

"Did they swim?"

"All the time," said Finbarl, his fragmented memory uncertain of facts. But what did truth have to do with a good story?

Aminatra tiptoed into the cool water, her robe hitched up. She closed her eyes, relief ebbing away the soreness of a day's walking. "We can't stay too long. We're exposed down in this valley."

Finbarl risked another teasing splash. "We've crossed one human in all our time here and she's turned out okay. Ambushed in paradise! Just our luck."

Aminatra turned towards the 'okay' companion, now prostrate, lapping up the river water as though a beast.

Ten minutes later, with water pouches filled and bodies refreshed, they set off again, climbing the steep slope to the plain above. By the time they reached the top, Karlmon was moaning. "My shoes are rubbing."

"Mine aren't," replied Aminatra with a smug smile. "But I didn't swim in the river."

"Where's Maddy?" asked Finbarl, unwilling to comment on the discomfort of his shoes.

"She's coming."

With consummate ease, the girl darted up the sharp gradient, holding a strange creature between her fingers.

"What is it?" asked Aminatra, intrigued by the silver scaled beast glistening in the sun.

"I don't know," confessed Finbarl. "I've seen nothing like it. Could it be a fish? That's what used to live in rivers. Huck … Whatever-his-name used to catch them in that book."

"A ffffiiissh," repeated Aminatra, enjoying speaking an unfamiliar word. "Can we eat it?" She mimicked eating to Maddy, who nodded in reply.

"Why weren't there ffisk in the river at Athenia?" enquired Karlmon, as he sniffed around the funny-shaped animal.

"Fish," corrected Finbarl. "I don't know. Perhaps the water was too cold for them."

"How do we cook it? Do we cook it?"

"We'd better not ask Maddy," said Finbarl. "I imagine she keeps it simple. But if we remain walking along the side of the river, we'll be able to hunt fish whenever. How hard can it be to trap one?" He offered his open pouch to the Ferral, who dropped their meal into its recesses, unaware of the opportunity to laugh at Finbarl's boast.

The landscape again changed in the company of a water source. It reminded Finbarl a little of home, where the Tourney valley erupted with life within its frame of arid scrubland. Here lush, noble trees dominated the upper edge of the river valley, not daring to spread too far from the fertile strip but providing generous shade to the trekkers. Elsewhere, grass covered the ground, interrupted by bushes and saplings. Despite the heat, walking was easier, allowing them to make significant distance as the hours of the afternoon passed.

"What's that funny smell?" asked Karlmon, as they halted for a brief rest.

"It's not Maddy, is it?" suggested Finbarl, having picked up the strange odour a while back.

The Ferral recognised her name and looked between her companions with a pique of interest. Karlmon sniffed around her. "It's not Maddy. Though she pongs." His little nose continued to twitch as he followed its lead around the party. "It's Finbarl!" he declared, pulling his face away in disgust.

Finbarl sniffed across the front of his thawb, the odour present but its source still a mystery. It smelt stronger to his right, and he realised his bag housed the guilty party. He swung it off his shoulder, pulling the opening apart. A pungent stink flooded the air. "Cronax!" cursed Finbarl. "What the ..." He pulled out the fish. The afternoon sun had done its worst.

Karlmon approached, testing with his own senses, reeling away in disgust.

"Throw it away!" cried Aminatra, holding her nose. "It's gone off."

Finbarl didn't need telling twice, lobbing the carcass as far as possible. Only Maddy appeared unaffected by the aroma, gasping in shock as her catch flew through the air. A pained shriek left her mouth before she sprinted off in pursuit. The others watched with a mix of amazement and disgust as she sat over her prey, ripping it apart with her teeth, sparing them a look of displeasure.

"I think we've upset Maddy," said Aminatra.

"I think my bag and everything in it will never smell nice again," moaned Finbarl. "She's welcome to it. There's no way I'm eating that."

"Well, we've nothing to eat now," said Aminatra. "And we've annoyed our huntress."

Finbarl shrugged. "She'll come around if she survives the food poisoning. I'm going down to the river to wash my bag."

Chapter Eight

Maddy slept soundly through the night and, at first light, disappeared in the company of Karlmon.

"She appears unaffected," observed Finbarl.

"Her stomach can no doubt cope with far worse," said Aminatra.

"I meant, she isn't holding a grudge."

"Children don't. They forget tantrums with the next distraction."

"I suppose you're right. Let's get our things together so we're ready to go when they get back." Finbarl lifted his bag. "Cronax! It still stinks. Everything still stinks."

As the miles passed, so the river grew. The valley sides flattened until they walked level with the flowing water. From see-through and pure, the river morphed into a muddy brown. Karlmon lost the desire to swim, the river no longer the benign play area but a menacing torrent, roaring its intimidating warning. His one foray into its murky waters with its tugging currents revived recent memories.

While the waterway snaked across the landscape, the group took a straight path, leaving the river's company, rejoining a few miles on. When the land rose again, they skirted around the hills, losing contact for days, until the tributary valleys led them back to the primary channel.

"I can hear the river," called Finbarl, after one such diversion.

"Me too," echoed Karlmon, running ahead to get the first sighting. At the top of a shallow rise, he skidded to a halt, turning with surprise on his face.

"What is it?" asked Aminatra.

Karlmon ran back to the adults. "There's a man."

"A man!" repeated Finbarl, rummaging in his bag to retrieve the gun.

"A Ferral?" pressed Aminatra.

"No, he's wearing clothes. Strange clothes."

"Stay here!" commanded Finbarl. "I'll look. Try to explain to Maddy." If she didn't scare them off, she may attack.

Maddy inspected a necklace fashioned from glass beads found among the river's pebbles by Karlmon. Showing little inclination to speak, she hummed in a pleasing, almost lyrical way.

Aminatra raised a hand with an open palm, added a finger to her lips to ensure silence. Maddy crouched in huntress mode, losing her 'normal' girl qualities. "Make sure she stays put," whispered Aminatra to Karlmon.

The boy ran to Maddy's side, taking hold of her hand and pointing to the ground. She growled, the instruction counter to her instincts, but trusting Karlmon.

Finbarl crept towards the ridge, nervous and unprepared, despite hoping for this day since leaving Athenia. To encounter someone from a different civilisation drove them on. He carried a wishful image of Mandelaton: a utopia of enlightened people, of learning and liberty. But what if they harboured ill will? What if they found a worse civilisation than Athenia?

Flat upon the crisp brown grass, Finbarl peeked over the lip. It was a man! Finbarl struggled to contain a laugh, triggered by Karlmon's withheld fact: the man was having a shit. It seemed somehow wrong to spy, but the man's attire fascinated Finbarl. A pair of multi-coloured, baggy trousers hung around his ankles, while over his torso he wore a vibrant red top with tassels across the chest. Most impressive of all, the hat. With a broad, open back, it folded to a point at the front, decorated on one side with an array of bright and bushy feathers. Finbarl fought the urge to call out, fearing any man would panic while so vulnerable. He held on until the man secured his magnificent trousers around his waist.

"Hello!" called Finbarl, climbing to his feet, stepping down the slope, his gun out of sight behind his back. "I am a friend. Mandelaton?"

The man froze, uttered a strange word, then sprinted away in obvious terror. Finbarl cursed, taking one step forward, considering pursuit. After further thought, he spun around, reclimbing the ridge. "He ran away."

"Why?" called back Aminatra.

"I don't know!" exclaimed Finbarl. "Maybe a strange man emerging from nowhere."

"Maybe I should have made first contact?" suggested Aminatra, joining Finbarl on the ridge. "A woman's less threatening."

"You wouldn't want to see what I saw," said Finbarl.

Aminatra looked concerned. "Why? Are they monster-like?"

Finbarl laughed. "No, he was having a dump." Aminatra's admonishing fist struck his shoulder.

"So, what do we do now?" asked Aminatra, as Maddy sprinted past.

"We follow," determined Finbarl. "I suspect Maddy can pick up the trail."

With the river so close, providing a natural barrier, tracking the man proved easy. Just thirty yards on, through a narrow thicket of trees, they found themselves on a grass bank, opening on to the river.

On a thin strip of golden sand stood five men, all holding an array of weapons. Behind them, tilted at a forty-five-degree angle in the shallow water, lay a large man-made object.

"It's a boat!" gasped Finbarl, recalling images from books once read.

One man, not ten yards away, shouted something unintelligible, waving a machete towards them. Finbarl gripped his pistol. Theirs had been a bold approach, marching up to a group of strangers. He prayed it hadn't been a mistake. The men appeared to lack guns, but their machetes and axes conveyed a menacing intent. Two bullets remained within the chamber of Finbarl's pistol. Was now the time to use them?

"We mean you no harm," called out Aminatra, Bokanda's machete remaining untouched on her belt. "We come from a long way away." She held Karlmon for his protection and to show children were among them. Maddy's intimidating snarl neutralised the gesture, but Aminatra's diplomacy triggered an excited conversation between the men.

"What do we do now?" asked Finbarl.

"We wait," said Aminatra. "We're guests in their land and need to prove we're no threat."

The oldest man took a step forward. "Alo, I am Captain Tarlobus Mendine. We are traders. Ou are ya?"

Finbarl and Aminatra exchanged puzzled glances.

"Did you understand that?" asked Finbarl.

"Yes, and no. My brain says I shouldn't have, yet it seemed familiar."

The man spoke again. "I am Captain Tarlobus Medine. Speek yar language."

"I understand him," announced Karlmon.

"So do I!" declared Aminatra, a smile forming to replace her concern. "I am Aminatra. This is Finbarl, Karlmon and Maddy. We are travellers."

"Aminatra," repeated the man as best he could. "Alo. Wiere ya from?"

Aminatra pointed east. "From across the mountains."

This provoked a flurry of animated chatter among the men, as the man called Tarlobus translated.

"Long way," said Tarlobus in response.

"Yes, long way," concurred Aminatra. "Where are you from, Thalibas Meden?"

The mispronunciation forced a smile from Tarlobus. "Riufer," he said to blank faces. "Riufer," he repeated, pointing to the water.

"Oh, river!" exclaimed Finbarl. "He's saying they've travelled down the river."

Tarlobus nodded his head. "Yee, riufer. Wiere ya go?"

"Mandelaton," answered Aminatra. "We're seeking Mandelaton."

Tarlobus shrugged before relaying to his companions, who shook their heads.

Behind Finbarl and Aminatra, Maddy paced in her animal-like nature.

The activity caught the eye of the traders. "Wat she?" asked Tarlobus, nodding his head towards the girl.

"What she?" repeated Aminatra, her mind struggling to decipher.

"What is she," suggested Finbarl, as he turned to see what intrigued them.

"Oh, she is friend," said Aminatra. "She is Maddy."

"Mardy," repeated Tarlobus, before adding, "strange."

"Yes, very strange," said Finbarl with a grin, eliciting a laugh among the men on Tarlobus' translation.

"Corm, join oos!" beckoned Tarlobus. "We eit."

"Not nice, Finbarl," chastised Aminatra in a whisper, "but keep it up, it's making us friends."

Finbarl, Aminatra and Karlmon climbed down onto the sand, approaching the men, leaving Maddy prowling alone. Convinced their visitors posed no threat, the traders' weapons now lay on the ground, while the group dispersed. A couple waded through the water to the boat, returning with a box. Tarlobus motioned for his guests to sit on the sand. "We eit," he repeated.

With a confirmatory exchange of glances, Finbarl and Aminatra led Karlmon down to the beach. The welcoming mood dispersed concerns, and Finbarl slid his gun into his thawb. The box contained a rustic red pot and plates.

"Dis Corelye," said Tarlobus, introducing the man carrying the box. "Captain's first mate."

"Hello, Corelye," said Aminatra, recognising only the name from the sentence.

The man, his blond hair equal in length to Aminatra's, looked blank, failing to respond.

"Not speek language," explained Tarlobus, scratching at his scruffy grey hair.

The idea others spoke unfamiliar languages never occurred to Finbarl. While the Mandelaton letter contained some unfamiliar words, he understood it all, and the books he read as a child were all in one dialect.

"What language do you all speak?" asked Aminatra.

Tarlobus sighed as though the question pained him. "We all speek Talifian, bot Corelye e speek Atticas. Bortell und Malto speek Deluqic. Gidhaert," he thumbed towards the youngest among their group, "e speek some of yar language. All speek language of ome city. Captain Tarlobus speek every language."

"Including ours," said Finbarl.

Tarlobus nodded. "Yee, dat odd. Ya speek ancient language of scholars. Forgot by most, bot still used by dem."

"You said 'city'?" enquired Aminatra. "Each man is from a different city? How many cities are there?"

This time Tarlobus shook his head. "Na, Bortell und Malto from same city: Deluquine. Bot, yee, dere are many city."

"How many?" pressed Aminatra.

Tarlobus thought hard. "About ... fowell." Unable to translate, he held up both hands, flashing ten fingers followed by four.

"Fourteen!" exclaimed Finbarl.

"Yee, sorm big, sorm small."

"Civilisation," said Finbarl with reverence. "What city are you from?" Before Tarlobus answered, the young crewman with a beard of colourful beads and rings through his ears arrived with bowls of olives and dry bread. "Thank you."

"Gidhaert of Parodis," explained Tarlobus. "Say alo!"

The man eyed each of the interlopers. "Hello, I am Gidhaert Wilboon. You speak the tongue of the scholars? Have you been to Parodis? Is it not the best city there ever was?"

Tarlobus laughed. "Der only fing a Parodisian loves more dan deir city is demselves. Gidhaert miss breakfast to preen imself."

Gidhaert fired an annoyed glance towards his captain. "A Parodisian prides themselves on their appearance. Is it not a sign of superiority?"

"Bah!" Tarlobus reinforced his judgement with a spit.

"Parodis," mouthed Aminatra, her eyes enthralled by Gidhaert's decorative beads and bright clothes. "It sounds wonderful. Like paradise. We've travelled from beyond the mountains to the west."

"Dey tell us already," grumbled the captain to his crewmate. "Wiy ya not listen?" He spoke in a softer tone to Aminatra. "We go to

Parodis. Captain Tarlobus, na city. Born on riufer ... river. Trader. I sell from one city to another. Eit!"

"A trader," repeated Finbarl, biting into an olive. "Incredible. Trade was dead in Athenia. No one to sell anything to; nothing to sell."

"Parodis trades with all. It has the most marvellous markets," said Gidhaert.

"From across moontains, ya say?" began Tarlobus. "Wat dere?"

Finbarl smiled, a little in shame. "Nothing. Just desert, Ferrals, and death."

"There are some marvellous people there," corrected Aminatra, wiping a little olive oil from the corner of her mouth. "But it's a hard life. We thought we were alone."

"Then you'll love Parodis," declared Gidhaert.

Tarlobus sprayed a string of incomprehensible words in the young man's direction. With a frown, Gidhaert retreated to the boat.

"Sailors should be working, not talking," explained the captain. He then nodded to the grassy bank. "Ya not alone. Wiy girl not eit?"

Maddy sat on the grass examining her body, as was her way.

"She's a Ferral," explained Finbarl, conscious their host showed no reaction to the word. "They're not from Athenia."

"She'll find her own food," added Aminatra. "She's a remarkable huntress."

Tarlobus shrugged again, unconvinced Maddy ate at all, given her wiry frame.

"How far is the nearest city?" asked Aminatra.

Tarlobus held up eight fingers. "Duite days on river. We ere for ... um ... fur. Unter sell fur to us; we sell to city. Not many corm dis far west."

"How many days' walking is that?" enquired Finbarl.

"Ya want go to city? Many, many weeks' walk. By riufer duite days."

"Yes, but we don't have a boat."

"Captain Tarlobus ave boot: der Medino," exclaimed Tarlobus with a hearty laugh, gesturing towards the vessel.

"The Medino?" questioned Aminatra.

"Name of boot," explained Tarlobus, tapping his chest. "My boot. Captain Tarlobus as room for friends."

Aminatra and Finbarl looked at one another and smiled. "Did you hear that, Karlmon? We'll be going on a boat."

Karlmon crunched into some dry bread. "I've never been on a boat before," he said with enough hesitation to suggest he didn't understand what it entailed. "Can you swim?"

Tarlobus laughed again, scaring the boy. "All Mendines can swim! Taught as baby." He put his hand out about a foot off the ground to show his meaning. "Bot wiy swim wen ya ave boot?"

Karlmon frowned, not sure what to make of Tarlobus.

"We drink now!" declared Tarlobus, at ease with his guests. He turned towards the boat and yelled, "Malto, che filto vin!" A moment later, the man they had first encountered wandered across carrying an urn. He seemed uncomfortable in their company. Perhaps, Finbarl considered, embarrassed at having run from them. After his departure, Tarlobus tapped the side of his head "Malto, not good up ere. Malto und Bortell, not trust."

Finbarl glanced across at the pair, wondering what Tarlobus meant.

"Ya drink!" Tarlobus poured a generous amount of liquid from the urn into four mugs, passed them around and raised his own. "We drink to friendsip!"

Awkward silence followed as Tarlobus' solitary mug remained aloft. The captain nodded in encouragement until Aminatra understood and lifted her mug.

"Slutree!" cried Tarlobus and, with considerable force, hit his mug against Aminatra's, causing the fluid to spill. To Tarlobus' delight, Finbarl and Karlmon followed. The captain downed his drink in one. The Athenians sipped but finding it pleasant guzzled the rest. "Is good?" enquired Tarlobus.

"Is good," answered Finbarl, enjoying the alcoholic beverage warming his throat and stomach.

Karlmon starting coughing, making Tarlobus erupt with mirth.

"Peraaps too strong for boy?"

The man known as Corelye called over and Tarlobus nodded. He turned to his guests. "Der tide as turned. We make ready to leave."

"The tide?" asked Aminatra, unfamiliar with the word.

Tarlobus searched his memory for the words to explain. "Water rise und fall und rise again." Aminatra's face remained confused. "We must get on Medino," continued Tarlobus. "Ya soon see tide."

With Tarlobus yelling instructions, the crew scurried about adjusting ropes and fixings. All the shouting and orders reminded Finbarl of life as a guard in Athenia. The boat, an inanimate bystander to date, righted itself amid the rising water. Watching from the beach, Finbarl studied the long, graceful design. Low in the water but wide and stable, it rocked on the surface. A tall pole occupied its centre with a wrapped canvas bound at a right angle. An open space occupied the front, with boxes stacked across, while a small hut sat towards the rear.

"Ya corm on board now," instructed Tarlobus from the deck. "Bring yar friend." He pointed to Maddy on the bank.

Aminatra waved to the girl. "Come on, Maddy! We're going on the boat." She remained unmoved. "Karlmon, go get Maddy." If anyone could get through to the girl, he could.

The boy leapt up to the grass bank. Finbarl and Aminatra craned to hear as Karlmon spoke to his friend, pointing in the boat's direction.

After some time, Karlmon walked back. He turned, beckoning her to follow. At last, she edged forward, only to stop again. Karlmon repeated his part, taking a few steps, encouraging Maddy to follow.

"For Cronax's sake!" cursed Finbarl. "What's the matter with her?"

Gradually, they made it to the sand.

"Corm!" called Tarlobus from the boat. "We must go! Tide!" He pointed down at the rising water.

"Come on, Maddy!" urged Aminatra, as the Ferral crouched once again.

"You and Karlmon get onto the boat with the bags," instructed Finbarl. "I'll convince Maddy."

Aminatra examined the face of the girl for signs of fear or stubbornness. "Okay. Karlmon, you take my bag. I'll take Finbarl's."

"Come on, Maddy!" cried Karlmon with desperation as he waded into the water. Gidhaert took the bags, offering a hand to pull them up. "It's okay, Maddy," called back Karlmon from the deck. "Look, we're okay."

"Maddy," cooed Finbarl. "We must go on the boat. It will take us to a city. We'll be safe there, I promise." Except for her name, the words meant nothing to the girl. "Maddy, please! We don't want to leave you." Her face remained unmoved.

"We must go!" shouted Tarlobus.

Finbarl clasped Maddy's arm, tugging it, but she pulled back and he released her. "She doesn't want to go!" cried Finbarl towards the boat. "What should I do?"

"We can't leave her!" yelled Aminatra.

"Maddy!" screamed Karlmon, now in tears.

Finbarl turned back to the Ferral. "You're one of the family now," he said, grabbing her by both arms, lifting and throwing her over his shoulder. Her limbs thrashed as a fearful howl escaped her throat and Finbarl smiled in memory of their earlier encounter.

The crew on the boat observed, half amused, half uneasy, as Finbarl carried the writhing girl towards their vessel.

"Ya know ow to treat yar women," crowed Tarlobus, unaware of the poisonous look from Aminatra.

"Here, take her!" urged Finbarl as he stood next to the bobbing vessel, the water past his stomach.

Gidhaert looked undecided, inspecting the strange girl at close range for the first time.

"It two-man job," said Tarlobus, between laughter. "Bortell, il requir por manue lilet!"

Bortell, the largest of the crew, two inches taller than Finbarl with a doughy, harsh face, ambled over. The water rose, lifting the boat higher. Finbarl stretched to lift Maddy as high as possible, allowing the two men to grab a flailing limb each. Sight of his crew flinching from the girl's blows caused Tarlobus to laugh even louder, his demeanour in marked contrast to the sombre Aminatra and Karlmon beside him. Bortell dropped their reluctant cargo's legs to the deck, with one final flying foot catching Finbarl in the face.

"Bravo!" cried Tarlobus. "Ya ave already earned yar passage." He stepped to the side, offering his own hand to Finbarl. "My men ave deir ands full," he quipped, pulling Finbarl on board. "Now ya must calm ya beast. Sailing serious business." He nodded to Bortell to leave the girl in his crewmate's custody and get back to work.

Easier said than done, thought Finbarl as he watched the Ferral struggling under Gidhaert's hold. "Aminatra, dear," said Finbarl, collapsing on the deck, rubbing his sore chin. "I think this is perhaps one for you. I'm not sure I'm in Maddy's good books."

Aminatra laid a hand on his shoulder. "You did the right thing," she reassured. "Who knows what's going on in her head? It must be strange for her."

"We're on a boat," said Finbarl. "It's strange for us all." He paused for a moment. "Hey, we're on a boat!" Amid the drama, the unfurled canvases caught the wind, propelling the boat across the water. The bank drifted away, the boat picking up speed as the river grew deeper and deeper. Finbarl marvelled at the beauty of the boat and the river. Oh, to have travelled so in Athenia, he pondered. How different things might have been.

"Ouch!" Gidhaert reeled away from Maddy, cursing in a foreign tongue, with Aminatra trying to calm the girl.

"What happened?" asked Finbarl, knowing the answer.

"Maddy bit him," replied Aminatra. "It's his own silly fault for standing so close after he released her."

Finbarl smiled in apology, as the girl retreated to the wall of the hut, crouching in the angle.

The crew exchanged looks of amusement, except Gidhaert, nursing his wound at a safe distance from Maddy.

"Sha not say much," called out Tarlobus, now seated at the rear of the boat, holding tight to a bar of wood.

"Maddy can't talk," answered Aminatra, before adding with defensive pride, "but she's very intelligent."

"Wiere sha from?"

"The mountains," said Aminatra. "She was alone, so we adopted her."

"Sha reminds me of ... wolf," said Tarlobus, digging deep to think of the correct word. He translated for his crew, receiving a chorus of guffaws.

Finbarl thought the same but felt protective. "She's very human, just rough around the edges."

Tarlobus shrugged and spat into the river. "Captain Tarlobus once wrestle a wolf."

A silence followed; Finbarl was uncertain how to respond to such a random brag.

"Boy!" Tarlobus called to Karlmon. "Corm, Captain Tarlobus show ya ow to steer boot."

Karlmon hesitated.

"Go on, Karlmon," encouraged Aminatra. "It'll be fun."

"But what about Maddy?" he replied.

"If you look occupied and happy, then Maddy will relax and settle down," explained his mother.

Karlmon shuffled round the side of the shallow hut, shy eyes reluctant to fall on Tarlobus.

"Old on to side!" cautioned Tarlobus, as Karlmon walked down the narrow strip of deck. "We not wan ya falling in."

The boat rocked in the current, causing Karlmon to stagger towards the edge but, heeding the captain's words, his hand found a secure grip on the rail.

Tarlobus stood, the bar still in his grip, motioning for the boy to sit. "Now, old dis between yar arm und grip der end wit yar ofer and."

Karlmon copied the captain's actions, struggling to understand his accent. His face lit up as he sensed the pressure of movement within the bar.

"It called tiller und controls der rudder," explained Tarlobus, pointing into the water behind while still easing the tiller. "Pull left to go right und right to go left." He nudged the tiller left and to Karlmon's delight the boat banked and turned. Tarlobus released his hand. "Now, ya pull it back so we go straight. Easy now!" With his hands free, the captain removed his impressive hat, placing it on his extra crew member. "Dis belong to Heronus: a famous admiral!"

"Look mother! I'm steering the boat," laughed Karlmon, his shyness gone as the hat slid over his eyes.

Aminatra smiled, noticing Maddy perk up with interest at the sound of her friend laughing. "She'll be all right," she commented to Finbarl. "Though keep your distance for a while."

"Where would you have me go?" replied Finbarl.

Chapter Nine

"Look, birds!" cried Aminatra, taking a break from scrubbing the Medino's deck. A large skein of honking geese flew above.

Finbarl and Karlmon eased themselves up from their own scouring duties. "How many?" asked Finbarl. Despite their jobs, life on board the boat felt serene after months of hiking across difficult and dangerous territory.

Karlmon tried counting. "Thirty or thirty-one."

"Tirty-one," echoed Tarlobus, watching from his vantage point at the tiller. His broad smile reflected the jovial affection he had developed for his extra crew members. They worked as payment for their passage, but with the boat over-crewed and they under-skilled, tasks were minimal and easy.

Bortell also watched, mumbling under his breath, resentful at the captain's benevolent attitude, in stark contrast to his tirades against his permanent crew.

"Maddy, birds!" Karlmon called out, pointing to another flock of geese.

Still unsettled, Maddy undertook no duties. She sat on the roof of the hut, watching the workers below, her natural inclination to roam curtailed by the limits of the boat. With a cursory glance, she inspected the geese, licked her lips, then curled up to examine something within her hand.

"What you got there?" asked Aminatra, intrigued as the object flashed in the light.

As expected, no reply came, and Maddy continued to stare with fascination, turning it over and over between her fingers.

"It's a piece of metal," commented Karlmon. "She likes anything like that. Shiny stuff."

"Where did she get it?" asked Aminatra.

Then Gidhaert spotted Maddy's curio, letting out a distressed cry. He stepped closer but stopped, unwilling to confront the girl. Instead, a high-pitched, indecipherable complaint flowed toward Tarlobus.

The captain spared a glance toward Maddy, then growled back at his crewman. With a further hesitant glare towards Maddy, Gidhaert tugged his beard and cursed, before retreating below deck.

"Ya creature as taken one of der lad's rings," called across Tarlobus. "Captain Tarlobus tell im, if e want it back be man und take it." A sly smile formed between beard and moustache.

"We'll try to get it back for him," said Aminatra.

"Good luck," said Finbarl. "If it makes her happy, may be best to let her keep it."

"Hasn't she stolen it?" asked Karlmon, standing by Maddy, examining the ring for himself.

"Er, well, yes and no," answered his mother. "It's not hers to take, but she doesn't understand what property is. We must teach her about wrong and right."

"Shame," commented Finbarl. "She's the most honest person I know."

***

As the sun paused for a last breath of day, Finbarl sat by Aminatra, legs dangling over the boat's side, water lapping beneath them. Anchored for the night about 100 feet from the bank, they rocked in the gentle current. Karlmon coaxed Maddy into playing a restrictive game of chase around and over the hut, while the crew played cards beneath deck.

"We've made it," declared Finbarl. "We've contacted another civilisation. Our journey's over."

"We haven't seen this civilisation yet," replied Aminatra, swinging her feet in the cool air.

"Yes, but there are several cities. Healthy trade. This boat! It belongs to an advanced civilisation."

The boat impressed Aminatra with its tiny hut leading to a spacious cabin within the hull, but she remained sceptical. "The boat could be a hand-me-down from a past age? They don't possess anything else more advanced than Athenia."

"But Captain Tarlobus is a man of the world: learned, a traveller, free to go where he wants. Are those not qualities we seek?"

Aminatra shrugged. She never took anything for granted. "He seems a fine man, but what about Mandelaton? That's the city we hoped to find. They've never heard of it."

Finbarl, distracted by a small bird skimming the water surface and flitting away, shook his head. "Sorry, you were saying?"

"Mandelaton!"

"We've been heading for the only place we knew existed," said Finbarl. "Now we've learnt of other civilisations. The letter never said they were the most superior civilisation."

"The fact they reached out said they were superior," challenged Aminatra. "Why have no other cities tried crossing the mountains?"

"Fair point," agreed Finbarl. "But perhaps they've tried. We just found the Mandelaton letter. What other evidence were the Wardyns withholding from us?"

"Okay," said Aminatra, "but Tarlobus, this man of the world, would have mentioned it. He didn't seem interested."

"So pessimistic," chided Finbarl. "Let's focus on the future. Imagine what we'll find when we get to these cities."

"Karlmon!" yelled Aminatra, causing Finbarl to jar away as the sound hit his adjacent ear. "Careful!"

"Sorry, he's being reckless," Aminatra explained to Finbarl. "He thinks he can swim, but he can't. Don't want him falling in."

"A little warning would be nice," chastised Finbarl, poking a finger into the offended ear. "Now, what do you want in your city?"

Aminatra pondered for a second. "No walls, no food shortages, and no guns."

Finbarl nodded. "Not seen a gun so far and I'm avoiding mentioning mine. Maddy was a surprise to them, so no Ferrals. Why would they need walls then? And if they can travel wherever they want, food must be plentiful."

"And what do you want?"

Finbarl recalled the archaic books of his youth and the amazing possessions of the ancients. "A flying machine!"

"Finbarl!" laughed Aminatra. "Be realistic."

"No, they existed. I've seen pictures. So, why not this civilisation?"

"I know that," stressed Aminatra, "but with flying machines, they'd have flown over the mountains to visit Athenia. All we've seen in the sky are birds."

"Suppose you're right," Finbarl replied with disappointment. "How about books for everyone?"

"I like that," said Aminatra, placing her folded arms on the handrail and resting her chin within them.

Raised voices from the card game broke the serenity. "Tarlobus doesn't sound happy," commented Finbarl.

"He enjoys shouting," said Aminatra.

Gidhaert emerged from the hut, his face red with anger. He stepped towards the seated couple. "Bad loser!" With raised hands accompanying his cryptic words, he vanished to the rear of the boat for privacy. His brooding presence brought Karlmon and Maddy's game to an end and they joined Finbarl and Aminatra.

"He's not happy either," said Aminatra.

"They've been drinking," commented Karlmon, sliding his body between his mother's and Finbarl's.

"What makes you say that?" asked Finbarl.

"We could hear and smell them through the walls," replied Karlmon. "It reminded me of when the guards drank. Kept us awake in the barracks."

Finbarl nodded, recalling his days back in Athenia when he and his colleagues drank themselves silly on the local beverage: Kywaczek.

Then Tarlobus emerged from the hut, staggering across to them, reeking of alcohol. "Ya're fine woman, Aminatra," he declared.

Finbarl's hackles rose, but Aminatra's hand patted his thigh.

"Ya're locky man, Fffinbarl," added the captain.

"Why thank you," said Aminatra, always the diplomat. "Is everything all right? You sounded angry."

Tarlobus laughed, provoking a little snarl from Maddy. "It's noffing! A captain keeping crew in order. Appens all time." He stood silent for a moment, focussing his mind to keep himself steady. "We sleep now. Tomorrow, danger. Captain Tarlobus take ya ffrough ... cataracts."

"Cataracts?" repeated Finbarl, confused.

"What's cataracts?" asked Karlmon.

The captain fought to find the words, but with alcohol befuddling his mind, he failed. Instead, he waved his hand up and down and repeated the word. "Cataracts." Aminatra and Finbarl exchanged a bemused glance. "Ya sleep, bootiful lady," continued Tarlobus. "Tarlobus will look after ya."

With that, he staggered away, vanishing into the hut, thumping the doorframe with a final drunken lurch. Maddy snarled again.

"What was that all about?" asked Finbarl.

"He was rather sweet," said Aminatra.

"I mean danger and cataracts, not his soft spot for you."

"No idea," answered Aminatra. "But he's right, we should get some sleep. Whatever tomorrow holds, we need to be ready." She yawned with exaggeration, before adding, "And some of us need our beauty sleep."

Chapter Ten

Despite Tarlobus's mysterious warning, Finbarl slept well. The last three nights he'd enjoyed a deep, restful slumber, something lacking for a while. They slept up on deck, under the stars: a luxurious domain compared with the uneven, living floor of the mountains, jungle or plain. Life on the water appealed to Finbarl.

Smoke and the aroma of food stirred him. He opened an eye, spying Corelye cooking over a portable stove. The crewman appeared closest to the captain.

"Eat!" Corelye said, spotting Finbarl shaking his limbs free of sleep. With his Athenian vocabulary exhausted, he held up some meat on a prong.

While the others slept, Finbarl wandered over, his blanket wrapped round his shoulders. "Thanks. What is it?" he asked, picking a chunk of white meat off the fork.

"Eat!" repeated Corelye.

The meat burnt Finbarl's hand. He flipped it from one to the other, blew hard and popped it in his mouth. Still too hot, Finbarl juggled it around his mouth, exhaling a cooling breath. With a delicate bite it broke up, releasing a soft and succulent flavour. "Mmm, it's good," he mouthed, still managing the heat with a gaping mouth. "A little muddy, but nice."

"Mmm," echoed Corelye, surprising Finbarl with another word he understood. "Fish."

"Fish!" exclaimed Finbarl. "Cronax, it tastes better than it smells!"

"Fish," repeated Corelye, keeping their communication simple.

"Yes, fish. Mmm," answered Finbarl, rubbing his stomach, accepting another piece.

"What's mmm?" asked Aminatra, strolling over to join them.

"Fish," answered Finbarl, prompting Corelye to repeat their shared word. "It's nice. Not like anything I've had before." Finbarl passed her the piece cooling in his hands.

"Oh, yes," said Aminatra, letting the flavour sink in. "A little muddy, but I like. Maddy's one must have been off."

"Don't remind me," said Finbarl. "I can still smell it every time I open my bag."

Captain Tarlobus's voice boomed from the stern, and they peered over to see him supervising Bortell and Malto raising the anchor. As the captain let forth another instruction, Gidhaert unfurled the sails, capturing the light morning breeze. The boat glided off at the start of their day's journey. A heron inspected them with lofty disdain from the bank, before stabbing the water to capture breakfast. In the arid lands of Athenia, nature seemed against them; here, all felt as one.

"Secure down der cargo!" yelled the captain, waving his hand towards the Athenians.

"With what?" asked Finbarl.

"Anyfing ya find. Make sure nofing loose or we lose!"

Finbarl shared a nervous exchange. "Is this to do with last night's warning?"

Aminatra shrugged. "Best do what he says. There's a ..." She paused, placing a hand on her chest. Her face drained of colour. "Excuse me!" Dashing to the boat's side, Aminatra vomited into the river.

"Are you all right?" asked Finbarl, comforting with a rub of her back.

"Must be the fish," commented Aminatra, wiping her mouth with her sleeve.

"Not all agree wit life on der water," laughed Tarlobus. "Gidhaert sick wen e join oos. Nofing make Tarlobus sick."

"Go!" urged Aminatra to Finbarl, as she gulped down the cool river air. "Start securing things down. I'll be fine in a minute."

"Are you sure?"

"Go!"

Finbarl found a coil of rope by the mast and began threading it through the handles of some crates. Tarlobus wandered forward, inspecting his efforts, nodding his head in satisfaction. Behind, the crew dashed back and forth, tightening ropes, securing anything loose. As the land on either side rose, squeezing the waterway into an ever-narrower channel, the vessel picked up pace.

Tarlobus shouted an array of commands. Corelye lowered the sail, Gidhaert and Bortell leaned over the side, retrieving four large oars stored on braces. They placed them into oarlocks, and Corelye and Malto joined them, each holding an oar.

"Too dangerous wit sails," explained Tarlobus for the benefit of the Athenians. "We soon in Puela Gorge. Need more control."

Anxiety showed on the faces of the crew, but ignorance left Finbarl and Aminatra confused.

"What do you mean by dangerous?" asked Aminatra.

Tarlobus laughed. "Dangerous for lesser captains darn Tarlobus, bot we okay. Ya sit round mast though or we say goodbye."

Frustrated but trusting, they complied. "Karlmon! Maddy!" called out Aminatra. "Come here! We must stay away from the side." Karlmon skipped across, while Maddy remained on her perch. Aminatra waved encouragement, but the girl refused to move.

"Try food," suggested Finbarl, waving a piece of dried meat in the air.

"Really, Finbarl!" Aminatra sighed. "We must be patient and try to communicate as though she's one of us. If we treat her like an animal, she'll behave like one."

But the bait worked. Maddy spotted the treat and hopped down, taking the meat.

"You feeling better now?" asked Finbarl with a smug smile.

"Hmmm," answered Aminatra, rolling her eyes.

***

Tension rose within the crew. Their actions carried an urgency but their voices a quiver. It all seemed at odds with the changing nature of the river. While cliffs now loomed to each side, they veered away, creating a wide, open expanse. The river lost its purposeful drive, spreading out to a serene lake. Only when Finbarl looked straight ahead did it all make sense.

The cliff walls cut in at almost a right angle, intent on blocking the valley. A sharp, narrow 'V' ripped down the middle, allowing the river to squeeze through. The sedate, brown waters of the lake churned into a bubbling white cauldron. Finbarl's muscles tightened as the boat lurched forward, as though gripped and pulled by an invisible force.

They entered the narrow corridor accompanied by the roar of charging torrents, burying the shouts of the crew. Up the bow went, crashing back down, dipping left, then rolling right. The crew struggled with their oars as Tarlobus grasped tighter to the tiller, yelling unheard instructions to his men. Finbarl craned his neck, trying to understand what was happening. Tangled vegetation dappled the cliff face. It was hard to focus as the boat raced down the angry gorge. Finbarl held tight to the mast, his torso tossed in all directions as though riding a bucking camel. His eyes caught the foliage-adorned rock, causing his brow to crease in confusion.

"What's happening?" cried a fearful Karlmon, breaking Finbarl's train of thought.

"I'm not sure," answered Finbarl. "The river's narrowed with the same amount of water trying to get through. Tarlobus assured us we'll be all right. We must stay out of the way."

"Let's sing a song!" encouraged Aminatra, a smile hiding her own fear.

Green on the other side.
Gold from my past.
Colours in these other places,
Never seems to last.

Her voice wavered, but after a verse, as the others joined in, she sang with confidence.

It's better where I came from.
Better in my dream.
Better over distant hills.
Better than this seems.

The crew, distracted from their efforts by the melodic accompaniment, received a stinging rebuke from Tarlobus.

Land of my fathers.
Blue skies overseas.
Tempting me far from home,
Away from reality.

It's better on an island.
It's better in-between.
Better where I've never gone,
And better than what I've seen.
So, all this doubtful thinking, it leads me to conclude,
That life at any time and place is wanting to improve.

The boat lurched left and then down, bringing the singing to an abrupt halt. Maddy tried to rise, but Finbarl calmed her with a hand to her shoulder. The gesture sufficed where once only forcible restraint had worked. She adjusted herself into her familiar crouched-ball posture and stared ahead.

A harsh, grating noise sounded to the right, leading to an explosion of undecipherable shouting from Tarlobus toward Malto. The crewman looked terrified as he attempted to gain control of his oar.

"Hang on to the mast!" cried Finbarl over the deafening roar of the river, the boat tossing and turning.

"What if the boat sinks?" yelled Aminatra, clutching Karlmon between herself and the mast.

"We'll be all right," stressed Finbarl, trying to do the same with Maddy, but sensing her reluctance. "Tarlobus knows what he's doing."

Then the noise faded, and the boat steadied. "Did I not tell ya trust Tarlobus?" declared the captain. "Ya ave a bootiful voice, Aminatra, though was a sad song."

Finbarl and Aminatra released their white-knuckled grips from the mast, reclining in relief. Around them the crew members collapsed to the deck, exhausted. Only Tarlobus gained energy from the drama, regaling the boat with an imperial strut.

"Was that it?" asked Finbarl.

"Puela Gorge!" answered Tarlobus. "Fast water und rocks mean we go fast. It over! Now need to find damage." The captain walked over to the prostrate Malto, planting a boot in his side, cursing as he did so. "Not all rocks avoided!"

"But that didn't look like a natural gorge to me?" queried Finbarl. "The cliff looked ... well, it looked man-made! Nature's just reclaimed it."

Tarlobus bowed. "Man-made. Natural. Still a gorge und Tarlobus get us frough safe."

"But it was huge!" pressed Finbarl. "What was it? How did they make it?"

This time Tarlobus shrugged. "Der past only leaves problems for today. Once riufer eld back by giant wall. Wiy? Captain Tarlobus not know."

Finbarl rose to his feet, shaking his head in wonder, looking back at the fractured barrier. He offered a hand to Aminatra. "You still feeling sick? Cronax! I am!"

"No, but Cronax!" exclaimed Aminatra. "I'm glad that's over."

They glanced over the hut to the bubbling cataract now behind. It looked less terrifying from the calm water beyond. Tarlobus disappeared below with Bortell and Corelye, the noise of his banging and cursing carrying up to the deck. Malto sat nursing his bruised ribs, while Gidhaert lowered the oars back into their braces.

"Hope it's a one-off," commented Finbarl. "I wonder how they got up it in the opposite direction?"

Before Aminatra offered her view, Tarlobus reappeared. He threw another curse towards Malto, who flinched at the prospect of further assault, but the captain restrained himself, instead turning to Aminatra and Finbarl. "Is good. We iyt rock bot no leak. Need to moor to check ootside. Ya get to go on land again." He yelled directions to his crew, sending them scurrying about setting the sail and manning the tiller.

"Did you hear that, Maddy?" asked Aminatra. "We're going to land."

The Ferral tilted her head, curious at the mention of her name.

An hour later, Tarlobus guided the vessel into a pocket of calm water, dropping the anchor. A busy exchange took place between the captain and Corelye, ending in the latter taking over the mantle of shouting at the put-upon Malto. The sorry sailor removed his shoes, jumped overboard and vanished beneath the water.

Finbarl and Karlmon rushed to the side to observe. Malto's head re-emerged, the water lapping around his shoulders.

"Is mistake," explained Tarlobus. "E get cold checking."

At the captain's nod, Malto pinched his nose and dived under the water. Aminatra joined the spectators, engrossed with Malto's antics. Tarlobus paced behind, mumbling to himself. When Malto resurfaced, the captain leaned above the beaming crewman, listening to his findings then replying with another string of curses.

"Der fool say na big damage. We okay. Lucky for im, eh?" explained Tarlobus.

Finbarl and Aminatra nodded, not understanding Malto's error. "When can we go ashore?" pressed Aminatra.

Tarlobus burst forth with another set of instructions, prompting Malto to throw his arms up in disgust. "Ya can go now," said Tarlobus. "I tell Malto to carry ya."

"That's unnecessary," said Aminatra, unsure how a man up to his neck in water could carry her. "But he can take Karlmon."

The boy wrinkled his nose in disappointment. "I wanted to swim!" he protested but jumped into the water before Malto with a whoop. The sailor turned his head, avoiding a splash to his face, still catching

Karlmon. Another splash to the side surprised everybody. Maddy, escaping the confines of the boat, paddled through the shallows to the shore.

"Do you think we'll be able to get her back on board?" asked Finbarl, as he lowered himself into the chilly water.

Aminatra watched until both Karlmon and Maddy made it to land. "I hope so." Mimicking her son, she jumped in front of Finbarl, who caught her and guided her to the shallows, where Aminatra waded the final few metres. Behind, with raucous laughter, the crew were stripping naked on deck.

"It's good to be on land again," commented Finbarl, gripping the front of his thawb and wringing out the water.

Karlmon and Maddy vanished into the trees, their pent-up energy seeking an outlet.

"Don't go far!" cried Aminatra.

"They'll be all right," reassured Finbarl. "Tarlobus knows this land. He wouldn't have landed here if there were dangers. And Maddy can handle herself."

Aminatra acknowledged the point but, like all mothers, still wanted her child in sight. "We should gather food. We don't know how long Tarlobus' generosity will keep us."

"You're right," agreed Finbarl. "At least the land looks fertile. I don't think they need our help at the moment." He looked behind to see the crew wading towards the shore, carrying their clothes in a bundle above their heads.

"Do we need to tell Tarlobus what we're doing?" asked Aminatra.

"No, they're not going anytime soon, and they won't leave without us."

Again, Aminatra shrugged, unconvinced, but acquiesced. "Let's go in the direction of Karlmon and Maddy. I would prefer it if they were in sight."

A fig tree, its harvest of ripe fruit spread between branches and floor, attracted a troop of gibbons and squawking birds. With Finbarl's and Aminatra's approach, the animals retreated.

"There's plenty to go around," reassured Aminatra, as the apes chattered with disdain from a distance, their annoyance turning to alarm when a third human arrived.

"Karlmon, what have you been up to?" asked Aminatra, as the boy wandered over.

"Just exploring," he explained.

"Where's Maddy?"

Karlmon shrugged. "She climbed a tree and wouldn't come down. So, I left her."

Aminatra sighed.

"Perhaps we should find her?" suggested Finbarl. "Entice her down with some figs."

"Aeeeekkkk!" A distant scream sent the watching gibbons scrambling up the nearest tree and the regrouping birds to flight.

"What in Cronax's name was that?" cried Finbarl, his darting head trying to pin down the source.

"Did you bring your gun?" Aminatra dragged a reluctant Karlmon to her side.

Finbarl shook his head. "It's in my bag on the boat. I didn't want to get it wet. Make your way back to the boat! I'll investigate."

"Shouldn't we stay together?"

"Okay, stay close behind me and be ready to run if you have to." They hurried towards the source, scanning the surroundings for signs of danger. After 100 yards, raised voices carried from their right. "That's Tarlobus!" whispered Aminatra.

"Come on, he'll know what's happening," urged Finbarl.

They found the captain with Malto and Bortell; the latter was animated, clasping a blood-soaked arm.

"What's happened?" cried Finbarl, skidding to a halt.

Tarlobus looked less than pleased to see them. "Ya girl, sha attack Bortell!"

Vibrant scratches adorned Bortell's cheek, blood spreading on his sleeve. He let forth a burst of angry, incomprehensible words in their direction.

"What did he say?" asked Aminatra.

"E say sha joust attacked im for na reason. Like wild beast."

Finbarl scratched his chin. Maddy would attack like a wild beast, but only if provoked. "Where is she?" Tarlobus translated the question for Bortell, who replied with another explosion of angry words, pointing to a thick clump of trees.

"What was he doing in there?" asked Aminatra, conscious it was a distance from the boat. The question seemed to stir doubts in Tarlobus and his tone changed as he translated again. This time a heated exchange took place between the captain and his bleeding crew member.

"E say e look for wood for stove," said Tarlobus.

There was an ample supply of wood nearer, leaving the answer sounding hollow.

Maddy emerged from the trees and, seeing Finbarl, Aminatra and Karlmon, made her way towards them. She stopped on sighting the ship's crew and snarled.

"It's all right, Maddy," reassured Aminatra, beckoning her closer.

Maddy crept forward a few more paces, her eyes locked on Bortell, the snarl permanent. At ten yards' distance she halted again, a smudge of blood visible around her mouth, while her left cheek glowed a sore red.

"Did you assault Maddy!" challenged Aminatra. "You got what you deserve, you Fer ..." She stopped short of using the old Athenian slur. "You barbarian!" The tone compensated for the weak insult.

Finbarl screwed his fist into a ball, ready to land a blow on Bortell, but Tarlobus held up his hand. "Enouf! We deal wit dis. We don't know wat appened. Could be self-defence."

Aminatra missed a breath. "She's a young girl! It's indefensible."

Tarlobus looked flustered. "Sha not like any girl I know."

"What was he trying to do to her!" yelled Aminatra.

"Na, na, na!" said Tarlobus, his face an awkward red. "I speak to Bortell. Ya ave my word."

Aminatra's hackles remained up.

"It could all be a misunderstanding," Finbarl said, trying to lower the temperature. If they lost the crew's protection, they would be in trouble. "I think Bortell's learnt his lesson not to mess with Maddy."

The words irked Aminatra but gave her time to consider the wider picture. "Tell your men to keep away from Maddy! That girl's capable of ripping your throat out if she doesn't like you."

Tarlobus absorbed the words with a glance at the crouching Maddy, her tongue licking at the blood around her mouth. "I believe ya," he said. "Now, we move on. Back to boot. Friends again."

An uneasy mood hung over the boat. Only Tarlobus behaved as before, barking orders and encouraging Karlmon to develop his sailing skills. Maddy, somehow enticed back aboard, sat in her sullen posture atop the cabin. Bortell observed her with a mix of hatred and fear, while the other crew members kept a respectable distance.

"I thought we were safe," commented a disheartened Aminatra to Finbarl.

"We are," he reassured. "They've learnt their lesson and Tarlobus seemed genuinely upset."

"Tarlobus carries on as though nothing happened."

"We don't know what happened," stressed Finbarl. "Maddy can't tell us, and she doesn't seem too upset. I've seen camels easier to read than her."

Aminatra glared, unamused by the analogy. "It could be more sinister! Maddy isn't upset because she doesn't understand what that beast tried to do. I'd hoped we'd left such barbarity behind us in Athenia."

"It's one man," sighed Finbarl. "You want to judge them all on his behaviour?"

"We can judge a civilisation on how it responds to such behaviour."

"We're in the middle of nowhere. Who knows how far from civilisation! If he or anyone else tries anything else like that again, I'll find a home for one of my remaining bullets."

"Oh, how bloody civilised!" yelled Aminatra, storming off to find solace in Maddy's silent company.

Finbarl cursed to himself. What in Cronax's name did Aminatra want him to say?

Chapter Eleven

T ime passed, while distractions and necessity thawed the atmosphere on the boat. Unfamiliar sights and experiences continued to surprise the Athenians. On the fifth day, a vast herd of deer crossed the river before them. A hundred heads ploughed through the water in a determined column, joining a hundred others escaping the churning waters for dry land. The approaching boat panicked the creatures, their speed increasing, but failed to dissuade those still starting their crossing.

Tarlobus hollered a command to lower the sail, allowing the barge to drift in the current and the deer to complete their journey from one bank to another.

"Smoke!" called out Karlmon a few miles further on.

To the crew's amusement, the Athenians gathered on the port side, cheering at the sight of distant figures tilling the fields around the cottage from which the smoke originated.

"What is this place?" asked Finbarl.

Tarlobus shrugged. "Na name. Still long way from city. Bot in territory of Parodis."

At the mention of Parodis, Gidhaert perked up. "I'll take you into Parodis, if you wish. It is beautiful. I will visit my family and friends."

Finbarl saw the smile on Aminatra's face and answered in the affirmative. "Yes, please. Is it far?"

"Two more days on riufer," answered Tarlobus. "I trade dere for day, pay river toll, den travel on."

"Will they expect unfamiliar people?" asked Aminatra.

Gidhaert looked confused by the question. "Of course! Parodis is on the river, with traders and pilgrims passing through all the time. Though no one who dresses like you."

Aminatra blushed, glancing down at her attire. It had never occurred to her their clothes would set them apart. "Will there be food for us?"

"Arvest good dis year," said Tarlobus, "but ya need pay for food."

"Pay?" queried Finbarl. "What does that mean?"

Tarlobus rolled his eyes and uttered something in his own tongue before answering in theirs. "Ya need exchange somefing of value for food."

"Like a token?" suggested Aminatra.

Tarlobus frowned. "Na, like mooney or another product. Did ya not ave mooney?"

Aminatra and Finbarl shook their heads in unison.

"Yars must be strange land," said the captain.

***

The evening arrived accompanied by a brief shower of rain before the clouds drifted away to expose the stars. Finbarl closed his eyes, ready for a good night's sleep, his mind racing off to the life awaiting them. In trying to conjure an image of Parodis, memories of Athenia surfaced, his only benchmark. They had walked away from Athenia as it burnt, but it still symbolised a place of safety. To be among and working with others was to be strong. Yes, Parodis was like Athenia, but better. That was his last conscious thought before his heartbeat synchronised to the gentle, rhythmic breathing of Aminatra by his side and he joined her in sleep.

Finbarl's dreams wandered a strange path. The contentment fuelling his sleep became lost and corrupted by black figures above, oppressive and mocking. One moment he laughed amid his family but was then naked and alone. A noise crossed the world of reality into his subconscious. It occupied an illogical place. His conscious mind intervened and, in a flash, he sat upright, awake.

"What ... what is it?" Finbarl stuttered, looking up at a shadowy face that moments before haunted his sleep.

To Finbarl's side, a muffled squeal escaped from Karlmon. The boy struggled amid the clasp of a stranger, his mouth covered by a gloved hand. Beyond, Finbarl made out Aminatra's slumped body held under each arm by two further silhouettes. Adrenaline coursed through Finbarl as he tried to climb to his feet but, as he pushed up on his right arm, a foot lashed out, and he collapsed back down. An intense stab of pain shot through the arm. Agony and confusion swirled in his mind, as an object, a mere smudge in the darkness, struck his forehead. The blink of terrifying reality dissolved into dreamless unconsciousness.

Chapter Twelve

A throbbing, agonising beat accompanied the meaningless words that awoke Finbarl. He opened his eyes, the light compounding the pain in his head. Over him stood Corelye, his outline blurred through Finbarl's groggy eyes. The sailor spoke again, repeating his previous line. Only one word triggered recognition: Aminatra. Finbarl struggled to sit upright; a nausea swept through him as pain exploded from a vague source. The name of his wife stirred broken memories. As his hand sought the source of his headache, he recalled fragments of the night.

"What happened?" asked Finbarl, his fingers feeling their way over the tender lump on his forehead. He willed his other hand up to assist in the examination, but it disobeyed, limp and useless by his side. The befuddled world made no sense.

Corelye's excited tone conveyed some measure of the drama, but his language none.

As Finbarl's sight sharpened, he noticed Corelye's expression flicker in alarm as he stepped back. With a pained rotation of his neck, Finbarl turned to see Maddy crouching by his side, her features sympathetic.

"I don't suppose you can explain what happened either," said Finbarl, looking into the youngster's eyes.

Maddy emitted a plaintive sound and nuzzled her head on Finbarl's upper arm.

Something bad had happened. Finbarl sensed that much. "Where's Aminatra? Karlmon?"

Again, Corelye answered with the familiar word of 'Aminatra' amid an incomprehensible sentence, his eyes fixed on the unreadable Maddy.

"What in Cronax happened?" demanded Finbarl, as he tried to push himself to his feet. His raised voice set off a thumping pain in his head, competing with the searing pain the action triggered in his arm. "Ferralax!" he cursed. "My arm!" He collapsed back down, clasping his limb with his other hand.

"It brooken," came a familiar voice.

"Tarlobus! Thank Cronax. Someone to tell me what's going on."

"I get splint for ya arm," explained the captain, waving the materials in the air. Tarlobus knelt by Finbarl, mindful of Maddy by his side, and examined the arm.

"What happened!" pressed Finbarl.

"In time," said Tarlobus, his voice as quiet and soothing as Finbarl could remember. "Bot ya arm bad. Need fixing. Will urt."

Finbarl opened his mouth to demand an explanation, only to find a stick shoved in longwise.

"Bite down!" ordered the captain.

Finbarl's eyes met Tarlobus' and he recognised the portent of remorse within the captain's and bit down as instructed. "Argghhh!" The pain defied description as Tarlobus grabbed Finbarl's arm on either side of the break, then pulled and pushed in a sharp movement.

Maddy backed away at Finbarl's scream, her teeth exposed, her body poised to attack the inflictor.

"No, Maddy ..." A swirling nausea overwhelmed Finbarl once again.

"Old im!" instructed Tarlobus, one eye on Maddy, as Finbarl fainted backwards. "It body's way of coping."

Corelye held Finbarl upright by the shoulders, while the captain laid out two sticks and some bandages.

"We elp Finbarl," explained Tarlobus with a nervous smile towards Maddy, who remained unmoved.

Corelye laid Finbarl down, as the captain lifted the sticks and placed them on either side of Finbarl's limp arm, cooing all the time, "Good girl. All good." As soon as Tarlobus secured the bandage round the splints, they edged back to a safe distance.

Maddy moved forward, her snarl hidden, and crouched next to the prostrate Finbarl, her eyes lost and sad.

***

"Cronax!" Finbarl shot upright, his mind trying to recover a grasp on his place in time. "What happened?"

"Ya faint," said Tarlobus. "Reset yar boone."

"I remember," gasped Finbarl, looking down at his bandaged arm. "Cronax, that hurt."

"Ere." Tarlobus offered a mug. "Drink!"

Finbarl sniffed at the liquid within and, reassured it possessed the potency to do him good, downed it. "Wow! Could have done with that before you did my arm."

"Ow arm?" enquired the captain.

"It's ..." Finbarl stopped, turning to offer a reassuring hand to Maddy. "What about Aminatra and Karlmon? What in Cronax's name happened?"

Tarlobus looked Finbarl in the eyes, holding the silence too long. "It bad news," he began. "A small boot paid uos visit. Dis fool," he nodded towards Gidhaert. "E attacked, und knock oot by Bortell und Malto. Na time to raise alarm. Der dirty, fieving cheats!"

"I don't understand. Where's Aminatra and Karlmon?" Overwhelming panic consumed Finbarl.

"Goone," answered Tarlobus.

"Gone! What does that mean?" cried Finbarl, his face draining to white.

"Adonelisians!" vented Tarlobus. "Not good at all. I believe Bortell und Malto ...," he spat in disgust, "... ave traded yar woman und boy to slavers."

"Slavers!" exclaimed Finbarl, as Maddy brushed her head on his neck. "What's a slaver? Why? How do we get her back? Where is Bortell? I ... I ..."

Tarlobus laid a calming hand on Finbarl's shoulder. "Sorry, my friend. Dey long goone. Der Adonelisians, violent, warlike scum. Dey capture people, und force dem to work. Ya can't just get Aminatra und boy back. Dey don't welcome strangers und yar arm. If ya go to Adonelis, ya dead. Bortell und Malto, once paid, dey drink mooney away in bar."

"I'll kill them!" raged Finbarl.

Maddy interpreted his anger as aimed towards the crew and began circling Tarlobus and Gidhaert.

"I not blame ya," said Tarlobus, "bot ... Ya girl looking dangerous?"

"Maddy," called Finbarl in a soothing tone. He smiled, stroking Tarlobus' sleeve as a gesture of friendship.

"Sha good fighter," commented Tarlobus, his eyes following Maddy as she returned to Finbarl's side. "Kill one raider. Dey take ya if sha not old dem off before we drove dem away."

"She's very protective," remarked Finbarl, stroking Maddy's hair. "So, what do we do?"

"Best fing ya do, accept fate. Tomorrow we be in Parodis. Ya start new life. Many stolen by Adonelisians: none corm back. Dey may be lucky und now in good ousehold. Sha fine woman und Karlmon ealthy. Dey get decent price for dem."

Tarlobus's stoic calm and pragmatic rationalism shocked and angered Finbarl. "I have to do something!"

"Wat ya do?" asked Tarlobus.

"I don't know," admitted Finbarl, examining his lame arm. "We can't do anything until daylight. Will you help us find them?"

With a sympathetic smile, the captain held up his hands. "Na, I not cross Adonelisians. Ya friend, but I just trader. Ya go to Parodis. Dey enemies of Adonelis. But dey tell ya wat I told ya. Aminatra und boy lost."

"Parodis," repeated Finbarl. A chilled wind caught his face, and he stopped to take a deep breath. "Right!" he declared. "We'll go to Parodis. Someone there will help us!"

Tarlobus nodded his head, recognising Finbarl's stubbornness. "Gidhaert can take ya. E from Parodis." The captain hurled a command toward Gidhaert, and the crewman shrugged. "E introduce ya to some people," confirmed Tarlobus.

"Thank you," said Finbarl, his mind racing ahead. It seemed simple. He had once united a disparate group of prisoners to overthrow the Wardyns of Athenia. Now he would find the words to win over the civilised people of Parodis. Yet beneath this certainty, weakness and helplessness weighed, the agony of his loss unbearable.

Chapter Thirteen

As Aminatra stirred to consciousness, it occurred to her she felt sick. Her gut confirmed the prognosis, and she retched. A vague recollection of a rude awakening surfaced, then a memory of a hand covering her mouth, then nothing. She looked down at a dirt track in the darkness, her stomach bumping on something uncomfortable, ambling along the path. She spat, removing the bitter bile, then tried craning her neck to survey her position. The movement triggered wooziness, her blood-filled head dangling down. A pungent aroma hinted she lay over a creature of some sort: too low to be a camel. Her mind instructed her hands to adjust and upright herself, but they wouldn't move. Through befuddled thoughts, she concluded something bound her hands. Panic refrained from overwhelming her confusion, and whatever put her to sleep kept her passive. She wriggled her ankles, discovering something shackled her legs too. An inner voice demanded she scream for help, but her body lacked the will: its overriding preference for sleep. Voices invaded her dreamy thoughts. Fighting the urge to close her eyes, she opened her mouth to call out. She felt a strange, numb-like sensation, as though detached from her body. A sound emerged, but not the words her mind forged, just a slurred, meaningless moan. The external voices got louder, and soon Aminatra's bleary eyes focussed on two sets of sandals pacing beside her. She struggled to lift her head to look at their faces, her weakness overwhelming. Unintelligible words drifted through Aminatra, her mind attempting to grasp and interpret them, but only becoming confused by the effort. Then the beast came to a standstill; Aminatra's stomach appreciated the relief. She tried to speak again, but a piece of soft material, pressed over her nose and mouth, curtailed the attempt. Unconsciousness overwhelmed her for the second time that night.

***

Aminatra's senses revived to the sound of a crackling fire. Her nausea subsided; the motion ceased. Her heavy eyelids opened, and she winced at bright, flickering flames in the surrounding darkness. She sat against a tree, her arms and legs still bound. Voices murmured in the distance, beyond her sight. Her addled mind shaped a vague notion of earlier, but it hung confused between dream and reality. A burst of birdsong hinted dawn drew near. Aminatra ran her tongue across a dry palate. The residue of vomit lingered. The unpleasant taste triggered a coherent memory, and what she thought was a nightmare came to life. Important questions sprang into her thoughts. Where was she? Who were those men? What had happened to her? Where were Karlmon, Finbarl and Maddy? She summoned the energy to struggle in her bindings but to no avail: they were too strong, and she was too weak.

Contrasted against the light of the fire, a man approached. This time, she saw his face. It was Bortell. He grinned.

Aminatra's first attempt at speech failed as her dry mouth cracked into a cough. She tried again, words at last emerging but in a slur. "Whasht's gwing on?"

Bortell spoke in his own tongue. What he said meant nothing to Aminatra, just as her words meant nothing to him.

"Where'sh Karlmon? Finbarl? Maddy?"

The names triggered recognition. He laughed, showing off a crooked row of teeth, and whispered something unfathomable. Someone called his name, and Aminatra watched as he departed without another word. Unable to make the other men out in the light, she estimated five. A thought struck her they were the crew of the boat, but the silhouettes were wrong, with Tarlobus's rotund body absent.

Aminatra's faculties slowly returned. Fear and anger aided the process: the cold shudder of dread stirred her senses. Confusion, however, still dominated. With a blank in her memory, horrors filled the gap. Was she the only one left alive? Had the others suffered? She wanted to cry, but life had weaned her off such distractions. What she craved was revenge: to break free from the ropes, exacting a Ferral-like vengeance.

Laughter erupted, followed by an exchange and shaking of hands. Two broke away, departing into the darkness. Aminatra recognised one as Bortell. The remaining men approached, the light of the fire reflecting in warm licks upon their attire. They stood in an intimidating line before Aminatra, the details of their unusual costumes now clear. She had seen nothing like it before. Smooth metal plates covered their chests, held on by a leather jerkin. Beautiful, ornate armour covered the fronts of their legs and arms. To Aminatra, it seemed an excessive use of precious metal, but the grandeur and nobility fascinated her. The polished surface allowed her to make out her own distorted reflection. She cringed inside at her sorry state.

One man bent down, and she steeled herself to look him in the eye. His harsh face, possessing two parallel scars on each upper cheek, inspected her with unfeeling brown eyes. The man uttered something incoherent, aimed at his companions. They stooped to examine their captive, their faces marked with the same deliberate scars, their hair cut in the same manner, cropped down the sides and back. It gave them a brutal, threatening appearance. Each man smiled but showed no friendship.

"Who are you?" she spluttered through the fear. "Why have you taken me?"

The men straightened, beginning a conversation, ignoring her. They spoke fast. An odd word sounded familiar, but Aminatra understood nothing. Each possessed a sword sheathed at his waist. Aminatra willed her hands free to snatch a weapon and draw blood from these cowards, but the binding remained fast. One drew his sword and crouched; Aminatra's reinforced courage crumbled. Was this the end? She flinched, withdrawing her knees. Angered by the action, the man grabbed her ankles, yanking the legs out straight. Aminatra yelped, closing her eyes in fateful expectation.

The pain never materialised and, on opening her eyes, she saw the rope cut and loose by her feet. Were they letting her go? The man's stern face scuppered such hope. He grasped the binding between her wrists and pulled Aminatra up, her legs wobbling like a newborn lamb's. Yanking on the bindings, he forced Aminatra to follow. A donkey awaited.

Fragments of the night draped over a creature surfaced, and Aminatra realised the poor beast had borne her through the darkness. Its benign expression conveyed no grievance. A load already weighed on its back, ruling out a return to the undignified position of the night. Instead, the man connected a harness around the donkey's neck to her own bindings with another length of rope. Aminatra's stomach churned in sickening recollection at her internment in the prison at

Athenia. Only the beast leading her differed. The full gravitas of her situation struck home: she had lost her freedom again!

"Why are you doing this to me? I've done you no harm!" Despair swamped her.

"I'm thirsty!" A faint voice emerged from the darkness behind.

Aminatra swung her head round. A second donkey stood ten yards away, awaiting its own load. In its wake stood four dejected figures connected by a rope, prisoners like herself. At the rear, the smallest. The only recognisable figure and unmistakable to Aminatra. "Karl-mon!"

Chapter Fourteen

Finbarl sat at the boat's bow as it glided through the water, his legs dangling over the side, as he once had with Aminatra by his side. Despite being under-manned, Tarlobus left him alone. There was little he could do anyway with his strapped arm.

On Finbarl's lap lay Aminatra's bag, open with her few possessions exposed for his melancholic contemplation. He smelt her on everything, even the copy of *Animal Farm*. They hadn't read together since boarding the boat, distracted by the narrative of the river. But he wondered if she perhaps read alone during those rare moments, trying to better herself.

Maddy found solace on the roof of what Finbarl now considered her hut. She sat staring to their aft, over the head of Tarlobus, pining for her absent friends. Finbarl considered joining her, but his own pain pushed him to solitude. Loss provided a frequent companion in his life, but to have lost Aminatra and Karlmon tortured his heart.

The passing world, along the river's diverging banks, grew more interesting with each hour. Other boats passed, then small farmsteads appeared, the fields occupied with several labourers and beasts of burden toiling in the sun. Then the first village, a collection of huts surrounded by grazing cattle and ploughed fields. Finbarl found distraction in the spectacle. The freedom they enjoyed amazed him.

Hundreds of people went about their work without fear in the open countryside. It was his and Aminatra's dream. If only she were here to see this, thought Finbarl. It was hard to reconcile his contradictory fascination and sadness.

"*I'm hungry.*"

Finbarl turned. Karlmon stood before him, a beaming smile on his face. "I'm not surprised," answered Finbarl. "The way you've been chasing Maddy all day."

The boy sat down next to him, his head resting on Finbarl's shoulder. Finbarl handed him a wild carrot foraged on their last trip to land.

"Where's your mother?"

No reply came, the daydream shattered by a noise astern. Finbarl sat alone, carried along but left behind.

***

"We be in Parodis wifin der day," remarked Tarlobus.

Finbarl combed Maddy's hair, as Aminatra used to do for the girl. It appeared to calm her. He looked up at the captain and acknowledged him with a half-smile. "And I still can't persuade you to help? Could you not take us further up the river, nearer to Adonelis?"

"Impossible," replied Tarlobus. "Wen we at Parodis, ya see chain crooss riufer."

"A chain! Why?"

"Protection und control," explained the captain. "Stops Adonelisians raiding up riufer und allows Parodisians to collect toll from travellers."

Finbarl frowned, trying to understand the strange dynamics of the land.

"Adonelis still long way from riufer," continued Tarlobus. "Ya go to Parodis, get better. Best way."

"Look Maddy!" exclaimed Finbarl, pointing to the riverbank, half listening to Tarlobus. "Another village and a horse."

Maddy followed the line of Finbarl's finger, looking with curiosity at the scene.

"I've never seen a real horse before, just pictures in books. See, there's a man riding it!"

The horseman, dressed in a lavish range of brightly coloured clothes and with a large hat, trotted along the edge of a field, occupied by workers.

"He's a Terratus: landowner. All this land is his," explained Gidhaert, hovering behind the captain.

"Are all those people his slaves?" asked Finbarl, fearful of the answer.

Gidhaert laughed, his personality warming the closer they got to his home city. "No! There is no slavery in Parodis. Everyone is free. They pay rent to the landowner."

"Rent?" Finbarl didn't understand, but hearing the word 'free' reassured him. "This is Parodis?"

Tarlobus shook his head at Finbarl's naivety. "Dis Parodis territory. Ya know city wen ya see it."

The man atop the horse spotted their boat and watched them keenly, trotting closer to the bank. Finbarl waved. The rider remained unmoved, as though in thought. His hand crept up, then flagged left and right with a furious intent.

"Is that a Parodisian welcome?" queried Finbarl.

Tarlobus mumbled under his breath. "E wants somefing. Captain Tarlobus not want to stop."

"Will he be able to help me?" asked Finbarl, impressed by the rider's noble appearance.

"My friend," declared Tarlobus. "Ya in too much of urry. Wiy ask one Terratus, wen ya find undreds in city."

"How big is Parodis?"

"It is the biggest city in Taliphia!" declared Gidhaert with pride. "There are many who live there. Including hundreds of Terratus and thousands and thousands of people."

"Are we stopping?" enquired Finbarl, conjuring an image of Athenia, his only reference point for a city.

"Hmm." Tarlobus weighed his options.

"We should, Captain," urged Gidhaert. "Word will get back to Parodis if you don't."

Tarlobus spat overboard. "Der pamp is right. Captain Tarlobus not upset a Terratus. Bad for business."

Captain Tarlobus vanished to the rear, cursing and shouting orders. The mainsail swung forty-five degrees, catching the breeze, as Tarlobus angled the tiller, sending the Medino towards the bank.

"What's a pamp?" Finbarl asked Gidhaert.

"An insult," answered the youngster through gritted teeth. "What jealous outsiders call Parodisians or anyone else who dresses with style."

"Why do you put up with that?" ask Finbarl.

"Money!" explained Gidhaert, before adding, "And to learn. Captain Tarlobus is the best. One day I wish to own a fleet of trading craft."

On the shore, the Terratus dismounted, walking his steed to the water's edge. He waited with patient expectation as the horse drank.

"I wonder what he wants?" said Finbarl, waiting at the ship's bow with excitement. "He looks splendid. A dozen men like him on their horses will terrify any Adonelisian."

"Have you ever seen one?"

"An Adonelisian? Well, no, but you said Parodis was the greatest of cities."

"Oh, it is," declared Gidhaert. "Wait until you see the buildings. They touch the clouds."

"The clouds!" whispered Finbarl to himself.

"But the Adonelisians are fearsome warriors," continued the sailor. "They'd kill their own mother if she looked at them wrong."

Finbarl frowned, glancing again at the waiting Terratus "How does Parodis thrive if the Adonelisians are so dangerous?" he asked. "A chain alone cannot hold them back. All this land looks so vulnerable."

"Because we're superior," answered Gidhaert without pause. "Smarter, with better weapons, a greater cause, and not forgetting the Unumverum."

"The Unumverum?"

Instead of answering Finbarl's query, Gidhaert lost himself in thought. "I suppose control of the river is essential too," he said eventually. "It gives us economic strength. We trade with everyone, and we have many friends in the other cities, all dependent on our goods. Even the Adonelisians rely on us, and they wouldn't dare attack. If Parodis snaps its fingers, then all other cities would join us in defeating them."

"Why would they want to attack you?" asked Finbarl.

"For the same reason they can't," answered Gidhaert. "Our wealth and power. Oh, and to get their hands on the Unumverum."

"What is the Unumverum?" Finbarl tried again.

"A wonder of the ancient world and a marvel of our time," declared Gidhaert. "I'll show you when we get to Parodis!"

With the lowering of the sails and splash of the anchor, the Medino bobbed in shouting range of the shore.

"Ow can Captain Tarlobus elp, noble sir?" bellowed the captain, strolling to the side. "Peraaps a tinboo or a pontel for yar lady wife?"

"Transport to Parodis," replied the Terratus.

"Forp," swore Tarlobus, his smile remaining unperturbed. "Of course. An onour. But yar orse?"

"To be left here at my villa," explained the man. "I planned to ride back tomorrow, but when I saw your vessel, I thought …"

"Ya ffought ya'd get free passage, ya lazy pamp," muttered Tarlobus for the benefit of his crew. "Are ya ready to corm aboard now?"

"No, I must stable my horse and inform my household. Wait here."

Tarlobus's cheeks grew red, eyes darkening. His crew awaited the explosion. Instead, the fake smile returned. "Ya urry, now. Captain Tarlobus as people waiting for im."

"Of course. Of course," promised the man. "I won't keep you long." He clasped the horse's reins and led him away towards a single-storey building.

The explosion came. "Der nerve! Captain Tarlobus not pick-up service! I'll squeeze im for every pownlet, forping pamp. Get back to work, ya lazy sqits!"

The crew scurried away, leaving Finbarl and Maddy alone with the captain.

"Do you not want him aboard?" asked Finbarl with trepidation.

"Na," snapped Tarlobus. "Ow ya say? Creature dat suck life."

"Er, mosquito? Parasite?"

"Yee, yee. Parasite. Not work, not pay. Just eit."

With nothing to do but wait, Finbarl grabbed some sleep, missing Tarlobus's display of frustrated pacing. He awoke to find Maddy sleeping across his legs. A wave of pride washed through him as he watched her. She had grown so much as a member of their family. No one had changed more or overcome so many challenges.

As pins and needles tickled Finbarl's right leg, he eased Maddy's head onto a bag and shook his limbs in relief. "What am I going to do with you when we reach Parodis?" Finbarl asked his sleeping companion. "I want you to stay with me, but will you understand a city and its ways?"

Maddy shuffled, making a small hum, as though responding.

"You're so far from home now, if you ever had a place you thought of as home. Perhaps I could teach you to speak. Would you like that?" This time, only the rhythmic breathing of sleep answered.

"At last!" Tarlobus grabbed the side rail. "'Not long' e say. Captain Tarlobus lose good money waiting."

The Terratus stood on the bank, adorned in new, equally impressive clothes, with a bag over his shoulder. "My cook made me eat before the journey," he said as way of explanation for his tardiness.

"E's changed and eaten!" cursed the captain under his breath. "Maybe bathed too."

"Send your boat to collect me," instructed the man.

"Na, boot," called out Tarlobus. "Ya must wade to us."

"I can't," exclaimed the Terratus, looking down at his yellow, embroidered trousers. "Can one of your men carry me?"

Again, the captain flushed a bright red, his knuckles whitening as his grip tightened on the rail.

"I'll go, captain," offered Gidhaert.

"Den go!" hissed Tarlobus, his eruption of expletives saved for another day.

"I see what you mean," said Finbarl, easing himself up as Gidhaert jumped into the river.

"Tarlobus as na time for spoiled children."

The increased activity awoke Maddy. She stretched each limb, one at a time, then watched with bemusement one man carrying another on his shoulders through the water. The Terratus held his boots in his hands, his trousers rolled up to his knees, urging caution from his human mule.

"A hand, if you please," requested the man with raised arm as they reached the Medino.

Captain Tarlobus stared back, unmoving.

"Take mine." Finbarl offered his one good hand and pulled the man on deck.

"Why, thank you," said the Terratus, inspecting Finbarl with a curious eye. "What strange clothes."

Tarlobus pushed himself forward. "I'm Captain Tarlobus. Ou do I ave der pleasure of carrying?" His anger buried beneath a syrupy accommodation.

"Ah, Captain, you do me a great service. I am Yelvito De Parmsoli. You have a fine vessel. I hope I haven't inconvenienced you too much?"

"Not at all," lied the captain, an eye following the sodden Gidhaert as he climbed aboard. "Captain Tarlobus always appy to elp a man in need."

"Excellent. Then a cup of chee would be most welcome."

"A cup of chee?" repeated Tarlobus, through a hollow smile. He yelled a command in another language.

"What an unusual aroma," commented Parmsoli, his nose hunting the source, stopping at Maddy. "Hello, what's your name?"

Maddy sniffed in return, inspecting the new face.

"Maddy can't speak," explained Finbarl, as the mast unfurled, setting them on their way again.

"You're not from Parodis and yet ..."

"I know," said Finbarl. "Somehow our language is the same as your scholars. Are you one?"

"No," laughed Parmsoli. "It is a convenient language to communicate between peoples. You look like you've been in the wars?"

Finbarl glanced down at his arm. "The Adonelisians."

The name triggered a reaction. "On the river? Their audacity is breathtaking. The Senorium will hear of this. It's about time someone taught them a lesson."

"Yes," exclaimed Finbarl, spotting an opportunity. "They took my ..."

"Ah, here comes the chee. Forgive me; chee should always be enjoyed in silence. Helps one rebalance."

***

With the afternoon sun bearing down, they rounded a bend in the river. A line of buildings along the waterfront hove into view. "Parodis!" cried Finbarl, jumping to his feet, startling Maddy.

Parmsoli laughed. "That's not Parodis but Vilenso, a small town. We are still hours from Parodis."

"But it's as big as Athenia," gasped Finbarl, counting the buildings as they spread back from the river.

Parmsoli shrugged, unsure what Finbarl wanted him to say.

"Is Parodis bigger?"

"Much, much bigger," answered Parmsoli. "There are many such small towns in Parodisian territory. Each provides food and goods to sell in the city. Parodis then trades with the other cities."

"And Adonelis? How big is it?" pressed Finbarl.

Parmsoli laughed. "Not as big as Parodis, but much bigger than Vilenso. I've never been there, but you hear stories."

Finbarl blew out his cheeks. Such huge scale he'd never imagined. It also put his headstrong plans to charge into Adonelis and rescue Aminatra and Karlmon into perspective. What hope did he have when up against so many people? "Tell me about Parodis. What's it like?"

"It's the most amazing place in the world!" declared Parmsoli without hesitation. "The finest buildings, the tastiest food, the most beautiful women and the finest army and navy."

"An army? Strong enough to defeat Adonelis?"

"Of course! Did I not say the finest? I serve as a magor. Won a few feathers in my time."

Grabbing the opportunity, Finbarl relayed the story of Aminatra and Karlmon's kidnap and his plans to get them back.

"Oh, dear," responded Parmsoli. "One hears of such things but tries to block them out. Very tricky situation."

"But could the army help? Do you have influence?"

"I do indeed," declared Parmsoli. "But it is the Senorium who decides what the army does."

"What's he like? Can you talk to him?" A memory of Athenia's Governor Elbar formed in Finbarl's head.

"The Senorium is not a man," explained Parmsoli. "It's an assembly of 200 men and women, voted for by the citizens of Parodis."

"I don't understand. How can so many make one decision? How do people know who to vote for?"

"What a simple man you are," remarked Parmsoli. "We elect members of the Senorium to specific roles for a year. I hope to run myself next year. There is a lot of discussion, then the Senorium itself votes on a decision and the government enacts it."

Rather than take offence, Finbarl nodded his head, confused. "So, how do I get my family back?"

"Not a clue," confessed Parmsoli. "Though I've always found money helps with most things."

"Money: something I don't have," mused Finbarl.

"Well, Parodis is a good place to make some. I wish you luck." Parmsoli clasped his hands behind his back and wandered off, as though inspecting the boat.

Finbarl screwed up his nose and sighed. "Sounds like this is going to be harder than I thought, Maddy."

The girl perhaps agreed, tilting her head with a thoughtful look.

***

"We soon in Parodis," boomed Tarlobus, startling Finbarl. "Dere is much to do dere. Dere is much to do now!"

The crew shot from one spot to another, as Tarlobus continued yelling towards his put-upon men. Maddy, mimicking a trait picked up from Finbarl, shook her head in annoyance.

"This is truly a world beyond my understanding," said Finbarl to Maddy. "So many people; such different clothes and ways. Why would they take Aminatra and Karlmon?"

The familiar names stimulated interest from Maddy.

"Tarlobus and Parmsoli have tried to explain it to me, but I can't understand what I've yet to see. You can buy and sell anything and, in places like Adonelis, that includes humans. Values change, so one day you can buy it, the next you can't! Some people can buy anything and others nothing. Life was simpler in Athenia. Perhaps I can get money to buy them back?" As the thought popped into Finbarl's head, he looked at Maddy to gauge her reaction. Her unresponsive face deflated his enthusiasm. "We'll get them back somehow. I promise!"

From the rear of the boat, a rich voice crooned a song. Finbarl turned as another baritone joined, then a third. The crew, led by Tarlobus, belted out an upbeat melody as they worked. Even the idle Parmsoli joined in, much to the captain's surprise.

"It tradition," called out Tarlobus in explanation, as the others continued with the next verse. "Wen journey nears end, sailors celebrate safe return wit song." He rejoined the singing in perfect time, before adding, "Ya sing chorus!"

While the words were meaningless, the repetitive chorus seemed simple, building to a crescendo before returning to the verse and its pleasing rhythm. As the next chorus approached, Tarlobus waved his hands, conducting his choir, urging Finbarl to partake. He mumbled along, unconfident with his pronunciation, but provoking a burst of approval from the captain.

For the next hour, the singing continued. Sometimes a crew member sang solo, often a tune with a mournful edge. Corelye owned the best voice, although the captain sang with the most passion. Between the sad songs, they all partook in raucous singalongs, some comedic and others crude, if Finbarl understood the accompanying hand gestures. Finbarl felt uncomfortable enjoying himself, but it pleased him to see Maddy's bemusement-tinged pleasure. It also encouraged him to assist with the work as best he could with his one good hand, making ready for landfall.

"Parodis!" cried Gidhaert, overflowing with emotion. The singing stopped. All looked to the river's bend ahead.

Finbarl could not see the city, just rising smoke and two towering needles side by side. "What are they?"

"Just wait," urged Parmsoli, joining Finbarl at the bow. "When we're round the … Look!" The tips of another pair of needles appeared above a hill. "A wonder of the ancient world. They're the original columns for a mighty bridge spanning the river. Have you ever seen anything so high?"

"They do reach the clouds!" gasped Finbarl.

"Bridge still exist over riufer," explained Tarlobus, "bot not original."

"How has it survived so long?"

Tarlobus shrugged, turning to Parmsoli. "Wiere did a Terratus learn to sing sailor songs?"

"Oh, in my childhood. Papa employed an old sailor to maintain our villa. He entertained the family."

"Hmm." Tarlobus stroked his beard. "Wat ya do in city, Finbarl?"

"Get money," he answered, his eyes stuck on the needles. "Gidhaert has promised to introduce me to some friends."

"Ya not elp my friend?" challenged the captain, facing Parmsoli again.

"Oh, that I could," said the Terratus. "Alas, I won't be around long."

"But you have money and friends," pressed Tarlobus, folding his arms.

"I do. I do. It's all a little bit awkward at present. Money's tied up with a New Harbour venture. You know the sort of thing? All dependent on getting a competitive price. But I will have words with my contacts in government. These things take time."

Finbarl only half listened. A steep cliff rose as the waters disappeared round a sharp corner. On the top of the cliff, their first sight of Parodis itself, beside the majesty of the bridge towers.

"Cronax!" exclaimed Finbarl, his mouth agape. "It's huge! It's magnificent!" Hope welled inside: surely the people who built such grandeur could help him get Aminatra and Karlmon back. The cliff face housed some dwellings hewn deep into the rock, with fragile wooden walkways connecting them, hanging over the water. Finbarl spotted people spinning wool from a terrace and weaving baskets in the shade. Above towered the surface buildings, their stone walls solid and painted in vibrant blue or white. An aura of wonder and power emanated from the city.

Passing beneath the bridge, Finbarl craned his neck to examine the wood structure, gently swinging between the pin-like towers, dozens of ropes connecting the two. It had never occurred to him that such structures were necessary, let alone possible. The scale overwhelmed him.

"Two other columns once rose from the depth of the river," explained Parmsoli. "The ancients' bridge would have been more stable than ours. The water has long since destroyed them. You can't cross the bridge now when the wind blows. It rocks like a cradle!"

"The towers look so delicate, yet so strong. Does much else survive from the Golden Age?" asked Finbarl.

Parmsoli shook his head. "Nothing to compare to this, though their footprints are everywhere. The bridge's material is a mystery."

"Lower der mainsail!" commanded Tarlobus.

"We'll be docking soon," explained Gidhaert, unknotting the rigging.

"Docking?"

"Landing," translated Parmsoli, patting Finbarl on the back. "We've arrived! Our paths must soon diverge. I wish you every success in getting your family back. You can rely on Yelvito De Parmsoli to raise this within my circles."

"Thank you," said Finbarl, shaking the offered hand. "You give me hope."

Chapter Fifteen

Aminatra stroked her sore wrists on her cheek, managing a fleeting nibble of the binding. Throughout the march, she worked at fraying the rope, but hopes of escape vanished when Adonelis came into view. The morning light caught the bleak, imposing walls ringing the city. Only the scale impressed Aminatra. This was not the utopia they sought, but a larger version of Athenia. She glanced behind for the umpteenth time to check on Karlmon and offer him hope with a reassuring smile. He looked tired but managed a smile back.

For some time they had passed by people heading away or towards the city. Some were traders, some were warriors bearing the symbolic facial scars, and many were like themselves, trudging without choice under the brutish command of a captor. None of the free paid the prisoners the slightest attention, and dread built within Aminatra as their path encountered the victims of Adonelisian terror, their limp bodies hanging from stakes and trees.

At the confluence of roads before Adonelis, a congested stream of travellers waited before the enormous gates. Never had Aminatra seen so many people, heard so much noise.

Shouting erupted behind. Without warning, her captors shoved Aminatra to the side as two horsemen trotted past. Those still in their path received a sharp sting from stick-wielding riders. Aminatra mouthed a silent curse at them before her donkey moved forward, tugging at her binding. They filtered down into a single line while the guards on the gate inspected them. She spotted the grim decorations adorning the walls, decapitated heads, and looked away in disgust. With a word from one captor, a guard waved their procession through into a broad avenue.

The comparison to Athenia proved inaccurate. They shared walls, but Adonelis was no 'make-do' city but a construct of intimidation and grandeur. Aminatra scanned her surroundings with mouth agape. People scurried like ants in every direction. A thin line of twin-storeyed buildings lined both sides of the spacious avenue, their style uniform and neat. Soon, they gave way to fortified dwellings, a familiar frontage complemented by towers. Compared with the cramped and chaotic Athenia, it shouted order and purpose. Aminatra pondered if Parodis and perhaps Mandelaton shared such a style and appearance. Yet despite her awe and wonderment, she soon noticed it lacked character and colour. The stark, grey walls seemed well-built but, with no variation or decoration, they melted into the background without interest. Even with their limited resources, the people of Athenia always brightened their buildings. Yet one building did impress. A vast square base of sloping walls led up above the surrounding homes, supporting a smaller tier that in turn angled up to yet another floor. Atop, only just visible, rested a crowning building. On each side, endless stairs climbed to the summit. Aminatra craned her neck as they passed by, wondering at the strange markings upon the walls and characters who appeared part of a story. It impressed and struck fear.

Emerging into an enormous square, Aminatra appreciated the true scale of Adonelis. The road split to form a ring around an expanse of grass and statues. Everywhere on the sunburnt grass, scar-faced men groaned and grappled in acts of one-on-one violence: wrestling, sword fighting and staff jousting. Each bout ended in respect, the combatants parting and bowing to the other, then resuming their entanglement. Training, Aminatra surmised, as she noted the lack of women so far. Some had waited at the town gates, their faces covered as though battling an Athenian sandstorm. The streets, however, appeared a male domain.

The train of prisoners soon departed down one of many roads sprouting like tendrils off the square, each disappearing into the distance with a sentry of uniform, grey buildings.

"How does anyone find their way when every street looks the same?" asked Aminatra of the prisoner attached to her. As with all her questions on the trek, the man returned an uneasy smile, unable to understand a word she said.

One of their guards yelled a curt instruction, directing the donkeys and their human chain into an enormous courtyard. In the middle, under a section of awning, a small stage faced towards another set of closed gates. Along the four outer walls ran benches, a metal tube running parallel above the ground; two sides were already occupied with abject-looking souls, their ankles chained to the tube.

A guard untied Aminatra and her fellow captives from the donkeys. With sword drawn, he forced them to join the wretched prisoners on the benches. Then, with frightening efficiency, a man daubed a painted symbol on each prisoner, chained their ankles to the pole and cut the binding around their wrists.

"Ah, it's good to move my hands," said Aminatra, rubbing at the burns left by the rope. Her neighbour nodded his head, recognising the universal language of relief.

Aminatra observed still more prisoners arriving in their wake. Further trains of sorry captives were processed and lined up on the benches. There they sat in silence for the next hour, while the Adonelisians busied themselves within the heart of the courtyard. Aminatra stood to view Karlmon, lost among his taller companions, but a volley of verbal abuse followed by a blow from a stick convinced her sitting hurt less.

"What happens to us now?" asked Aminatra. As if in answer, a horn blew. The gates at the far end of the courtyard opened. People flooded in, buzzing with excitement, gravitating to the outer edges, working their way along the line of seated prisoners.

"What are they doing?"

The first of this curious crowd reached Aminatra. Dressed in a plain brown tunic, he paused, grinned and yelled back to a colleague, who wrote something on a scroll. By the time Aminatra opened her mouth to ask a question, he was gone, moving on, stopping again, sometimes yelling. Others followed, dressed in similar, sombre clothes, working around the benches, assessing and recording. At the centre of the courtyard, excited chatter engulfed the organisers as they watched the new arrivals with interest.

After another half hour, a voice boomed from the stage, prompting silence and stillness. The noise erupted again as the visitors made their way towards the stage, congregating around it. A passageway remained between the ordered crowd, through which an armed guard forced a group of stumbling captives. Aminatra watched, curious and terrified. The compère continued to shout, inviting members of the crowd onto his platform to poke and prod at the prisoners. Then a loud conversational ritual between the man and those gathered took place. One word, 'soldemir', repeated itself, becoming familiar to Aminatra's ears. On each utterance it brought an exchange to a close, the prisoners led away to stand in new, nervous groups behind the Adonelisians.

When Aminatra's turn came, the man who chained them to the tube disconnected them with equal skill. He shooed them along towards the stage. Now free of ankle and wrist restraints, Aminatra considered escape, but too many people blocked her path to the gate. Where would she go if she got beyond the courtyard?

All the prisoners brought in with Aminatra lined up on the stage. Karlmon stood in the second row, behind Aminatra, just to her right.

"Mother!" he whispered.

"Karl!"

"Are you all right?"

Aminatra fought the urge to turn her head. "I'm okay. We'll get out of this. Don't worry!"

"Where's Finbarl and Maddy?"

"I ..." As Aminatra tried to answer, a woman, eyes peering above a veil, grasped her lower jaw and pushed her upper lip back with a stick, inspecting her teeth. At her side, a guard armed with a whip persuaded Aminatra to accept the indignity. Next, she held a hand to Aminatra's stomach, mumbling something incomprehensible but appearing pleased.

Several others followed, a few passing Aminatra without a glance, some prodding her as though a plump chicken. With the inspections complete, they left the podium while the master of ceremonies spoke in hushed tones with colleagues.

"What's going on?" Karlmon's voice quivered.

"I don't know," whispered Aminatra from the corner of her mouth. "I think we are being traded."

"Like metal at Athenia?"

Aminatra smiled at the odd analogy. "Yes, I suppose so."

The conductor boomed out again, bringing an end to their conversation. He hovered by the first prisoner in the row, his hand on their shoulder. Words poured from his mouth as he pointed at those in the audience, who shouted back. Then he cried, "soldemir!" and moved to the next pitiful captive, repeating the ritual.

With Aminatra's turn, the man stood before her, animated and pointing at her unusual thawb. Her exotic appearance stirred the onlookers, a number yelling what Aminatra now understood to be bids. After an eternity, the man shouted "soldemir" and passed to the next in line.

Aminatra held her breath as Karlmon's turn arrived. From the corner of her eye, she caught the man waving his hands, holding up the material of Karlmon's thawb. A few bids kicked off proceedings and then silence. Eyes turned to the individual responsible for the last bid, standing to the fore, his hand thoughtfully stroking a neat beard. The seller pushed past Aminatra to the front of his platform, bowing with melodramatic gratitude to the buyer. He cleared his throat and addressed the crowd. The silence turned to chatter as the seller stirred up applause. Aminatra used the distraction to steal a glance back at Karlmon.

"If they separate us," she whispered, "make sure you can recognise who takes me away. If we get the opportunity to escape, it will help us find each other."

Karlmon looked confused. "Why will they separate us?"

"It's only for a short while," reassured Aminatra. "Ouch!" A stick brandished by a guard whipped against her thigh. She straightened as the man further admonished her with a stare. "I was talking with my son!"

The man said nothing but opened his mouth to show off a tongueless palate. He pointed at Aminatra, drew his finger over an imaginary tongue and smiled: the threat clear. Aminatra shivered. Even in Athenia's brutal world, she had never imagined such barbarity.

When the seller reached the end of the second line, the guards man-handled the prisoners from the stage. A man reading a scroll directed each purchased commodity to a waiting group. Aminatra kept her eyes on Karlmon as a man grabbed her arm, leading her away.

"Mother!" cried out Karlmon, moving in the opposite direction.

"Be strong!" called out Aminatra. "We'll be together again soon."

The man gripping her arm released it and Aminatra flinched in readiness for a blow. Instead, he spoke, inspecting her with intense curiosity: "You speak Anglicus!"

"You understand me?"

"I do," confirmed the man, "but you're not from Parodis."

"Parodis!" exclaimed Aminatra. "No, but we were heading there. Do you know Parodis? Can you help us get there?"

The man laughed. "I know Parodis well. Who isn't familiar with the city of their birth?"

"Then you can help us! Do you know Captain Tarlobus?"

He shook his head. "I know no one of that name. I have not lived in Parodis since they captured and sold me into slavery, like you. Some ten years ago."

"You're a slave too!" Hope evaporated, despair refilling the hole.

"We must continue to move or both of us will suffer the whip!"

They joined a group containing the woman who examined her teeth earlier and three other slaves. The Parodisian spoke with his female companion, referring to Aminatra, who craned her neck in search of Karlmon among the crowd. She heard his sobbing, but the multitude of bodies hid him from sight.

"Where are they taking my son?"

The Parodisian turned, annoyed by the interruption. "Be grateful. The Royal House purchased him. That man is the chamberlain to Prince Andolis. Your boy will join his household in some capacity."

"Will I be able to see him?"

"You'll do as your master sees fit! Nothing more, nothing less." The man folded his arms.

"Who is my …," it pained Aminatra to say it, "… master?"

"General Hal Malic. An eminent man and warrior! Friend to the king. Now, enough questions. My name is Huut. I run Master Malic's estate. This here is Peli." The woman at his side gave a curt nod. "She runs the kitchen. That is where you'll be working."

"My name is Amina …"

"Silence!" Huut raised his hand. "Forget what others called you before. The master will name you. The past is meaningless; your life is meaningless. You serve the master; your life is his."

"But …"

"I said silence! You must learn to obey, or they will punish you. The only reason I've not whipped you is because of your condition."

"My condition?" Aminatra asked, compelled to disobey again.

"Peli tells me you are with child. That's why you went for top price and why the master will be pleased."

"Pregnant," spluttered Aminatra. "I … No, I'm …" Her denial faded as maternal instinct recognised signs from the last month. A light-headed nausea swept through her at the realisation she would bring another child into this nightmare.

Chapter Sixteen

Overwhelmed by the sights, sounds and smells around him, Finbarl spun in circles, trying to absorb it all. The odour triggered memories of Athenia and human conurbation. New, unplaced aromas mixed with the familiar pungent reek of waste and sweat. His nose twitched in search of the tantalising flavours, only to be distracted by the visual splendour. Vast buildings of marble surrounded the square, their colourful facades decorated with intricate patterns and carved attributes, while towering columns supported the roofs. The view from the river failed to do it justice. Nothing in Athenia compared to this.

Reflecting the grandeur of the architecture, the people of Parodis hurried past in their vibrant and varied clothes. Each displayed a range of glistening jewellery on fingers, ears or hair. Most ignored the unfamiliar visitors; some called out a greeting to their guide, Gidhaert. Others cast a discerning eye over the unusual girl who snarled and snapped if they went too close.

Everything was new to Maddy. Fear and bewilderment flooded her senses rather than wonder. She clung to the back of Finbarl's thawb, only letting go when his rotating undermined her attempt to hide.

"There are more people in this square than I have ever met," declared Finbarl. "Some will help me, I'm sure. How tall is that building?

How do you dye such a rich red? What does that sign say?" He fired a dozen such questions toward Gidhaert.

Their guide, so reticent aboard the boat, burst into life within the confines of his hometown and free from Tarlobus's personality. "That large building is the Guildhall. Over there you have Lorthonia's statue. On the fourth Monday of Maimon, a grand procession takes place to celebrate his victory over the Pegonians."

The names and details meant nothing to Finbarl, but he followed Gidhaert's pointing finger, listening with fascination.

"Look! Look!" shrieked Gidhaert. "The Kilshare."

A column of horsemen appeared, riding two by two, their uniform a glorious mix of armour and decoration. The sun glinted off the former, charging the line with electric majesty.

"Guards?" enquired Finbarl, watching with envy, his own drab clothing now a sorry, torn and ragged garment about his shoulders.

"Cavalry," corrected Gidhaert. "The Kilshare are one of the finest regiments in the army. All boys wish to grow up to become a Kilsharie. The feathers denote how many battles each man has fought and won."

Finbarl scanned the line, noting the considerable amount of plumage some were adorned with. "Are you at war a lot?"

Gidhaert laughed. "Oh, no. When I say 'battles', I mean tournament battles. I'll show you the arena later."

"Can I hire this Kilsharie to raid Adonelis?" asked Finbarl.

"No, no. They are in the service of the government, not mercenaries. Ah, see the dome in the distance! That's the Cathedral of the Unumverum."

Drawn between admiring the potential of Parodisian's military and the mysterious Unumverum, Finbarl completed another spin, to Maddy's annoyance.

Already crowded streets somehow filled with more people as Gidhaert led them away from the square. A gentle wind cooled the stuffy air, bringing Finbarl's attention to several flapping banners hanging off the front of buildings. Indecipherable lettering covered the white material.

"What do they say?" asked Finbarl.

"They ..." Gidhaert considered how best to translate. "They represent the mantra of Parodis. Our philosophy. That one says, 'Don't dream your life, live your dreams'." He dismissed a few as unworthy of translation, then pointed to another. "This one says, 'If people are trying to bring you down, it only means you are above them'."

Finbarl smiled. "Yes, I like those." He noticed colourful posters covering the walls. "And those?"

"Same thing. That one with the child says, 'You're special because there's only one you.' Some advertise things to buy."

"Very positive."

"We believe that for society to succeed, individuals must reach their full potential. Where I'm taking you, they'll explain it better than me."

"Can I put up a sign seeking help to get Aminatra and Karlmon back?"

"Money, Finbarl. You need money. First to advertise your message and then to pay those you wish to help you."

"Yes, I've heard of money. Money to write a message. How odd. I don't have to pay to speak?"

"Err..." Gidhaert floundered under the barrage of strange questions.

A sneeze from Maddy broke the awkward silence. For the first time within Parodis, she broke from Finbarl's tail, following her nose to the source of a new, compelling aroma.

"Wow, what's that smell?" Finbarl's own nose twitched in appreciation.

"That, my friends," declared Gidhaert, with a touch of Tarlobus in his mannerisms, "is the spice market. Come! I'll take you through it. There is more than spice."

"Stay close!" cautioned Finbarl to Maddy as they entered a narrow, bustling street. "If we lose Gidhaert, we'll never find our way back to the river."

Noise, colour and odour overwhelmed, with goods crammed onto and between packed stalls.

"We call this Spice Lane," declared Gidhaert, squeezing through those working their way in the opposite direction.

A volley of cries flew from each side; salespeople caught the ears of both interested and disinterested parties. Maddy whined. Her aromatic intrigue was subsumed under this alien onslaught. The buildings lining the road cut out the light, adding to the claustrophobic atmosphere. She retreated to Finbarl's side, her hand gripping his, as once she'd seen Karlmon do.

"Are they angry?" enquired Finbarl, reassuring Maddy with a smile.

"Ha," laughed Gidhaert. "No, they're haggling."

"Haggling?"

"Yes, negotiating over the price."

"Why?"

"Err ... I ..." Gidhaert pondered the question. "To get the best price ... I suppose."

Finbarl shrugged, only half understanding, but with his eyes bewitched by the multitude of colourful products on sale. "What is that?" He pointed to a sandy-coloured powder.

"Turmeric," explained Gidhaert. "To flavour and colour food or to dye clothes. It stains."

"And that?"

"Saffron. A sweet flavouring made from petals. Very nice!"

"Can we try some?" asked Finbarl.

"Do you have twenty pownlets?"

"Pownlets?"

"Money!" said Gidhaert. "Saffron's expensive. It's shipped here from the north. Only the rich can afford it."

Finbarl looked perplexed. "Pay for flowers? I don't understand money, nor do I have any. How do I get some?"

Gidhaert appraised his companion with disbelief. "You earn it. Find work."

"Doing what?"

"I don't know!" exclaimed Gidhaert. "Ah, watermelons." An impressive pyramid of giant green balls stood to their left. "They're so refreshing on a hot day."

"Do we need money for them?" enquired Finbarl.

An exasperated Gidhaert let out a sigh. "Everything costs money."

"So, not only do I need it to buy help and rescue Aminatra but also if we're to eat?"

"Come on," urged Gidhaert, eager to move on from the endless questions. "We're heading to the cathedral." He pointed to the most prominent building in the city.

"Hey, Maddy!" cried Finbarl. "We're going to the dome on the hill." They had first seen its summit from the river, but it had seemed a normal building among others. Once within the city walls, it shone as the focal point, its true scale exposed. It was visible from everywhere and, Finbarl supposed, you could see the world from it.

How Finbarl wished Aminatra and Karlmon were there to witness that wonder of humankind. Never had his imagination conjured a vision so grand. Even the books read of the Golden Age had not prepared him for it. Was it like that in the past?

They climbed a long, gradual hill, leading to the cathedral. The clothes worn by the people on the street changed. Loose, flowing robes of uniform cream replaced the competitive colours and adornments of the main square.

"Scholars of the Unumverum," explained Gidhaert before Finbarl asked. "I'll take you through Halloan Park. It is the most inspiring place in the world."

Finbarl struggled to imagine what could be more inspiring than all he'd already seen.

Halloan Park comprised a main path weaving between hillocks, each mound half dug away with curved steps, on which sat a mix of students and ordinary Parodis citizens: an audience for the scholars on their stage at the base. They gripped their robes and waved hands, orating and arguing, receiving applause and nods.

"Oh, Master Jolick is speaking!" cried Gidhaert. "We must listen for a while. He's an Unumverum Honry. Your language is the tongue of the scholasti. Come!"

With all the steps occupied around Jolick, they climbed the grassy mound and stood above.

"Power is a constant," began Jolick, pacing round his stage. "Divided and allocated to affect us mere mortals. The larger the segment, the stronger the gravitational pull, limiting the freedom of the individual. We must never allow ourselves to become another Adonelis or Deluquine. Ruled by kings, oppressed and stymied."

A student from the audience raised his hand. "Master Jolick, how should power be divided between the great cities? What if one gets too powerful? What if Parodis is that one?"

Jolick smiled. "It's Pocquet, isn't it?"

The audience member nodded, delighted at the recognition.

"Ideas occupy the universe of power through their ownership by individuals. The more people believe in something, the more powerful it becomes. We can't afford to allow the beliefs of Adonelis or Livorian to gain power and crush the individual. Encourage our own philosophy to grow and foster freedom for all. We want the world to understand as we understand. Do you understand?"

A murmur of agreement and laughter rippled across the steps and Gidhaert nodded his head. "Isn't he magnificent?" he whispered to Finbarl. "Did you understand what he meant?"

"I think so," answered Finbarl, still trying to digest the words. "Will the scholars know the best way to get my family back?"

"Come on!" beckoned Gidhaert, ignoring the question. "I have to be somewhere after I've delivered you. The Medino sails in a day."

They descended the hillock, joining the path. Finbarl slowed his pace as they passed each speaker, hoping to hear and learn. For some, a fiery debate seethed among the audience. Others elicited dreamy adoration. One scholar stood out, with his scruffy clothes, bald, shiny head with tuffs of wild white hair to the side and excitable gestures. He held court to a handful of people.

"Why so few?" enquired Finbarl.

Gidhaert sniggered. "It is the price we pay for freedom of speech. Poor old Master Bartarnous. He's a little crazy, though a Unumverum Honry too. Just look at him! Stains on his tunic. Always warning of weakness and complacency within Parodis society and the dangers we face. It's outrageous when we have the Unumverum."

They stopped on the path. "You promised to show me and explain the Unumverum," said Finbarl. "What is it?"

"Soon, soon," pledged Gidhaert. "Oh, listen! Bartarnous is off on one of his whinges."

"... monsters grow." Bartarnous twitched and waved his hands, his eyes staring, lost. "Vanity is the seasoning in the recipe of personality. Too little and you create something bland and unappealing; too much and you create something unpalatable and overpowering. We are born unique, but not special."

"You see," whispered Gidhaert. "The fool speaks madness. He has his followers but, as far as I'm concerned, any man who can't dress himself shouldn't be taken seriously. He talks of vanity, but look at him! Bartarnous wants a ... I don't know what he wants!"

All the speakers sounded wise and magnificent to Finbarl. Something about Bartarnous reminded him of Dul-biblex, the Athenian librarian, but he nodded in agreement and followed in Gidhaert's wake as he took off again.

On passing Bartarnous, Finbarl looked into the scholar's eyes. They stared back but never locked, flickering in all directions as though possessed. The old man's nose twitched, and he scratched his wild white hair, before returning to his sparse audience.

"So," began Finbarl, trotting to catch up with Gidhaert, "all is spoken of in the park?"

"That's right," enthused Gidhaert. "No subject is barred, however controversial or foolish."

"And anyone can speak?"

"Well, no. Only the scholars trained amid the Great Cathedral. Who would want to listen to me philosophising?" Gidhaert sniffed at the notion.

"But you can still say what you want?"

"Of course. When the drinks flow at the bereo hall, I often do!" He now laughed aloud, causing Maddy to hiss. With a more sober manner, he added, "But, not if it offends anyone."

"What's a bereo hall?"

Gidhaert patted Finbarl on the back. "I've never known anyone ask so many questions."

Chapter Seventeen

"You sleep here!" instructed Huut, as he showed Aminatra around the villa. Along a corridor wall, several arched cavities infiltrated the bricks, reminding Aminatra of kilns. Hair protruded from some, occupied with the heavy breathing of the sleeping. "You share your bed with Lexi and will work on alternating shifts." He tapped the crown of Lexi, eliciting a grunt.

Peli, her veil now removed, hung on Huut's shoulder, gabbling in his ear, encouraging him to explain details to the new slave. "The bucket in the corner is for you know what," continued Huut. "All slaves of this section share it and you agree among yourselves who cleans it out."

Aminatra's face remained unmoved. She had conceded this life would have no benefits, just hardship. Even the wilderness of Athenia seemed preferable. Her thoughts focussed on escape. An opportunity would arise, and she needed to be ready to take it.

Peli passed Aminatra a small bundle of clothes.

"Put these on!" instructed Huut. "I'll burn your old ones. You'll wear the veil whenever outdoors in public. It is a crime not to."

"Why?"

"Because!" snapped Huut, before a sigh. "Because their disciplinary code says warriors should have no distractions, such as that of the flesh."

"Why don't men wear veils, then? Don't they understand how they distract us women?"

"I don't make the rules or agree with them: just follow them," answered Huut, the new slave's sarcasm floating over him. "Now change!"

"Where?"

"Where what?

"Where do I change?"

"Here!" exclaimed Huut. "Slaves have no privacy."

Aminatra turned her back to Huut and lifted her thawb over her head. She glanced behind, pleased to see Huut's eyes averted. Peli stared at her with impatient eyes. The new garments, a grey, short-sleeved tunic and skirt, itched but were not displeasing to Aminatra, who had worn nothing but a thawb.

"Remove your footwear!" ordered Huut. "You'll have no need for them around the estate and it will make you less inclined to try running away."

"But ..."

Peli, already on her knees, lifted one of Aminatra's legs and prised off a sandal, then the other, before throwing them towards the chamber pot.

"Now to the kitchen," said Huut, ignoring Aminatra's protesting face, leading them down the corridor. "This is where you will do most of your work under Peli's supervision. I suggest you learn to communicate with her as quickly as possible."

"Will you teach me?" enquired Aminatra.

"No!" snapped Huut. "After today, our paths will hardly cross. You'll learn out of necessity. If you can't do your work, well, the master will have no use for you."

The kitchen was a hive of activity. A raging, open fire stood at one end of the large room, with twenty slaves dashing back and forth amid shouts and curses. Adding to the stifling heat, several concealed stoves lined the middle, each covered with a bubbling pot. Peli shouted something towards Aminatra above the general noise.

"Your lessons begin," explained Huut. "She says, 'You work hard, or you don't eat'."

"I know how to work hard," retorted Aminatra. "What do I have to do?"

"Chop, cook, wash. Anything you're told. Peli will demonstrate later." Huut wiped the sweat running down his brow. "Now, I'll take you to meet the master."

Grateful to leave the humid air of the kitchen, Aminatra kept in step behind Huut, the cold of the stone floor acute upon her bare soles. He led her through a maze of corridors, plain except for statues of warriors, then across a courtyard and into a grand reception room with ornate, wood, latticed windows allowing a refreshing breeze to pass through.

"You only speak to the master if he asks you a question," explained Huut. "You don't look the master in the eye. Understand? You do whatever he commands."

Aminatra nodded as her eyes surveyed the room. A strange mix of austere functionality and beauty touched everything. The furniture, minimal and spaced out, possessed sharp right angles and no padding, but a flourish of intricate carved decoration adorned the legs. On the pure-white ceiling, delicate patterns swam from corner to corner.

"The master is unusual amongst Adonelisians," commented Huut, noticing Aminatra's fascination with the surroundings. "He has an appreciation of beauty."

"You admire him," said Aminatra, recognising Huut had let slip a confidence.

"He is my master," answered Huut, the guarded slave once again. "Now, silence!"

A half hour of silence passed. They stood waiting, Huut with patience, Aminatra in frustration.

"When is he coming?" she asked, no longer able to hold her tongue.

Huut spared Aminatra a discerning glance. "When he's ready. The master's routine sometimes gets disrupted if he's summoned to the palace or a client comes seeking a tricky ask."

"Client? I thought he was a general in the army?"

"The master is patron to many. They come to him to assist with legal disputes or other problems. In return, they give him their loyalty. Now, sil ..."

The door swung open and two large hounds bounded in, their initial instinct to explore the smells along the wall evaporating at the sight of the two slaves. A deep bark accompanied their dash towards Aminatra.

"Remain still! Show no fear!" urged Huut through the corner of his mouth. His own face flushed with concern.

The hounds stopped a yard short, their noses assessing the unfamiliar scent of Aminatra, a growl signalling their decision. She fought the impulse to run, her memory recalling how the Ferrals circled before they had attacked her in the prison.

"Ka! Walag! Dem shiloto j'a tullim!" An authoritative voice, as though by magic, set the dogs at ease. They sank to the ground, their eyes losing their threat.

Aminatra could not help but glance towards the voice's owner. A sharp tap on her shin from Huut's flicked foot reset her eyes forward, but she had seen the unmistakable figure of the master. He was a large, well-built man with dark skin and rich black hair. Aminatra estimated his age as forty, his face a contradiction of uncompromising brutality and benevolent sensitivity. His cheeks adorned what Aminatra now understood to be the ceremonial scars of the warriors. Other scars dotted his brow and chin, while his flattened nose carried the tale of a past break. Yet his eyes, wide and light, held no malice.

General Malic, accompanied by two men who hovered behind either shoulder, lowered himself on a chair before Aminatra. He sat upright, his hands on his thighs, his arms locked straight. His eyes slowly surveyed Aminatra as he conversed with Huut in his native tongue.

"The master is interested in where you come from," said Huut. "I have informed him your land lies beyond distant mountains. He wants to know the name of your home."

"Athenia," answered Aminatra, unsure of what to do with her eyes. They instinctively tried to focus on Malic, but she instead turned them on his black tunic. She recognised the word 'Athenia' repeated as the conversation proceeded without her.

"The master wishes to know if Athenia is a rich land. How big is your army?"

Aminatra frowned. She had never quantified Athenia before, having never lived elsewhere. "Life is hard there. This land is more fertile. We had no army, just guards."

"Guards?" pressed Huut.

"They imposed the law of the Wardyns and protected us from the Ferrals."

"Wardyns? Ferrals?" Huut appeared keen to answer his master, frustrated at having to mine for further answers.

"The Wardyns ruled Athenia; the Ferrals are a people with savage ways who attack Athenia, but ..."

Huut cut her short with a wave of his hand as he translated. The master fired back a question.

"The master asks what weapons these Ferrals possess."

"Err, none. They throw stones." As Aminatra's answer left her mouth, Malic laughed. Her eyes connected with his, assessing the truth that lay behind. "You speak my language?"

Huut gasped at the impudence of the new slave, but Malic smiled.

"Very astute," said the general, his accent strong but understandable. "Huut has taught me the tongue of the scholars. It pays to understand your enemy. Why do you speak as they do?"

"I don't know."

Malic pondered the answer. "Very well. Your name is Athenia from now on." He leaned back, addressing one of his assistants, then stood and straightened his tunic. "You are with child?"

"I think so," answered Aminatra, feeling self-conscious.

"A boy would be preferable," stated Malic, rising to his feet.

Aminatra opened her mouth but realised it was an instruction, not a conversation. "I already have a boy. His name is Karlmon. The prince bought him."

The general nodded. "I saw him this morning when I visited the king and his son. Your boy is to be Prince Andolis's playmate. An honour."

"I ... Well, yes, it is." Aminatra did not understand what it meant but appreciated it could be worse, grateful for the additional knowledge.

She sensed a change in Malic's tone as he addressed Huut once more, then departed through another door, the dogs whipping ahead of him. One of his shadows followed; the other remained.

Huut turned, a sombre edge to his face. "I told you to respect the master. Why didn't you?"

"What do you mean? He seemed happy. It made no sense since he speaks my language."

"It is not the master's place to punish or express himself to a slave. You never look him in the eye again, nor speak when not spoken to! You will also always address him as master when you speak to him!"

"Punish?" queried Aminatra, as she noticed the remaining assistant remove and straighten a leather strip from his belt.

"Touch your toes as I do!" instructed Huut, bending down.

With trepidation, Aminatra did as told.

Swish! Crack! From the corner of her eye Aminatra caught a pained wince erupt on Huut's face. Ten cracks followed. She frowned, unsure why Huut paid the price for her disobedience. Then a further crack, and pain shot from the back of her thighs, up her spine and exploded in her head. A restrained cry escaped from her mouth. She bit her lip, trying to stay silent as the next blow came. Three further lashes inflicted their damage, and Aminatra braced herself for the sixth.

"It's over!" said Huut, straightening like an old man.

Aminatra lifted a leg, touching behind to where her wounds throbbed. She grimaced, glaring toward her punisher. His face passive, he refastened the whip on his belt and departed without a word.

"Cronax!" cursed Aminatra. "That hurt. Why did they punish you? And why more than me?"

Huut raised his head, regaining his composure. "I am responsible for your failures and discourtesy. My back suffered the blows. When you have given birth, you will also receive ten lashes if you fail again. And worse is possible!"

"Worse?"

"A slave who listens to what they should not will lose their ears, one who sees what they should not, an eye, and one who speaks falsehoods, their tongue: one who betrays the master, their life."

"How barbaric!" gasped Aminatra.

"That comment loses you your tongue, if an Adonelisian hears you," warned Huut. "They are a brutal people, but they live by principles and standards and are honourable. In choosing their own path in generations past, they followed the doctrine of Sym La Panau. He blamed the collapse of civilisation on the weakness of man and argued that humanity could only rise again if people lived virtuous lives, foregoing worldly distractions and focussing on discipline and strength as a brotherly bond. His temple dominates the city."

"Ah," acknowledged Aminatra, visualising the multi-tiered building she marvelled at on her first day in Adonelis.

"You will only hear them speak the truth, no matter how frank, never a lie. They believe themselves to be superior to all others. Parodis represents everything they despise."

"Slavery is not virtuous. Nor is whipping a pregnant woman."

Huut ignored the comment. "I sensed the master liked you, but you broke the rules." He reached behind, rubbing the back of his tunic. A faint smudge of blood covered his fingertip. "Not a word of this to anyone else, or I will beat you myself! You can return to the kitchen, Athenia. Find Peli and start work."

Chapter Eighteen

"Cronax!" Awe burst from Finbarl's lips, reverberating through the vast expanse of the cathedral.

"Gidhaert raised a finger to his lips and whispered, "This is a place of learning and home of the Unumverum."

With head tipped back and mouth agape, Finbarl stared up, following the painted piers to the distant arches supporting the roof. Central to all was the dome, supported by the building's rotunda heart. Cornice decorations surrounded the rim, leading to sumptuous, patterned tiles. The outside overwhelmed him, but the interior triggered a spiritual euphoria. All his dreams of a better world came to fruition with this symbol of achievement. Life in Athenia squeezed out all hope in a benevolent deity; here he could believe. Temptation won through and he closed his eyes and cried, "Beautiful!" listening to the echo until it faded.

Maddy hunted for the bouncing sound with curious eyes. Even she seemed to find some wonder in the surroundings.

"Shh!" Gidhaert waved them on, acknowledging the critical stares of others with an apologetic shrug. "I have friends here; they work for the scholars. They will be better able to help you than I. But first the Unumverum."

At the heart of the cathedral, under the dome, another building rested. Its walls were made of white marble, gilded with gold-leaf inscriptions, and curved into a perfect circle, with stained-glass windows somehow fitting at even spaces. A delicate gold spear finished off a conical roof of blue and red zigzag tiles. Intricate mosaic designs ringed the floor around.

"This is the window to peek through," advised Gidhaert, leaning in, pressing his face against a yellow pane. He stepped back, nodding his head with an enthused glow. "Take a look."

Finbarl shut one eye and peered through. "It's a book?"

"Oh, yes," concurred Gidhaert, still nodding like a child disclosing a secret. "It is *the* book! When the world of old collapsed, the survivors of Taliphia swore they would start afresh, forget all the evils that had led us to ruin, and build anew."

Listening intently, Finbarl noticed the men with swords guarding the entrance, their eyes on Maddy as she ran a finger across the floor patterns.

"But, of course," continued Gidhaert, "it's impossible to forget everything and not wise to do so. So, our ancestors put all worthy knowledge in the Unumverum and established the Honry scholars as guardians and interpreters."

"Explains why it's so thick," commented Finbarl. "So, you built the city following their instructions?"

"Well, over many generations, yes."

"But it doesn't mention things like guns or flying machines?"

"Guns?" Gidhaert's blank face looked back.

"Never mind."

"Flying machines. How imaginative. But why?"

"Never mind," repeated Finbarl. "What if someone invents something new?"

"That is not likely," replied Gidhaert. "After all, the book has already told us what we need to know. However, should it happen, we ask the scholars to decide if it fits within the sanction of the Unumverum."

"Does that occur often?" Finbarl stepped back to allow Maddy an uninterrupted route with her finger along a mosaic. "Sorry, but if not, I don't understand what the scholars do other than talk at the park. Won't you be in danger if another city develops a better weapon?"

Gidhaert winced, pained by Finbarl's ignorance. "They translate what the Unumverum means to our everyday lives, advise on and shape our laws, provide moral leadership and guidance." The young sailor paused, glowing with pride, stroking his beads. "The Unumverum is more than a guidebook from our past; it is also a guidebook for our future. In times of crisis, our ancestors steer us, their prophecies bringing victory and peace."

Finbarl laughed. "You're joking? You mean, you learn from their mistakes?"

Anger coloured Gidhaert's cheeks. "No, I mean, it tells us precisely what to do. It sees into the future. You should not disrespect the Unumverum! It's proven its worth for hundreds of years. When the Pegonians fought us, the scholars found the text pertaining to the event and, through interpretation, advised our generals on what to do to defeat them. Or when the rains didn't come in Korrahu, the Unumverum spoke of the drought and guided the Honry to an aquifer. The future's laid out within its pages, but you need the blessing and wisdom of the Honry scholars to understand it. Only they have access."

"That's incredible," exclaimed Finbarl, taking another look through the glass. "Can they use it to say if I get Aminatra and Karlmon back and how?"

"No, they will only consult the book when a crisis affects Parodis, not for an individual's woes."

"Could I not read it myself?" pressed Finbarl. "If it is in my tongue, then I can understand it. The scholars need not know."

"No!" spluttered Gidhaert, his tone rising an octave. "This is a sacred book, Finbarl. No one must access it other than those ordained to do so. If such a sacrilege were to occur, then the very future of Parodis would be at risk.

"Now, come! Enough of such silly talk. I will take you to meet my friends." Gidhaert ushered them away, leading them down spiralling stone stairs to a room full of chatting men and women.

On sight of Gidhaert, three men and two women hurried over, exchanging hugs and handshakes. They conversed in their colloquial tongue, ignoring Finbarl and Maddy. Gidhaert appeared a different person to the put-upon Medino sailor, laughing and animated.

After a few minutes, Gidhaert turned. "These are my friends: Lhaluma, Pet, Favo, Dae and Allus."

The group nodded, smiling towards Finbarl, eyeing Maddy with interest.

"Hello, my name's Finbarl. This is Maddy."

"Gidhaert's told us all about you," replied the man known as Pet, his Anglicus accented but understandable, his hair a striking ginger. "You've travelled a long way, but speak the tongue of the scholars?"

"Yes. Parodis is amazing. I thought all people spoke as I do until we met Captain Tarlobus."

"The scholars' tongue is an ancient one," said Lhaluma, tall and lean with a beaded beard running down to his chest. "It's all other languages that have veered away from it over centuries. How odd that yours has not."

"And your journey's not been without its difficulties, we understand?" enquired the shorter of the women, Allus, her hazel eyes soft and friendly.

A flush of regret coloured Finbarl's cheeks. He had let the wonders of Parodis beguile him, subsuming the reason he was here. "Yes, the Adonelisians took my wife and son. I need help to get them back." He lifted his strapped arm, as though to prove the severity of his situation.

This triggered a flurry of exchanges between the group in words not meant for Finbarl's consumption.

"Gidhaert said you may help," pressed Finbarl.

"Our friend Gidhaert," said Lhaluma, adjusting a shiny brooch on his lapel, "has either been exaggerating our ability or you have misunderstood. We are but servants to the scholars. You need an army to win your family back."

"They know nothing of this world," added Gidhaert. "My captain informed them of the futility of saving someone from the Adonelisians." He turned to Finbarl. "All my friends can offer is to help you find your feet in Parodis. The best Parodis may afford you is the chance to hire some foolhardy mercenaries to raid Adonelis, but you need money for that. Lots of it."

"And that's possible?" asked Finbarl, confused but hopeful.

"With time and luck," said Pet, whose lucid eyes reminded Finbarl of his old friend, Gauret.

"I must go!" declared Gidhaert. "I have business to do: a new cloak to buy and the latest beads from Jurdurin."

"What colour cloak?" asked Dae, herself wrapped in a blue one.

"I haven't decided yet," said Gidhaert. "Perhaps green."

The choice ignited an excited discussion in their natural tongue. An awkward Finbarl stood, forgotten again.

"They tell me blue is the colour this season," announced Gidhaert. "I have been away too long!"

"I don't understand," confessed Finbarl.

"Why, Finbarl," cried Pet. "If you are to become a Parodisian, you must learn style is everything." The others laughed. "No self-respecting Parodisian will leave their house without the finest and latest fashion. Our dear Gidhaert here is quite the disgrace in his drab working clothes!" This caused more hilarity.

Still not comprehending, Finbarl looked down at his thawb. "This is all I have."

"Money!" declared Dae, touching Finbarl's cloth with disdain. "You must earn some money."

"But I'll need the money to buy the ... er ... mercinaras."

"Mercenaries," corrected Pet. "No Parodisian mercenary will follow you if you don't have the right clothes! A Pegonian might!" The laughter continued.

"Don't worry," said Allus, sympathising with the straight-faced visitor. "We'll help you find a job and you can sleep at the cathedral dormitory until you're settled."

"What about Maddy? She is not ..."

"There's a women's dormitory too," cut in Allus.

"No, I mean, she's different. She won't work or sleep where told."

Gidhaert uttered something incomprehensible, stirring a snigger in the others.

"What did you say?" challenged Finbarl.

"Nothing," answered a red-faced Gidhaert. "I just joked Master Bartarnous might help."

"Why?"

"Well," said Gidhaert, shifting uncomfortably. "He like's a lost cause."

"I see," said Finbarl, the joke lost on him. "Do I find him in the park, or does he come here?"

"Either, but ..." Gidhaert threw his hands up. "Oh, it doesn't matter. I really must be going. I wish you luck, my friend." He shook Finbarl's hand, spared a nervous glance at Maddy and edged past her, out the door.

"So," said Pet, after an awkward silence, "tell us about your world!"

"But over a drink with a papim," added Favo, speaking for the first time in a deep, gravel voice to suit his bulkier frame.

"Oh, yes!" cried Allus. "Have you tried papim?"

Finbarl shrugged.

"It's a cake. Parodis is famous for it."

They ushered Finbarl and Maddy back up the stairs and through the cathedral. Outside, the heat under the sun contrasted with the cool air of the building. Finbarl looked back at the towering edifice as they strolled down the hill, still enraptured by its magnificence.

Short of Halloan Park, they turned in the opposite direction, onto another open patch of grass. People sat in small groups on the ground, talking, eating and drinking. Athenia had no space to offer for such relaxation, no abundance of food to enjoy in such quantity. Stalls occupied the edge, a huddle of people crowding before each.

"I'll get them!" announced Dae. "Will ... Mmmaddy ... want a cake?"

"Does it contain meat?" asked Finbarl.

Dae exploded with a shrill laugh, causing Maddy to flinch. "No, just flour, egg, butter, honey and seeds."

"You can try it with her. She hasn't eaten for a while." Finbarl watched with curiosity as Dae wandered across to a stall, squeezed into the crowd and, with shouting and waving, made a transaction.

She returned carrying a wooden board loaded with cups and cakes. Finbarl's eyes widened, his stomach alive with anticipation.

They sat in a circle, with the cups passed around. Maddy examined the offering but refrained from taking it, unsure at the steaming content. The cakes lay in the centre, teasing Finbarl's taste buds with their aroma. Finbarl sipped at the drink, the heat catching him unaware.

"Blow on it," suggested Allus. "Let it cool a little."

Finbarl smiled, feeling the fool at his naïve and clumsy ways.

"What is the name of your home?" asked Lhaluma, stretching his long legs out.

"Athenia," said Finbarl. "It is far west, through forests and mountains." He watched Dae blow on her drink and take a sip and copied her. Now cool, the flavour came through. A bitter edge accompanied a fruity tang. It was nice. "Maddy." He raised his cup towards her. "Good. You like."

She seemed to understand and sniffed at the cup on the ground before her. Finbarl blew with exaggeration in his cup to demonstrate. She mimicked, then lapped at the liquid.

"She drinks like a dog!" exclaimed Favo.

"Is she from Athenia?" asked Lhaluma.

"No," explained Finbarl. "We discovered her on this side of the mountains. She's what we call a Ferral. They're a primitive people. Many live around Athenia, though."

"A Ferral." The group repeated the name with interest.

"Does she talk?" enquired Pet. He picked up a slice of cake and bit into it.

Finbarl watched as two others followed his lead, then felt confident enough to do the same. "No. Ferrals lost the power to speak long ago." He took a large mouthful of cake, closing his eyes as the sweet honey tantalised.

"You look like you needed that!" quipped Pet.

"Mmm, mmm." A muffled nonsense emerged from Finbarl's stuffed mouth. With a gulp, he tried again. "Since I lost Aminatra and Karlmon, I've hardly eaten."

"That's your wife and son?" asked Allus.

"Yes, I miss them terribly."

Pet leaned across, gripping Finbarl's shoulder. "You'll get them back. Why did you leave Athenia?"

"That's a long story!"

"Parodisians love a good story," said Dae, clapping her hands.

"Particularly with papim!" chipped in Favo, eyeing the last piece.

For the next hour, Finbarl told his story: his life as a guard, how he met then betrayed Aminatra, rediscovering his mother within the prison, his fall from favour and imprisonment, losing his mother, falling in love with Aminatra, their struggle to free themselves from the drug Jumblar and finally the failed attempt to save Athenia. The group sat, enthralled.

"And so, we sought a better life over the mountains," concluded Finbarl.

"That's incredible," said Allus, wiping a tear from her eye.

"I think we may have discovered a way for you to earn money!" declared Pet, climbing to his feet, taking the stance of an orating master. "If we can teach you to speak Parodisian, then the people of this city will pay good money to hear your stories."

"Oh, yes," agreed Favo, stuffing the last papim in his mouth. "They love to hear tales of distant lands and strange people."

"Strange people?" queried Finbarl.

"I mean ...," Favo leaned in with a conspiratorial whisper, nodding towards Maddy, "... the Ferrals!"

Chapter Nineteen

"**W**oud! Kwip ut, Athenia!"

The familiar, harassing voice of Peli cut across the kitchen. Aminatra dropped her chopping knife and scurried to the woodpile. Gathering an armful of logs, she lugged them to the fire, placing them at its side. The flames warmed her cheeks as she leaned forward to add three logs, feeding their persistent hunger, satisfying Peli.

Aminatra's new name took some getting used to. Raps from Peli's large wooden spoon speeded the process. Strange, shouted words attached to a half-familiar name meant nothing to her until stinging utensil strikes roused her into action. She now listened carefully, recognising the name, learning the associated words and actions. It was not how she envisaged acquiring the language, but it proved effective. The beatings became less frequent as she became more efficient.

Aminatra's body also adapted to the rigours of the work. She rose an hour before dawn, woken by a rap on her skull as a slave stirred all those asleep amid their cells. While the major fire in the kitchen remained tended throughout the night, the stoves required relighting. Aminatra's first task was to clean and restock them, which was a dirty job as it proved impossible to avoid thick soot from covering hands and arms. She then mopped the floor, which she enjoyed because of its extravagant use of water: something she never experienced in Athenia. As other slaves hurried about their own roles, Aminatra hummed to herself, pushing the mop into its bucket, sweeping the floor, swirling the head around and around. No one seemed to mind her humming. Even Peli acknowledged it with a smile.

The first prepared meal of the day was a thick, gloopy sludge made from oats, berries and milk. Aminatra stirred the cauldron until the consistency reached sufficient thickness. She even got to sample it, ensuring the mix was satisfactory, the heat appropriate. With one meal complete, they began preparations for the next. No time for rest or idle thoughts. They often worked late into the night if the master entertained guests, not collapsing in sleep until they had cleaned and stacked the crockery. The portions the slaves received for their labour were miserly in comparison. However, for a girl used to life in Athenia, the variety and quantity proved enough.

Huut appeared at the door and called out an instruction to Peli. She yelled in turn, targeting her team with specific directives. Aminatra was certain she heard her given name within them. She repeated the phrases in her mind, memorising the words, watching her peers, construing the meaning of their actions. They lined bowls on trays, ordering them by the cauldron. Time to serve breakfast. Aminatra prodded her tongue into a spooned sample and nodded, satisfied it was hot enough. Then, with a large ladle, she dispensed the sludge into the bowls. Speed was essential. If the food arrived cold, all could expect a beating. As they filled each tray, a slave rushed it on its way, only stopping by the door to learn from Huut where to take it. Aminatra remained to carry the final tray. She filled a bowl, examined the cauldron, noting plenty remained for the slaves, then wiped her hands on a dirty cloth. The tray carried four bowls, which was nice and light compared with some.

"To the master's chamber, Athenia!" instructed Huut, who followed in Aminatra's wake as she set off down the corridor. "How go your language lessons?"

"I'm learning," she replied. "It's slow progress, but I'm getting there."

Despite Huut's haughty declaration they would not speak after that first day, Aminatra suspected he enjoyed speaking in his old tongue. In fact, he had become quite chatty whenever she delivered food to the master.

"You are doing well, picking up your duties, not making mistakes."

"They aren't hard to learn, just difficult to do at speed and for so many hours, particularly with a mother's burden."

"If you show ability and competence," said Huut, ignoring the reference to Aminatra's pregnancy, "then other, better opportunities will arise. I started in the fields, but my education impressed and now I'm a senior slave."

"How long did it take you to learn their language?"

"Not long," answered Huut. "While it is quite different to the tongue of the scholars, it has similarities to Parodisian. Yours is a greater challenge."

"What did you do in Parodis?" asked Aminatra, eager to learn all she could from their chats.

"A scholar," reflected Huut. "They captured me just after I qualified."

"What happened?"

"Oh, it hurts!" exclaimed Huut, convincing Aminatra he would divulge no more, but with a sigh, he continued. "With its control of the river, Parodis has dominant influence across many of the cities of Taliphia. We dominate commerce and, in the slipstream of trade, our scholars travel to spread wisdom and enlightenment to others. Cities like Adonelis or Mammu vie for the hegemony of this land. While I visited Camptex with a mission, the Adonelis raided, forcing the city under their orbit and massacring, or enslaving, anyone who didn't submit or was from Parodis! At the wrong time and place, as they say!"

"And do you hope to escape one day and return?"

Huut, disappointed, looked down at Aminatra. "You'd do well to forget such thoughts and concentrate on your work here. Now, no more talking!"

They entered the master's private chamber, Huut leading with a gentle knock to the black sheen door, holding it for Aminatra to glide through with the tray.

General Malic sat at the head of the long rectangular table, Lady Malic opposite, their son and daughter on either side. The boy, Klout, was in his late teens, older than the girl, Bethu, who was perhaps two years Karlmon's senior. Both sat upright, presented neatly, quiet and disciplined. Their hair mirrored each respective parent: his shaved from an inch above his ears downwards, hers a tidy bob down to her neck.

Huut announced himself and ushered Aminatra forward. This moment always caused her nerves: holding the tray in one hand, while presenting the bowl with the other. A spillage with either would lead to severe punishment.

"Morn vu glori, marstoc," said Aminatra, with a well-practised phrase, as she placed the master's bowl before him, her eyes locked on it.

"Ah, Athenia! Our girl from the mountains." Malic smiled at her, waiting while she produced a spoon and sampled his breakfast before him. "Huut, do these people have the qualities of good workers?"

The tall slave stepped forward. "If Athenia is typical, I believe they do, Master."

"Maybe I will visit one day. Would you like to go home, Athenia?"

Aminatra circled the table, noticing the pair of hounds asleep beneath it, and presented a bowl to the mistress of the house. "That would please me, Master. Though the environment is not welcoming." She understood Malic's words and intent, wishing to ingratiate and dissuade with her answer.

Lady Malic clicked her finger, impatient at the slave's distraction and strange words, her own bowl untested for poison. Aminatra bowed and spooned a morsel into her mouth. As she moved on to the boy, Klout, a sharp exchange passed between wife and husband, Aminatra recognising the tone from her arguments with Finbarl.

The general laughed. "Your mistress doesn't like me talking with a slave in her own tongue. I told her I speak to whomever."

Aminatra smiled with unease, unhappy to be the topic of discussion, trying to digest the sample from Klout.

"I'm among the most powerful men in Adonelis. Others fear me, but not my wife! Did you fear your husband, Athenia?"

"I love and respect him," answered Aminatra.

"Oh, he lives, does he? Not a slave here?"

"I don't know if he lives or is dead, but you didn't capture him with Karlmon and me."

"Most likely dead then," replied Malic, tucking into his breakfast. "We'll have to find you a new one when that baby is born."

A wave of nausea welled within Aminatra as she held a spoonful of Bethu's breakfast before her lips. She took a deep breath and swallowed the sludge. "Thank you, master."

As she and Huut backed towards the door, their duties completed, Aminatra felt the stern eyes of Lady Malic on her. When out in the corridor, Huut confirmed it.

"I fear our mistress may not have taken to you. Be careful!"

Chapter Twenty

Finbarl sat on the edge of his dormitory bed, scratching his head. By his feet lay Maddy, deep in sleep, hair tied up, making her seem like a normal teenage girl. As on the previous night, he had bid her a goodnight by her own bed in the female dormitory, walking back to his own quarters alone. And, as before, she had followed him to sleep on the floor by his bed. The other occupants expressed their disquiet at such behaviour. 'Sorry' was the first word to learn in the native Parodisian tongue.

Everything had been going well. The group befriended on his first day helped him to settle, showing him around, introducing him to others and teaching him the ways and language of the Parodisians. But the problem of Maddy remained. She either clung to Finbarl or hid in darkened corners. Every noise made her start; each new person provoked a snarl. He would not give up on her, but something needed to change.

Unable to sleep, Finbarl threw on his thawb and crept out of his room. Too much swirled through his mind. Then there was the soft bed. It was so luxurious compared with the straw mattress of his Athenian days, but his body favoured the familiar. He looked back to ensure Maddy remained undisturbed and stole out of the dormitory.

The first light of morning fell on the deserted streets of Parodis. Finbarl stretched his arms and yawned. The city still made him wonder. Its buildings reflected a warm dawn glow, appearing as though built from gold, their long shadows cast over the roads. A faint smell of baking bread drifted his way. Others were up and at work already.

Dawn was the best time to explore the city. If he kept the cathedral dome in sight, there was little chance of getting lost, despite the multitude of streets. He strolled down the hill, towards the centre of the city. A glint of the distant river caught his attention, and he wondered about Tarlobus and his crew. Were they once more riding the currents, travelling to faraway places, trading between cities? And of Parmsoli. Had the Terratus made progress among his friends in power, as promised? "It won't be long, Aminatra," he pledged aloud.

"Hello!"

The voice startled Finbarl. He swung around, trying to locate the source.

"Who's that?" asked the mysterious individual.

Finbarl craned his neck, shielding his eyes from the low sun as it peeked over the roof. A row of buildings stood back from the street, constructed from a rugged grey stone. Amid the fourth window along on the third floor, a face appeared, surrounded by a distinctive white mane. Stepping into the shadow, Finbarl made out the familiar features of Master Bartarnous. "Good morning. My name's Finbarl. I'm a visitor to Parodis."

"I heard you talking. Like me, you enjoy the early hour and sharing your thoughts with the silence," said Bartarnous, his eyes staring towards Finbarl as they had at Halloan Park. "It is so conducive to contemplation and clarity. Fewer noises to distract."

"I suppose so," answered Finbarl.

"Did you visit the park the other day?" asked the scholar, his head twitching back and forth. "Word has been echoing through the cathedral of newcomers from a distant land who speak in the tongue of the scholars."

"Yes. We're from the west," replied Finbarl. "From beyond the mountains."

"You and a strange creature: half-human, half-beast."

Finbarl half-smiled. "You mean Maddy? She is all human. There were four of us: my wife and her son. But the Adonelisians kidnapped them."

"I see," said Bartarnous, nodding in a strange up-down-sideways motion. "That is a long way to come to suffer such. You must share some chee! I've many questions I wish to ask."

Finbarl hesitated, recalling the low regard in which Gidhaert and his friends held the scholar and unnerved by the old man's inability to keep still.

"Come!" pressed Bartarnous. "Stories you may have heard about me are as nothing to the quality of my chee." A beaming smile broke through.

"Thank you," answered Finbarl, surveying the building for an entrance.

"The door to my left," instructed Bartarnous, pointing down. "It's open. Up the stairs to the top. I'll be waiting for you." His head disappeared inside, but his voice still carried. "From across the mountains! Who would have thought it?"

With a tentative push, Finbarl opened the door, his head leading with a curious examination before his feet followed. Oil-burning lights mounted on the wall exposed a plain hall with a staircase on the left. The stone steps, worn over time, tilted one way and then the next, not unlike life aboard the boat, considered Finbarl as he climbed. True to his word, Bartarnous awaited at the top.

"Welcome!" cried the scholar, squeezing Finbarl with a surprise hug, the waves from his twitching body flowing through to his guest. "I am Povar Bartarnous. You have come so far. We must cement our two people's friendship. May I?" Without awaiting an answer, Bartarnous ran his fingers over Finbarl's face.

Finbarl's arms hung limp at his side, uncertain if they had a role in this ritual. Should he mimic his host and feel his face? "I'm Finbarl," was all he could think to say in response.

Releasing his visitor, Bartarnous motioned Finbarl towards an open door. "I can hear the water boiling. The chee will be ready soon! What material is that, Finbarl?" He rubbed his fingers on the thawb.

"Linen," answered Finbarl.

"I see," mulled Bartarnous. "It's light. Is it cool in the sun?"

Finbarl shrugged. "I've only ever worn a thawb. It is what it is."

"So it is," laughed the host, gesturing for Finbarl to sit by a small round table by the window. "And your arm is in a splint?"

"The Adonelisians attacked us on the river. They stole my wife and son."

"Your pain must be great."

Unconvinced the scholar offered a solution to his plight, Finbarl gave a terse reply. "It is."

The room contained little, but all fascinated Finbarl's wandering eye. Books fought for space on a short, wall-mounted shelf. A small cupboard housed an odd collection of knick-knacks, while positioned to the middle of the far wall, catching the morning sun through the window, hung an object of wonder.

"What interests you to make you silent?" asked Bartarnous.

"The picture. I've never seen anything like it!" gasped Finbarl. "It's so real; so beautiful."

"You think so?" said Bartarnous. "An old student of mine painted it: very talented, I'm told. Not at his studies, but with a brush."

"Why?" asked Finbarl.

"Why what?"

"What is its purpose? Why did your student create it and why do you display it?"

Bartarnous chuckled. "That's an excellent question. Does it not improve the room?"

"Oh, yes," concurred Finbarl.

"Then that must be its purpose. Ah, here comes the chee! This is my servant, Alusto," said Bartarnous, introducing the young man carrying the tray of drinks. "A fine brewer of chee, but he's no painter!"

Finbarl laughed, infected by his host's guffawing. The servant smiled, as though familiar with the joke. He passed a cup to Finbarl and gripped Bartarnous's wrist, guiding it to the other cup. The scholar's eyes never left Finbarl as his fingers crept around the vessel. Finbarl frowned, confused by the behaviour.

As Alusto departed, Bartarnous sniffed at his steaming cup. "Ah, there is nothing quite like a hot chee in the morning. Is this not exciting? Two peoples meeting."

"How did you become a scholar?" asked Finbarl. "Are you priests?"

"Yes," answered Bartarnous, then smiled, adding, "and no." He sipped his chee and let out a satisfied sigh, wiping his lip with a sleeve. "There's so little we know about each other. Today I will tell you of Parodis and the scholars; tomorrow you will return and tell me about your land and people. Each morning, before the world awakes, we will sip chee and swap stories. What do you say?"

Finbarl raised his cup, as taught by Tarlobus. Any initial suspicion of Bartarnous was washed away by his friendly manner, "I would like that." He could sneak out of the dormitory at first light, and no one need ever know his destination or companion.

Bartarnous leaned on the windowsill, his head turned to the outside. "So, where to begin?"

"How did your people survive the collapse of the Golden Age?" asked Finbarl.

"Golden Age? You mean the age of the bridge builders?"

"When civilisation ruled the world."

"As far back as that, eh." Bartarnous scratched his chin. "Not a clue! We call it the Lost Age. They left us ruins, but not much else. What emerged was one people: the Taliphians. All the cities are descendants of the Taliphians. A more argumentative people you will not come across." The scholar punctuated his tale with a laugh and an involuntary jerk of his head. "Civilisation crumbles to its knees, and what did we do? We argued!"

Finbarl laughed politely, accompanying his host, reflecting on his own ancestors' less-than-perfect response to the past.

"So much knowledge and learning already lost and people were angry and confused. But what direction should we take? In one year, Mossili and his followers fall out with the others, pack up their bags and set off to found their own settlement. Fifty years later, Pegon has a sulk and takes his disciples off to establish their new home. Then the founder of Parodis. After a thousand generations, everyone has stormed out, founding the fourteen city states you see today, each with their own philosophy and all still arguing. I often joke ...," Bartarnous paused for breath between laughter, "... I often joke even those who remained at the original settlement felt obliged to leave in a huff until the place was empty!" Tears now flooded down Bartarnous's cheeks.

Finbarl laughed too, unclear at what. "When was the Unumverum written?"

"Not a clue." Bartarnous wiped a sleeve across his dampened cheeks. "Needless to say, it's the source of most of the arguments. Those that wanted to follow its lead to the letter, those that wanted to use it as an occasional reference and those that wanted nothing to do with it. Of course, that was before someone discovered it could also see into the future. Then they all wanted to follow it, or at least possess it."

Sipping at his chee, Finbarl followed Bartarnous's flickering eyes, which never rested. He faced Finbarl but somehow always looked through him.

"Alusto! More chee!" yelled Bartarnous. "Where was I? Ah, yes. So, a community called Parodis emerged as custodians of the Unumverum. Disciples to its words and its mysteries. Difficult years followed as people rallied against the past, burning books, wrecking machinery, caught up in the fervent idealism. But with the past erased, people realised finding their way to the future was not as easy as they thought. Somehow, the Order of Honry emerged. I guess they were just the smartest who could turn the words into a framework for living. They passed on their wisdom to the next generation and, over time, they established themselves as scholars and guides. With years of study, they discovered the true power of the Unumverum. Knowing the future gave Parodis its confidence and stability to flourish."

Alusto arrived with another tray of chee, swapped the cups and vanished again.

"So, you dismantled your old civilisation and rebuilt a new one," reflected an enthused Finbarl. "That is what my mother proposed. Parodis would impress her."

"She did not come with you?"

"No, she died," said Finbarl. "You would have liked her ... and Dul-biblex. He looked after our library. I don't think burning your books would have agreed with him, but he would appreciate you keeping the best of the past through the Unumverum. What does it say about the future? Will I find Aminatra and Karlmon?"

"I wish it were that easy," sighed Bartarnous. "The text is meaningless until the right context unlocks it. We only consult when a crisis arises and the Senorium requests it. Even then, there is much discussion as the Honrians come to an agreed interpretation."

"Gidhaert said much the same," lamented Finbarl. "What about the other cities? Do all have scholars and share a copy of the Unumverum?"

"They certainly managed to forget the past, but scholars and the Unumverum are unique to Parodis. Each went their separate way, but not without relationships and trade. The Unumverum is Parodis's alone and closely guarded. Our city has always led the way, but you can't stop ideas with borders. Other cities adopted the wisdom of the Unumverum by copying us. That's not a bad thing."

"And religion?" enquired Finbarl. "You sound like a priesthood."

BOOM!

Finbarl flinched at the sound of a distant explosion, its deep rumble vibrating through his bones. Bartarnous's reaction involved a twitch but little sign of disturbance.

"What was that?" asked Finbarl, standing to inspect the scene from the window.

"Pay it no heed," said Bartarnous. "It is the mine at Lanfil Flash. Commonly known as the Flash."

"What do they mine?"

"Metal," came the terse reply.

Finbarl continued to stare out the window, intrigued by a new sound and talk of metal.

"You were asking about religion and a priesthood," continued Bartarnous. "It's complicated. The Unumverum demands equality and liberty for all. Every citizen of Parodis believes what they wish. You can worship a pumpkin if you so desire. I prefer to eat mine."

"That's incredible!" exclaimed Finbarl, sitting himself down again. "Anything at all? Even if it contradicts the rulers?"

"The people choose our rulers: the rulers represent our people."

"I think I understand," said Finbarl, trying to equate it to the Wardyns from Athenia, but finding no parallels.

"There are limits," continued Bartarnous. "A citizen's beliefs and actions must not lead to the errors made by our ancestors. Scholars police this, judging whether a decision or opinion has consequences that threaten our future. In government, all decisions are run past a second chamber of scholars, who debate and determine if a law is appropriate. A citizen can believe in any god they desire, but the scholars provide the moral direction."

"And do the scholars all agree?" asked Finbarl, part aware of the answer already.

"Interpretation, by its nature, invites disagreement, but some of us disagree more than others." Bartarnous laughed again, but this time it carried a sad lilt.

Finbarl sipped his chee, watching his host, waiting for him to elaborate.

Bartarnous stared out the window and sighed. "Over my lifetime a dangerous shift's taken place, from a community willing to sacrifice to protect liberty, to a city of individuals willing to exploit this liberty for their own needs. The city's wealth brings benefits, but it unbalances us. It worries me. The city is in peril."

"I don't know about that," challenged Finbarl. "It's an incredible place. The people are kind and generous. What unbelievable riches, metal everywhere. And, of course, you own the Unumverum. Everything is better than where I came from. Perhaps when I tell you of Athenia, you'll better appreciate what you have."

"Perhaps the Unumverum will set us back on the right path," mused Bartarnous, his usual enthusiasm missing. "Oh, there are worse places to live than Parodis, but ..."

"AAHHHH!" A scream from the next room cut the scholar short.

"What was that?" demanded Finbarl, climbing to his feet.

Alusto burst in, clutching his hand. "She bit me! She bit me!" With a nervous check over his shoulder, he cowered behind Bartarnous.

"Who?" pressed the scholar.

"Her!" shrieked Alusto, pointing to the door with his bloodied finger.

Finbarl gripped the chair, ready to use it as a weapon, and then relaxed. "Maddy!"

The Ferral stood in the doorframe, sniffing her surroundings, inspecting those in Finbarl's company.

"Who is it? Your interesting friend?" asked Bartarnous, sniffing the air, uncertain whether to laugh.

"She has a remarkable way of finding anything, including me!" said Finbarl. "Don't worry, she won't harm you."

"But she bit me!" protested Alusto, waving his finger as proof.

"Well, I wouldn't advise you touch her," added Finbarl. "Not unless she likes you."

"I only tried to stop her barging in on Master Bartarnous!" yelled Alusto.

Maddy snarled, disturbed by the aggression.

"It's all right, Maddy," calmed Finbarl. "These are our friends." He went over to her and placed a reassuring hand on her shoulder. "This is Master Bartarnous and Alusto."

"Does she not talk?" asked Bartarnous.

"No, the Ferrals lost the power to talk many generations ago."

"A Ferral," repeated Bartarnous. "Describe her to me?" He aimed his request at Alusto.

"She bit my finger!"

"Oh, be a Terratus!" chastised the master. "I hear she is nothing more than a girl. The bugs in my bed will bite deeper than her."

"She's not like any girl I've seen before!" moaned Alusto, as he sucked on his damaged digit.

Finbarl guided Maddy to the window, and she looked out as though seeing a new world. Inclined to investigate, she lifted a leg to climb on the windowsill.

"No, Maddy! You can't go out!" Finbarl pulled her back, smiled and signalled danger with his hand.

"You describe her to me, Finbarl," requested Bartarnous.

Finbarl looked deep into the scholar's flickering eyes. "You can't see!"

"The master is blind," confirmed Alusto. "You've only just realised?"

"I've never seen a blind person before," answered Finbarl, shocked by the disclosure.

"Well, that makes two of us," chortled Bartarnous. "Do they not have such people where you come from?"

Finbarl shuffled awkwardly. "None who live beyond a few years. They could not survive, so ..."

"So, they kill them," stated Bartarnous, finishing what Finbarl couldn't.

"I presume so," said Finbarl. "I don't know. How have you survived?"

"Life is not about fulfilling a template," declared Bartarnous. "It is just about living. I can only live the life I'm given. But it is my life and not one that others should take away from me! Without the distraction of sight, I can see further into the soul of man than most: beyond the pride and vanity."

"You move as though sighted," observed Finbarl.

"As you move without thinking," replied the scholar. "My bruises focus the mind."

"Why do you have a picture on the wall and books?"

"Why, to improve the room. You appreciate it through sight, I through your reaction. Alusto reads to me. Now, tell me of Maddy."

"We named her after my mother," explained Finbarl, describing Maddy as best he could, his adjectives far more sympathetic than those he might once have used for a Ferral.

"So, she does not differ from you or I?" asked Bartarnous. "Really, Alusto, you led me to believe she was a monster."

"There is something unworldly about her, Master! She watches me now as though a wolf would a lamb."

"She differs not in appearance," concurred Finbarl, smiling towards Maddy. "Only in behaviour. Though her eyes do possess a ..."

"Your story must be fascinating," cut in Bartarnous. "You must bring Maddy to our morning rendezvous. I would like to learn about you both: this wolf and the shepherd."

"It looks like she'll come if you wanted her to or not," quipped Finbarl.

Alusto snorted his disapproval.

"Oh, Alusto, don't fret so," said Bartarnous. "You've nine other fingers, and I'm sure I'll have learnt all I need by the time she's nibbled six of them!" A familiar outburst of laughter followed as the scholar rolled in his chair.

PART TWO

Chapter Twenty-One

"We're surrounded! Save the last bullet for yourselves!" A hundred eager eyes stared at Finbarl. He allowed the silence to stretch, building the tension in the dim light of the hall. "The Ferrals crept closer and closer until we saw their blood-stained teeth. We fired our weapons, killing dozens, but others sprang up as though from the rocks themselves. Each guard whispered a prayer." Finbarl paced in a tight circle, addressing his entire audience. "We accepted the loss of our souls to these man-eaters. I angled my weapon under my chin, preferring suicide to being eaten alive." The audience gasped as one. He had them in the palm of his hand. "'Yasheee!' A sudden cry ripped down the valley, from beyond the Ferrals. I lowered my weapon and cried 'Cronax!' From a cloud of sand emerged three camels charging towards us, their riders shooting and hollering, dispersing the Ferrals. Some savages scattered but others, fearless as always, remained unmoving, trampled by the unstoppable beasts. As the camels reached us, they slowed but a fraction. I noticed one rider was not a guard but my love, Aminatra, thinking nothing of her own safety. Those of us still alive grabbed a passing saddle, I to Aminatra's. They carried us away from the danger, our feet dragging on the ground. The Ferrals howled in frustration; their feast lost. I scampered up to straddle the camel, holding tight to my love and saviour. We lived to fight another day!" Finbarl collapsed into a bow.

The audience cheered, followed by the adopted chant of 'Cronax', their raised bereo mugs saluting the storyteller. Favo and Pet wandered through the crowd, hats in hand, collecting payment for the evening's entertainment. Money flowed as freely as the drink, and soon the hats bulged.

"Another excellent night!" declared Favo, showing Finbarl his collection.

"And it's not over yet." Pet grinned, patting Finbarl on his back. "You take what we've made so far back to the safe," he instructed Favo. "I'll collect payment for part two of tonight's extravaganza."

They tipped the coins into a bag and loaded it on Favo's back.

"Hurry now!" urged Pet. "And stop for nothing. The streets aren't safe."

"I know! I've done it before." Favo adjusted the bag until comfortable, then slipped through a side door, into the night.

"You okay?" asked Pet of Finbarl.

"Sure," he replied. "Just a little hot. Could do with a drink."

"Anything for the star of Parodis."

As Pet vanished into the crowd, fighting towards the bar, Finbarl collapsed onto a chair. Sweat covered his brow. A bead ran down his clean-shaven chin, dripping to the floor. He wiped his face with a sleeve and undid the top few buttons on his brilliant-green shirt. Being a storyteller was demanding work, but it was worth it. After four months of intense language tuition, the city adopted him as one of their own. Now, six months on from his arrival, Parodisian crowds flocked to hear of his daring deeds in the strange land of Athenia. They were deeds owing as much to fiction as fact, but ones that paid well.

In the early days, he regaled the bereo halls with true stories, but meeting demand was his first lesson in entertainment and economics. The audience expected new, evermore exciting stories. Danger, suspense and fear, mixed with escape, heroics and romance, sated their appetite, drawing in ever bigger crowds. The Ferrals provided the perfect baddies and Aminatra the romance. He did this all for her. Each night a different bereo hall and each night a good purse. "A few more months," Pet assured him, then he would have enough to hire mercenaries and rescue Aminatra.

"Here, get this down you." Pet returned, passing across a mug of frothy bereo.

When first Finbarl sampled the liquid, he recoiled at the bitterness, now he drank it like water. He took a large gulp. "Thanks. I needed that."

"I've arranged for the landlord to keep you filled up for the rest of the evening."

"What would I do without you?" declared Finbarl, raising his mug in appreciation. They were sincere words. All his friends had helped him so much since his arrival, but Pet took him under his wing and understood his needs. He arranged the work, the venues, the promotion, even the clothes Finbarl now wore. Finbarl scratched under his collar, still not used to the constricting attire. Only his beardless chin now distinguished him from his fellow Parodisians, and Pet proposed that to retain "an exotic aura". Most importantly, Pet looked after Finbarl's money concerns. The whole concept still confused Finbarl, so he was glad to let Pet collect the fees, buy the clothes, the drink and pay the rent for his new room.

"You stay there and enjoy your bereo," encouraged Pet. "I'll get stage two going."

Finbarl nodded with reluctance. His left eye twitched with a sense of unease, but past objections were overcome by the chance to make more money, bringing Aminatra's rescue closer.

"Ladies and gentlemen!" cried Pet over the noise. "Hush! Hush! Ladies and gentlemen! Your attention." Silence spread around the room until all waited in anticipation. "Refrain from your carousing to experience the thrill of your life! For a mere ten pownlets, you can look into the eyes of danger, sense the odour of fear and feel the exhilaration of standing before death." Pet lowered his voice to a discreet volume. "Ladies and gentlemen, who among you is brave enough to enter a room with a live Ferral? Step this way! Step this way!"

As an excited buzz filled the hall again, Finbarl took two large gulps of bereo. It appeared to dull the shame a little. He looked away from the disorganised queue by the door.

Pet stood at the side, encouraging others to join. "Have your money ready and your nerves reinforced."

'It's all for Aminatra! It's all for Aminatra!' Finbarl kept repeating the justification in his head.

The door creaked open as the first customers giggled at the prospect of the thrill. Then came the shrieks and gasps as they disappeared inside.

Closing his eyes offered Finbarl no relief. He still saw the image of what awaited them: a stripped Maddy locked in a cage, a leg of raw meat dangled within reach. Then, as people passed through goggling and provoking, the meal pulled away out of grasp, stirring the Ferral to anger. The paying customer received the show the impresario had promised. Familiar reactions filtered through to Finbarl's ears: the gasps and shrieks, the laughter and bravado. 'It's all for Aminatra!'

***

The cool night air did nothing to stir Finbarl from his drunken state as he staggered back to his room. Maddy followed behind, oblivious to his complicity in her evening of humiliation. She had let Pet know her feelings with an attempted bite as they parted ways outside the bereo hall, Finbarl dragging her away. This would be the last time he put her through this torment, Finbarl told himself, the alcohol no longer dulling his feelings but exaggerating his self-disgust.

A figure emerged from a side alley, their features hidden by the dark.

"Evening," remarked Finbarl.

No reply came. Instead, the character whipped a hood over their head and brushed past Finbarl. As they passed Maddy, she hissed, recoiled and bared her teeth. The figure turned, the light catching his face. Sunken eyes examined the Ferral with dispassion.

"Sorry," said Finbarl. "She's harmless. You just caught her by surprise."

Again, no reply came. The man turned and scurried away, eliciting a further hiss from Maddy and a shrug from Finbarl.

"I am sorry." This time Finbarl addressed his apology to Maddy, hoping she understood the sentiment if not the words. "I won't lock you up again. When we have Aminatra and Karlmon back, you'll understand."

As always, the mention of the familiar names evoked a plaintive hum from the girl.

"Pet estimated we made over 700 pownlets tonight."

"That's a good night's return." A voice emerged out of the darkness, speaking in Finbarl's native tongue.

Finbarl spun round, wobbling left as limbs ignored his brain's drunken commands. "Who's there!"

"A friend," came the soft reply, as a cloaked figure stepped out of the shadows.

"Oh, Bartarnousshh!" slurred Finbarl, trying to regain his composure. "I wondered why Maddy allowed you so near without reacting. She's hissing at others."

"Hello Maddy," greeted the scholar, allowing the girl to rub her head against his shoulder in affectionate recognition. "I like to walk at night. Others have less advantage over me." He sniffed the air. "You've been enjoying the local brew."

"Grateful fans," answered Finbarl.

"I've noticed Maddy hasn't been herself recently. We've been progressing so well with our chats. Developed a genuine bond. Has something upset her?"

Finbarl looked away with guilt. "D'know."

"Hmm." Bartarnous's eyes somehow found Finbarl, seeing to his very soul. "She is a remarkable woman. Intelligent, sensitive, caring, inquisitive and courageous. Did you know she can count? I've had her adding lentils. Just basic arithmetic and not conducive to my favourite soup, but impressive. However, she remains vulnerable: in the complexity of humans, not the essentials of life. Many get lost on the road to their potential, exploited and corrupted. She is lucky to have someone such as yourself looking after her. Eh, Finbarl?"

The question pierced Finbarl, cutting through his defences. "I ... I ... It's all for Aminatra! Maddy understands."

"You've taught her to speak, have you?"

"It's none of your business!" shouted Finbarl, defensive aggression replacing the maudlin self-pity.

"Money is a mistress you must be wary of," warned Bartarnous. "She promises much, seduces you, can bring some happiness, but stirs jealousy, distrust, greed and true blindness."

"What are you talking about?" Finbarl dismissed the advice with an exaggerated waft of his hand. "The only jealousy I see is yours!"

"But you look through a flagon of bereo," countered Bartarnous. "You must choose your friends better."

"At least I have friends!"

"Mine is indeed a lonely road, but following the truth is not always a popular route. Life is full of teachers, but the first lesson you must learn is which ones to trust. Those that say what you want to hear teach nothing."

Finbarl shook his head, his mouth ajar in drunken confusion.

"Goodnight, Finbarl," said Bartarnous, turning and walking away. "I'll see you for our next breakfast chat. Take care of yourself." Out of the darkness followed, "And Maddy."

Chapter Twenty-Two

"Show me!" demanded Peli, resting one knee on a low-lying stool.

Aminatra complied, folding back the collar of her tunic to expose a hidden lining of embroidery.

"Oh, that's beautiful, Athenia," exclaimed Peli, folding her knee until she sat on the stool.

"It's simple but effective," explained Aminatra, rubbing the stitches. "Took me a few nights. Not always easy in such poor light."

"You've done a fine job, and it's invisible with the collar straight." Peli encouraged Aminatra in this covert act of embellishment on her otherwise bland uniform. A rebellious secret: an indulgence to stir pride.

Aminatra lay a grateful hand on Peli's. The angry, snapping matron of the kitchen was in fact a friendly, angry woman, caring towards her fellow slaves, bitter at her enslavement. Each rap of her wooden spoon was a fast-track lesson in survival. The shouting that once intimidated lost its threat with a new language learnt, exposing the encouragement and affectionate pet names within the commands. As Aminatra's pregnant belly grew, so too did Peli's motherly devotion. She helped create the extra-large tunic Aminatra now wore, with its expansive pleats, trading her secrets in cocking a snook at the Adonelisians with a simple needle and thread.

"May I?" asked Peli.

Aminatra smiled, familiar with the request, guiding Peli's hand to her stomach. "Did you sense that?"

"Yes," said a gleeful Peli. "It kicked!"

"She's been kicking all morning."

"She? You know it's a girl?"

"Only by her behaviour," answered Aminatra, squinting as the sun's rays broke through the glassless window. "This one's well behaved. Karlmon was a little devil and fidget." The women laughed, revelling in a shared experience.

The eyes of the other kitchen slaves followed the frivolous interruption.

"Get back to work!" growled Peli, rising from the stool. "The master will not be happy if his supper's late, my children. Don't let my wavering standards distract you from your duty."

Light laughter rippled across the kitchen as the work picked up. All recognised the risk of failing the master.

Aminatra, assigned to lighter duties, rose, returning to her workstation to knead the bread dough. She had no time pressure, happy for the dough to rise in the heat of the kitchen, ready for baking in the early hours. But her back ached. She longed to lie down to take the weight off her feet.

Frenetic activity continued around her, the volume growing as the deadline for the master's and his family's dinner approached. The mistress insisted on a special feast for the returning General Malic.

"You're getting good at finding the best quality products from the market," remarked Peli, examining an aubergine. "They'll cheat you if they can. Honourable people, my arse."

"I enjoy going out and wandering about the city," said Aminatra. "Even if I only waddle."

"Still no sign of your boy?"

"No," answered Aminatra, kneading with increased fervour. "But there are so many people. I may have walked past him and not noticed. Or he looked right at me, not recognising his own mother behind the veil."

"The veil has its advantages. Sometimes it's nice to go unnoticed."

"I want to be noticed by Karlmon!" snapped Aminatra. "Sorry, I didn't mean ..."

"I know."

"It's just, all I see is armed men. Men marching, men training, men fighting. Bloody men playing at war. Where are the children playing? The faces of women, smiling, laughing, crying? This isn't a society. It's an army justifying its own existence."

"I think you've killed the dough," said Peli.

Aminatra looked down at the shredded sticky remains. "Sorry."

Huut's head appeared at the door. "The master's ready for his dinner. Are we?"

"A week of late-night pot scrubbing for anyone who's not!" yelled Peli.

"Ready!" came a chorused response.

"Then let us not waste time," urged Huut, clapping his hands in encouragement. "Athenia, can you deliver laundry to the mistress's bedroom? You'll find them stacked for collection at the washroom."

Peli folded her arms, testing her sternest look. "Resurrect the dough first."

Aminatra didn't mind either task. A stroll would do her back some good. She sprinkled a covering of flour onto the table and reintroduced the pieces of dough to each other.

As the last delivery of supper vanished out the door and the kitchen madness subsided, Aminatra brushed her hands, removing the flour, rinsing them in a bowl of water. It wouldn't do to dirty the mistress's fresh linen.

She found the pile of folded sheets where expected, loaded them to rest on her bulging stomach and ambled towards the mistress's bedroom on the other side of the villa. With evening supper engrossing most, the corridors were quiet, with only the occasional slave shooting past to fulfil an unexpected demand. Aminatra cut through the courtyard, taking her time, the gravel path uncomfortable on bare soles. She stopped to admire the flowers and shrubs. A red rose released its fragrant perfume. How a climbing rose would improve those grey walls, thought Aminatra, inspecting her surroundings. She bent down to bury her nose amid the petals, savouring a moment of pleasure. The garden, harnessed by Adonelisian discipline, still found room for nature to obey its own rules. Between the harmonious, established horticulture sprouted discreet but beautiful weeds. Aminatra always looked out for them, sometimes picking a blossom and pinning it to the inside of her tunic. She identified with these underdogs, struggling in the world of favoured perennials and nurtured flowerbeds but somehow surviving.

"Poison!" A scream shattered the peace, originating from the master's dining room.

Aminatra froze, unsure what to do.

A door flew open, and a slave shot out, his face white and aghast. He noticed Aminatra before him. "Mistress Bethu is poisoned! She cannot breathe. I must find Huut. Where is he?"

While only understanding a few words from the blurted sentence, Aminatra recognised enough and shook her head, ignorant of the estate manager's whereabouts.

The man flapped with indecision, picked a direction and sprinted away, hopeful his quarry lay on the route.

Torn between returning to the kitchen, out of the way and out of trouble, or heading towards the trouble, Aminatra stood still.

Further screams emerged from the dining room. "Bethu! Poison! Who would do such a thing?"

Aminatra recognised the mistress's voice. She dropped the linen and ran, as best her body could, into the dining room. On the floor lay the writhing eight-year-old, hands pressed against her throat, eyes bulging out of a blue face. The family stood paralysed around her. General Malic, sword drawn, looked for an invisible foe. His bodyguards shuffled around the edge of the room, useless and in fear at the consequences of failing their master. The hounds whimpered in a corner.

Mistress Malic's hands clasped the face of her son. "Are you okay? They've not poisoned you too?"

"I'm fine!" cried Klout, trying to break free. "Where's Huut?"

Their eyes turned to Aminatra as she burst in, hope dissolving to disappointment.

"Poison!" screamed the mistress again, as though for Aminatra's benefit.

"Have they found that blasted man yet!" cursed the master. "If she dies, he'll pay!"

"No one else feels ill?" asked Aminatra, conscious she spoke out of turn.

"No!" wailed the mistress. "This is the cruellest attack. Taking my daughter and leaving me to suffer her loss!"

"What did you eat?" Aminatra waddled to the side of the gasping Bethu, easing herself down to clasp her hand.

"We had finished our supper and ate nuts to accompany conversation," answered Malic, his tone a mix of anger and confusion.

"Nuts?" questioned Aminatra. "Quick, help me get your daughter on her feet!"

"Why?" demanded Malic.

"Just do it!" yelled Aminatra. "I can save her!" As she uttered the words, Aminatra realised she could promise no such thing. She had a theory picked up from reading *Hamner's Definitive Medical Guide*. Even if her diagnosis proved correct, she had never tried the procedure before. If she were wrong or failed, death would be her reward.

Malic bent down, his eyes surveying Aminatra with suspicion. "What witchcraft do you possess to save our daughter?" He lifted Bethu to her feet. She no longer writhed; her strength was gone.

"It's not witchcraft. There's no poison," explained Aminatra, as she took the body from the master and wound her arms from behind, clasping hands together across the girl's tummy. "My bump's in the way." With a tight squeeze, she jerked the small, limp body against hers, cringing as it pushed against her unborn child. Nothing! She readjusted her hands, lowered them, and squeezed again with more force. A projectile shot from the girl's mouth, followed by the wonderful sound of a hungry gasp of lung-absorbed air. Aminatra released Bethu into the arms of her father, who watched in amazement as colour returned to her cheeks.

"Master!" A breathless Huut appeared at the door.

"I've found it!" declared Klout, holding up the discarded projectile. "It's an almond."

"Master, I heard word of poison," gasped Huut. "What happened?"

General Malic remained speechless, lowering his rasping daughter to a chair.

"Bethu got a nut stuck in her throat," explained Klout. "This slave saved her life."

Huut looked at Aminatra and then back at his reticent master. "Is Mistress Bethu better?"

Malic cracked his knuckles. "She is now, thank Sym La Panau. Where were you when we needed you?"

"I was at the stables," said Huut. "Overseeing preparation for your trip today, Master ... as instructed. I came as quickly as possible."

"Of course. Of course," said Malic, trying to regain composure. "Your services were not required. Athenia has served us well." He smiled towards Aminatra. "You can name your child Bethu as a gratitude from us."

"Thank you, Master," answered Aminatra, underwhelmed and confused.

"We still can't rule out poison or attempted assassination," declared the mistress, still to show the slightest affection to her recovering daughter.

"It was an accident, Mother," responded Klout.

"I've eaten a hundred almonds, but never suffered such an affliction! They could have planted large nuts to choke Bethu, or God forbid, Hal or you."

"They, my dear?" questioned General Hal Malic. "Bethu is small and should chew her food. No oversized nut can damage if chewed properly."

"Maybe," huffed the mistress, "but who provided such dangerous almonds? You must punish someone!"

"We'll discuss later," instructed Malic. "Huut, carry Bethu to her bed and arrange for her chambermaid to care for her throughout the night!"

"Yes, Master." The slave lifted the child in his arms. "I'll organise a honey and poppyseed solution to rebalance her body."

Malic nodded. "Everyone, leave us!" He waved the bodyguards out, guiding Aminatra to the door, before whispering. "As reward for saving Bethu, I will allow you to forego punishment for your earlier insolence. Make sure Lady Malic doesn't find out."

"Err, thank you, Master." Aminatra hid her disbelief. Anger clashed with acceptance that this was General Malic's idea of generosity.

Chapter
Twenty-Three

A groggy Finbarl sat on the floor, a mess from emptied bags spread before him. The hangover felt familiar, as did regret at last night's behaviour and his determination to change. His stubbled chin rested in one hand, another reached for his old thawb. He always returned to his Athenian possessions when seeking clarity. They stirred memories of his mother and her spirit, of Aminatra and Karlmon. This thawb has gone through much, he mulled, running his fingers over the material, recalling happier times.

The items sprawled across the floor lay in stark contrast to the relative wealth and luxury secured through his new life in Parodis. With the help of Pet, his walls and cupboards now displayed the dividends of success and fame: items of pottery, a sword and breastplate, brooches and a range of clothes. He had never appreciated so many clothes were necessary for so many situations or changed them so often to meet an elusive fashion standard. They symbolised his success and were badges worn to broker further progress up the social status ladder. It was not, Pet explained, just money he needed to secure a following, but the outward display of wealth. People required proof of someone's success to offer their allegiance.

Finbarl lifted Aminatra's spare thawb, brushing it to his cheek. Not a day passed without him thinking of her. Guilt at his impotence ate into him. Did Aminatra believe he had deserted her? What would she think if she discovered he lived so well?

"Oh, Maddy, what should I do?"

The question to his mother stirred her namesake. She perched on the windowsill. As Finbarl laid the thawb back down, she slithered down to the floor, retrieved the garment and returned to her vantage point. Her nose twitched at the familiar odour of lost kin, and she crumpled it against her bosom, emitting a lamenting hum.

Amid the mess, the pistol caught Finbarl's eye. An urge swept through him to fire the pistol to release all the anger, frustration and shame he felt.

A rap at the door broke the tension. Maddy sprang to her feet, ready to pounce. Finbarl grabbed the gun, buried it in a bag and shoved it under the bed. He told tales of firearms to his audiences but never confided he possessed such powerful technology. "Come in!"

Pet and Allus appeared in the doorway, grins on their faces. "Morning, oh master of storytelling," greeted Pet.

"You don't look so good," observed Allus.

"I'm fine," lied Finbarl. "There's something I need to tell you."

"Excellent," cut in Pet. "We have a surprise for you. Someone wants to meet you."

"Who?"

"It's a surprise," stressed Pet.

"I'm not sure I'm feeling up to anything today," said Finbarl.

Pet frowned, confused by such reluctance. "You don't understand. There isn't really a choice."

Stubborn eyes stared back at Pet.

"Hello Maddy," said Allus, breaking an awkward silence. "You going to join us?"

Maddy remained unmoved, staring at their visitors as though contemplating prey.

"Is she okay?" asked Allus, her voice now edged with nerves. "She won't attack?"

Finbarl sniffed. "You're far too close to make an interesting challenge for her. She would prefer a pursuit or ambush."

"Don't tease, Finbarl!" pleaded Allus. "There are stories spreading across the city. Parents don't want their children near her."

"Hmmm, I know," grumbled Finbarl. "I started the bloody things! It doesn't help she's taken a dislike to redheads and snarls every time she sees one."

Pet, his attention on the mess, missed the insinuation.

"That's why I've made my decision," continued Finbarl. "You won't tell me who I am to see, but say I must come with you?"

"You won't regret it," said Pet. "I promise."

"Oh, please Finbarl," cooed Allus. "It's most exciting."

With a glance at Maddy, Finbarl rose to his feet. "Very well. I'll tell you about my decision on the way."

***

"But you can't!" protested Pet, absorbing the news from Finbarl as they strolled along a cobbled path.

The fresh air stirred Finbarl from his melancholy, his mind no less fixed but his manner now that of a belligerent guard of Athenia. "Maddy is family. She's made such wonderful progress since we first met. That cage is setting her back and degrading. I'm not putting her in there again. That's final."

"But the money!"

"People will still pay to hear my tales."

"Not as many and not enough," pressed Pet. "Where do the eyes fall of those that pass us in the street? Not upon you, but on the mysterious girl they've heard stories of."

Finbarl inspected the faces of those walking past. None spared him a glance, their attention caught by Maddy prowling behind. "It's wrong to create lies about her."

"But the money!" repeated Pet. "Each sale in life depends on a little lie; each stallholder in the market claims their products to be the best."

"Well, that's silly. They can't all be the best," stated Finbarl. "Wouldn't it make more sense for each to be truthful? That way, people would know where to get the best produce."

Pet laughed in disbelief. "That must be a strange place you come from. It's a competition. You outdo your rivals: grow better crops, sell more products, make more money, buy better clothes. If you can't manage the first, be good at the rest."

"This is the strange place, and I'm not changing my mind."

"There must be another way Finbarl can make more money," urged Allus, always the peacemaker. "We have to help him get Aminatra and Karlmon back."

Finbarl smiled at Allus, grateful for her support.

With a nervous twist of his beard, Pet mumbled under his breath. "I can make you a fortune," he declared with a change of mood. "It is not without risk, but I know people who can guide us."

"And it doesn't involve exploiting Maddy?" asked Finbarl, his interest piqued.

"Shamcora!" cried Pet, alarming all around. "It is the most exciting thing you will ever see. Horse and man racing at speed. Huge crowds, danger and thrills."

"But I can't ride a horse," said Finbarl. "Is it like riding a camel?"

"No, no," laughed Pet. "You don't race; you bet on the race."

"Bet?"

"You back a team with money to win. If they do, you make more money."

"I don't understand," confessed Finbarl. "What am I buying?"

"Well, I ... er."

"Luck," said Allus. "What Pet hasn't told you is you can also lose your money if your team doesn't win. Scholars and students are banned from gambling. We do not understand these things well ourselves."

"Bah!" retorted Pet. "The law is ambiguous around those who work for the scholars. Anyway, I have watched many a race. A man with but one pownlet to his name can become a wealthy one if he backs the right team."

"I still don't understand," said Finbarl. "But it sounds most promising. With my earnings so far, I should be able to generate great wealth. Why did we not do this from the start?"

"Because the wealthy man can be left with nothing, too," cautioned Allus.

"You worry too much," said Pet. "I will take Finbarl to a race. We'll talk to my friends. They'll give us some tips." He gripped Finbarl's shoulder. "Bet small and see how you do."

"Yes, we'll do that," said Finbarl, pleased at having resolved one problem with a perfect solution. "When can we go?"

"Patience! You've got to meet ... Ha, almost let slip. No matter. You'll soon guess when we ... Ah, there it is!"

They turned a corner, their road opening onto a busy square. Finbarl had wandered this way before, ogled at the beautiful buildings, wondered at the colourful crowds. The fountains impressed him the most, with their flamboyant display spraying water skywards, the rainbow mist enthralling and mysterious. To an Athenian, they appeared pointless and wasteful and yet joyous and symbolic. Humanity controlled the water, not the other way round.

"Have you guessed yet?" asked Allus, as they guided Finbarl up a broad skirt of steps to a towering row of columns.

"No," admitted Finbarl, captured by the majesty of the building.

"This is the Senorium," explained Allus. "Home of the government."

"They wish to see me?"

"Well, no. The Primora has requested your company."

"The Primora." Finbarl repeated the name as though a sacred word. "You've explained them before. The people have chosen them to rule."

"That's right," said Pet. "Primora Dimi has governed for two terms. She is from one of the best families."

"Parmsoli must have made good on his promise," contemplated Finbarl. He shook his head, still bewildered by the concept of democracy. "What happens to those who didn't vote for her?"

"You do ask some silly questions," said Pet. "Nothing happens to them. It's a secret who you vote for, anyway."

"But you once said you voted for her?"

"That's right," said Pet. "She has the support of the Scholarium. Her family is very generous with donations. We all voted for her."

"I fear I'm as confused with democracy as with gambling."

Allus giggled. "Old Bartarnous would say they have much in common."

They entered a cool hallway, its high ceiling as impressive as the cathedral's. Men and women in lavish white tunics scurried back and forth, stopping to speak with or collect papers from the more sedate people in the rich apparel of the Terratus.

"The Chamber is not sitting," observed Pet. "The Senorium undertake their business here or at inns nearby. Come! We must not be late for the Primora."

They strode down the long corridors of the Senorium, only slowing to encourage Maddy not to explore the many recesses and rooms along the way.

Two gigantic wooden doors opened before them. "Welcome." A pair of secretaries ushered them through.

The Primora arose from her chair, a perfect smile greeting her guests. "You arrive at a momentous time. News has just arrived that the Livorians have agreed to an exclusive trade deal with us."

"Congratulations, Primora," cried Pet. "Another victory for Parodis and your leadership."

"They have made a wise choice," chuckled the Primora. "Ambassador Gipsemi and his fleet will get a well-deserved parade on their return."

"The Livorians will soon see the benefits of our friendship," said one secretary.

"Indeed, they will," agreed the Primora, her interest now on Finbarl and Maddy. "And talking of friends, I am delighted to meet our travellers from across the mountain."

"Forgive me, Primora," said Pet. "Allow me to introduce Finbarl and Maddy. They have no other given names."

Finbarl bowed as instructed, while Maddy explored the unfamiliar smells and sights of the office.

With her eyes following Maddy, the Primora spoke to Finbarl. "I am told you come from a dangerous land, parched and unwelcoming."

"The rain refuses to pass the mountains," answered Finbarl. "We hung on, but it was a world of walls and hardship."

"I see. And what do you make of Parodis?"

"You have everything Athenia doesn't: food, freedom, beauty and integrity. I'm so grateful for the friendship and kindness of this city. Everybody has been so helpful."

The Primora clapped her hands in appreciation. "Thank you, Finbarl. Parodis is a great city. Our peoples could be trading partners and friends. What does Athenia trade?"

"Err, nothing. We have no one to trade with. The prisoners brought salt in exchange for ...," explaining the mysteries of Jumblar was too complex, "... food."

"Don't worry, my secretary will make an appointment for you to talk to an official. Trade is such an effective way to build friendship. We may offer protection from ...," the Primora studied her notes, "... Ferrals, I believe you call them? Of which, your friend here is one. Is that right?"

Finbarl nodded, a huge grin on his face. "If only Governor Elbar and the Wardyns were alive to see your traders arrive at Athenia. He would have died from shock!"

"Governor Elbar? Wardyns?"

"Forgive me. I'm indulging in fantasies. The people of Athenia would be so grateful to connect with civilisation again. It's what Aminatra dreamt of!"

"Oh, yes, Aminatra," said the Primora, the smile adjusted to one of sympathy. "I understand she is your wife and held captive with her son in Adonelis. Very sad."

"My friend, Parmsoli, will have told you all," began Finbarl, excited his chance had come at last.

"Who?" asked the Primora. "I don't believe one knows a Parmsoli." She looked to her secretary for confirmation.

"No, Primora."

"Never mind," continued Finbarl. "If you could help with getting them back, then Aminatra and I could guide you to Athenia. We know the route through the mountains. Perhaps a dozen horses and men to raid Adonelis at night. That's all I need."

Primora Dimi tapped the air with an authoritative knuckle. "You have the government of Parodis's full backing in rescuing your family. We stand behind you. Justice must be achieved and the illegal duplicity of the Adonelisians held to account."

"Maddy!" Finbarl exclaimed, turning to seek a hug, trying not to twirl her round in a jig of delight. "We're going to rescue Aminatra and Karlmon!"

The Ferral yelped at the unexpected invasion of her space, slipping from Finbarl's arms to disappear under a large table.

"However," continued the Primora, ignoring the drama, "this government's position is not to engage in private ventures, which may bring danger to the city or its citizens. We can, therefore, not be seen to support you or offer you the materials to aid your mission. You have my word we will do everything we can to foster a conducive atmosphere for success." She waved towards her secretary. "I thank you, Finbarl, for meeting me today. It has been fascinating to hear from you and Maddy. If you'll excuse me, other business of state awaits."

As Finbarl opened his mouth, a queue of questions poised for release, the secretary ushered them out of the office and along the corridor.

"Someone will be in touch about discussing trade options," promised the secretary, as he left them on the front steps of the Senorium.

"I'm confused," said Finbarl. "Is she going to help me rescue Aminatra and Karlmon or not? What's a 'conducive atmosphere'?"

Pet laughed. "Sorry, Finbarl. The Primora is a seasoned politician. She's promised you everything, while promising nothing. It is good that she knows of your plight, though."

"But why would she say she would help us but offer nothing?"

"Oh, Finbarl," sighed Allus. "It isn't easy for you, is it?"

"An adroit politician never commits to anything," explained Pet, beginning the descent down the steps. "That way, they have wriggle room. They sugar their words, so you swallow them, but …"

"Wait!" cried Finbarl. "Where's Maddy? Oh, Cronax! I think we left her in the office!"

"Forp!" exclaimed Pet, sharing a new curse with Finbarl. "Is the Primora in danger?"

From shock, Finbarl's mouth morphed to a grin. Then laughter erupted.

"It's not a laughing matter, Finbarl!" stressed Allus. "If the Primora gets hurt, we could get into real trouble."

"Maddy won't hurt her," reassured Finbarl through his tears. "Though I'd pay to watch that secretary try to evict her."

A small grin crept onto Allus's face. "We'd better help him then!"

Chapter Twenty-Four

A strange sound disturbed Aminatra's daydream, the courtyard acoustics exacerbating her confusion. There was a Ferral-like quality to its primitive angst. It originated to her left, escaping the private quarters, cutting the gentle evening atmosphere. Another wail followed, higher in pitch. Someone younger expressed themselves. Aminatra retreated to the kitchen, unnerved. More primordial sounds pierced the window, combining into an unworldly harmony.

"What's going on?" asked Aminatra, greeted by a solemn silence in the kitchen.

Peli shook her head. "I'm not sure. It's not good news. This is their mourning ritual. News must just have arrived."

"A family member?"

"I don't think so."

The slaves crowded by the windows, listening to the continued laments, watching for signs of activity.

"Master Malic's guards are going frantic!" observed a voice.

"Let me see! Let me see!" Peli pushed her way through her colleagues. "They're changing into battledress and arming themselves. Something serious is going on!"

At that point, Huut thrust his head in the room, his face drained of colour. "The king is dead! King Gordian II died in the night!"

All turned in unison, gasps escaping from open mouths. Even Aminatra gaped in shock. She could not say why. It seemed instinctive. Some slaves joined the wailing, others sobbed.

"What does this mean?" asked Aminatra, facing a sombre Peli. "Why are they arming?"

"I don't know."

Huut's voice cut in. "The king's death means political turmoil. His son is too young to take over the reins of power. It leaves a power vacuum. Always a dangerous time."

"Karlmon!" gasped Aminatra. "Will he be safe?"

Huut's pursed lips gave away his doubts. "It's complicated. If those in the late king's inner circle can transfer power safely, then all will be well. Master Malic is key, as the king's favourite. He would make a good regent, protecting Prince Andolis's rights. But ..."

"But what?" demanded Aminatra.

"Another faction revolves around the queen," explained Huut. "She is the king's second wife and stepmother to Prince Andolis."

"Why would that be a threat?"

"She has a son of her own. Two years younger than Prince Andolis." Huut left the fact hanging for Aminatra to interpret.

"I don't understand," said Peli, saving Aminatra from exposing her own ignorance.

"It's all to do with power," explained Huut, keen to share his own insight. "With Prince Andolis acknowledged as King Gordian's successor, then Queen Fantoneli loses her power. With the prince out of the way and her own son recognised, she can rule in his name. A living Prince Andolis is not in the queen's interest."

"Then I must rescue Karlmon now!" cried Aminatra.

"You'll do no such thing. These matters don't concern you. Your duties remain in this kitchen. If your boy survives, then having a dead mother will do him no good. Master Malic will determine how to protect the prince."

"Ouch!" Pain shot through Aminatra's stomach. Her head swam as she staggered back.

"You've upset the girl!" growled Peli, grabbing hold of Aminatra's arm. "Make room! Find a seat for her. She should avoid stress in her condition."

Huut backed away, uneasy around such concerns. "Quite right. The master will not be happy to lose the baby now he's named it."

"To hell with the ma ..." Peli bit her tongue. "Make yourself useful. Find a damp cloth."

"I'm fine," declared Aminatra, her voice weak. Peli eased her down onto a crate. "Just a little woozy. It'll pass."

"Baby's not coming?"

"No." Aminatra's tired smile reassured Peli. "Thank you."

Huut edged towards the doorway. "I must ensure the estate's perimeters are secure. The master will want to be ready for any eventuality."

"What is it about men and birth?" mulled Peli aloud, as she flapped a towel to cool Aminatra. "The most ferocious warrior will retreat at the very mention of it!"

"They don't like to see women braver than them," opined Aminatra, receiving a laugh from the kitchen staff and a knowing wink from Peli.

***

Twilight coloured the sky a darker shade of blue as the temperature dropped. A bat ventured out in search of an early meal, while beautiful birdsong belied the frenetic human drama bubbling around. Aminatra waddled up the path towards the stables. Despite Peli's protestations, she insisted on getting out of the kitchen. The cook gave in, sending her with bread and fruit for the slaves tending the horses.

"Coming through!"

A line of slaves rushed past her on the track, followed by a soldier striding at his own pace.

"Any of that for me?" he asked, spooking Aminatra.

"No, sir." Aminatra bowed her head, averting her gaze. "They have tasked me with delivering to the stable boys, sir."

"Pity. I've not had a nibble since the sky fell in."

The friendly tone surprised Aminatra, and she spared a glance. "Master Klout! I didn't recognise you."

"I had no such trouble, Athenia. Your bump is as big as Mount Halipto! Are you due soon?" The general's son yanked at his breastplate, adjusting it.

"Not for a month. Are you going to fight?" Aminatra froze, realising she had broken a rule. "Sorry, Master Klout. I did not mean to speak out of turn."

A smile responded. "You're forgiven. Just don't do it round father or mother. This damn armour!" He shifted and tugged. "Adonelisian men are supposed to welcome discomfort, but I fear a Mossilien once ravished my mother. It's the only thing that explains me!"

Aminatra blinked in shock. She had never heard an Adonelisian talk with such a flippant and disrespectful tone and wondered if this was the nature of teenage rebellion in this city. "You have Master Malic's eyes and his courage." Flattery was always a sensible tactic.

"True, but not his discipline. It's not for the want of beatings. My tutor did his best to thrash it into me, but I learnt at an early age to pretend. You put on a facade to the world but live your lie beneath. I sense you have a free spirit, too. Do you understand what I'm talking about?"

"I do. It is in everyone, but most cannot access it or fear doing so." Emboldened, Aminatra allowed her eyes to study the young man's face. He was but a teenager, a few years older than Maddy. Without the facial scar, his skin was unblemished, smooth and rich in colour. Life's brutality had yet to erode his youth. "Have you ever lived anywhere else or seen other cities?"

A bitter laugh escaped Klout's mouth. "The only other city I've seen is Camptex. My father took me after his army captured it. All I saw was ruins and death. A year later, I met a Campton slave, Litviola. She told me of the city before its destruction. The most beautiful woman I ever ..." His voice trailed off.

"You had feelings for her?"

"I loved her. She loved me. Love is weakness according to Sym La Panau."

Aminatra hesitated to ask. "Where is she now?"

"Likely dead," pined Klout, his Adonelisian traits preventing tears. "Father sold her. Someone told him about our relationship. It could never have been but ..."

"I'm sorry. Stolen love is not a wound you can heal. If you knew your girl was alive and where she was, would you try to rescue her?"

"Of course. I have often thought of going to Hethvarn in search of Litviola."

"Hethvarn?"

"The home of the dead."

Reaching out a hand, Aminatra dared comfort the boy. "You must not think the worst. When I lived in Athenia, I lost my boy. I never gave up with hope. And despite the odds, I found him. I've lost him again, but Cronax, nothing will stop me getting him back."

"But you're a slave."

"You've enslaved my body but not my mind!" declared Aminatra, becoming bolder with every sentence. "Nothing you ever do will take away my free spirit."

Instead of growing angry, Klout let out a deep sigh. "I'm confused," he admitted. "The Adonelisians are the chosen people. Sym La Panau teaches us that. But he never says why. You saved my sister's life when we stood around and watched. I'm supposed to be this perfect man, but why do I feel so useless?"

"You're not useless," reassured Aminatra, recognising her own insecurities when a teenager. "Just trapped. Trapped in a lie. I've seen it before. Help me rescue my son. Show me you want to break free. Prove to yourself you have the strength to be something more." Aminatra shivered, exhilarated and terrified by the audacity of her words.

The noise of the stables reached their ears: shouts of the grooms readying the horses, soldiers growling commands, the animals neighing in distress.

"I can't!" said Klout. "My father must safeguard his position and that of Prince Andolis. He summons all his followers to join us. We are to march to the palace to show our respects to the dead king. We will have the upper hand if we secure the prince. Others will back father. I cannot let him down."

"But with the prince secured, you can save Karlmon too!"

A horse galloped towards them, Klout guiding Aminatra off the path to safety. "One of the messengers. I must get ready. We ride out soon." A sterner Adonelisian face looked at Aminatra. "I can promise nothing. My duty is to my father and the prince. With the prince safe, your son will be safe, but still a slave."

Klout strode off, summoning a groom with a curt wave of his hand, as Aminatra pondered, trying to interpret what the last few minutes meant. Despite his ambiguity, Aminatra sensed hope.

Chapter Twenty-Five

"Come on!" Finbarl was on his feet, punching the air, unsure what intoxicated him. Those massed around did the same, their intensity somehow infectious. Below in the arena, a cloud of dust chased the source of their excitement. The crowd rippled as the horses passed, accompanied by cheers and groans. Saliva foamed from the steeds' mouths. Each sinew strained under the encouragement and whips of their riders. A light wooden frame, connected to the equine beasts by leather straps, stretched behind, down into the churning dust, where it joined a metal axle. Wooden wheels, no bigger than hands, spun at either end, jolting with violent impact across the dirt. Balancing on the axle, a rider gripped tight to a set of reins, their face hidden behind a scarf, glasses and a layer of dirt.

"Wahoa! We're gaining!" Pet nudged Finbarl. "Go Green!"

The four racers steered into a corner, each adorned in their team's colour, matching their fans in the crowd. Wheels slid against the centrifugal forces, left reins tugged harder, the right eased.

"I can't look!" squealed Dae, covering her eyes with a hand, peeking through her fingers. "They're about to hit each other!"

"Keep going, Green!" yelled Finbarl, oblivious to Dae's concerns.

Somehow, all four came out of the corner unscathed, onto the long straight. In the lead and neck and neck were Red and White, Green a head behind, Blue less than a nostril back again.

"One more lap," cried Llahuma. "One more lap, Green! Come on!"

"White's trying to cut across!" yelled Pet. "Push now, Green!" He turned to Finbarl in a more restrained manner. "If he wins that line, we won't be able to pass him. Our man's got to go for it now. Let's hope he has something left."

Finbarl shook with excitement, willing his rider on with each jerk and punch. "Cronax!"

"Aaahhhh!" Dae screamed, joined by half the crowd.

"A wheel's shattered," howled Llahuma.

Red shunted to the right, its axle collapsing as a wheel splintered, the fragile metal ring holding it together useless. The rider spun skywards as screams turned to gasps. Limbs, tied to the axle for necessity, twisted with a sickening motion, unprotected by the padding of the upper body. The horse, pulled by the madness behind, stumbled, unable to take the next corner, pushing White as it did so.

Unaffected by the catastrophe unfolding, Pet hugged Finbarl, jumping with excitement. "Green has a gap. If we avoid the wreckage, we're through!"

Finbarl gulped, shocked by the carnage, caught in the thrill.

"The money's ours to lose now!" cried Pet, as the Red's rider crashed to earth, rolling and entangled. Avoiding the others was his only good fortune.

White now occupied the outside, the rider struggling to coax the horse back to the competitive line, its supporters' groans drowned out by the cheers of the Greens and Blues as they vied for the lead.

"The padding will protect him?" questioned Dae, the only one in the group concerned about the lifeless Red rider. "Now I know why Allus volunteered to stay behind with Maddy."

"A little," reassured Pet, craning his neck as people jumped up in the row in front. "There are also weights packed in there to stop them flying at each bump. Not conducive to a soft landing!"

"I feel sick," wailed Dae, turning away.

"They get paid for the risk," observed Llahuma, biting into a pastry. "No end of youngsters wanting to become a Shamcora racer. Who wouldn't want to be worshipped by the ladies? GO ON, GREEN!"

Into the final straight, Green and Blue battled for the finishing line, their riders' whips cracking the last drops of energy from their horses. White tailed by a length, while Red remained unmoving across the arena, surrounded by those eager to get the track ready for the next race.

Finbarl held his breath, fists gripped tight. The suspense was excruciating. Pet's hand rested on his shoulder, bobbing and squeezing encouragement for their horse to his right.

"Come on! Come ON! COME ON! YESSSS!"

A roar erupted, flags of green burst into life as other colours faded to the background.

"We won!" cried Pet. "You won, Fin!"

Adrenaline coursed through Finbarl's body. He felt the thrill of a flight from a pack of Ferrals, but without the personal danger. "How much?"

"Well, not that much," confessed Pet. "You only put on a small amount." His mind calculated the odds. "Eighty-five pownlets. That's not bad. One win out of three races."

"There's one more race, right?" considered Finbarl. "If I place my winnings on that, how much would I win?"

"Your horse has to win first," observed Llahuma.

"If it wins?"

Pet leaned forward, stretching his neck to read the bookie's board. "Green is five to one. That would be … 510 pownlets. Not bad."

"What about another colour?" asked Finbarl. "Any larger odds? I've bet on Green every race so far."

"Huh," Llahuma tried to cover his disbelieving laugh. "Green is our team. We back them through thick and thin."

"It's a bit more complicated than you may think, Fin," added Pet, resting his hand back on Finbarl's shoulder. "Loyalty to a team is, well, like a birthmark. You can't change it. Those of the Scholarium are Green. To betray the team would be to betray the Scholarium and your family."

"But I'm not of the Scholarium?"

"Err, no. But you've pinned your colours to our mast. The rivalry between colours can get out of hand. You don't wear your colours out of the stadium. Not unless you want to be stabbed. Riots broke out a few years back over a disputed race. This is a serious business for Parodisians."

"Not all Parodisians," remarked Dae with a sniff.

Finbarl frowned.

"You need to study the form, pick the Greens who will win for you." Llahuma nodded his head, pleased with his own advice.

"How much do the riders earn?" Finbarl's eyes drifted in thought. "You said it pays well."

"You can't be serious, Finbarl," gasped Dae. "Look what happens when things go wrong!"

"Dae's right," added Llahuma. "Those guys have been riding since young. You wouldn't stand a chance."

"Then it will have to be eighty-five pownlets on the next race," declared Finbarl. "Green to win!"

"That's the spirit!" cheered Pet, as an eerie sigh escaped from the crowd. An official draped a blanket over the head of the fallen Red rider, shaking his head, as others lifted the limp body and carried him from the arena.

***

Finbarl and his friends stood atop the stairs outside the stadium, a mass of people pushing past on their way home.

"Oh, well," sighed Finbarl, tearing his betting slip in two.

"He was too hesitant on the corners," lamented Llahuma. "You'll know not to back him next time."

"Keep moving!" yelled an official.

"Come on, let's drown our sorrows," urged Llahuma, joining the flow down the steps.

"Or celebrate what might have been," said Pet.

"I'm not in the mood to celebrate anything," said Dae.

"I ..." A rumble of excitement down in the square stopped Finbarl. "What's happening?"

A young lad ran across the paving slabs, a bundle of papers under one arm, a single sheet waved above his head. "Brutal attack! Brutal attack! Read it here. Brutal attack!" People swarmed around him, exchanging a coin for a sheet.

"Let's find out what's going on!" cried Dae, dashing off to join the throng.

"Stay here," suggested Llahuma. "We don't all need a newp."

"A newp?" queried Finbarl.

"A news leaflet." Pet reclined on a step, his arms behind his head. "Bad news, no doubt. I prefer ignorance."

Dae wandered back, engrossed in her acquisition.

"Well?" pressed Llahuma. "Put us out of our misery!"

"Oh, it's terrible," rued Dae. "I wish I'd never read it!"

"Told you," chirped Pet with a grin.

"They've found a body. Mauled and disfigured. A murder!"

"Pass it here!" urged Llahuma, his long arm outstretched. "Are they linking it to previous attacks?"

"Who would do such a thing?" Dae wiped her nose on her sleeve. "Even the Adonelisians aren't that barbaric. Only a monster!"

"Yes, an Adonelisian would have the decency to chop your head off before mutilating you," quipped Pet.

"Oh, Pet! You can be such a ... What's your word, Finbarl?" asked Dae.

"Er, ferralax."

"Yes, a ferralax! You can be such a ferralax sometimes."

The insult washed over Pet, who turned onto his side, resting his chin on a hand. "Which poor tok got mushed this time?"

As Dae released an exasperated sigh, Llahuma peeked over the top of the newp. "No names, just a middle-aged man from the Neeva district."

"Could it not be a big cat or bear?" asked Finbarl. "I read tales back in Athenia, where they attacked humans."

"Don't know what a bear is," replied Llahuma, "but no lion would venture into the Neeva district. And I've never heard of a creature that steals jewellery!"

"This is the Parodis Butcher," clarified Pet. "It's the fifth attack of the year. Some sicko getting thrills from killing innocent folk. Though, if they will go out at night in the Neeva ..."

"Oh, I'm off home if you're going to continue being so insensitive," snapped Dae. She swung her scarf round her neck and stormed away.

"I think you upset her," stated Finbarl.

"She's too sensitive," countered Pet. "That's her problem. A little light banter never hurt no one."

Finbarl bit his tongue, trying not to rise to Pet's immaturity. "Let's catch her up!"

Chapter Twenty-Six

A hot, suffocating night weighed on the city, the gentle breeze failing to relieve the stifling atmosphere. Aminatra paused, catching her breath, wiping her sweaty brow. A madness consumed her, compelling her onto the streets during curfew. Hurried boots and shoes of soldiers and horses rapped across the paved city. It wasn't safe to be out. Around the corner, the flickering light of a flaming torch appeared. Aminatra pressed herself into the shadowy recess of a doorway. Her pumping blood drummed in her ears. What had she been thinking to venture out?

A shadow cast itself on a wall, then a silhouette figure appeared. Orange flickered on their armour, identifying a soldier. He walked at pace, uninterested in his surroundings. But Aminatra could bear it no longer. She turned to the door, refusing to watch, hoping her blindness translated to invisibility. Illogical, but everything she did tonight owed itself to a lunacy.

Time, ill-defined on this night, tormented Aminatra as she waited for news of Karlmon. Malic and his entourage had departed for the palace hours back. Patience had its breaking point. Aminatra reached hers, slipping from her sleeping berth under a chorus of snores, driven by a crazy notion of rescuing Karlmon. How easy it was to escape the near-deserted estate, then on to the streets. However, squeezed in this secluded corner, with bulging stomach crushed to the wall, forced doubts to the surface. Pregnancy and nefarious activity didn't suit each other.

With the lane empty again, Aminatra pressed on. Clouds, trapping the muggy air, imposed disorientating darkness. She struggled forward, palms supporting her ripe stomach.

A faint rumble travelled through the ground, building in volume. Aminatra's heartbeat increased. She backed up the street, seeking another shadowy sanctuary. A familiar wooziness returned, and she slid to the floor, cursing her foolishness.

The rumble grew to thunder as General Malic appeared on his horse at the head of his mounted followers. Aminatra's eyes strained, searching for Karlmon among the mass, but their numbers blurred in the darkness. Malic's slumped shoulders hinted at frustration. 'Where are you, Karlmon?' mouthed Aminatra to herself, resisting the maternal urge to shout and demand her child back.

With the cavalcade passed, Aminatra climbed to her feet, supporting herself against the wall. Tears welled as failure and despair engulfed her. Her choices had withered to one: return to the estate. A brief window of opportunity offered itself to sneak back in undetected while the soldiers stabled their horses. She staggered back along the route to the estate with forlorn thoughts of Karlmon.

***

"Where have you been!" demanded Peli in a whisper, rolling in her cell as Aminatra returned to the slave dormitory.

"You're awake?"

"I wondered if you were giving birth, all the groaning and huffing you made!"

"Sorry." The snoring from the other cubicles suggested Peli exaggerated.

"They *will* execute you," warned Peli, easing herself out of her cell. "Once you give birth, you'll be meaningless to them."

"I know." Aminatra sat on a low stone bench, stretching her back. "I thought I could rescue Karlmon myself."

Peli lowered herself next to Aminatra, massaging her shoulder blades. "That was stupid. How far did you get?"

"Not very. Oh, that's the spot!" She grimaced with satisfaction. "Master Malic has returned. He didn't look happy. I've got to find out what's going on!"

"Huut's your best chance. He hears all sorts of things. But you won't get anything until tomorrow."

"That may be too late," said Aminatra, trying to keep her voice restrained. "I may have another source."

With a shrewd nod, Peli sighed. "What madness have you got in mind? You should get some sleep. Think of the baby!"

"How can I sleep not knowing Karlmon's safe?"

"You have a stubborn streak, Athenia. It's what makes you a wonderful mother." Peli vanished down the corridor, a finger raised to stress her imminent return.

"There," she declared a minute later, holding out a jug. "If you're going to wander the house at night, at least pretend you're doing something. You can say someone's requested water."

"You've done this before," commented Aminatra with a grin. She climbed to her feet and hugged her friend. "I may lose everything tonight, so it's worth risking everything."

Peli laughed. "That may explain how you've survived this long. Or you were born under a rainbow. Good luck. I'll cover for you as best I can."

"Don't take any risks for me," pleaded Aminatra, as she walked off down the corridor, the flickering torchlight catching her frightened eyes. "I'm taking enough for the both of us."

Unlike earlier, the estate now buzzed with activity. A soldier hurried past Aminatra, his mind shaped by orders, the slave a part of the background. Aminatra watched him to the end of the corridor, wondering what information he possessed. Elsewhere voices carried, edgy and intense, polluting the air with foreboding. Descending a small flight of stairs, Aminatra turned right, towards the Malic family's bed chambers.

"Halt!"

Aminatra jumped, spilling water from the jug.

A hostile face appeared from the shadows, the glint of armour exposing his status. "What are you doing?"

"Master Klout requested water, sir. I have instructions to bring it."

The soldier's facial scars creased as he examined Aminatra. "The master is at the guardhouse taking refreshments with his father and men. Why would he ask for water for his chambers?" His face pushed closer.

A few seconds of eternity passed as Aminatra sought an answer. She clutched her stomach, moaning with a melodramatic flourish. "Oh, my waters have broken! I think I'm giving birth." She nodded down to the spilled liquid.

The sinister eyes of the guard turned panic-stricken. He stepped back as though avoiding the plague. "You should return to the slave quarters! Send someone to clean up your mess!"

"I will, sir," said Aminatra, backing away, adding a faint groan for effect.

Around the corner and out of sight, Aminatra leaned against the wall and let out a deep breath. A few more shocks like that and she would give birth.

She made her way north towards the guardhouse, unsure what to do once there. No excuse would justify her presence. She sought Master Klout in isolation, not surrounded by his father and armed men. The feelings of earlier resurfaced. It had been a stupid idea from the start, and she was in no state to succeed. Three soldiers appeared at the end of the corridor, turning in her direction. She lowered her head in due deference, hoping they would pay her no heed.

"Athenia?"

Aminatra looked up to see Master Klout.

"What are you doing up at this hour?" he asked. "Surely, even slaves must sleep."

With subdued eyes Aminatra answered. "If you will permit, Master, I've been tasked with bringing you a message."

"Of course. What is it?"

"It's of a private nature, Master. I have instructions not to share with anyone but you."

Klout presented an awkward smile to his companions. "How intriguing. Gentlemen, if you don't mind. These are indeed unusual times."

Without complaint, the two soldiers wandered off with a smirk.

"What is it?" hissed Klout. "You put me in a difficult situation."

"Sorry, Master." Aminatra looked the young man in the eyes, exploiting the vulnerability exposed at their previous meeting. "Please tell me what happened at the palace. Did you find Karlmon?"

"You dare stop me to ask such a question!" The tone reflected his father's, but his eyes offered no threat. "I should have you whipped."

"Forgive me, Master. Exact whatever punishment is appropriate, but please tell me the answer!"

He assessed Aminatra for a moment, surprised by her gall. With a sweeping inspection of the corridor, he leaned in. "I can't answer your question. Father's plan to secure the prince ran into a problem: he's vanished!"

Aminatra gasped, turning pale. "You mean the queen's killed him?"

"No, no," reassured Klout. "She doesn't know where he is. The prince has run away. No one knows where they are. The queen is furious. Father isn't best pleased either. He can't secure the support he needs in this vacuum of uncertainty. The queen has the upper hand and has ordered father to remain at home."

"Is Karlmon with him?"

"The whereabouts of slaves was not discussed, but it's possible."

"Where could they be? Why would they run away?"

Klout shrugged. "He's his father's son. The best educated boy in the realm. Perhaps he understands the political situation better than we thought."

"How can we find them?"

"You ask too many questions for a slave ... for anyone! Father has his agents offering rewards for information, but time is against us. In two days, he must offer fealty to the queen or face the consequences."

"The consequences?"

"Civil war or suicide."

"Suicide! What will he do?"

"I don't know," confessed Klout. "All options cause our family great suffering. We can but pray to Sym La Panau an ally finds the prince. Now, I must go! We cannot speak like this again."

"But you will keep me informed?" asked Aminatra with hope.

Klout looked past Aminatra in thought. "You will become my mistress."

"I ..." Aminatra shuddered, lost for words.

"Don't worry," said Klout, with a laugh. "I'll expect nothing of you. We'll talk and no more. No one will question you coming to my room. It is the perfect solution."

"So ... So ... But I'm pregnant! Who will fall for such a ruse?"

"You overestimate your importance. Others will see nothing but a man and master exercising his right for company."

Aminatra almost gagged in disbelief. "And I climbed a mountain to find this 'civilisation'?"

"Sorry?"

"Nothing, Master. I was reminiscing about better times. Should I tell people?"

"No need. I'll sow a seed to spread the rumour across the household. This little rendezvous may already have set tongues wagging. You must nurture it, but never admit to it."

"Is this how you started with Litviola?"

Klout flushed. "There is a limit to the impertinence I can accept, Athenia. Don't forget your place!"

Aminatra bowed in apology, his reaction answering her question.

Chapter
Twenty-Seven

"A mouse, you say?" reflected Bartarnous, standing by his window as a cool breeze ruffled his hair.

"Yes," said Finbarl. "I found her playing with it one day. Playing is the wrong word: caring for it. Once she might have toyed with it, then eaten it, but now she feeds and talks to it in her own unique way."

"Most interesting. And the Ferrals of your world did not domesticate animals?"

"No, they hunted them and ate anything ... I think." Finbarl checked his past prejudices. "Do you suppose this is another sign of Maddy becoming more like us?"

Bartarnous turned, stroking his chin. "I think she has always been like 'us', just adapted to suit her environment. It may be nothing more than loneliness. She's very much alone in this sea of people."

"She has me," countered Finbarl. "You're her friend and there's Allus."

"An old, blind man who studies her, a young woman too afraid to hold her hand and a father figure who spends time away betting on the Shamcora. Company indeed!" Bartarnous shuffled around the table, on which Maddy lay curled up, oblivious to her central role. "And how goes your relationship with the horses?"

Finbarl looked sheepish. "There are good days and bad days, but I'm learning."

"What is it you're learning?" asked a sceptical Bartarnous, sitting down as he allowed Maddy to nuzzle his arm with her nose.

"Well, which riders have talent, which are lucky ..."

"I see. So, you are banking your own luck on someone else's? I wish you my own with that strategy. It is your money, after all."

"Ah, well ... err ..." Finbarl managed a grin, contradicted by doubt-filled eyes. "Pet won't let me touch my savings but introduced me to a lender. It's his money I'm betting with."

Bartarnous spluttered out a jet of chee. "A loan? Scandalous! And how did you secure a loan to bet with?"

"I don't understand it. Pet negotiated based on my securities."

"Your securities," echoed Bartarnous, wiping the wall with his sleeve. "The only securities in your possession are savings and the clothes on your back. How much interest do they charge?"

"Twenty percent. I'm told that's reasonable."

Bartarnous whistled. "A blind man would avoid that deal a mile off! Your naivety will be the death of you."

The twitching, inquisitive snout of a mouse appeared from Maddy's pocket, ears sampling the strange noises, its delicate toes pulling it up. Maddy stretched her forearm, forming a bridge for the rodent to scurry along. Every few seconds it stopped, whiskers vibrating with curiosity, before dashing on to its next inspection.

"But I'll soon win the money to pay it back, and some more," continued Finbarl, one eye on the mouse with casual interest. "Pet says I need to be patient."

"The fool lives off chance." The criticism softened by Bartarnous's smile. "Do you trust this Pet? He appears rather good at telling you what to do with your money. Lies and money are well acquainted."

"Oh, yes. He's been so supportive since I came to Parodis. Of all my friends, he's the one who's made things happen."

Bartarnous sucked on his teeth, his eyes somehow scrutinising Finbarl.

Meanwhile, the mouse sat on Maddy's palm, stretching upwards on its rear legs in search of food. With a biscuit crumb between her lips, Maddy bent her neck, allowing her friend to pluck the morsel.

"Our furry companion here trusts Maddy because of the food she feeds it," observed Bartarnous, somehow sensing the scene before him. "Is it not also trusting of a trap with its lure of food?"

"What's your point?" asked Finbarl, a little tired of his mentor's advice.

"You can't always spot the difference between a friend and a foe when focussed on the food."

"The starving man will get food wherever he can," rebutted Finbarl, happy to stick with metaphors.

"That's not my point," sighed Bartarnous. "Just be careful."

To Finbarl's relief, Alusto entered the room carrying a bundle of papers. Suspicious eyes scanned the prostrate Maddy. "Your students' essays, master."

"Ah, thank you," said Bartarnous, taking the bundle. "What news from the market this morning?"

The question stirred the servant, his face twitching with intrigue. "There is word of another brutal slaying in Neeva. A child, no less! The mood is volatile."

Bartarnous shook his head. "A child! The poor parents. If the Terratus don't act fast, the mob will."

"I thought the Terratus were landowners?" queried Finbarl. "What's their role in catching a murderer?"

"It's a matter of law," explained Bartarnous. "To be a landowner, you must acquire a certain level of wealth and, with that status, you're responsible for upholding the law. They won't be apprehending anyone themselves. Their duty is to organise others."

"I say, let the mob deal with this monster!" declared Alusto.

"I've seen what a mob can do," reflected Finbarl, haunting memories of a burning Athenia floating to the surface. "It's like a single being overwhelmed by blind hatred, lashing out at anything and everything. Only destruction and agony are left in its wake."

"Never liked the term 'blind hatred'," mused Bartarnous. "Infers vision somehow makes you wiser." He chuckled. "But, no, our friend is wise. We must trust in the law. I rely on familiarity and order: chaos is true blindness."

Alusto muttered under his breath, spotting the mouse scamper across Maddy's shoulder. "Master! I have just rid this flat of vermin. Must we bring others into our house?"

Something in the way he said 'vermin', his eyes directed at Maddy, roused Finbarl. "What do you mean by that?"

"They bring disease and eat our food."

Finbarl stared at the servant, still unsure where he aimed his vitriol.

"Maddy has full control of her mouse," reassured Bartarnous. "She feeds it and will take it with her. It calms her. You don't want an unhappy Maddy. Eh, Alusto?" He burst out laughing, causing Maddy to sit up to inspect the animated scholar.

Only Finbarl saw the burning anger on Alusto's face. "Things have been going missing again, Master. Pens and small knick-knacks." This time, the target of Alusto's accusation was clear.

"Maddy!" sighed Finbarl.

"Bah! It is all replaceable," said Bartarnous, unfazed by the theft. "It appears to be a compulsion. I wonder what she does with it?"

"She has a nest with a pile of pretty items in my room," confessed Finbarl. "All are safe and I'll return them ... one day. It keeps her happy and occupied."

The servant snorted, whipped around and vanished out the door.

"We had a whole larder ruined by a family of mice a year back," recalled Bartarnous, his smile at odds with his memory of the discovery. "For such small creatures, they enjoy a prodigious appetite."

"We should probably go," said Finbarl, glancing out the window to assess the sun's shadow. "Before Maddy borrows anything else."

"Of course, of course!" Bartarnous waved the bundle of papers. "I have much work to do myself. Alusto will read these to me, and I will spend the rest of the morning tutting and cursing at my students' prose and arguments."

"You must find it hard teaching but not being able to read," observed Finbarl as he climbed to his feet.

"Not as hard as my students find learning and writing. We all carry our burdens. To communicate with clarity is a far greater gift than not having a choice in how I communicate. Does our Maddy not speak ever so clearly without words?"

Finbarl chortled. "She does. Particularly when upset."

A placid Maddy slipped off the table, stirred by Finbarl's movement.

"We could learn lots from her in the art of communication and reading people," mulled Bartarnous. "Her innocence is an open book. I must confess, I'm surprised at how far I can see into her from such an economy of sounds and touch."

"You're just happy she searches that mane of yours for ticks," teased Finbarl. "Come on, Maddy!"

Chapter Twenty-Eight

A minatra held a bowl of hot milk in both hands. As was her habit when concentrating, she chewed her tongue, eyes locked on the liquid. Small steps suited her condition as she made her way down the corridor. Two female slaves approached in the opposite direction. They split, passing either side, merging again with a conspiratorial giggle. Aminatra ignored them. Attitudes throughout the estate had changed in the last few days. People treated her differently. Guards refrained from lewd comments or slapping her behind. Peli possessed an air of distance, while others exchanged unsubtle innuendo in her company. She suspected the cause, but no one spoke of such matters.

"Don't dawdle," instructed Huut, as he passed by. He hadn't changed at all, too busy to care or comment.

Aminatra ignored him too, content to keep her own pace and the milk in the bowl.

"I bring refreshments for Mistress Bethu," said Aminatra, lifting her cargo a fraction for the benefit of the guard.

He snapped to attention and gave the faintest of nods. Yet a further sign news of Aminatra's fictitious relationship with Klout had taken root.

"Mistress Bethu," called out Aminatra, as she knocked and pushed the door open. "I have your warm milk. Just as you like it."

The girl sat in bed, a candle flickering to her side, a single parchment in her hand. "Put it here," she instructed, pointing next to the flame. "I'm reading Sym La Panau. Most only start with him when they're ten."

"You must be an excellent reader, Mistress." Aminatra studied the wall tapestry hung behind the bed, its central embroidered figure purporting to be Sym La Panau, his face angry and a fist raised.

"I am. Do slaves read?"

Aminatra placed the milk down on a small table, causing the candle flame to wobble. "Some can; some can't. I can read in my tongue, Mistress."

"But not Sym La Panau?"

"No, not Sym La Panau, Mistress," answered Aminatra, the philosopher's eyes watching her from his needlework vantage point. "What does he write about?"

The question caught Bethu off-guard. "Err, he talks of weakness and fear. They caused the collapse of civilisation in the past and we cannot succumb to them again."

"I see, Mistress. He sounds like a wise man. I would love to hear you read some."

The girl considered her parchment, her eyes exposing doubts. "Not tonight, Athenia," said Bethu with an exaggerated yawn, slipping under her covers. "I'm tired."

"Of course, Mistress." Aminatra bowed, an unseen smile declaring a minor victory. "I hope the prince is safe and able to sleep soundly."

"Oh, yes. Me too." The call of sleep proved less pressing now for little Bethu. She sat up again, reaching for her milk. "I'm a year older than Prince Andolis. I want to be a princess one day."

"Where do you think he is, Mistress?"

"Mmm, just right," cooed Bethu, sipping at her milk. "I don't know. He never left the palace. I met him once, but I don't remember it. Father tells me the prince kissed my cheek. We were babies. A good omen, though."

"But he can't still be in the palace, Mistress." Aminatra cared little for Bethu's memories, hoping only to extract a nugget of intelligence shared among the family.

"Mother thinks he's held captive by a family. But why would they do that? If he came to us, we would help him." Bethu's milk moustache undermined her serious frown. "Father refuses to discuss the matter. He shouts a lot since the king died."

"Everyone's on edge, Mistress," said Aminatra, realising the girl knew as little as she did. "These are worrying times."

"Father will make things right. He always does. Here, I've finished." Bethu handed Aminatra the empty bowl. "You may leave me now. I'll dream of being a princess tonight."

"Very good, Mistress." As Aminatra backed away, Bethu blew out her candle, leaving the room in darkness. Aminatra loitered by the door and enjoyed the silence. Despite her inculcated superiority, Bethu still possessed a kernel of childish innocence. The latter reminded Aminatra of Karlmon. She liked to listen to his breathing as he dropped off to sleep.

Back in the corridor, Aminatra considered visiting Klout for further news, but the idea of another knowing grin from the guard, or sly comment across the kitchen floor in the morning, dissuaded her. She wanted to be alone.

Outside in the fresh, still air of night, Aminatra wandered away from the house, back into the darkness.

"Look out!" A pair of jogging soldiers appeared out of the murk, almost knocking Aminatra over. They were gone before she could grovel an apology.

"You look out, you ferralax," she said instead, enjoying the opportunity to speak her mind. She continued walking. The noise of mobilised troops invaded everywhere on the estate. "I wish you would just fight your little battle, kill each other, and let me be."

At the estate boundary, Aminatra paused for a rest. A small stone bench invited her to sit. She closed her eyes, listening to the strange mix of silence and mayhem. The moment belonged to her. A rare taste of freedom. She opened her eyes as a moth fluttered past, drifting up towards the hazy moon. A bat swooped, grabbing the moth, shattering Aminatra's serene state. That was life: a struggle towards the light and then death. She rose, refreshed in nothing but bitterness, as memories of tragedies and torment resurfaced.

A distant cry floated in from beyond the boundary walls. Aminatra turned, her thoughts on Karlmon, as she examined the charcoal-shaded stones, picturing the world on the other side. Amid the regular contours of the wall, a patch of wild foliage draped down one section. It didn't deserve a second thought and yet ... Aminatra reached her hand into the growth. The plant offered no resistance and soon she felt the familiar sensation of wood. She pulled away the tendrils, exposing a derelict door, one hinge broken, the plant escaping through the gap at the top.

Intrigued, Aminatra waggled at the latch. Rust grated on rust, but it moved. She pulled on the handle, and the door gave a little before possessive plant tendrils halted the advance. Bouncing the door back and forth, she hoped to ease it open, but nature held tight. With the light too poor to know what difference she made, Aminatra yanked away strands of growth. It didn't matter what lay behind the gate.

A forgotten and secret exit appealed to Aminatra. Such knowledge would be vital when the day came to escape. Again, she tried the door. It opened a foot. Not quite enough for the tummy. She felt along the top, finding a tight, restrictive ligature. Keen not to remove all the cloaking foliage, she eased one end from its bindings. Another few inches of give and Aminatra squeezed herself through the gap.

A dark alley welcomed Aminatra. She strolled along the path, straining her eyes to explore the surroundings. Arriving at a junction, she looked one way and then turned to examine the other.

"Cronax!"

Chapter
Twenty-Nine

"S he's taken my earring!" growled Favo. "Give it back!"

"Maddy, give Favo his earring back!" said Finbarl with a stern eyebrow.

Maddy retreated to a corner, her eyes cherishing the new knick-knack.

"Let her play with it," suggested Finbarl. "I'll retrieve it for you tonight when she's asleep. She likes studying them. I think she's trying to understand the colours and tricks of the light."

"That's too late," complained Favo, striding towards Maddy. "I need it now. I can't go to the theatre without my favourite earring."

"Don't …!" Finbarl's word of warning hung in the air.

The large fingers of Favo enclosed around the lithe wrist of Maddy, yanking her towards him. Favo's towering frame loomed over the petite Maddy, but three limbs and a mouth remained unrestrained. With amazing dexterity, Maddy spun and leapt, transforming from victim to attacker, riding the shoulders of Favo. Her nails dug into his cheeks, eliciting a scream.

"Get her off! Get her off!"

"Finbarl, do something," screamed Lhaluma, a mere bystander until now.

"Maddy! Stop it!" snapped Finbarl. "Maddy! Stop it now!"

Her eyes caught Finbarl's, reading his grave expression. She slid off the panicked Favo, bounding out of the door with her prized gem.

"Madd ... Oh, what's the point?" sighed Finbarl. "She's gone for the day. Cronax knows where she goes."

"She attacked me!" cried Favo, touching his raw wounds. "And stole my earring!"

"You should know better than trying to take something from her," said Finbarl, too familiar with Maddy's ways to feel sympathy for Favo.

"But she took something from me!"

"Look on the bright side," urged Finbarl, with a knowing smile. "She didn't bite or kill you. That means she likes you. Anyway, you have plenty of other earrings."

"That was my favourite!" Favo, his face flushed, spun on his heels, and stormed out of the room.

"Poor Favo," commented Dae, stepping out of Lhaluma's shadow with Maddy gone.

"It's only a bit of glass," protested Finbarl to the sombre faces now focussed on him. "Maddy likes to order them by colour and size.

"A Parodisian prides themselves on their appearance," said Lhaluma. "You should know that by now. Poor old Favo will have to buy a newer, better one or miss the theatre."

"I know, but still don't understand. In the prison, a piece of glass was only good for trading for food. Nice hair and a bangle didn't help you stay alive."

"You and your forping prison!" exclaimed Lhaluma. "This isn't some barbaric backwater. It's important to be seen at social events and to stand out. We have to think beyond where our next bath is coming from. You have no control over that dirty ape."

"Why you ..." Finbarl gritted his teeth. "Oh, forget it! I'll try to find Maddy and get your precious lump of melted sand back! You can spend the day washing and preening." With that, Finbarl departed with the same dramatic flourish as Favo.

***

Finbarl stood at a junction and was faced with a dilemma. Which way had Maddy gone? The usual crowds hurried past, intent on going somewhere.

"Have you seen a young girl? About this high." Finbarl raised a hand to his shoulder. "Long hair. Plain tunic. Moves with ... well, she's different."

The passer-by assessed Finbarl with a cursory glance and shook his head.

"Where would you go, Maddy? What does a Ferral need?" Finbarl kicked a stone in frustration. Parodis was big. He hadn't appreciated how big. Each street looked the same, while all its eyes seemed shut. How could no one notice Maddy? She didn't comply with the rich pageantry of the Parodisians, coiffured and flamboyant, designed to make each individual unique. Yet, ironically, only Maddy stood out. In their obsession with individualism, the Paradisians had succeeded in becoming indistinguishable.

"Excuse me," said Finbarl, catching the eye of a woman with a child. "I'm looking for a young woman, about so high. She has a grey tunic on. Skinny and wild-looking."

The woman mulled over the description, then shook her head. "Sorry."

"Yes, we have," contradicted the child, a girl of maybe six. "She ran past us on the stairs. I want to run that fast."

Still looking doubtful, the mother shrugged. "I don't remember, but we've just come down the Antoturk stairs. You know, linking Hedstrom plaza to Kalehelm Rue."

Finbarl took his turn to look unsure. "How far?"

"Turn left and left again after a hundred yards."

"Thanks."

"That was about fifteen minutes ago," added the woman. "Pippella's been playing in a fountain."

Finbarl winked at little Pippella, bidding the mother a good day. He found Pippella's fountain, envious at missing the opportunity to bathe his tired feet, and pushed on to the stairs. At their base, he stopped. "Oh, Cronax!" The wide sandstone steps went on and on: one hundred high. "Of course, you ran up them!" He cursed Maddy in absentia and began the ascent.

"City life has made you soft," Finbarl said to himself between gasps, as he surveyed Hedstrom plaza at the summit.

People criss-crossed, stopped to chat, or sat in the sun enjoying a snack or drink. Far too busy for Maddy, decided Finbarl, trying to get his bearings. Maddy craved silence and space. Nowhere within the city offered such conditions during the day. Finbarl spared a glance skywards at the tower of the Terratus Hall, then shook his head. The roofs and high points of Parodis would appeal to Maddy, but word of her antics would have reached Finbarl by now. No, he decided, the countryside was the only plausible destination for a stir-crazy Ferral. He examined the skyline, trying to work out the city's nearest exit point. The needles of the bridge towered over all else, only a few hundred feet to the south.

"This way to the bridge?" Finbarl fired the question towards several people as he fought his way through the crowd. "I don't suppose you've seen a teenage girl come this way?" A shrug, a vague point or aloof disinterest met his enquiries, but Finbarl ploughed on, the route to the bridge becoming more obvious with each step. No one admitted to sighting Maddy.

One road led down towards the harbour, while another sloped up to the bridge. A steady line of people headed along each. Finbarl dismissed the former route, conscious of Maddy's dislike of boats. The bridge both intrigued and intimidated him. It possessed an alien-like presence belonging to another time and place. So tall, so vast. As he climbed the road, the supporting needles seemed to grow in height. He cranked his neck, feeling woozy as he followed their line upwards. Suspension ropes hung from each, his eye following them down until they connected to the wooden bridge. It felt inadequate compared with its ancient counterparts.

"Is it safe?" asked Finbarl of a passing man.

"For what?"

"Err, crossing."

"Safer than swimming and cheaper than a boat," replied the man, pushing on over the chasm, a loaded basket balanced on his head.

Finbarl dared a glance down towards the brown, rushing river water, jerking his eyes up and away in fear. He had dreamt of flying machines, yet to walk through the air seemed unnatural. His mind tried to argue Maddy hadn't come this way, but logic suggested she had. Beyond a small settlement on the other side of the river, an open khaki landscape beckoned, devoid of people.

Air drawn into his lungs quivered with trepidation as Finbarl took his first step on the wooden slats of the bridge. He pressed down, reassured by a firmness, and took another step. A woman passed him, loaded with a huge bundle of clothes. Her motion echoed through the walkway and up Finbarl's legs. Clasping the handrail, he froze.

"First time?" called out a man, nearing the end of his crossing.

Finbarl nodded his head, braced for further ripples.

"Best way is to keep moving. If you stop, the fear glues you down. Don't think: move."

A sheepish smile acknowledged the advice as Finbarl's knuckles turned white. "Keep moving," he repeated. Behind, he heard the man chuckle 'first time' to another, and realised he was the source of ridicule. Another deep breath, a gritting of teeth, and Finbarl willed his legs on. For a second, they refused to obey, but at last complied, striding in long gaits as Finbarl's eyes stared to the horizon. He repeated the mantra, 'keep moving', with every step, forgetting to breathe. Without a central support, the bridge wobbled with increased severity the further out he got.

"Steady there!" called out a passer-by. "You're rocking the boat. Small steps."

A boat? The swaying stirred memories of life aboard ship with Captain Tarlobus. Something about those better days calmed Finbarl. His pace slowed; his stride shortened. Aminatra and Karlmon were there with him, rocking on the gentle flow of the river.

"Ten pownlets, sir."

The demand shattered Finbarl's fantasy. He had somehow reached the other side. A uniformed man stood before him; a barrier blocking the exit.

"Sorry?" said Finbarl.

"Ten pownlets. The toll. If you can't pay, you can't cross."

Finbarl opened his mouth to argue. "But …" Another thought pushed to the front. "So, you would see everyone who crosses?"

"None get through without paying," declared the tollkeeper.

"Have you seen a young, skinny girl, about so high?" Finbarl lifted a hand to his own shoulder. "She would have had no money."

"Then she wouldn't have got through."

"But have you seen someone of that description?"

The tollkeeper pondered the question. "I've not turned anyone back today. Are you to be the first? You're creating a queue."

A line of impatient faces awaited Finbarl's inspection. "She's very agile and resourceful. Could she have bypassed you somehow?"

A laugh erupted from the tollkeeper. "Only if she's a monkey."

Finbarl reached into his pocket and held out ten pownlets.

***

Night had fallen and failure and frustration multiplied Finbarl's fatigue. He leaned against a wall, rubbing the soles of his sore feet one at a time. Back in Parodis, he made his way through unfamiliar streets, heading home but hoping the elusive Maddy might at last appear.

"Argghh!" A scream cut through the darkness, startling Finbarl, setting off a chorus of barking. The sound echoed between buildings, confusing Finbarl as to its source. He looked around, hoping to find a harmless explanation or someone to share his concerns with. The streets were empty.

"Hello!" Finbarl called out. "Is everything okay?"

Only a dog answered with a further bark.

With reluctance, Finbarl went to investigate. He approached a narrow lane shrouded in darkness. As he turned the corner, a hooded figure emerged, bumping into Finbarl.

"Sorry," said Finbarl. "Did you ..."

Faint light from a distant lamp caught the side of the figure's face. A cold, sunken eye stared at Finbarl, then vanished, consumed in the darkness. Finbarl shivered, unnerved by the encounter. He pressed on into the alley, his shadow stretching as he left the light in his wake.

"Hello." Finbarl's voice lacked confidence, oppressed by the dark. There was no one to be seen. Finbarl progressed deeper along the lane, his eyes adjusting, scanning the nooks and adjacent alleyways. Instinct told him to turn around and head home, but an object caught his attention.

A bare foot jutted from the shadows, still and pale. Finbarl sensed a chill, alert to danger. His eyes flickered left and right. The soundtrack of Parodis never afforded absolute silence, but a tense lull weighed on the moment. "Who's there?" he asked, his fist screwed to a ball.

No reply came; the foot was unmoving.

"Are you all right?" Finbarl edged forward, his breath tickling with fear. "I ..." He froze. The shadow hid the detail, but not the story. A dead, male body lay before him, with vacant, lifeless eyes staring out. Finbarl crouched down, testing the pulse with a forlorn hope. A grim, dark film covered the body's neck and torso, recognisable as blood even without colour.

A wave of uncertainty consumed Finbarl. This wasn't his city. It lacked the rigidity of Athenia or the order of the guards. Chaos mixed with purpose. It was both thrilling and frightening. A cry exploded from his mouth. "Help! Help!"

The dogs responded, stirred to a frenzy with each repeated plea. A few angry voices shared their views on a disturbed night. Then the warm, flickering light from a flaming torch appeared at the end of the lane, getting closer and closer. Finbarl ceased his cries, waiting for the approach of help. The beaded beard of a Parodisian man appeared, eyes agog in terror.

"Someone's been attacked!" gasped Finbarl. "They're dead."

The man's eyes grew wide, his mouth ajar but unable to speak.

"Can you alert the authorities?" pressed Finbarl. "Come on, man! I need your help."

"Is it the Butcher?" He pushed his torch towards the body, reeling as the light exposed the vivid red.

"I don't know," said an exasperated Finbarl. "That's why we need someone in power. They can determine the facts and, if it is, search for the culprit."

A strange, squeaking wail emerged from the man's throat, transforming into a full-blown cry. "It's the Butcher. The Butcher! The Butcher has struck again!"

"Oh, Cronax!" Finbarl climbed to his feet and yanked the torch from the man's hand. "Give me that!" He ran the light down the dead body, studying the wounds. The dark shadows cast by the torch gave the features an angular, unfamiliar appearance. Only the haunting eyes seemed human, dancing flames reflecting on the lenses.

Excited voices stirred from all directions, getting louder and louder. "Down here!" cried the man. "It's the Butcher! Their jewellery's gone." Dark figures approached, then another torchbearer, then still more people. Soon, a crowd blocked the lane, pushing and jostling to view the body. Questions and speculation ricocheted back and forth, tears and sobs erupting amid the growls for vengeance.

"Does anyone recognise the victim?" asked Finbarl, filling the vacuum of authority through habit.

An indiscernible rumble of answers flowed from the crowd, un-familiar names filtering through to Finbarl. And then one response caught his attention.

"It's one of those servants to the scholars."

Finbarl stepped towards the crowd and looked back on the corpse, the shadows dispersed by a multitude of torches. "Cronax!" cried Finbarl. "It's Favo!"

Chapter Thirty

A young boy, about nine, stood in the darkness, his ragged clothes at odds with his noble posture and fine, polished shoes. "Who are you?" His question hinted at disdain.

"Amin ... I'm Athenia," answered Aminatra. "What's your name?"

The boy stared blankly, as though he didn't understand. An awkward silence followed.

"What are you doing out during curfew?" asked Aminatra, bending to the boy's height with sympathetic eyes. "It's not safe. Who's your master?"

Anger creased the boy's brow. His head darted around, seeking a solution to his frustration. Unable to contain it any longer, he spluttered out, "I have no master! Do you not recognise me?"

"Er, no."

Shocked, the boy clenched his fists. He seemed confused and lost, as though awaiting instructions.

"I belong to Master Malic," explained Aminatra, pained by the phrase but eager to connect with the boy. "You're outside his property. Tell me your name, so that I might know who you are."

Some anger drained from his face. "Then I am where I hoped to be. You address Crown Prince Andolis, son and heir of Gordian II, heir of Heliola, Gordian I, Etiopius, Neso III, Temkin the Conqueror of Juell, Mattyk IV, Mat ..."

"You're safe," cut in Aminatra, sensing Andolis intended to list his full ancestry. "Everyone's looking for you. Where's Karlmon?"

The interruption confused the boy still further, the protocols and pageantry of the palace his hallmark for communicating. "I... that name is not familiar to me. You are a strange and rude slave. I'll punish you for your ... your insolence."

Aminatra paid little heed to the threat, delivered with a lack of conviction. "Are you alone?"

"I have Atlas and Coloss with me," declared Andolis, assuming all knew their names. "They seek a way into General Malic's estate."

"The main gate is round the corner," said Aminatra, pointing along the high wall that circled the estate. "I can show you."

"I don't wish to be seen," added the crown prince. "You are a regrettable occurrence in that respect. I will have your tongue removed to ensure silence."

A nervous smile flickered as Aminatra assessed the situation. "But I can get you in. No one will see you. I am a trustworthy servant. Master Malic can vouch for me."

"I'm glad to hear it, but it is simpler if you never talk again. It won't prevent you from continuing to be trustworthy. Ah, here comes Coloss."

A dark mass grew and grew until a giant of a man stood before them, panting for breath.

"Life in the palace has made you unfit, Coloss," commented Andolis, looking comically precarious chastising the towering figure before him. "Did you find a way in? This slave says she can do so. Do we trust her?"

The giant shook his head, eyeing Aminatra as he did so. She wondered which question he answered. A hand then reached out, gripping Aminatra's throat and squeezing. Her eyes bulged, locked on those of her silent assailant, while her mouth opened, hoping to plead for her unborn baby. Only a pained rasp emerged. She clasped his fingers with hers, trying to prise them free, but it was no competition. A wild swing of a foot to his shin triggered little more than a grunt.

The prince, watching with a casual disregard, stepped closer. "Can you show us a secret way in? Coloss will end your life if you lie."

Coloss smiled as he lifted Aminatra off the ground in his vice-like grip.

With feet flapping and gagging for breath, Aminatra attempted to nod. Her vision blurred.

"Mother?" Another voice sounded, familiar and welcome.

A fragile smile formed on Aminatra as she drifted into unconsciousness.

***

Through the fog of recovery, Aminatra recognised the same bulbous features occupying her vision prior to blacking out. Coloss's hand no longer gripped her throat but flapped, creating a gentle breeze.

"Karlmon?" she wheezed, disorientated and confused on the cobbled road. "Was that my Karlmon?" She spoke Athenian.

A young, fresh face darted in front of the giant. "Mother! Oh, Mother! Are you okay? Coloss meant no harm. He doesn't know his own strength. I've told him off. You've got fat!"

Aminatra shook her dazed head and gathered Karlmon in a hug. "I've missed you so! Oh, my baby. Have they treated you well?"

"Oh, yes. I've had a wonderful time. Until yesterday, I played every day."

"I don't understand. Are you not a slave?" Aminatra ran her fingers up Karlmon's coarse, woollen top and onto his cheek.

"Of course, but that's not a bad thing. These clothes are nothing like those I wore in the palace. They were bright and shiny. Where are your shoes? And I eat so well. I'm allowed whatever the prince has. Figs, mangos, ora ... They must feed you well, too. Do you know what a ...?"

"The prince," interrupted Aminatra, allowing Karlmon to catch his breath. "He meant his goon to kill me. Are we safe now?" She squeezed her tender throat.

"Ando is my friend!" cried a hurt Karlmon. "He wouldn't harm anyone ... except his enemies. And Coloss is no goon. He's the prince's bodyguard. He doesn't talk ... well, he can't; he has no tongue."

Aminatra gasped. Her eyes darted to Coloss, then the diminutive figure of the prince in the background. Passive, regal eyes watched. "He ..." Aminatra stopped. There was no reason to tell Karlmon of the prince's threat.

"Enough talk in your strange tongue," said Prince Andolis, his indelicate choice of words unnoticed by all. "It is not safe here. We must get inside General Malic's stronghold."

"Can you help?" enquired Karlmon to his mother.

"Of course. Help me up! And I'm pregnant, not fat. You're going to have a brother or sister."

"A brother!" repeated Karlmon. "We can play together at the palace."

Aminatra sighed. "What happened? Why is the prince having to hide?"

Karlmon let his mother lean on his shoulder. "I'm not sure. The king died, and I thought Ando then became king, but ... I don't understand it all. A man told Ando the queen planned to kill him. Why would she do that? They instructed Coloss to bring him here and Ando wouldn't come unless I came too."

"Atlas! Tell your mother to hurry!" demanded the prince.

"You're Atlas!" said Aminatra, straightening her tunic. "They stole your name, too. I'm referred to as Athenia."

"They named me after some mountains," declared Karlmon. "I prefer it."

"Hmm, I don't know about that, but your prince is right. It's not safe out here. Follow me!"

Aminatra led them down the narrow alley along the side of Malic's property, following the tall, fortified wall that ringed the compound. "There's the gate," announced Aminatra. "It's unlocked."

"What's on the other side?" asked Prince Andolis. "No one must see me."

"Er, not much," answered Aminatra. "The path goes through the herb garden. I thought you wanted help?"

"Only General Malic must know of my presence. My stepmother will have spies in the household. Baltimor told me I should only trust Malic. Your mother should address me in accordance with my status, Atlas."

"Who's Baltimor?" enquired Aminatra of Karlmon in a whisper. "And how does one address a prince?

"He was a friend of the king. Like I will be when Ando is king. And you ..."

"Cronax! It's stuck!" cursed Aminatra as she tried the gate. "The vines must have fallen and blocked it."

The prince whispered to his bodyguard, and Coloss stepped towards Aminatra with a determined glare.

She stood frozen, a dread filling her stomach.

"Out of the way, Mother!" encouraged Karlmon. "Coloss will get us in."

With a sway and a huff, Coloss piled his shoulder towards the gate. A grating squeal signified movement. One more shove and it gave, sending the gate swinging open.

Coloss turned, smiling at Aminatra, just as he had when squeezing the life out of her. Aminatra grimaced and released the breath she hadn't realised she held. "He seems to enjoy his work."

"Well done, Coloss," said Prince Andolis. "Now, find me a safe place to hide, Atilas's mother! I look forward to seeing General Malic's face when he's told of my arrival."

"My name is Athen ... Aminatra!"

"Why does your mother refuse to address me properly!" complained Andolis.

"Shhh!" Aminatra held a finger to her lips. "Or we'll be discovered. There's a place you can hide. It's not far."

The procession of four crept through the unlit herb garden, the fragrance of lavender and jasmine a calming companion on the fraught night. Aminatra led, with Coloss at the rear. How she was going to hide that lumbering mass, she didn't know.

Despite the hour, voices carried across the estate. A blurred figure dashed from one point to another in the distance. With darkness their cover, no one should take the prince's party for anything other than members of the household going about their business.

Aminatra took them in a wide arc, as far from the principal residence as possible, through the gardens, past the smithy's closed workshop and towards the stables.

"Where are you taking us?" whispered the prince. "There are too many men around."

"That's the stables," explained Aminatra, indicating the twin line of huts facing each other. "It's been crazy with activity since ... since news of your father's death. We can skirt round the back. Just need to get our timing right. Now! Come on!"

Aminatra waddled at speed from the shadows, across an open stretch of ground flecked with the light from flaming torches at the edge of the stables. Karlmon followed in her wake, making it to the safety of a shielding fence.

"Right, now ... Cronax! Where's that prince of yours?" Aminatra turned to see Andolis frozen in a crouch at their starting point. "What's he doing?" She beckoned him with a frantic wave.

"He's scared," suggested Karlmon. "Ando never goes beyond the palace. I'm the only one who could persuade him to leave."

"Does he want to be safe or not?" huffed Aminatra.

Karlmon attempted his own encouragement with a wave. The prince jerked forward, only to freeze again. "He wants to move but can't!"

"Then we go to Plan B," said Aminatra. "They stay in the shadows, and I bring Master Malic ... or try to bring him. There's no guarantee I'll even be able to speak with him. You run back to them and ... Woah!"

A juggernaut bounded towards them. Coloss carried a distressed-looking prince under one arm, gambolling in awkward fashion across the open space. Aminatra bit her lip, glancing toward the stables, expecting to hear a call to arms.

Only the ragged breath of Coloss broke the silence as he careered into the fence, his ability to stop as ungainly as his running. He released the prince and hung his head low.

"Thank you, Coloss," remarked Andolis, brushing his tunic clean of invisible dirt. "Far quicker." A furtive glare exposed his embarrassment.

"We're out of sight now. You shouldn't have to ask to be carried again," said Aminatra with a wry smile. "This way!"

Behind the stables lay an enormous mound of manure. They squeezed past, the ground squelching under their feet. Vents of warm, stewing air wobbled in the faint moonlight. The prince pointed his nose away, cringing in disgust.

"We're here!" announced Aminatra, nodding towards two arched huts surrounded by a low wall.

"Where?" demanded Prince Andolis.

"The pigsties," said Aminatra, pointing at a bed of trampled straw. "It's okay. Only one's occupied. They served poor old Napoleon up for the Feast of Jampo."

"Like from the book!" exclaimed Karlmon.

"That's right. And I named the other one Snowy."

"But where are we to hide?" pressed the prince, looking confused.

"Well, Snowy won't appreciate you sharing her sty, so you can occupy this one."

Andolis shook as though malfunctioning. "I'm a prince! No, I'm the king! I can't stay in a pigsty. How dare you! I demand you find me a room with a bed. The shame of it! I'd rather die than stay here."

"Keep your voice down or death could be an option," hissed Aminatra. "Look, it's dry and I can get you some fresh straw to keep you warm. I'm told pigs are very clean animals. This is the best place to remain unseen. I feed Snowy, so few others need to come this far out, and I can bring you food, pretending it's for your neighbour."

"General Malic will have something to say about this! He'll punish you for my treatment."

"Ando, my mother is trying to help you," said Karlmon. "It will only be for a short while. Who will think to look for the supreme king of Adonelis in a pigsty? It's the safest place."

Prince Andolis looked to Coloss. The man returned a solemn nod. "Oh, very well," conceded the prince. "But only for a day. No longer. And your mother has still to address me appropriately!"

As Coloss scrambled through the sty entrance to review their temporary home, his bulky frame hugging each side, Aminatra took Karlmon to one side. "You're growing up fast. He seems to trust you?"

"We're friends. I told you."

"But do you trust him? These people are brutal. They don't see us as humans. Remember how we considered Ferrals before we met Maddy?" Aminatra took a deep breath. "Now I have you back, we can try to escape. Forget Master Malic. I can steal shoes and other stuff. The city is in turmoil. We won't have a better time."

"Ando calls me his brother. He isn't perfect, but I can't leave him to die. I'm happy here. And you must call him Most Supreme and Beloved Light."

Aminatra didn't know whether to laugh or cry. "You're a slave, Karlmon! A worthless slave! Don't you see the barbarity that takes place: the heads on spikes, the handless servants, the blind beggars, the tongueless bodyguards? Who do you think cut out Coloss's tongue?"

Karlmon processed the information, it still not fitting to his own view of the world. "I assumed he was born that way. He loves Ando."

"You're living your prince's lie, my darling. Remember what happened to Snowy and Napoleon when they took over *Animal Farm*?"

Tears trickled down Karlmon's cheek, reminding Aminatra he was but a child. She drew him in, pressing him against her bosom.

"You deserved your time of play," she said, stroking his hair. "But we can't stay here. They will split us up again."

"Please tell General Malic the prince is here," begged Karlmon. "I don't want him to die! We can escape then."

The thought of leaving her boy's side again sickened Aminatra, but, despite her better instincts, she nodded. "Help your prince get comfortable. I'll see if I can somehow get the master to come alone."

Chapter Thirty-One

F inbarl lazed on the grass slope, his eyes closed, the sun warming his face. The typical bustle of Halloan Park provided the background noise, as the scholars' voices carried to their students, while the murmur of the latter ebbed and flowed in response. Beneath Finbarl, curled in a ball, slept Maddy, unperturbed by her adventures of yesterday. Where she went remained a mystery. When Finbarl traipsed into his room in the early hours, there she was, sitting on her favourite windowsill, admiring her stash of baubles. She sniffed the air, as though recognising the macabre legacy of Finbarl's night. He shared his tale, the trauma and tragedy, trying to make sense of it all. She listened attentively, giving Finbarl the impression she understood. It tied up the strangest of days.

Now, occupying the stage before Finbarl stood Bartarnous, his audience as sparse as usual. Finbarl hoped a lecture might distract his thoughts from the night's horrors, but his mind soon strayed. The grim, drained features of Favo stared out, while Finbarl racked his memory for clues from the scene. Had he looked the Butcher in the eye with that momentary collision? The face failed to form, only that hollow eye. All his instincts, forged as a guard in Athenia, stirred his determination to punish a wrongdoer. The conflict and guilt of once having punished the innocent departed in the face of such senseless cruelty.

An indecipherable shout piqued Finbarl's attention, cutting through the rich baritone of the purveyors of wisdom. He prised open an eyelid, his gaze falling on Bartarnous. The scholar danced to the tune of his intricate arguments, waving his hands, shuffling backwards and forwards, rolling his head.

"... when I say all actions are at root selfish, I don't refer to the overt world, where we demarcate kindness and meanness with ease, but the layers below where we have but one aim: to survive and perpetuate our genes, protecting our offspring. No action, despite ..."

Content the shout belonged to the random cacophony of the city, Finbarl lost interest and closed his eye again. He stretched his toes, touching the soft wool of Maddy's tunic. As she arched her back to push him away, he tickled, feeling that fatherly bond which had helped him through his loss.

"FINBARL!"

This shout carried loud and clear. Finbarl whipped upright, twisting to scan for the source. Other heads among the students craned to identify the disturbance. Who dared break the sanctity of Halloan Park?

"FINBARL!" A head appeared above the mound, red and angry. It was Lhaluma, with Pet and Dae in his wake. Their eyes locked on Finbarl as they stomped in his direction.

"What's up?" Finbarl climbed to his feet, his brow knotted with confusion.

"You dare disturb my lecture!" barked Bartarnous.

"Be quiet, you old fool!" retorted Lhaluma. "Have you not heard? The Butcher has taken one of our own: poor Favo. Attacked and ripped in some disgusting alley."

"I know." Finbarl sighed. "I discovered the body. He …"

"And you didn't tell us!" cried Dae, her cheeks reddened from tears. "We found out from a chee vendor."

"I'm sorry. It happened so late. I'm still processing it myself."

"But you found time to sunbathe!" accused Lhaluma.

"Now, look here! This has been upsetting for me. Favo was my friend. It's terrible what happened to him, but he's not the first good friend I've lost. The best way I know how to cope is to work out who did it and get justice."

Finbarl's words triggered a secretive contretemps between Pet and Lhaluma, while Dae stared towards Maddy.

"I said I'm sorry," repeated Finbarl.

Lhaluma broke off his conversation, stepping up to face Finbarl, prodding him with a finger. "And who do you think did it?"

Finbarl became aware a crowd built up around them, focussed on him. "The Butcher is the most logical suspect. While I've not seen the other crime scenes, I understand the throat is the point of attack. It was savage."

"Savage," echoed Lhaluma, his tone now agreeable, half addressing the crowd. "Can you be more specific about the suspect? After all, you were close at hand when it happened. Or so I'm told."

Finbarl nodded. "Well, that's what I've been wondering about this morning. I may have seen them. We bumped into each other."

"How convenient. Do you want to hear my theory?"

"Of course! That'll help. Share all we know with each other. It may assist me to recall something."

"Oh, good," said Lhaluma, his sugary-sweet delivery perplexing Finbarl. "Our monster has the mind of a wild beast. Don't you agree?"

Finbarl hesitated. "I suppose so."

"They take what they want, when they want it," continued Lhaluma. "When someone tries to stop them, they get angry. I suspect each of the Butcher's victims has upset them."

"You could be right," agreed Finbarl.

"But they bury their anger, letting it fester, until they can hold it no longer. Their fury erupts in an orgy of violence. Which leaves just one question: how do they evade discovery in a busy city?"

Finbarl nodded. "Good point. I wond ..."

Ignoring Finbarl, Lhaluma pressed on. "They will vanish for lengthy periods, never telling their families where they go. During this time, they float around the city, unseen and unnoticed, because they have the skills of a hunter. With patience and guile, they stalk their prey, watching and waiting. When the moment comes, with the streets empty, the light gone, she glides in for the kill, then vanishes back into the dark. What do you think?"

"You said 'she'?" queried Finbarl with a frown. "The Butcher won't be a woman. In my experience, only men resort to such barbarity. Don't get me wrong, women can kill, but with more subtle methods."

"In your experience?" repeated Lhaluma, his voice wobbling with anger again. "That's funny, because you've told many a tale of barbaric women and taken many a pownlet from hard-working folk for it."

"Oh, the Ferrals? Yes, never upset a female Ferral, but I confess my tales did embell ..." Finbarl froze. "Hang on! You've ... Maddy's not the Butcher. That's ridiculous. I mean, look at her!"

Maddy, now awake, remained curled in a ball, curious eyes watching the drama.

Dae could hold back no more. "Yet you told Favo only yesterday that she must like him, or she would have killed him."

"I was being flippant!" Finbarl rolled his disbelieving eyes. "I'm not saying she wouldn't give a grown man a nasty bite and a few scratches, but only if provoked. A big man like Favo would have little problem overpowering her."

"Not if she surprised him," countered Lhaluma. "Don't you find it coincidental that the attacks started when you arrived in Parodis?"

"Rubbish! I'm sure the first attack happened long before ..."

"He's right!" A stranger, listening in the growing audience, aired his view. "I went to one of his shows and saw her in that cage. She ate raw meat. The Butcher eats her victims!"

"I've seen her on the streets at night," called out another. "Unsupervised. Not on a leash."

"They eat humans! I heard him say so."

"It was a show!" protested Finbarl, sensing the situation getting out of control. "I embellished to entertain. We used to believe the Ferrals ate human flesh, but that was our prejudices. No one had eaten Favo. You have my word!"

"She's the Butcher! The savage girl's the Butcher!" One voice cried it and soon the crowd echoed it until the entire park boiled in anger.

"You must tell Maddy to run for her life!" pleaded Bartarnous, feeling his way to Finbarl's side. "There is violence in their voices."

"It wasn't Maddy!" implored Finbarl. "I saw her when I got home last night. There was no blood on her tunic."

"Tell her to run! Run now! The mob are not interested in rational arguments. They are after blood."

Emboldened by the baying mob, Lhaluma made to grab Maddy. She flashed her teeth in a snarl, causing him to hesitate, convincing the 'jury' still further of her guilt.

"She's blood on her teeth! Claws for fingernails! Horns!" The accusations grew wilder and wilder.

Lhaluma tried again, meeting Finbarl's fist on the way.

"Get away from her! Run, Maddy! Run!" Finbarl pleaded with his eyes and waved the teenager away.

With one final snarl, Maddy turned and ran, the action an authorisation for the mob to give chase. A glance over her shoulder convinced Maddy of their intent and she increased her pace to a sprint. Bodies flashed past Finbarl, their focus on Maddy and vengeance.

"Go, Finbarl!" urged Bartarnous. "You must go with the mob. Cause confusion. Delay them. Allow time for the authorities to catch her. That is her only chance. If the mob gets her first, they will kill her."

Before the scholar finished his advice, Finbarl ran within the sea of people, a silent soul amid a roaring fury. A multitude of unfamiliar faces surrounded him, each adorning the look of blind anger. Finbarl wondered how many had ever met Maddy.

The Ferral disappeared, her natural agility giving her the advantage. Still the mob pursued, their thunder and accusations attracting further Parodisians to the cause. Soon, hundreds marched through the streets, some armed with swords, bows or just a stick.

"There she is!" came the occasional cry, redirecting the horde. They moved towards the heart of the city and the river. "Kill the Butcher!"

Finbarl now understood Bartarnous's suggestion. "She's down here!" His lie caused a moment's hesitation. Others took up the cry and the mass veered left down an empty street.

The mob showed no sign of losing its cohesion or anger. People emerged from their houses, intrigued by the uproar, merging with the flood. It reminded Finbarl of Puela Gorge, fomenting torrents fighting forwards, squeezing through the streets, catching all in their wake, roaring with fury. Something about the primordial spirit thrilled him: hundreds becoming one in mind and spirit. Yet the screams inside kept him focussed.

With little concern for where they had been, it came as a surprise when the mob spilled into the main square. As people spread out, the scale and size dissipated their energy.

Finbarl scanned the square, hoping not to see Maddy. It was impossible to spot anyone in such a crowd. The grandeur of the buildings ran contrary to the feral mood. A mounted troop of Kilshare formed before the trade hall, sticking out above the heads of the mob. Their swords glinted in the light and Finbarl felt less certain their intervention would guarantee justice. The mob's attitude to them also appeared ambivalent. Some cheered the knights, with their glamourous and flamboyant uniform, confident they would find the fugitive; others heckled, fearful of losing their own chance at revenge.

"She's escaped to the countryside," opined Finbarl to the women by his side. "Long gone. I'm heading back home to celebrate."

The woman eyed him with a mix of suspicion and disappointment. "Do you think so? The Kilshare can still catch her."

"See if others agree," suggested Finbarl. A content smile formed as he watched the chain reaction of regret trickle through those around him. How easy it is to control something that a moment ago was out of control, he thought to himself.

As Finbarl pushed his way through the crowd, spreading rumour and sowing disillusionment, another wave rippled from the other side. It grew louder and louder, fuelling the faded ire, until it erupted around Finbarl.

"SHE'S ON THE BRIDGE! SHE'S ON THE BRIDGE!"

The glum faces of those about to return home creased again under the spell of hatred. Fists pumped the air and bestial howls escaped as a febrile gravity drew the mob together once more. The Kilshare struggled to control their horses in the maelstrom, mere spectators of the growing disorder.

Finbarl found himself too far back to influence the head of this serpent as it wound its way up to the bridge. Shoulder pressed against shoulder and, despite his efforts, he could push no further forward. He jumped, trying to make out what lay ahead, but soon that was impossible as more pushed from behind.

"Is she there?" Finbarl asked out aloud.

Shrugs and shaken heads answered him. "I can't see." "She can't escape now." "She was never here!" "Stop pushing!"

Confusion reigned. The mob reached the head of the cliff, hesitant before the narrow suspension bridge. Despite the majestic towers, the platform, raised a hundred feet above the river, appeared fragile and worn. A few ventured on to the bridge, feet wide apart to balance as it rocked in the wind. On the other side, a small, curious crowd gathered, blocking the far end.

Finbarl remained in ignorance, helpless within the heart of the mob.

"SHE'S TRAPPED!" The words echoed through the mob, triggering a cheer and another surge. Each wished to land a blow to the Butcher.

"There she is!" screamed a woman in front of Finbarl.

Finbarl followed her pointing finger, tilting his head. Shimmering on one of the massive support ropes at the highest section of the bridge was Maddy. Hand crossed hand with grace, her bare feet gripping and gliding up the rope. There was nowhere to go but up. Finbarl held his breath.

With their prey in sight, more pushed on to the bridge, each body increasing the swing.

"I'll get her!" A man slipped a knife between his teeth and pulled himself up the same rope. Those below egged him on with a wild cheer. His limbs lacked the mobility and poise of Maddy. With the bridge careening to the rhythm of more and more people, he lost his nerve, clinging tight to the tether line, going neither up nor down.

No sympathy resided amid the mob and soon booing accompanied thrown objects. "Help!" pleaded the man, his eyes fixed to the depths below.

"Coward!" shouted the next man foolhardy enough to climb. "Let a real man show you how."

"Stop it! Stop it!" shrilled his predecessor. "You're shaking the rope."

Ignoring his pleas, the man pulled himself up, his eyes locked on the frozen obstacle above. "You had better get moving. I've got vermin to kill."

"No! I can't hang on much longer. Help me! Pleeease!"

As the bridge jolted at the extreme of its pendulum arc, the first man lost his grip. "Arrrrgghhh!!!" He plummeted, his legs clattering the man below, dislodging him, before both bodies struck the edge of the walkway with a sickening thud. They spun down, screams fading until lost to a distant plop.

A horrified hush descended on those near enough to witness the tragedy. "Move back!" one urged. "There are too many people on the bridge. It can't hold this many."

High above, on the rope connecting to the high point of the furthest tower, roosted Maddy. No one could see her hurt and confused expression as she observed the mayhem below.

Those too far back, unaware of the tragedy or the frightened girl they bayed after, saw a gloating creature perched near the heavens, aloof and uncaring. Their fervour increased, their determination for vengeance pushing them still further forward.

"Hang on Maddy!" mumbled Finbarl to himself. "You're safe up there." He had pushed himself to the edge, away from the unrelenting surge. Atop the cliff, a strip of land allowed a few to seek refuge from the crush. Most appeased themselves with vitriolic encouragement. Finbarl made out the blockage on the other side of the bridge, as more people hovered there to witness the drama. "What can we do?" He aimed the question at his mother. "The mob will lose patience, but someone will always be available to guard each end. They'll starve her down. What would you do?"

No answer came, no hawk soared to point Finbarl towards a solution.

A lull transcended on the mob. Realisation their prey was beyond reach diffused their urgency. A few on the bridge backtracked to the cliff, only to find other curious souls eager to replace them. With a rhythmic sway, the bridge continued to rock its occupants.

As the crowd quietened, a strange rumble emanated from beneath. Before Finbarl worked out its source, the ground shook. On the other side of the river, the edge of the cliff face crumbled, spilling into the water below. Screams added to the confusion and panic.

"WHAT'S HAPPENING?" cried Finbarl over the noise, falling into a young man next to him.

"IT'S AN EARTH ...," the rumbling subsided as the world composed itself once more, "... quake."

"I've never ..." Finbarl froze at the sound of further screams.

The oscillating bridge danced to a new rhythm, further energised by the vibrations of the earth. Up it swung, arcing at the vertical, tossing its terrified occupants into the air and down to their fate in the water. Finbarl looked away, unable to watch the carnage as dozens fell into the green soup below. A panic flared at the bridge's edge. Those attempting a retreat provoked the immovable mass on terra firma to push back. Faces vanished behind the cliff edge, etched with horror, their screams stifled as bodies bounced off protruding rock.

Limp cadavers splashed at the foot of the cliff, the river stirred to a white fury of consumption.

Finbarl looked to the tip of the central tower, relieved to see Maddy still there. But then ...

TWACK! TWANG!

One of the key ropes snapped, releasing its latent energy in a vicious lash. The boards of the bridge disintegrated, drifting down like matches, floating away amid the first bodies to resurface. With the tension gone, the towers wobbled. Only a little, but enough to scare away any birds resting there and Maddy.

Unwilling to endure her terror any more, Maddy leapt from her roost. She fell in silence, twice as far as all others, feet first and in control.

"MAADDYYY!" yelled Finbarl, watching in horror. He rushed to the cliff edge just in time to see Maddy break the surface and disappear. "Noooo! Maddy." He collapsed to his knees, tears streaming. Hope kept him transfixed on the water. Rescuers from the town were already helping the lucky ones out of the water. Only a few survived, but enough to foster hope.

Ten minutes passed and still no sign. The river now only released the dead. Finbarl rolled onto his back and screamed to the heavens. "Aminatra, I'm sorry! I couldn't protect her. Oh, Maddy."

Chapter Thirty-Two

"Where's Huut?" asked Aminatra, standing in the kitchen doorway, firing her question into the pool of activity.

"I'm behind you."

Aminatra turned to find the estate manager in the corridor, his arms folded.

"What are you doing up? Slaves without sleep are no good for their master."

"The baby was kicking. I couldn't sleep." A pang of guilt surfaced. Not at the lie but at the recent neglect in her thoughts and actions for her unborn child. She rested a hand on her stomach, hoping it conveyed love.

"What do you want of me? I'm busy. You're not the only one deprived of sleep."

"I must speak with Master Malic ... alone." A sheepish smile tried to win over the estate manager.

Huut's eyebrows shot up. "Must you? And why would a lowly slave need to do that?"

Aminatra considered telling all to Huut but realised she couldn't take the risk. "I ... I can't say. You need to trust me. It's very important."

"You need to trust me, said the assassin to the bodyguard."

"Sorry?"

"No slave ever talks to the master alone. Not even me." Huut's eyes narrowed as he noticed something. "What's that on your neck?" He leaned in.

"Oh, nothing." Aminatra put a hand to her throat. "Pregnancy sometimes causes bruising around the body."

"Really?" An unconvinced Huut continued to examine Aminatra. "That's new to me. Now, why do you wish to speak with the master?"

"Forget it. I spoke out of turn. Pregnancy makes you say things."

"Yours is truly the strangest pregnancy," commented Huut, his face a picture of scepticism. "Why don't you lie down? If you can't sleep, then at least get some rest."

"Good idea." Aminatra smiled, retreating towards the slaves' chambers. A glance over her shoulder found Huut still watching her. "Suspicious know-it-all!" she muttered to herself.

Out of sight and alone, Aminatra paused by a statue, resting a foot on the base, rubbing at a tired calf muscle. Her body needed rest and sleep, but her mind raced with the chance to escape. She felt torn between grabbing food and dragging Karlmon with her to find Finbarl and Maddy or fulfilling her promise and informing Malic of the prince's fate. The boy was a brat, undeserving of rescue. She enjoyed provoking him. And yet, she couldn't break a promise to Karlmon.

She turned to face the statue. "What do you think?"

Marble eyes stared back, the narrow lips unmoving.

"I can't let Karlmon down, but how do I get to see the master?" Her eyes ran down the young, adult warrior, dressed in military uniform, athletic, virtuous and heroic, representing all the Adonelisians held dear. "Of course!" she exclaimed. "Why didn't I think of that?" With a bow of gratitude, she bade farewell to the stone confidant.

Despite the hour, the estate still buzzed with activity, but no one noticed Aminatra as she waddled through the torchlit corridors.

"Master Klout has requested my company," announced Aminatra, standing before the guard by the family's quarters.

"I thought you had given birth?" the guard challenged, his eyes on Aminatra's stomach.

"It was a false alarm," confessed Aminatra, cursing her luck the same guard was on duty. "I'm due any day now, but when the master demands my company, I come." She winked, cringing inside at the seedy behaviour.

"Yes, of course." Seedy worked. "He's in his chambers."

Aminatra tapped on the door, awaiting a response.

"Enter!"

"Master, you wished to see me." She said it loud enough for the guard's ears, then slipped through, closing the door behind her.

"Did I?" Klout sat on his bed, a typical functionary Adonelisian design with built-in discomfort. Dressed in his armour, the boy had a melancholy frown on his face.

"I need your help, Master," began Aminatra, stepping to the heart of the room. "I bring important news for your father."

"What news?" asked Klout, perking up, rising to his feet. "Being alone and wallowing in doubts is not good."

Assessing the stark decor, Aminatra did not doubt it. "I must speak to your father alone. Can you arrange that for me?" Aminatra held her breath, half expecting the answer.

"Tell me first, Athenia! What news is so precious that only my father must know. Is it of the queen? Or perhaps the prince?"

Silenced followed as Aminatra weighed her options.

"Have I not trusted you?" continued Klout. "I threaten no consequences if you don't, but you must tell me. There is no other way if you wish to speak with Father."

With a slow nod, Aminatra agreed. "I've found the prince. He's safe and well hidden."

"What! That's wonderful news. Why the secrecy? With the prince safe under my father's guidance, the queen can't but recognise him as the rightful heir to Gordian."

"Perhaps," said Aminatra, "but the prince understands spies live among your father's men. He only trusts General Malic."

"Spies!" Klout struggled with the revelation. "I can't believe that, but ..." He scratched his chin. "It makes my head hurt to think the queen might want Prince Andolis dead, but Father's convinced."

"I've seen what power does to people," said Aminatra, recalling its intoxicating corruption from her days in Athenia. "Good people with nothing became monsters when given a gun."

"A gun?"

"Never mind. Will you help?"

"Of course. Where is the prince? Is he alone? Is he well?"

"He is. My son's with him, and some lump called Coloss. I'll tell all when I see your father.

***

"Father, may I speak with you?" Klout found the general with ease, accessing rooms without challenge, mixing with armed soldiers without fear, entering the meeting room with confidence. Only Aminatra's slowness of stride frustrated him.

"What is it?" snapped General Malic, standing at a round table covered with scrolls and surrounded by officers. "I'm busy. Can't it wait?"

Klout leaned into his father and whispered in his ear.

"Leave us!" The general now addressed all others. "I wish to discuss something in private with my son. What's she doing here?" His steely eye rested on Aminatra.

"To serve drinks while we talk," answered Klout.

Malic weighed up the reason, his gaze never leaving the slave. "Very well. I have a sudden thirst."

Puzzled expressions crossed the faces of the departing, but none questioned their general. His face remained stern. "Well, what about the prince? I can't afford to be distracted with gossip from the slave quarters. I presume Athenia has heard something?"

"She knows where he is," declared Klout, happy to impart positive news. "He's safe and looked after by Coloss."

"Is this true?" Malic's expression softened, now more curious. "How do you know?"

Aminatra lowered her eyes. "I have spoken with him, Master. He asked me to bring word to you and only you."

"And yet you told my son?"

"Would you speak to me otherwise, Master?"

Ignoring the riposte, Malic clasped Aminatra by each shoulder. "Where is he? Take me to him! You've done well, Athenia."

"I've hidden him in one of the pigsties, Master."

"You've hidden him where? A crown prince of Adonelis in a pig house!" His face reddened, but then a smile broke through. "Ha, ha! This I must see for myself. It's about time our kings relearnt what it takes to be a ruler of the Adonelisians. They've grown soft in their palaces."

"Can I come, Father?" Klout hovered, eager to please the general.

"I will go alone with the slave," answered the general, "but you are party to this secret and can help. You must follow a distance behind.

Ensure no one sees or follows us. The queen has her ears and eyes in my home!"

"But who would betray you, Father? Each man would rather die than lose their honour in such a manner."

"That is the Adonelisian way," agreed Malic. "But even the finest food rots. Particularly when an insect lays its eggs within."

"Does the queen not possess honour?"

"She's a woman. Emotions overwhelm them."

Aminatra's passive face hid the contemptuous sneer projected inside.

***

General Malic knelt before Prince Andolis, his head bowed, the grandeur of the gesture undermined by the surroundings. A piece of straw stuck out from the prince's hair: a pin popping his regal composure. Malic sniffed the air. A raised eyebrow acknowledged the rich aroma wafting across from their neighbour.

"It is good to see your majesty looking so well," commented the general. "Some feared the queen had already ... had already removed you from the line of succession."

"Does she really wish me dead?" asked Prince Andolis, more forthright in his language.

"Her aim is to rule through her own son. She understands you will wish to rely on wise counsel, as your father did."

"But she was always courteous and graceful when talking with me."

"While your father was alive, she played a role. Now he's gone we see her true face. There was only one woman I ever trusted, Sire. That was your own mother. May her memory last forever."

"I don't remember her well," sighed Andolis. "She was beautiful and well loved."

"Indeed, she was," agreed Malic. "And wise. She supported your father and helped him secure the throne but never once interfered in his rule."

Aminatra stood back, listening but more intent on enjoying time with Karlmon. He nestled between her arms, watching the ceremonious reunion.

"You're right!" declared Prince Andolis. "A woman has no place ruling."

"I told you they were barbarians," whispered Aminatra in Karlmon's ear, as she gave him a squeeze. He tilted his head up and back, smiling.

"The army understands that," said Malic, now on his feet, towering over the prince. "They will support you, but ..." A finger tapped his lips as he processed thoughts. "I must be honest with you, Sire. The situation is delicate. There are those seeking advancement and favour who would prostrate themselves before a false king to achieve their ambitions. It is important you don't play your hand too soon. Confusion has one advantage: it brings traitors out into the open. You must remain hidden for a while longer. I will encourage contrary rumours of your death and your survival, while building an alliance of those we can trust."

"But I don't like it here," complained the prince. "Can you not house me somewhere and ban others from entering?"

"I wish it were that simple," sighed Malic. "But while rumours abound, people will grow suspicious of a forbidden location. You've chosen a brilliant hiding place here, Sire. Your father would be proud. Imagine my shock when this slave informed me, but that only goes to show it never occurred to me. No, you must remain here. Only Athenia will visit with food. I will ask for the pig to be fattened for a feast. You have company with your beast and slave boy."

Aminatra clung tight to her referenced son, while offering sympathetic eyes to the vilified Coloss.

"You are right, General," mused Andolis. "I have chosen a brilliant hiding place. Ensure they bring the best cuts of meat and blankets ... and soap and fresh clothes ... and ..."

"I will provide what we can smuggle to you, Sire," said Malic, bowing his head and walking backwards. "Come Athenia! There is work to do."

"Our general pulled all the prince's strings, didn't he?" whispered Aminatra, planting a wet kiss on Karlmon's forehead. "Take care, and I'll see you in the morning."

"Goodbye." Karlmon hung to his mother's hand until distance tore their fingertips apart.

Klout awaited his father and Aminatra by the stables. "No one followed or saw you, Father. Is the prince all right? Where is he?"

The general strolled past, expecting his offspring to follow. "He is well but must stay hidden."

"Why?"

"Because I deem it appropriate!" snapped Malic. "You will ensure Athenia has access to quality food to take each day. Ask for extra portions. No one is to know where it goes. Your mother pays little attention, and your sister knows not to ask. Now, no more talk on this matter! I want you ready if the queen makes a hasty move."

"Yes, Father."

Malic halted, turning to Aminatra. "I'm half-minded to have your tongue removed to ensure your silence, but you did well. As well as taking food, you will convey messages between the prince and myself. But betray my trust, then the prince's neighbour will feed on your tongue and more!"

"Yes, Master," answered Aminatra through a dry mouth.

"Oh," began the general, walking on again. "I take it that was your son? Don't get any ideas of escape. There are many more punishments for him, should you try."

With that he strode away, leaving Klout and Aminatra flushed in their own bitterness.

"What did Father say to the prince?" asked Klout. "He tells me nothing!"

"Would he torture a child?" countered Aminatra, too angry for protocols.

"A slave is a slave," answered Klout. "You aren't planning on escape though, are you?"

"Of course not! I'm about to give birth."

"No, I suppose so. Now, tell me what they discussed."

Aminatra conveyed the general's thinking with a few summarised sentences.

"Strange," responded Klout. "Sym La Panau teaches us speed and surprise bring victory. An appearance of the prince with my father would evaporate all opposition. Most will favour Gordian II's heir to succeed."

"May I speak freely?" asked Aminatra.

"Go on."

"Your father has a strategy. He manipulated the conversation with the prince. I don't know what he plans, but he needs time for something."

"Well, you said he aims to sow confusion to draw out the prince's enemies and organise an alliance."

"Yes, but there's more. He doesn't respect the prince."

"Rubbish! My father is a loyal subject. Everything he does is with the prince's welfare in mind. Father was right. We should not talk about this further. I will stash food aside each day and bring to you on the second crow of the cock."

"Yes, Master," said Aminatra, wary of antagonising the boy further. "I need my sleep."

Chapter Thirty-Three

Bartarnous sat across from Finbarl, allowing his companion his silent despair. Dust floated amid the sun's rays, the light in turn highlighting Finbarl's tired features. He slumped forward on the table, his head buried in his arms. Alusto appeared in the doorway, rustling papers as a cue for his master. A wave of the hand sent him away again.

"They didn't even know her!" lamented Finbarl, not for the first time.

"Sorry," said Bartarnous. "A lie can be hard to put out when alight."

"I tried to find her." Finbarl wiped his sleeve across his running nose. "So many bodies! It was horrible. But she wasn't there."

"I know," repeated Bartarnous.

"Could she survive such a fall?"

"I don't know. It seems unlikely. The river will carry her body some way."

Finbarl gave a solemn nod, his mood turning to anger. "How could my friends betray her? I'll break Lhaluma's neck!"

"You'll do no such thing!" reprimanded Bartarnous. "He's bewildered and angry after Favo's death. Grief sparks irrational behaviour. You'd do well to give yourself time and them space."

"I've no one else to turn to," wept Finbarl. "People blame me for bringing Maddy to the city. They're accusing me of the deaths of all those people!"

"They've said that to you?"

"No, no. But I see it in their eyes. I'm ignored, shunned. A woman spat at me."

"There is much anger." Bartarnous stroked his beard.

Finbarl jerked up, puzzlement across his face. "Did the Unumverum not foresee this? Could you not have warned me?"

"The fate of the city is the focus. As tragic as this was, it does not threaten Parodis."

"Can it not identify the Butcher?"

"You know it cannot," said Bartarnous.

A commotion erupted in the hall, causing Finbarl to leap to his feet.

"What's going on?" demanded the scholar.

Allus burst in, her breath ragged. "Finbarl! You must come quick! They're raiding your room to take your property!"

"What! Why? Who?"

"Your debts have been called in. The Terratus have sent collectors."

Finbarl looked to Bartarnous. "I don't understand."

"As you said, people blame you," remarked Bartarnous. "Those you owe no longer trust you. You've the money to cover your gambling debts?"

"Pet has it. It's the funds put aside to fund Aminatra's rescue. I don't want to use it but ..."

"Pet's disappeared," said a sheepish Allus.

"What do you mean 'disappeared'?" exclaimed a disbelieving Finbarl.

"No one has seen him all day and his possessions are gone from his room."

"And my money?" pressed Finbarl.

Allus shrugged.

"Where's he gone?"

"A thief might find shelter in many a city not allied to Parodis," opined Bartarnous.

"I'll kill him!" yelled Finbarl. "What is this place? You possess all this freedom and yet use it to cheat others. Everyone's betrayed me!"

"Not quite all," corrected Bartarnous.

"No, sorry. Thank you, Allus. You don't blame me?"

"For what? Maddy didn't murder anyone. She was … sweet."

"I forgot you spent most time with her," recalled Finbarl. "So, what now?"

"Hurry!" urged Allus. "You must challenge those taking your things: discover the whereabouts of your money."

"Go, Finbarl!" added Bartarnous. "Don't waste time asking questions when action is called for."

"I know! I know! Come with me, Allus. I need a friend."

She shooed him from the room. "Run, Finbarl! Run! If you can't pay off your debts, then …"

Finbarl's longer stride carried him ahead of Allus, beyond hearing.

***

"What's going on?" shouted Finbarl, bursting into his room.

Three heads turned, each with an indifferent expression. One lobbed a brass cup onto a pile by the door.

Finbarl glanced at the heap, recognising his prized possessions. "I said, what's going on?" He reached out, grabbing the shoulder of the nearest man, pulling him round.

"Don't touch me!" The man, short and stocky, set his chin firm. "You'll only make matters worse for yourself."

"If you don't get out of my room, I'll make matters worse for you!" retorted Finbarl, shoving the man in the chest.

"You had better read it, Arturin," instructed the man.

His colleague unrolled a sheet of paper, clearing his throat. "Why, of course, Malmobo. As set out in paragraph 22.7 of the Debtors Act, the state authorises Brimnickle to confiscate all property of value of the named defendant, a Finbarl-no-surname, until the time the said defendant's level of debt is determined, and payments made to those owing. In the event full costs, including court fees, cannot be met, and no third party is identified to cover the debts, then the accused will be subject to para 45.1 of the Act. The named authorised confiscators may exercise all reasonable means to secure the property." Arturin rolled up the paper with a smug grin.

"And what in Cronax's name does that mean?"

"It means," said Malmobo, adopting the same smug grin as his partner, "it's the law!" He paused, sharing a laugh with the others. "But I must confess, I've always found one line frustrating in its vagueness. The one about 'all reasonable means.'" With that he landed a punch square in Finbarl's stomach, bending him double. "I mean, what is 'reasonable'?"

As Finbarl straightened, stepping forward to confront his attacker, another blow hit his side.

"Yeah," said Arturin, withdrawing his fist. "I've always taken it to mean whatever gets the job done. What about you, Olivar?"

Finbarl swung his head, trying to locate the third man. A kick to the back of his legs announced his presence. Finbarl collapsed to his knees.

"Don't care," laughed Olivar. "As long as we have fun."

"You see," said Malmobo, laying another punch to Finbarl's face. "Everyone interprets it different."

A spray of blood covered the wall as Finbarl toppled backwards.

"Finbarl!" Allus arrived. "Stop it! Stop it!"

"He obstructed us fulfilling our legal obligation," said Malmobo, kneading his sore fist. "I hope you stay out of the way."

"You've no right using force!" yelled Allus, falling to her knees to comfort Finbarl.

"And there you have it," declared Malmobo. "Another interpretation. No wonder the courts always take the bailiff's side. Very vague." The three men laughed again, continuing their scavenging.

Cradled in Allus's arms, tears mixed with the blood from Finbarl's nose. "I'll never get Aminatra back!"

"Don't give up," cooed Allus. "We're looking for Pet."

"Well, I think that's us done," announced Malmobo, loading the pile into boxes. "We'll index it all when it's valued and give you the receipt. Here's a copy of the ruling." He threw a slip of paper at Finbarl.

"Where's my bags?" mumbled Finbarl.

"What's that?" asked Arturin.

"Nothing," answered Allus on Finbarl's behalf. "Just go! You've caused enough hurt already." She urged Finbarl to silence with a subtle finger to her lips.

"Stupid clux shouldn't get in debt if he can't pay up," said Malmobo, heaving a box to his shoulder. "You got the rest?"

"Aye, boss," said Arturin. "See ya in court, Finbarl-no-surname."

Only the bedframe and a chair remained, neither of which Finbarl owned.

"Where are my bags?" Finbarl asked again, shuffling to sit upright.

"I don't know," said Allus. "Are those the ones you brought from Athenia? They didn't have bags in what they seized. Best you don't tell them of your other property. They'll take the clothes off your back."

"It's everything we carried," groaned Finbarl. "Books, clothes, my gun, memories."

"What's a gun?"

"Something I may need to rescue Aminatra and Karlmon." Finbarl wiped his sleeve across his face, leaving a sticky line of blood on the fabric.

"Let me stem that nosebleed," offered Allus.

"Thanks. I appreciate your help. Didn't think the day could get any worse. What's a clux?"

"Er, not a pleasant word. An insult to foreigners." Allus passed a white handkerchief.

"Thanks. Nice lads," commented Finbarl, climbing to his feet with a groan. "I'll be settling my debt with them. So, what happens now?"

"Not sure," admitted Allus. "What does the ruling say?"

Finbarl lifted the slip of paper up to the window. "Blah, blah, blah. How much? That can't be right."

"What?"

"Says I owe 55,000 pownlets. Where did they get that figure from? I never borrowed that much."

"Are you certain?" asked a hesitant Allus. "Your understanding of money has never been ... well, good."

"I can add," said Finbarl, reading the rest of the ruling. "I'm to appear in court in five days' time. Not had the best experiences of courts."

"You'll be able to challenge the figure. You've got records of all your loans?"

After an instinctive look around the empty room, Finbarl flushed red. "Cronax! Pet managed all that sort of thing for me."

"Oh, Finbarl!"

Chapter Thirty-Four

"You look like you spent the night wrestling an alligator," remarked Peli as Aminatra entered the kitchen. "Not get much sleep?"

"What's an alligator?" asked Aminatra, side-stepping the question on her nocturnal activities.

"Something you want to avoid," said Peli. "I got little sleep when expecting my third. It's the back. Couldn't get comfortable."

"Sleeping, sitting, standing; it's hard to relax. I want her out, but I don't want her out."

"I know what you mean. Poor little thing, born into slavery."

Aminatra's own fears echoed in the comment. She sighed. "Master wants the pig fattening. I'm to take it the best scraps."

"A feast, eh? Wonder what that's for. Didn't think the king's death was cause for celebration, but they're a funny people. Let me give you a hand. Can't have you carrying heavy buckets to and fr ..."

"No!" exclaimed Aminatra. She shook her head with a laugh, trying to downplay her reaction. "I'll be fine. The exercise does me good. Anyway, you're far too busy."

"And if you go pop in a pigsty?"

"I'll waddle back without my buckets," quipped Aminatra.

Peli laughed before her nose twitched in distraction. "What's burning!" She dashed to a stove, clipping the ear of the young slave standing by it. "You're putting too much wood in. It's too hot. If you've ruined Master's breakfast, he'll be having your testicles for lunch!" She lifted the lid off the vat. "Hmm, the edge has crisped. Move it off, spoon out the rim into a bowl. Then give it a good stir. Lucky I caught it."

"Yes, Peli. Sorry, Peli." The boy hung his head.

The cook returned to Aminatra, now peeling yams. "He'll learn," said Peli. "They're afraid the stove will go out, so put too much in. Sums up the life of a slave. Your boy can enjoy the overdone waste."

Aminatra's heart missed a beat. "My boy?"

"The pig! Who did you think I meant?"

"Sorry, all in a muddle today. Lack of sleep and worry." She yawned for effect. "Yes, he'll enjoy that."

Aminatra sat in silence, peeling away, pleased Peli no longer held the mythical relationship with Klout against her and thinking of Karlmon as the kitchen bubbled to a frenzy. Fatigue pulled at her, tempting her to doze, but she fought it. The fusion of smells awoke her stomach, which growled its usual protest. Huut appeared, sparing Aminatra a quizzical look, speaking to Peli, before vanishing again in a flustered state.

"Seems Master has no time to eat this morning and Mistress is not up to much," explained Peli, cursing their wasted efforts. "Mistress will eat in her quarters. I presume Master Klout and Mistress Bethu will eat as normal. Most youngsters can eat for two."

"Master Klout is at that age where he needs fuel to grow tall," added Aminatra, keen to ferment the cover story.

"I suspect he'll be taller than his father," remarked Peli. "He's a good lad. Somehow kind for an Adonelisian."

"He comes across as a typical Adonelisian to me," said Aminatra.

"Well, yes, but there's something about him. Not sure I would want to grow up as an Adonelisian warrior. They're just as brutal with their own as with others."

"Why are they such an angry, violent people?" asked Aminatra.

"Search me," said Peli, as she sampled a brewing dish. "I think they're just against things. You get people who take pleasure in disagreeing or disbelieving what someone who knows better tells them. They get a kick from others' misfortune and find happiness from being miserable."

Aminatra laughed. "I've met a few like that."

"Perhaps the founders were cantankerous old sods," continued Peli, enjoying her theory, "and embedded the behaviours in the city. They hate Parodis with a passion. Envy? Rivalry? Or just plain old being contrary? It explains a lot."

"Where did you find the time to become so philosophical?" teased Aminatra.

"Not in Adonelis!" Peli then shot off a volley of instructions across the kitchen, inspecting the freshly baked bread at the same time. "I must have picked up more from school than I realised. Silly, but I never enjoyed it. Didn't realise what freedom a good education provides and how important freedom is to get a good education."

"I never went to school," lamented Aminatra. "But I can read now."

"Not much good when we're not allowed anything to read."

"It saved Mistress Bethu. I learnt that technique from a book."

"Read any good books on escaping?"

"No," came the flat reply. The mention of escape provoked a pained memory of Master Malic's warning in the night. All Aminatra's enthusiasm and plans evaporated with his words. It felt like he occupied her mind, watching her from within. Would there ever be a better time to escape? But she could never risk Karlmon's life. They were stuck there for ever.

***

"He's eaten the lot!" complained a slave.

"Who?" enquired Peli.

"Master Klout. He asked for extra and wolfed it all. Where does it go? No scraps for us today."

Aminatra's ears pricked up.

"They're building up their energy for whatever," remarked Peli. "Except Master Malic. Air fuels the man!"

"I'll feed the pig now," said Aminatra, wiping her hands on a cloth.

"You sure you don't want a hand?" asked Peli. "One of the other kitchen slaves can help."

"No," answered Aminatra. "A heavy load will wake me up."

A smile returned to Aminatra's face as she lumbered up the path with her two buckets under the morning sun. Within each a pile of yam peel lay, enough to satisfy the pig, and the bowl of overcooked gruel. Passing Adonelisian soldiers ignored her as they hurried back and forth. The city remained in a state of bottled anxiety.

"Please be there," she whispered, approaching the agreed exchange spot. With a furtive glance around, she ducked into a clump of shrubs, feeling their stubborn branches pull her tunic. As planned, another bucket lay awaiting her, its chamber filled with the remnants of Master Klout's breakfast. It smelt delicious and temptation floated through Aminatra's mind, passing at the thought of her son missing out. She sprinkled the yam peelings from one of her buckets over the feast.

Three rugs lay folded beneath the container, a bladder of water to the side. Master Klout had done well. With two buckets in hand, she departed the shrubs, lopsided under the extra load, the rugs and bladder stuffed under her already bulging tunic.

Approaching the sties, only the pig emerged, with enthusiastic grunts welcoming the scraps.

"Sorry, it's this bucket for you," said Aminatra, hurling the yam and kitchen waste across the mud. The pig didn't seem to mind, and its nose pushed through the straw and dirt, shovelling up the peel.

"Psst. It's me. The coast is clear. I've brought you food."

Karlmon's face appeared first at the sty entrance, with a broad smile for his mother.

"I'm starving," came a voice from within, before the body of the owner barged past Karlmon. "Have you brought blankets? I couldn't sleep last night."

"Good morning, Prince Andolis," said Aminatra, smiling at Karlmon as he followed his companion out. "I have both food and blankets."

"About time. And clothes?"

"No clothes."

The prince cursed. "Show me what food you've brought!"

Aminatra lifted the bucket.

"You've brought my food in a bucket!" The prince's shout prompted Coloss to scurry out in alarm. "I can't eat that."

"I imagine Coloss has some appetite," said Aminatra. "Both he and Karlmon will find much to their satisfaction in here. You'll have to go without. And if you keep shouting, you'll attract unwanted attention."

Coloss's eyes brightened at the thought of food, while Karlmon glanced at the prince, aware a reaction would follow.

"I am his Supreme Highness Prince Andolis, son of Gordian II, grandson of ..."

"You said yesterday," cut in Aminatra, "but I still can't magic up a steaming meal on plates. This is the arrangement Master Malic made."

The boy's eyes narrowed. "How attached are you to your mother?" he asked Karlmon.

"Very!" answered Karlmon.

"Pity. She does so annoy me." Then, with a sudden lightening of his face, he said, "Very well. Show me what General Malic chose for my breakfast! And pass me that bladder. I'm parched."

Much to the neighbour's delight, Aminatra flicked the layer of yam peel into the next sty and swung the bucket, with Coloss taking hold, peeking down at the montage of edibles. He showed it to the prince, who nodded and said, "Atlas, try some of the chicken and bread."

As Aminatra passed across the bladder to the prince, she raised her eyebrows in surprise at his consideration.

Karlmon took a large bite from a chicken leg, stuffing what space remained in his mouth with bread. "Mmm, that tastes good!"

"Slowly," urged Aminatra. "You'll make yourself sick."

Prince Andolis waited until Karlmon swallowed and belched with satisfaction.

"I needed that," exclaimed Karlmon, rubbing his stomach.

"I shall now eat," declared the prince, grabbing the bucket back. Coloss watched from the rear, his eyes devouring each morsel passing other lips. "Now, try the water, Atlas," said Andolis, passing the bladder across.

The truth dawned on Aminatra, and she gasped in horror at Karlmon's unspoken role. "Be careful you don't choke, Your Majesty," she said with barely hidden contempt.

"What news from General Malic?" mumbled the prince through a full mouth.

"None," confessed Aminatra. "The estate continues to buzz with activity, but no news of the queen's plans come my way."

"Of course not," said Andolis, squeezing a pastry into his mouth. "You're a slave. Do all speak of me and my return?"

"I don't know. I'm just a slave."

"The water!" demanded Prince Andolis, ignoring Aminatra's insolence, sticking out a hand towards Karlmon and passing him the bucket. "Eat what you wish, Atilas. Coloss may have what remains."

Karlmon peered into the bucket to find little remained. "I've had enough, Ando. Here, Coloss, finish it."

The giant accepted the offer with a smile, scooping out the unappetising mix from the bottom in one hand. He sniffed and chomped from the edge, nodding with satisfaction with every bite.

"May I speak with Karl ... Atilas alone?" asked Aminatra.

The prince waved his agreement, gasping as he gulped down another mouthful of water.

Just out of earshot and sight, Aminatra retrieved the bowl of charred gruel from the second bucket. "I've saved you this. The prince didn't surprise taking more than a fair share."

"What about Coloss?" asked Karlmon, tipping the bowl until the gloop ran down his throat.

"I can't smuggle any to him," admitted Aminatra. "And anyway, I don't care about that brute."

"He's not a brute," protested Karlmon. "I've seen him save a butterfly. He only does brutish things for the prince."

"I see. And what does the prince make you do?"

"We just play."

"You understand he's not a genuine friend," said Aminatra with a grave face. "He allows you to eat his food to ensure it's not poisoned."

"Oh, yes," replied Karlmon, to Aminatra's surprise. "If I like something, I always say it has a funny taste and I need to try some more." He giggled.

"Brilliant. And if someone has poisoned it?"

Karlmon shrugged.

"Master Malic suspects we are planning to escape," said Aminatra, hugging her boy. "It is too dangerous to try now, but you must be ready. I'll bring some dry food. Hide it away from the others. I'll also smuggle another water bladder. They'll be essential if we're to survive beyond the city."

"And how will we find Finbarl and Maddy?"

"Hmm. We need to head north, locate the river. If we do that, we should be able to follow it to Parodis. Maybe they'll have heard of Finbarl and Maddy." Aminatra refrained from adding, 'if they're still alive'.

"Oh, yes," agreed Karlmon. "Maddy will make an impact wherever she goes."

Chapter Thirty-Five

"Cronax!" cursed Finbarl. "He's taken it all." Pet's room was almost as empty as his own. Ripped-up floorboards lay scattered, exposing a hiding place devoid of its treasures.

"How much was there?" asked Allus, her face a picture of sympathy.

Finbarl shrugged. "20,000 pownlets. Perhaps 25,000. Pet totted everything up. Said it was the safest place to store it!"

"Nowhere near the 50,000 you need."

"Nowhere near one pownlet now Pet's stolen it all!" Finbarl swung a foot at a loose timber, slamming it against the wall. "Sorry, I don't mean to take it out on you."

"That's all right," said Allus, laying a hand on Finbarl's shoulder. "I'm so ashamed of Pet. He could be a selfish idiot sometimes, but I never thought him a thief."

Strolling over to the window, Finbarl leaned on the sill, staring out across the city. "We're sure he's left the city? It's a big place. Plenty of hiding places."

With a sombre nod, Allus joined Finbarl by the window. "If he wants to enjoy his loot, Parodis isn't the city to flaunt it. Best place to make enquiries is down by the docks. Makes sense. If you want to escape, then the river offers the fastest and safest route out of here."

"Hmm." Finbarl narrowed his eyes, thoughts of revenge bubbling inside.

"We can go there next," suggested Allus. "Ask around. Try to find the boat that carried him. You've time before the hearing."

"But not time to catch up with Pet and ring his neck," snarled Finbarl. "Argh! Favo and Maddy are dead. All I think about is my money and trial." He hadn't felt that helpless since languishing in Athenia, bound and gagged and marched into the prison.

"Sorry, Finbarl, but you can't afford not to."

"Oh, come on. Let's try the docks."

***

Each time Finbarl visited the harbour, a thrill washed through him. It symbolised what humanity could achieve. Everyone moved with purpose, carrying huge loads of tradable goods, embarking and disembarking from the array of ships. So many indistinct sounds mixed with unfamiliar smells. What impressed Finbarl most were the vessels. Grand fighting galleys moored to the south in deeper water, lined with oars and towering sails, their sterns a graceful sweep before the broad deck, designed for warriors to amass. All activity revolved around the trading barges, not dissimilar to Captain Tarlobus's boat. They crammed into the piers at the heart. Dotted between them, small rowing boats nipped from boat to shore, boat to boat or shore to shore. Each had a character, somehow unique yet doing the same job.

"Where do we start?" asked Finbarl, intimidated by the scale and energy of the place.

"I don't know," admitted Allus. "I avoid the docks. The worst of life gravitates here."

"We'll ask," suggested Finbarl, looking around for someone with the appearance of belonging.

"Be careful."

Finbarl smiled, surprised by Allus's low opinion of docks. "Excuse me!" He called out to a man with the demeanour of a traveller, his clothes lacking the flamboyancy of a Parodisian.

The man turned, catching Finbarl's eye. A brief sentence of indecipherable words flew out of his mouth, while a harsh air coloured his features.

"A Deluquine," remarked Allus. "Not renowned for their friendliness."

"What did he say?"

She shrugged. "Nothing pleasant, I'm sure."

"Perhaps best to find a Parodisian. Ah, there's one. Excuse me!"

A short, stocky man, his beard beaded in the traditional Parodisian manner, stopped and smiled at them.

"We're looking for someone who sought passage on a boat in the last week," said Finbarl. "Who keeps such information?"

The man considered Finbarl for a moment. "Captains are supposed to report all crew and passengers to the harbour master." He spat on the floor. "Not all do, though. Money buys many a tongue."

"Thanks. Where can we find him?"

"Her," corrected the man, pointing to a hut at the end of a pier. "She's based there but could be anywhere. Busy lady. Who you looking for?"

"A man called Pet," said Finbarl. "A little shorter than me. Brown eyes. Long beaded beard."

"So, like half the men of Parodis. Good luck finding him." The man walked off, chuckling to himself.

"He would have been carrying a heavy load," called out Finbarl after him.

The man just laughed louder, vanishing into the bustling crowd.

"Everyone carries a heavy load at the docks," explained Allus. "Why didn't you mention his distinctive red hair?"

"Let's find this harbour master," grumbled Finbarl.

It proved a dangerous walk, pushing through the jostling stevedores, their angular loads capable of leaving a painful bruise. The hut had a weathered appearance, its wooden panels warping and in places crumbling to rot. A bright blue door lay ajar.

Allus stuck her head through. "Hello!"

No reply.

"There aren't too many women," observed Finbarl. "Perhaps it won't be too hard to find her."

"Can I help you?" A voice emerged from nowhere.

Finbarl and Allus swung around, the source still a mystery.

"Up here!"

They craned their necks to discover a face peeping over the hut's roof. "We're looking for the harbour master," said Finbarl.

"You've found her. Give me a minute to climb down and I'll come to you."

A moment later she appeared around the corner of the hut, straightening her leggings. "My viewing platform," she answered of an unasked question. "Helps spot the ships long before they arrive in port. The authorities are too cheap to build a proper tower. Now, you don't look like sailors. How can I help?"

"We're hunting for a passenger who may have sailed from here during the last week," said Finbarl. "Distinct red hair."

"Hunting? Is that so?" The harbour master picked up a dirty rag, rubbing her hands on it, her jovial appearance turning more suspicious.

"We understand you hold a list of all passengers."

"I do."

"Can we see it?" asked Finbarl.

"What's this passenger to you?"

"He stole my money."

"Did he now?" The harbour master's eyes followed the activity of the docks, only falling on Finbarl as she scanned toward the other direction.

"Yes," said Finbarl. "I really need my money back."

"I bet you do, but the answer's 'no'. Not my policy to share information with just anybody."

Finbarl fought to contain his frustration. "I'm in lots of debt. If I don't get the money back, well, I err … something bad may happen. Not sure what."

"Servenitude, I imagine," said the harbour master, her attention now fixed on Finbarl. "But the answer's still 'no'."

Allus, silent in the background, stepped forward. "You might appreciate a contribution to your tower fund?"

"I thought you were broke?"

"Finbarl is but I'm not," explained Allus. "We're not married or anything, just friends."

"I see." The harbour master allowed herself a smile. "I suppose I could permit a quick peek. The harbour needs that tower."

Allus counted out five coins and offered them on her palm.

"It has to be a tall tower," mulled the harbour master, pulling a disappointed face. "What if we're invaded and need to see what the enemy's up to?

"How about this?" Allus added five more coins.

"What did you say this passenger's name was?" The harbour master gathered the money in her grip.

"It's Pet," said Finbarl.

"Pet what?"

Finbarl turned to Allus, conscious he'd never enquired.

"His full name's Petro Lasson," said Allus.

"I once knew a Lasson," remarked the harbour master, retreating into the hut. "He had lovely teeth."

"This one won't when I find him." Finbarl curtailed his laugh at Allus's critical gaze.

The harbour master reappeared, carrying an open logbook. Her finger ran down a page. "Nope. No Pet or Petro Lasson recorded."

"There must be!" exclaimed Finbarl.

"Maybe he sailed under a false name," suggested Allus. "May we see? We might recognise a pseudonym."

"Help yourself." She handed the book to Allus. "Of course, it's more likely he just paid a captain extra to forget to record it. Happens all the time."

"And you let it?" asked Finbarl.

Evading the question, the harbour master asked, "You found your man?"

"No," answered Allus. "I mean, he might be in here, but ..." She shrugged.

"Cronax," muttered Finbarl.

"Where you from?" asked the harbour master of Finbarl.

Reluctant to engage in small talk, Finbarl brewed a surly response, only to find himself interrupted by a booming laugh.

"Eh! Dip dar farntano. I ear word 'Cronax' und fink to myself, only one man uses dat word."

Finbarl turned to discover Captain Tarlobus bearing down on him. Big, hairy arms engulfed Finbarl's torso, squeezing tight.

"Alo Symartha," said Tarlobus, winking at the harbour master before addressing Finbarl. "I've missed ya, my friend. Wiere is yar Ferral und wat news of yar lovely wife und boy?"

Finbarl reeled free of Tarlobus's grip. "C ... captain," he stuttered, refocussing on the surprise encounter. "Good to see you. Are you delivering more cargo?"

"Yee, yee. Trade is good. I ave full crew again. Trustworty men now. Und yar news?"

It hurt to think of Maddy, let alone talk of her fate. "Maddy died. It's been terrible. They blamed her for attacking people. It isn't true. They hounded her to death."

Tarlobus frowned. "Is sad. I like Maddy. True, sha scared me, bot sha good girl. Und Aminatra?"

"No news and little hope," Finbarl lamented. "That's why I'm here. I made lots of money, but a friend stole it. We're trying to find the thief." Realising Allus stood intrigued by his side, Finbarl motioned to her. "Sorry, this is my friend, Allus. She's helping me."

"Is good to find company wen wife lost," said Tarlobus, removing his hat and bowing before Allus.

"We're just friends," stressed Finbarl. "You may be able to help. We're looking for a man called Pet or ...?"

"Petro," filled in Allus.

"... who may have sneaked out on a boat sometime this week with a valuable load."

"I hope you've not been carrying undeclared passengers, Tarlobus," challenged the harbour master.

"Symartha!" exclaimed Tarlobus with a melodramatic smile. "Ya know Captain Tarlobus Mendine. An onest man. I always corme to visit my dear Symartha und pay my dues."

"Hmm," responded the harbour master.

"So, you've heard nothing?" pressed Finbarl.

"Ya must ask Corelye und Gidhaert. Corme! Dey be pleased to see ya." Tarlobus draped an arm round Finbarl's shoulder, steering him away. "Captain Tarlobus be back later, Symartha," he called out to the harbour master, "to complete my business."

"Er, you had better follow," Finbarl said to Allus, confused by the captain's behaviour.

Tarlobus squeezed tighter, leaning in. "I know of yar man," he whispered, checking over his shoulder to ensure they were beyond Symartha's hearing. "We took 'im down der riufer on middleday. A friend of Gidhaert, so a private arrangement. Passengers always trouble, except ya. Dat Terratus Parmsoli never pay Captain Tarlobus for lift!" He spat at mention of the name.

"Where did you take him?" Finbarl demanded, freeing himself from Tarlobus's embrace.

"What is it?" asked Allus, catching up.

"The captain ferried Pet! Three days back."

"I did," concurred Tarlobus. "Nat far. We drop im at Beemoff, about twenty miles up riufer."

The name meant nothing to Finbarl. "Will he still be there?"

"Na, it little more dan a berfing point. Ask Gidhaert. Dey spend trip talking. Gidhaert!"

Tarlobus's bellow pierced the raucous background noise of the docks. Gidhaert and Corelye emerged from below deck, half intrigued, half worried by their captain's summons.

"Look oo I've found," cried Tarlobus, as their faces relaxed at the sight of the captain's familiar companion.

"Finbarl! Allus!" Gidhaert smiled, beckoning all onboard.

"I've never been on a boat before," confessed Allus in a whisper.

"There's nothing to worry about," reassured Finbarl, mounting the gangplank, playing the experienced sailor. "It's a beautiful thing to glide on water."

Allus shuffled behind, pursued by Tarlobus, who shooed her on.

"What news of Parodis?" asked Gidhaert, shaking Finbarl by the hand. "Hello, Allus."

"Wat news, ya pamp!" exploded Tarlobus. "Yar miserable friend as stolen from Finbarl. Dat is news from Parodis."

Confusion descended on Gidhaert.

"Pet stole my money," explained Finbarl, his eyes searching the boat, triggering memories. "Lots of money. We're trying to track him down."

"Pet?" spluttered Gidhaert. "I can't believe it."

"It's true," said Allus. "I couldn't believe it either. Finbarl's in terrible trouble. Maddy's dead and Fin's ..."

"Pet killed Maddy?" Gidhaert drained with shock.

"No, no," corrected Finbarl. "It's a long story and there's no time. We must find Pet and my money. Where's he heading?"

With a puff of his cheeks, Gidhaert pondered the question. "I don't know ... Well, I can guess. He said he would stop off at Camptex. That means he'll be travelling through Adonelisian territory. I wondered why he was taking such a risk, but now it makes sense. Pet, a thief!"

"What do you mean, it makes sense?" pressed Finbarl.

"The authorities won't dare track him in enemy territory. Not unless they want to start a war. As long as the Adonelisians don't capture him, he's got away."

"Not from me!" growled Finbarl. "I'll track him. It's about time I visited the Adonelisians. I'll get back all they've taken from me."

"You're not allowed to leave, Finbarl," stressed Allus, the gentle rocking of the boat already making her feel queasy. "Not while you're in debt."

"Captain Tarlobus can smuggle me out. Eh, Captain?"

Tarlobus stroked his beard. "Na. If dey found oot, Captain Tarlobus banned from Parodis und ofer cities. Sorry, Finbarl."

Finbarl strolled to the side of the boat, staring out over the river in thought. His mother's spirit joined him in conversation, weighing up the options he put her way. After a moment, he addressed the expectant crowd. "Let's get this trial over with. Allus assures me it'll be fair. When they hear what's happened to my money, they'll let me off."

An awkward set of faces tried avoiding Finbarl's eye.

"That's right, eh, Allus?" pressed Finbarl.

Allus failed to answer. Her chin and cheeks rippled as though words bubbled inside, her face draining to white. With a dramatic lurch, she opened her mouth and vomited into the water.

"First time on a boat," stated Finbarl, as the sailors laughed.

Chapter Thirty-Six

"How much longer must I live like this?" moaned Prince Andolis, his tunic now stained in mud. "Has General Malic said anything? Why does he not visit?"

The barrage of questions and complaints had become a tiresome norm for Aminatra's visits to the pig houses. Her preferred response remained unspoken. "The situation's still tense. I'm not told much, but Master Malic fears it's too early and dangerous to expose you. He dares not visit and raise suspicion."

"Coloss smells like a pig! I'm minded to chop his nose off as punishment."

"Wouldn't it make more sense if you chopped your own nose off?" suggested Aminatra, glancing towards the giant for his reaction. A docile expression lingered. "Then you couldn't smell him."

The prince studied Aminatra, trying to determine if she was serious or not. "But that would hurt."

"I suspect it would, but not as much as having a tongue cut out."

"Why would I want my tongue removed? You do say some silly things. Perhaps I should cut your tongue out." This amused the prince. He giggled, looking to Karlmon, as though laying responsibility for his mother at his doorstep.

"No one should lose their tongue," said Karlmon. "If Coloss talked, I'm sure he would be interesting."

"But he's a slave," sniffed Andolis.

"I'm a slave," Karlmon stated, his chin quivering with the truth. "Do you not listen to me?"

"You're my friend, Atlas: my brother!"

"I'm a slave," repeated Karlmon. "My name is Karlmon."

Aminatra watched in silence, proud of her boy's bravery, fearful of where it might lead.

The prince turned to Coloss. "Would you like to talk?"

A slow nod answered.

"I suppose it would make my life easier," pondered the prince. "It can be a nuisance."

"Ooohhh!" Aminatra felt a sharp pain in her stomach.

"What is it?" asked Karlmon.

"Nothing, just a ... aahhh!" She bent forward, gritting her teeth at a further wave of pain. "Cronax!"

"What?"

"My waters have broken. I'm going into labour."

Prince Andolis sniffed with contempt. "What does this mean? Are you sick?"

"I'm giving birth, you ... aaargh!" Another piercing jolt trumped her insult. "Karlmon, sweetheart. You had better get help. Ask for Peli from the kitchen."

"You can't have it here!" exclaimed the prince. "I forbid it. No one must know I'm here."

With a resigned sigh, trying to control each agonising pulse, Aminatra nodded. "You're right. I'll head back to the house. It will be cleANERRGH THERE!" She sucked in a lung full of air, squeezing her eyes shut in pain.

"Can you make it, Mother?" Karlmon held Aminatra's arm, hoping it helped but helpless.

"Of coursSSSEEE!" She lowered herself to the floor, thankful for Karlmon's offer. "Scrap that plan. The contractions are too close together. This could be a short labour. I need one of you to help me."

The three males locked eyes, reflecting horror.

"Coloss, you must help Atilas's mother!" ordered Prince Andolis. "It's not the place of a king to ... er, assist. Nor of a child."

"Fine!" snapped Aminatra, getting onto all fours and pulling her tunic up. "Just make sure you're careful with those ..." She groaned, sagging her head to the ground, trying not to think of Coloss's hands. "Just be careful, please."

Coloss, the seven-foot giant, blinked with abject fear. His mouth opened, emitted a moan, and closed again.

"What does Coloss need to do?" asked Karlmon, his own face a picture of panic.

"You can help too," said Aminatra. "Hold my hand. You must not be afraid if I scream. Pass that stick! Place it between my teeth if the noise gets too much. Now, tell Coloss to kneel behind me. I'll instruct him what to do when the time arrives."

The snout of the neighbouring pig poked above the dividing wall, sniffing the air, intrigued by the strange noises.

"I'm hungry," announced the prince. "Coloss, pass me an apple!"

The giant's eyes remained fixated on Aminatra and the tiny emerging head. Those saucepan hands trembled, poised for action. His prince could wait.

***

Aminatra lay on a straw mat, too exhausted to care if the wailing of her new baby girl attracted unwanted attention. Sweat glistened on her brow, but a broad smile shone in the direction of her baby. Another body lay beside her, an unconscious victim of a delicate disposition: Prince Andolis.

"Thank you, Coloss," said Aminatra, cradling her newborn. "You were marvellous."

A dopey grin remained glued to the giant's face as he stroked the child with the tip of a finger.

"You were very gentle," commented Karlmon, patting Coloss on his back. "What's her name?"

"She was supposed to be a boy," said Aminatra. "Master Malic ordered it and instructed me to call him Bethu. But I've not considered her true name." She looked at her baby with loving devotion. Big, wet eyes gazed back, absorbing each fresh sight. "Libellia! Yes, she looks like a Libellia to me. No matter what the Adonelisians name her, she will always be Libellia."

Karlmon repeated the name to Coloss. "Libellia."

Coloss clapped his hands in agreement.

"How long have you been a slave?" asked Aminatra.

The dopey smile faded. Coloss held up eight fingers.

"Did it hurt?" Karlmon chipped in. "Having your tongue cut out."

"Karlmon! Don't be rude."

The bodyguard hung his head, a tear trickling down his cheek.

"I'm sorry, Coloss," said Karlmon.

"It must have been very traumatic," sympathised Aminatra. "Where's home?"

Answering stumped Coloss. He pointed east, then shrugged.

"A long way away?" suggested Aminatra, and he nodded.

"We're planning to escape," stated Karlmon, as though announcing a quiet walk in the country.

Aminatra glared in horror at her son, then dared a glance at Coloss.

The dopey smile had returned.

"Do you want to join us?"

Karlmon's innocence would be the death of them, thought Aminatra, as she tried to encourage silence through her eyes.

After a moment, Coloss's thoughtful nod turned enthusiastic, accompanied by an ape-like hoot.

"Finbarl's great," declared Karlmon, the fate of their escape already decided in his mind. "And Maddy. She can't talk either."

Aminatra considered Coloss, trying to understand the man who had throttled her, against the one who delivered her baby. Did she want him accompanying them on their escape? His size and strength would be to their advantage, but what of his trustworthiness?

"We're going to Mandelaton," continued Karlmon. "Finbarl found a ..."

The name sparked an eruption of 'ohs' from Coloss. He beat a palm against his chest, his mouth desperate to say something.

"Mandelaton." repeated Aminatra, awaiting further reaction.

Coloss obliged with short, sharp nods.

"You're from Mandelaton?" Aminatra dared to hope.

The biggest grin Aminatra and Karlmon had ever seen spread across Coloss's face, infecting their own.

"We're going to Mandelaton!" cheered Karlmon.

"Ooooww, what happened?" The prince awoke, groggy and confused. "What's Mandelaton?"

His companions laughed, their secret safe.

"You missed little Libellia's birth, your Supreme Highness," announced Aminatra, convinced Coloss would prove a trustworthy escapee.

Chapter
Thirty-Seven

F or a man raised to follow the rule of law, Finbarl still found the subject bewildering. He leaned forward, straining to decipher the words spoken by his own representative. They used his own tongue, but it made no sense.

"... adhering to section 27, my client acknowledges the litigant's claim to the money but offers a defence of maleficium."

The court bore no resemblance to that of Athenia; a calm and efficient mood was in stark contrast to Finbarl's last experience. He sat in the dock, the judge before him, silent but thoughtful. All the arguments prepared in his head seemed wasted after discovering an advocate spoke for him.

"My client had every intention of paying back his debts, and indeed had funds to cover most," declared Finbarl's advocate. "But claims one Petro Lasson absconded with said funds without my client's permission."

"And where is this Lasson?" enquired the judge.

"Not to be found in Parodis, my loor," answered the advocate.

"I see." The judge glanced down at a set of papers. "And is there any evidence for your client's wealth?"

The advocate adjusted her collar. "Er, alas, no, my loor. It is my client's great misfortune that he entrusted record-keeping to the same Petro Lasson. However, I can call on friends of my client to confirm his financial status."

A man stood up and cleared his throat. "Objection, my loor!"

Finbarl frowned, glaring at the stranger. Each time this man spoke, he painted Finbarl in a poor light, determined to prove him guilty. Had he somehow wronged him?

"If the word of a friend were to be trusted," continued the man, "then we would all be rich."

"Sustained," uttered the judge. "With no written evidence of a precise fiscal status, then your client stands on the edge of an Adonelisian sword. Do you have any further evidence in your client's defence? I've a lengthy list of cases to get through."

Finbarl egged his advocate on with a nod.

"No, my loor." The advocate turned and shrugged at Finbarl, before taking a seat.

"Very well," announced the judge. "With no means to pay your debt of 56,123 pownlets, the state will pay all creditors."

A tinge of hope lifted Finbarl's heart.

"You are now in the debt of the state," continued the judge. "I sentence you to servenitude for a minimum of five years. You will undertake payment through the auspices of the Office of Servenitude. Do you have anything to say, Mr Finbarl?"

Finbarl rose to his feet, as instructed to do so. "Am I free to go?"

"Did I not make myself clear?" growled the judge. "You are now owned by the state and will remain so until you've paid off your debt."

"I don't know what that means," confessed Finbarl.

With a heavy sigh, the judge turned to Finbarl's advocate. "I don't have time to explain every sentence. If you feel inclined, then please do so for your client or let him discover its meaning in his own time."

"Yes, my loor."

A hand gripped Finbarl's arm and motioned him out of the courtroom. He thought about resisting, but what would he be resisting?

"Sorry," said his advocate, greeting Finbarl in the corridor. "I did my best, but the judge was not in a sympathetic mood."

"What's happening, Mulwoa?" asked Finbarl. "I don't understand."

"You'll have to work for the state to pay off your debt."

"At what? For how long? Can I go home?"

The advocate sucked at her teeth. "The Office of Servenitude will decide where you work. For how long? Gosh, with your debt, you've a five-year sentence, but maybe longer."

"Five years!" The colour faded from Finbarl's cheeks. "I can't stay here for five years. Aminatra and Karlmon need saving. I'll leave Parodis tonight. They'll get their money back. I promise. But I'll do it my way."

"You don't understand," said Mulwoa. "You can't leave. Servenitude means you're obliged to work for the state."

"So, I'm imprisoned?"

"Gosh, no."

"So, why can't I leave?"

Mulwoa grimaced, trying to find the right words. "A farmer does not unyoke his oxen until the ploughing of his fields is complete."

"I'm an ox? Cronax, Mulwoa! I'm going home to rest and think."

"You can't. Technically, you don't have a home: it's the state's. Also, you're not allowed out in Parodis unless fulfilling your servenitude."

Colour returned to Finbarl's cheeks, the hue a bright red. "What on earth does that mean? Where can I stay if not in Parodis?"

"You are being punished, Finbarl. Defaulting on debt is a serious offence. You'll have to stay with all the other servenites in Meetro."

"And where the ferralax is Meetro?"

Mulwoa looked confused, her eyes dipping to the floor and back to Finbarl. "Why, below Parodis."

***

"Why didn't I know of this place?" remarked Finbarl, as much to himself as his burly escort. They descended a deep, winding set of stairs, emerging in a dark, cool tunnel. Its size overwhelmed Finbarl. "How did you build them? Tarlobus's boat could sail down here!"

The escort ignored the question, chewing on a piece of dried fruit. Dotted along the walls, oil-wick lamps flickered, exposing hunched figures.

"Who are they?" asked Finbarl, sniffing the pungent air.

"Your work colleagues." The escort spoke. "Change into these clothes!" He passed a bundle to Finbarl.

"And if I refuse?"

The orange light of a lamp exposed the escort's grin. "You starve."

"I hope they're my size," said Finbarl, stripping off his grand Parodis attire. He held up his new clothes, examining them in the dim light. A pained thought entered his mind. He had seen such uniforms around Parodis: the man collecting the horses' dung, those up scaffolding building the new market hall, others scurrying back and forth. Seen and yet unnoticed. "Is everyone down here a servenite?"

"All those in uniform and with a ripe smell."

"How many in total?"

The escort reverted to reticence. Instead, he pointed into the darkness.

"What?"

"Tell them you're new and they'll sort you out." With that, the escort walked back to the stairs, leaving Finbarl alone among a sea of hollow, staring eyes.

Finbarl gulped. "Hello ... My name's Finbarl. I'm new here."

Silence, broken by a distant cough.

"Who do I report to?"

A face emerged from the shadow. "I've heard of you, Finbar."

"It's Finbarl." His voice quivered with fear.

"A clux from beyond the mountains with a murderous girl." A man stood before Finbarl, his gaunt features exaggerated by the shadows.

"Maddy," said Finbarl. "She's innocent ... and dead."

"Aren't we all?"

"What does that mean?"

"Death is the best and quickest way to pay off your debt." The man smiled, exposing several missing teeth.

"I've challenged death before and come out on top." Finbarl's bravado belied his anxiety. "Shovelling shit holds no fear for me."

The man laughed before coughing consumed him. "Your debt's a little larger than a shit shoveller's if they sent you down here. They'll have you earmarked for the Flash with the rest of us."

"I've heard of that somewhere." Finbarl searched his memory. "Something to do with metal?"

"Oh, yes, something to do with metal," repeated the man full of sardonic weariness. "Why do I get the thick ones? All that holds Parodis up is beneath the ground. You'll find out tomorrow. Come! I'm to

waste my time showing you around the Meetro. They call me Balfour."
Reaching back into the shadow, he picked up a candle, lighting it from
a mounted oil lamp.

"What is this place?" asked Finbarl, willing to ignore Balfour's sour
insults. "Are you in the debt of the state?"

With the candle held before him, Balfour led Finbarl further up the
tunnel. "I'm not some corrupt clux! My crops failed, then my wife died
of mencoctitus."

"I'm sorry," said Finbarl. "Is that a disease?"

"Yeah, you wake up with mild symptoms and by the afternoon,
you're dead. Should have had the vaccine but, well, hindsight's a wonderful thing. Anyway, my wife worked, so with her gone and nothing
coming in from the farm, I couldn't pay my rent and the forping
Terratus brought charges. Watch your feet! There's all sorts of rubbish
down here and the odd body."

"But who farms your land now?"

"Some other sucker. Let's go down here." Balfour motioned the
candle to his right, the flame wavering in a draft.

"Another tunnel. How big is Meetro?"

"Forping big," answered Balfour. "Built by the ancestors. It covers
all the area beneath Parodis and beyond. Some tunnels have collapsed
or flooded."

"What did they build them for?" Finbarl, his eyes acclimatising
to the dark, surveyed the men and women scattered along the tunnel walls, huddled in malnourished groups, sheltering within simple
wooden structures with no privacy.

"To torment me," said Balfour with a huff. "Right, through here
…" He ducked into a small doorway, emerging in a rectangular room
lined with tables and benches. "This is the canteen. They feed us twice
a day. Nothing exciting, though I suspect exotic to you. All bland, but

who cares when you're hungry. And before you ask, it ain't free. They add the cost to your debt. Same for any tools you break."

"Why don't you just leave Parodis?" The question continued to ruminate in Finbarl's head.

Balfour shared a disbelieving stare. "And go where? There's too many bloody cluxes in Parodis. Why would I want to go live with them in their cities? Anyway, other cities don't dare harbour a Parodis servenite, and any that would are not places recommended for visiting. You'd be swapping one form of slavery for another."

"Slavery! But I didn't think Parodis had slavery."

"Ha! Slavery, indentured service, servenitude. Call it what you want. We're slaves to the system. You think you're going to do a few years and pay off your debt. Don't work like that, thicko. Slow work is punished with a fine. Talking on the job, it's a fine. When you're too sick to work, you'll be fined. And you will be sick. Look at these conditions. Those fines add up and convert into years. As I said, death's your best way out of here."

"Aminatra." Finbarl uttered his wife's name with a forlorn whisper.

"What was that?"

"Nothing. Just someone I miss."

"We have a saying down here: the lost and loved echo in the tunnels. On that note, I'll show you where we shit. Hold your breath!"

Chapter Thirty-Eight

Aminatra sat in a corner of the kitchen, lost in her own thoughts, tunic raised, little Libellia at the breast. The baby's presence brought a strange calm to the stuffy room. Peli refrained from shouting. The other slaves worked with a smile, cooing and winking whenever Libellia looked their way, chatting with a hint of festivity. New life was a joyous thing, no matter what that life might have in store. A slave's existence offered few compromises, and Aminatra found herself assigned to light duties for only a week, despite her aches, pains and tiredness.

"That's a rich head of hair," remarked Peli, holding her little finger out for the baby to grasp.

"I was similar when a baby," said Aminatra, adjusting her arms as Libellia wriggled. "It's funny how some are bald and some hairy."

"She's a pretty one. Why didn't you call out for help? My fault. Shouldn't have let you go alone."

"Nonsense." Aminatra watched her baby, unwilling to catch Peli's eye as she lied. "I guess no one heard me over the hubbub."

"You're so lucky it was an easy birth. Few babies can say they were born in a sty."

Aminatra smiled, pulling down her top as Libellia drifted off to sleep. A baking tray lay on the sideboard covered with a blanket, and

Aminatra placed her daughter on the material, leaving her naked in the humid air.

"How are you feeling?" enquired Peli.

"As one would expect. Cronax! I could do with a good night's sleep."

The general rumble of the kitchen ceased, absolute silence falling. Aminatra looked up in surprise to see Master Malic at the doorway, Klout and a nervous Huut behind him.

"Ah, Athenia, there you are!" Malic strolled over, surveying the room as though a new discovery. Sight of the baby caused him to pause. "I see you disobeyed me."

Aminatra eased to her feet, bearing a worried frown. "Sorry, Master? I don't understand."

"That is most distinctly a girl," he said. "Not a boy."

Words failed Aminatra.

"Not to worry," said the general, a stiff smile emerging. "You are good breeding stock and will provide many boys in the future."

The comment sickened Aminatra, but she replied with her own smile. "Thank you, Master."

"I have need of you. Leave your duties here and follow me!"

Aminatra bent to pick Libellia up.

"Leave it!" ordered Malic. "I said you, not your baby."

Nervous eyes flicked between Aminatra and Peli, conveying a mother's anguish. The cook gathered Libellia up, reassuring with a gentle nod. Aminatra blew a kiss, wiped her hands on her tunic and followed the general out of the room.

Silent questions passed between Huut and Aminatra, but not a word was spoken nor an answer forthcoming as the party left the house toward the stables. Huut carried a neatly folded pile of clothes, shiny and beautiful, at odds with the regimented, dour attire of the average

Adonelisian. The pace wore Aminatra down. She grimaced as her sore body objected.

Soon it became obvious where they were heading. They passed the stables, soldiers and stable lads sparing a curious look at their master, and into the unmistakable reek of pig waste. Huut's face contorted in confusion, while Aminatra's heart rate increased.

"Do you wish me to wait at the stable, Father?" asked Klout, confused himself. "To check if we're being followed."

"Unnecessary," snapped Malic. "The pretence ends today."

Klout turned to aim a surprised expression at Aminatra.

"Your Supreme Highness and Beloved Light!" called Malic on arrival at the pigsties. "It is General Malic, your loyal and loving subject."

Huut's mouth dropped as the prince emerged, his hair a mess of straw.

"My dear general," cooed the prince, brushing his stained tunic, straightening himself to present a regal air. "I was beginning to think you had forsaken me!"

The general bowed. "Forgive me, Sire. It has pained me every hour of the day to know you suffer here, but not without cause. The queen's made the error we've been waiting for. You shall no longer have to hide. Today, you lead a grand procession through the streets of Adonelis, calling the people to support you as the rightful king."

"What error? Tell me!" demanded Andolis, bursting with excitement.

"She has ordered the royal mint to produce new coins, celebrating her son's accession, with her own image on the other side."

The prince responded with a laugh that faded to awkward silence. "Er, why is that a mistake?"

Malic's smile showed patience, his eyes contempt. "She tries to establish legitimacy for her own position, Sire. The army and Adonelis will never accept a woman in power. I've had spies testing the mood across the city. Your appearance will bring relief and joy. My men follow you, and Generals Rhagcarta and Vuld commit to your cause. By the end of the day, I expect all but the queen to be behind you."

"This is wonderful," bleated Andolis, clapping his hands. "Are those new clothes for me?"

Malic snapped his fingers at Huut, who stepped forward, head bent low, and handed his pile to the general.

"The finest silk robes, Sire."

"My, how bright and splendid! I will change now."

"This slave can wash you, Sire," said Malic, indicating Aminatra with a tilt of his head. "The world must see you shine on your return."

"Absolutely," trilled Andolis, whipping his tunic off to stand naked before all.

"Water!" snapped Malic at the unexpecting Aminatra.

She hesitated, her mind racing for the closest source.

"The stables?" offered Klout.

It hurt to run, but Aminatra felt obliged, gripping her stomach and grimacing. An unusual silence fell across the stables, with doors open, horses missing. With little thought on the matter, Aminatra found a bucket of water and lugged it back to the sty.

"It's cold, Your Highness," she warned, dipping a rag in.

A flash of concern manifested itself on Prince Andolis's face, but he stood upright, determined not to flinch.

"A Prince of Adonelis shows no pain," declared Malic, allowing a creeping smile as the prince whimpered at the touch of the sodden rag.

"I feel renewed," announced Andolis, shaking in the fresh air as Aminatra finished the body bath. "Give me my clothes before I die from the cold!"

The loose silks failed to bring much warmth, causing Malic to frown. "You are a prince again, my Sire, but ... We can't have you shivering. People will mistake it for fear." He thought for a moment. "These clothes for the slave boy?" he asked Huut, signalling the bundle still in his arms.

"Yes, Master. Made of cotton."

"Excellent. Give them to his Supreme Highness. You can wear them under your silks, Sire."

"Slave's clothes?" questioned the prince, looking aghast.

"Necessity, Sire. There are no boys your age among my household."

"Very well," huffed Andolis. "Another sacrifice for my crown."

Another sacrifice of my Karlmon's, thundered Aminatra to herself. "Should I wash the others, Master?"

"Oh, do!" said Prince Andolis, before Malic could answer. "I couldn't bear to be reminded of this place by their smell."

Karlmon stripped first, giggling as the icy water tickled and agonised his body. As with his master, shivering consumed his body, but Aminatra rubbed him down with her own tunic, applying a mother's touch. She went to dress him again in his tunic.

"Don't!" cried Andolis. "Burn that tunic. I don't want to see or smell it again."

"But ..." began Aminatra, then stopped, aware of Malic's chilly gaze on her. "Yes, Supreme Highness."

"Both Atlas and Coloss must ride behind me with bare torsos," announced the prince, excited by his idea. "Two exotic savages from faraway lands in the service of, and in thrall of, their Adonelisian master. A show for the people, eh, General?"

"As you wish, Sire," came the dry response from Malic.

Coloss undressed with hesitation, the giant timid and uneasy at being naked. He stood before Aminatra, his hands large enough to protect his modesty, forlorn eyes lowered in humility.

"I'll start with the legs," said Aminatra, kneeling down. "I may need a ladder for the upper reaches." Her joke failed to raise a smile.

"Make it quick!" ordered Malic. "A savage cannot hide their savagery. Just get rid of the worst of that stink."

"What horse am I to ride?" asked Prince Andolis, strutting back and forth in his silks.

"The finest white mare I own, Sire," declared Malic. "I've had a number smuggled in during the nights to ensure a cavalry fit for a king."

**

A hundred horses ordered five wide pawed the ground, tossing their heads in nervous obedience, as a dozen drums built a deep, thudding rhythm. Behind, a mass of infantry, mixed with civilians and slaves, stood poised to march. To the fore, a line of white horses shone amid the grey of Adonelis, with Malic and the other generals astride and Prince Andolis central.

"Are you ready to claim your kingdom, Sire?" asked Malic.

"I am," cried Andolis, his high-pitched voice lacking the gravitas of his general, the horse far too big. "At the end of today, I shall possess both crown and the head of the traitor queen."

"We await your order to march, Sire."

The prince raised his arm, a silver sword gleaming in his grasp. "Forward, soldiers of the light!"

Each general mimicked the action, their swords raised. A cheer erupted as hooves dug into the sand and the column shuffled forward.

Karlmon, one row behind his prince and saddled on the same brown horse as Coloss, gripped tight to the mane, the noise and scale both exciting and frightening. Leaning to the side, he turned his head, hoping to spot his mother among those on foot. "I've never seen so many people," he commented to Coloss, unable to make out anyone familiar.

The giant smiled, nodding.

"Will there be fighting?"

The smile remained.

"We should have swords," said Karlmon. "How else will we protect Ando?" Coloss's hand patted his naked shoulder in reassurance.

Already others emerged from their homes, drawn by the commotion. Men ran forward, tears in their eyes, prostrating themselves before Prince Andolis. Women hurried to cover their faces, wailing in relief, throwing petals before the column. All joined the procession, its size growing on every street.

Aminatra found the crush of the crowd unsettling, her vision stymied by her veil, the precious bundle of Libellia clinging to her chest wrapped in swaddling. A moment ago, Peli appeared up ahead, soon lost again as eddies of human interaction mixed the column.

"Long live King Andolis!" The cry spread down the line, consuming almost all.

The eyes of a nearby soldier fell on the reticent Aminatra. "Long live King Andolis!" she cried. Coloss's bobbing head rose above all. Aminatra squinted, trying to make out Karlmon, but the bodyguard's bulk shielded him.

"It's a miracle," exclaimed the man jostling to the side of Aminatra. "I thought he was dead. The House of Gordian will again lead us."

Aminatra managed a smile. "Yes, we have the king Adonelis deserves."

"Don't talk to me, slave woman!" snapped the man. His hand gripped her throat. "I'll pull that tongue out myself."

He was no Coloss, his brow level with Aminatra's. Her eyes bulged in shock and anger. She swung her foot, catching her assailant on the shin. He gasped, releasing his grip. Sensing his confusion, Aminatra locked eyes and delivered a a slap to his face. As he staggered back, bounced and knocked by the progressing crowd, Aminatra slipped forward, escaping his sight and retribution. She smiled, a little of her well of anger and frustration vented.

Another mounted unit of cavalry arrived from a walled villa, their whooping signalling friendly intent. Priests descended the steps of the temple, singing the praises of both Sym La Panau and their prince, while children ran down the line of the column expressing a rare display of Adonelisian fun. Each street brought more followers, and Aminatra started to believe the coup would succeed.

"The palace!"

As they emerged into a great square, the volume of the crowd peaked. A tall, imposing building dominated the far side, its grey walls in keeping with the dour style of Adonelis, yet its lines and finish somehow impressive. Gates towered at its heart, tinted with bronze, drawing the attention. Before them stood a unit of soldiers, shields held to their bodies, spears to their sides.

A command from General Malic arrived at Aminatra's ears as an incomprehensible blur, but ahead it instigated action. The five white horses stood still while the cavalry behind spread out into two long rows, filling the width of the square. Those on foot followed, building an impressive wall of supporters staring across at the palace.

Aminatra saw her opportunity, squeezing forward and to the middle to stand ten yards back from Karlmon. "Karlmon!"

He turned and waved, an innocent smile on his face.

"Be careful! Stay with Coloss."

"Silence!" A cavalryman in the second row barked the command as General Malic raised his hand. The crowd obeyed.

"Your Majesty," prompted Malic, bowing towards the prince.

Prince Andolis shuffled on his saddle, gulped, and eased his horse forward. The clatter of horseshoes on stone was the only noise in the square. With a tug of the reins, he halted his steed halfway between his supporters and the palace guard. All eyes followed him.

"I am your king and master, the Most Supreme and Beloved Light, Andolis Gordian Heliola Etiopius Neso Temkin Mattyk Milonato, returning to my place of birth to claim my crown." The once squeaky voice found depth and power, carrying across the open space. "I bear you no ill will and seek nothing but your allegiance. You've done your duty, but now is the time to pick truth and legitimacy over the lies and transgressions of the murderer of my father, the charlatan and false queen, Fantoneli."

A gasp rippled across those gathered, the accusation heard for the first time. General Malic smiled, his script going to plan.

"Death to Fantoneli!" A single voice became a thousand, repeated until a chant.

The palace guards shifted with unease, their eyes looking at each other for guidance.

"Stand firm!" growled their commander, drawing his sword and facing his own soldiers. "It is not Queen Fantoneli who rules but her son, heir and legitimate son of Gordian II, King Gordian III."

"A usurper who does not stand with his army or the people of Adonelis," cried out Andolis. "I am the firstborn and am recognised by the spirit of Sym La Panau and all others." A sweeping arm demon-strated his support, eliciting a cheer.

"I have my orders, Sire," declared the commander, his voice leaking uncertainty.

"It is blood money you have!" General Malic trotted up to the side of Prince Andolis, his patience wearing thin. "An Adonelisian is nothing without honour and integrity. How much gold has blinded you to your duty?"

A grumble trickled through the guard, their discipline broken.

"Silence, you pathetic rabble!" shouted the commander, seeking to re-establish order. His flushed, angry face froze as shock etched itself on his features, the colour draining away.

"Long live King Andolis!" yelled a guard, withdrawing his blood-stained spear from his commander's back. Hesitation followed before guards and those before them joined in the cry, a red puddle spreading around the lifeless body.

"The day is ours," said Malic to the prince. "You did well, Sire."

"The day is mine," corrected Prince Andolis. "A throne holds one. But you are right. I did well."

"But, of course, Sire. Forgive my careless language."

"What now?"

"I suspect the queen's loyal followers remain within the palace. We must send the army in. Enough talking and no mercy."

"Make it so, General. I grow tired and wish to rest in my room."

Chapter Thirty-Nine

The bright morning light stung after a night in the tunnels. Finbarl held a hand up, shielding his eyes, breathing in the fresh air. A hundred servenites marched in a ragged column, Finbarl among them, nervous and intrigued. He rested the long handle of a pickaxe on his shoulder, his feet stepping on dry, wilting grass stretching into the landscape away from the river. After two miles over gentle, undulating terrain, the column climbed a long hill, coming to a standstill at its brow.

Finbarl gasped. Beneath, spanning the expanse of a wide valley, lay a hell. A devastated turmoil of grim, black earth and rubbish. Small craters littered the surface, stagnant water glistening within. Deep, carved channels cut across, while dark, voluminous holes punctuated at random points. No vegetation claimed a foothold in the depths, only upon a mountain of discarded soil looming at the valley's far end. A pungent odour permeated the air.

"Welcome to the Flash," said Balfour, squeezing to Finbarl's side. "What the city achieves in celebrating humanity, the Flash shames it."

"Cronax!" cursed Finbarl, rubbing his eyes, pointing to the distance. "Those tiny figures are people. There are hundreds of them."

Balfour followed his finger to a deep scar at the base of a hill. "Ah, those industrious ants, there to be trodden on by the boot of Parodis."

"Is that where we're going?" asked Finbarl, unappreciative of Balfour's euphemism. "What are they doing?"

"They're digging for metal. Not ore. There's not much of that left. No, my friend, they and we seek the waste of the past. The thrown-away detritus of a failed civilisation. If you thought they constructed Parodis on ingenuity and glory, think again. It's sweat, blood and rubbish."

"I don't understand."

"I envy you your ignorance, so I'm going to spoil it for you. This entire valley is where our ancestors got rid of their rubbish. It's a trash heap buried under a thousand years of time. They built big but, fic, they wasted bigger."

A shout from the front stirred the column to movement. They circled the valley for a hundred yards before a steep path led them down.

"Watch your footing," cautioned Balfour. "The edges crumble."

Finbarl lifted his pickaxe off his shoulder, gripped the head and steadied his descent using the shaft.

"Ignorant, but not stupid," commented Balfour. "You may last longer than a week."

"It's that dangerous?" asked Finbarl.

"Depends how lucky you are. Notice that smell?"

Finbarl nodded.

"Gas," said Balfour. "A by-product of trash. Builds up in pockets. You dig a hole and release it, then make a spark with your pickaxe ..." Balfour paused, letting Finbarl use his imagination.

"Err, bang?" said Finbarl.

"BOOM!" responded Balfour, his hands adding to his dramatic display.

"I may have heard them in Parodis," said Finbarl, recalling the time in Bartarnous's apartment.

"It's our way of reminding them we're here," said Balfour with his toothless grin. "And have you seen what acid does to a man's skin?"

Finbarl shook his head.

"It can burn through to the bone. Fic, you don't want to discover a pool of that when digging."

"Where's it come from?"

"God knows. Just another thing they threw away. Anyway, those are the fun ones. You've also got buried alive, crushed by an extraction wagon, or stabbed in a fight."

"I guess you're lucky," remarked Finbarl.

"The luckiest man alive!" declared Balfour with a laugh. "I get to work here every day." The laughing faded to a poignant silence. "Maybe the lucky ones are those that die on their first shift."

At the valley's bottom, a section of trampled earth allowed the servenites to order themselves into a square. Finbarl followed Balfour's example, standing idle in the third row. A man in the garish colours of Parodis faced them, his intense face focussed on a scroll.

"I've allocated you sector R7," he said, raising his head to gauge the reaction.

Disinterest answered.

"Row one and two," he continued. "Surface extraction. There's a marker where you start. Rows three and four ... Ah, you have a shaft."

A groan emanated from the selected.

"A shaft?" mumbled Finbarl from the corner of his mouth.

Balfour spat in disgust. "We'll be digging underground. Dangerous work."

"What, gas or acid?"

"Everything I warned you about."

"No talking!" yelled the official. "Rows five and six retrieval. All clear? Good. Ropes and ladders are in the usual location, and lamps and helmets are already awaiting you down the shaft. I see we have some fresh faces. Shirkers will be punished, talking will be punished, failure will be punished. Don't let me keep you. Go clear your debts!"

The parade of servenites broke with a disciplined know-how. Finbarl stuck with Balfour, following a sullen column down a sticky path around the edge of the valley.

"Why do we have to dig underground?" asked Finbarl. "Can't we just access from the surface?"

"Far too sensible," grumbled Balfour. "All the best metal is deep down. When a virgin area's started, they like us to find and extract that first. Impatient barstees!"

"How deep do we go?"

"More bloody questions!" Balfour responded. "Deep enough to make you wake up in a cold sweat thinking about it."

"No wonder they make us live underground. Gets us used to it."

"Hmmm."

"Is sector R7 far?" asked Finbarl, languishing at the back of the column.

Balfour lifted his spade, pointing to the north-east. "It's a grid. I take it a clux knows what a grid is? You'll find markers along the valley edges. Come on, don't dawdle. Not unless you want a fine."

With long strides, Finbarl caught up with the group, making its way down the valley's eastern flank. "Wouldn't it be quicker to cut across?"

"Quicker to what? Death? Give it a go. It'll save me from your forping company. They pump water up from the river to clean away the soil. It's a quagmire out there. You stray into the wrong place and the mud will claim you."

"I ..." The concept of sticky, wet mud confused Finbarl.

PTSSSHOOOLLL! A sudden noise whipped between the hills, alien and haunting.

"What was that?" Finbarl gripped his pickaxe, searching for the source.

Balfour laughed. "You really are an ignorant clux. That's a controlled release of gas. Someone's been lucky." He pronounced the last word with a sarcastic lilt.

"Oh, I see," said Finbarl, sniffing the air.

"Not all gas has an odour. That's why it's so dangerous. We have candles on our helmets. Keep an eye on them. The colour tells you everything, but not always in time."

"I'm home in Athenia!" lamented Finbarl. "The only metal there was that found buried. You just have a lot more."

"There's no doubting our ancestors' profligacy, but how long will it last?"

"How much of the valley have you mined?"

"You've seen it from on high," said Balfour. "There's not much lies untouched."

"So, things really will be as they were in Athenia," commented Finbarl. "Only without the Ferrals or prisoners."

"Ferrals?" queried Balfour but didn't wait for an answer. "Used to be just criminals worked the Flash: a just punishment for murder or rape. But the more successful Parodis became, the more metal it needed. Found a ready supply of workers in the poor, misfortunate and unlucky. Which are you?"

"All three, I guess," answered Finbarl.

"Join the club."

With the sun climbing in the sky, they cut in along a narrow path, skirting craters and shafts. A rich, dark soil exposed a weird mix of constituents, strange materials of faded colour, shredded yet holding to their original form.

"What's that?" asked Finbarl, pointing to one such tangle, its upper edges fluttering in the wind.

"Don't know. There's lots of it. Been there thousands of years and still hasn't broken down. But useless to us. Only thing we're looking for is metal."

A loose framework of wood ringed shaft R7, supporting a robust winch holding a simple structure able to accommodate four on uncomfortable seats. The servenites, familiar with their duties, broke into groups. Finbarl followed Balfour, circling the shaft, his nose twitching to an unusual flavour.

"Gas?"

"Probably," replied Balfour. "It permeates the entire area. Don't notice it after a while."

"How do you know when it's at a dangerous level?"

"Your head goes bang with the rest of you! Now, shut up and join the queue. We're going down."

Chapter Forty

"Look what they've done to the walls!" exclaimed Prince Andolis, entering the palace foyer. "My mosaics are ruined."

"That's blood, Sire," said General Malic, his tone patient. "Of those who obstructed."

"I want them punished. Those were my favourite pictures."

Malic drew a deep breath. "I will have their dead bodies mutilated, Sire."

"And I want new mosaics. Lots! One representing my victory today: my first battle as commander."

"Battle?" The general turned to the entourage behind, an eyebrow raised. "We give thanks to Sym La Panau for giving you the strength to lead us to victory, Sire."

"Where are my servants and slaves?" demanded Andolis, his eyes searching the empty corridors. "I'm hungry and wish to wash the stench of battle from my skin."

"All those within the palace are now dead, Sire," explained Malic, a hint of irritability entering his voice. "Those who served the queen could not be trusted."

"Then who will attend to my needs?"

"You have Coloss and your slave boy. I will lend you Athenia. There are always hardships to suffer after a battle, Sire."

"I see," said Andolis, his brow creasing in frustration. "Have I not suffered enough? That pigsty still haunts my thoughts."

"A monarch's life is one of sacrifice, Sire," said Malic. "Your people are grateful to you for following your father's example."

"Athenia!" Malic snapped his fingers.

"Yes, Master?" Aminatra hurried forward, past the brutish soldiers, clinging to Libellia.

"The king desires food and washing. You will find something suitable within the palace."

Questions flooded Aminatra's mind, but only one answer would do. "Yes, Master."

"Good. Have everything brought to the king's chambers and give that baby to someone else! Take that ogre, Coloss, with you. My men are still purging some corners of traitors."

***

Aminatra stood alone with Coloss. The king's entourage vanished round the corner, baby Libellia among them in the arms of her older brother.

"Find food, Athenia! Fill a bath, Athenia! Miraculously know where everything is in an enormous, unfamiliar palace, Athenia!"

Coloss smiled, patting his own chest.

"Yes, of course, you know your way around, but still ..." Aminatra straightened her tunic, attempting to get her thoughts and self in order. "So, go on. Lead the way."

Coloss guided her through a labyrinth of empty corridors, down a staircase and into the cooler depths of the palace.

"It's impressive," remarked Aminatra. "I thought Master Malic's villa was big. If only they would use brighter colours. Cronax! The blood is the brightest thing." The scarlet legacy of Malic's purge left stains throughout the palace.

They entered a cavern of beautiful arches, vanishing into smooth domes at the ceiling. Barrels and boxes hogged the floor's edges.

"A storeroom," surmised Aminatra. "What do we need from here?"

Coloss raised a finger, disappearing into the shadows at the far end.

"I'll wait here then," said Aminatra, the dark, unfamiliar surroundings playing on her nerves. She hummed a tune, her eyes inspecting the boxes. A glint caught her attention. Two glints, gone and then back. Aminatra gulped, recognising the pattern of blinking eyes.

"Who's there? Show yourself!" Aminatra searched for Coloss, hoping for his timely appearance.

A face rose, catching the light of a lamp. The frightened eyes of a young woman stared out. "Forgive us, Mistress. We hide through fear. They killed all before them. We have done nothing wrong."

"We? How many of you are there?"

Four further bodies emerged. One an emaciated man, the others teenage girls.

"You're slaves?"

"Yes, mistress."

"I'm a slave too," said Aminatra, noticing a mix of acknowledgement and confusion in their eyes. "Coloss! Where are you?"

Sight of the formidable, topless Coloss emerging from the darkness caused the group to shrink in fear.

"It's okay," said Aminatra. "He's with me."

"But ... but ..."

Coloss, carrying a large box, inspected the newcomers with suspicious eyes.

"They're palace slaves," remarked Aminatra. "Seeking sanctuary down here. They could help us collect food. What do you have there?" She leaned forward, sniffing a beautiful aroma.

Angling the box to the light, Coloss closed his eyes and opened his nostrils to the accompaniment of a smile, communicating as only he could.

"Soaps and perfume! You brought us here for that?"

The giant nodded, thrilled with comprehension.

"Cronax! Oh well, you know what the prince wants. Let's get the food now. Then we can let these good people escape."

"You'd do that for us?" asked the young woman.

"If I thought a rational argument would save you, I'd try that, but I've not seen rationality since I arrived. Come out of there! Do you know where the kitchen is?"

The woman stepped forward, encouraging her companions. "I do. But what if the soldiers see us?"

"You'll be safe in the company of Coloss." Aminatra indicated the giant with a tilt of her head. "All will have seen him in the company of Prince Andolis. What are your names?"

The woman flicked a nervous glance up at Coloss. "I'm Nanpol. This is Oona and Vee." She nodded towards two of the girls. "The others must introduce themselves."

"Curannie," said the other girl with a shy smile.

"Ugan." The man hung back, his voice timid, his head lowered.

"I'm Aminatra. We're seeking a meal for Prince Andolis." Her eyes remained on Ugan, wincing at the discovery of ragged lumps in place of his earlobes. "Er, who's going to lead the way?"

The kitchen was not far, and easy to find, their new companions familiar with the underside of the palace. Aminatra recognised the humid odour, hoping it matched General Malic's estate.

"Cronax!" Aminatra recoiled, gagging in horror.

Amid the shattered pottery and scattered cauldrons lay several slave bodies, pools of blood mixing on the floor with spilt food.

"That will happen to us if we're seen!" cried Nanpol, instigating a chorus of sobs from her companions.

"Shh!" Aminatra held a finger to her lips. "These kills are recent. The soldiers won't be long gone."

"If that is so, we must escape now," whispered Vee. "You have your food."

Aminatra went to answer but stopped, her mind calculating the options. "Where will you go if you escape the palace?"

The question triggered only frowns.

"You can't survive in Adonelis. Will you be able to get beyond the town walls?"

"We only need to hide until the killings cease," said Nanpol. "Then we can return to the palace."

"What, knock on the door and ask for your job back?" Aminatra made a tentative step into the room, tiptoeing between the mess and gore. "No, every palace slave is dead. It's just a matter of when."

"Then we might as well end our own lives now!" exclaimed Vee, trying to contain her emotion in a whisper.

"There may be another way," suggested Aminatra, digging through a cupboard. "Ah, this looks good." She pulled a bowl of dates out.

"Well?" pleaded Nanpol.

"There are two things in your favour. Firstly, with the palace household all but wiped out, who's left to recognise you, and, secondly, slaves go unnoticed anyway." She addressed the exception to that rule. "Coloss, do you recognise anyone here?"

The big man shook his head.

"So, what are you suggesting?" asked Nanpol.

"You stick with us. We pretend you're slaves from another household we've commandeered to get things in order. A bluff!"

"And if someone does recognise us? Can you imagine the punishment?"

Aminatra shrugged. "You'll be free one day. Believe in that. A lie is a risk worth taking for such a chance."

The palace slaves huddled together, whispering thoughts between themselves.

"Oh, give me a hand, Coloss, while they sort out their fate. Otherwise, we'll all find ourselves dead."

With less concern for the state of his feet, Coloss stepped through the mess, spreading bloody footprints across the floor.

"Try over there!" instructed Aminatra. "There may be some bread they baked this morning."

Nanpol appeared at Aminatra's shoulder, a furtive look on her face. "May we speak in private?"

Aminatra frowned. "Have you decided?"

"Yes, we'll join you. It is fractionally better than suicide."

"Good."

"But ..." Nanpol's voice descended to a barely audible whisper. "Your friend lied about not recognising us!"

"Coloss?"

Nanpol nodded her head, sneaking a glance in the giant's direction. "Ugan tells me he meted out his punishment, cutting off his earlobes."

"What!" Aminatra failed to restrain her voice. "Coloss! Get over here!"

"Nooo!" squealed Nanpol, retreating as Coloss lumbered over.

"Was it you who cut Ugan's ears off?" Aminatra stood with her hands on her hips, as though scolding Karlmon.

Coloss cranked his neck, observing the cowering Ugan, then shrugged.

"Cronax! How many people's ears have you cut off?"

His eyes searched the upper recesses of his memory and opened both hands, flashing his digits to signal more than Aminatra cared for.

"Oh, Coloss. Why?"

He hung his head, his eyes expressing hurt.

"I understand," said Aminatra, her tone more sympathetic. "You had no choice. The prince or another bully ordered you to do it."

Coloss's slow nods acknowledged his shame.

"What did Ugan do to 'deserve' it?" Aminatra aimed the question at Nanpol.

"Nothing! He said he was serving food when a sensitive discussion took place. Are you sure we can trust it?" Nanpol glared at Coloss, his humble posture giving her strength.

"Coloss has suffered at Adonelisian hands as much as any slave," said Aminatra, reaching out with a touch to comfort him. "He's lost his tongue but learnt how to survive. Sometimes that's our only weapon against them: to survive. One day a chance will come to destroy this wicked place, and it will be the survivors leading the charge in the name of the dead. We can trust you, can't we, Coloss?"

A single tear trickled to his chin, lingered and dropped to the floor. Coloss gave a solemn nod.

"Right, enough talk. Help me fix a meal fit for a king."

***

"Who are they?" demanded General Malic. His guards drew their swords, stepping forward to block the party.

"To ensure his majesty got the feast he deserves," said Aminatra, "I commandeered additional slaves from General Vuld's household."

Malic's eyes narrowed, assessing the unfamiliar faces. "Put the trays down and leave us. Not you, Athenia or Coloss."

Nanpol and the others backed out of the room, relieved the bluff had worked, uncertain on their future.

"There are no oysters," complained Prince Andolis, examining the platters of food, picking up samples to sniff at them. "Atilas! Leave that baby and try this food."

Karlmon handed Libellia back to her mother, whispering, "She's been crying a lot. The prince was not happy."

"She misses her mother," said Aminatra, gathering her daughter in her arms, the tiny face showing recognition and happiness. "I can recommend the olives."

Aminatra watched as Karlmon worked his way around the platters, his cheeks filling, his eyes growing with each pleasant taste. As he stepped back, Andolis pounced on the food, gorging with a noisy satisfaction.

"You must be hungry, Sire," observed Malic with an air of distaste.

Andolis responded with a belch.

"I trust you have everything you need, Sire? Athenia can bathe you after your meal. Your linen is fresh, and you have the company of your boy and bodyguard."

Raising a chicken leg, Andolis acknowledged, his attention soon drawn by a peach.

"Good," said Malic, edging towards the door. "Athenia. A word."

Aminatra passed Libellia back to Karlmon and hurried across. "Yes, Master."

Malic leaned in towards his slave, his voice secretive. "I must now focus on the business of state. You will stay with the king and meet his every need. Only you leave the room to collect what's required. No one else, not even his majesty."

"I don't understand, Master."

"I don't need you to understand. You do as you're told." With that, Malic motioned for his armed guards to depart. He followed them out, pulling the door shut. A click sounded.

Aminatra's brow creased. She looked across at Andolis, still sating his bottomless appetite, and tried the door handle. "He's locked us in!"

Chapter Forty-One

F inbarl drove an elbow forward, grunting at the effort. With his other hand he pulled his pickaxe. A single rail, running the length of the tunnel, dug into his stomach, causing discomfort. He brought his right knee up, digging his toes into the dirt, and pushed off, edging on a little further, relieving the pain. A small candle rested on the rim of his leather helmet, giving shape to the claustrophobic tunnel. He continued another five yards, until emerging into a larger shaft. Wooden beams supported the walls and roof, and Finbarl climbed to his feet.

"Why not make all tunnels this size?" he whined, rubbing at his sore back.

Balfour wiped a rag across his forehead, removing a grimy layer of sweat. "To annoy you cluxes!" He paused, sighed with extravagance, and continued. "When made to crawl, you know someone's died trying to make a normal shaft. Whatever's above is noxious. With trial and error, we bypass the danger.

"You work that wall. Give me your pickaxe and watch! I'll show you how to swing an axe down here." Taking the tool, Balfour pushed a leg back, and slid one hand to the bottom of the handle. "Keep the other hand loose, like this. Tilt at this angle and move your weight to your back leg." The axe crashed against the mine face, plunging deep.

"We call that a 'clean' strike. No debris, no metal. Pull the head up and waggle. Soil falls to the floor. I pile it onto the tray, and it gets drawn down the shaft and deposited on the surface. Think you can manage that?"

"Like this?" Finbarl asked, poised with the pickaxe.

"Bend your front knee. It's all about getting maximum power with minimum effort. Not bad for a clux."

Finbarl swung. A 'clean' strike. The candle flame rippled.

"Adequate. Now, waggle!"

"This is the hardest part," complained Finbarl, trying to retrieve his tool from the wall.

"You'll discover muscles you never knew you had when they ache in the morning."

The axe head gave way. Soil tumbled to the ground, covering Finbarl's feet. He paused, admiring his work.

"Don't stop! Straight again: swing, dig, pull. If we don't advance by five yards before lunch, it will be another month on your fine."

Finbarl swung, jerked, released, and swung again. "How do they know how much we've dug? Don't suppose they ever come down here."

"Ha!" Balfour turned and spat on the floor. "You see your comrades sweating away down there?"

All Finbarl could make out was shimmering candles, but the rhythmic crack and thud of pickaxe on surface sufficed as evidence. "Yes."

"Anyone of them could tell on you. Hell, as a forping clux, I could tell on you."

"Why?"

"Why do you think? A month added to your fine for slow work; a month removed for grassing. Pick up the speed! Don't swing too hard. Pace yourself."

"Cronax!" cursed Finbarl, his lungs burning with effort. "They've created a heaven and hell."

"Enough talking or one of those demons will have cause to celebrate."

Finbarl shook his head in disgust, unable to restrain himself from uttering one more word. "Cronax!"

***

The hours passed. As Finbarl flagged, Balfour took over with the pickaxe, leaving him to shovel the waste onto a tray. With a tug on a rope, the tray slid away, balanced on a single rail, vanishing into the narrow tunnel. Finbarl loaded another tray and began spading more soil on it.

A dull clang greeted Balfour's pickaxe. He released one hand, shook it and cursed. "Forp! The downside to finding metal. Goes right through you."

"Metal! What do we do now?" asked Finbarl, seeing no sign among the dark surface of their find, but sensing a familiar excitement.

"We call for help, build a support structure and keep on digging."

"How big will it be? What if it can't squeeze through the tunnel?"

"Oh, hadn't thought of that" Balfour squeezed as much sarcasm out of the phrase as he could. "We'll know when we've dug it out. If it's too big, we break it up down here. You thought digging was hard work! Likely to kill a forping clux."

Finbarl nodded his understanding.

"Why do you never rise to my insults?" asked a perplexed Balfour. "Been poking you since we first met."

"You're just an old curmudgeon," said Finbarl with a smile. "I've seen your type before. Bitter at the world, not me. Every insult contains the answer to my questions or offers advice. I think you like me."

"Bah!" Balfour sneered then stuck two fingers in his mouth and whistled. Bobbing candles approached in the darkness, sweating bodies appearing.

"What you got?" asked the first.

"Just clearing the face," answered Balfour, holding the axe by its neck, chipping away at the soil. A silvery surface emerged, flecked with a red layer that crumbled with the waste.

"Looks substantial," remarked another voice.

"I'll take centre," said Balfour. "Start digging three yards either side. No, make it four."

"What is it?" asked Finbarl, standing back out of the way.

"Too early to tell, but my gut says a vehicle." Balfour used his fingers to brush off clinging dirt. "Dug one out a few years ago."

"What sort of vehicle?"

"The sort that don't get dug out by talking!"

Taking the hint, Finbarl moved in with his spade.

With care, they ate away at the soil, exposing a warped metal surface. Wooden pillars now lined the walls, hammered into place as it threatened to crumble.

"It's at an angle," commented Balfour. "We're going to have to dig high. Never good for creating a stable tunnel."

Finbarl continued shovelling, his eyes following the progress with fascination.

"Yes, definitely a vehicle," remarked Balfour. "This crushed gap is where they sat."

"And they just threw it away?" queried Finbarl. "I don't ..." He froze. Something wasn't right.

"Balfour, your candle. It's flickering with a blue-green flame."

With a twitch of his nose, Balfour stopped. He scanned his companions. Their flames danced with similar hues. "Tools down: candles out! Everyone! Nice and gentle."

A surreal, slow-motion drama played out. The furious activity ceased as men snuffed out all flames and crept backwards, placing their axes and spades gently on the ground. Complete darkness surrounded them.

Finbarl licked dry lips. "I can't smell gas."

"Odourless. Can you feel your way to the crawl tunnel? We need to get out as quickly as possible."

A body bumped into Finbarl. Arms reached out, flapping in search of a surface. Finbarl wanted to scream; he was feeling disorientated and trapped.

"I've found it!" A voice pierced the darkness. "Follow my voice. Here, here, here, here ..."

Shoulders collided, nudging Finbarl towards the guiding voice.

"One at a time. Don't push!"

Finbarl recognised the rim of the crawl tunnel and eased himself onto his stomach. His heart thumped; his head spun. Behind, he heard a thud.

"Faster!" came a cry.

With gritted teeth, Finbarl wriggled on. Elbow forward. Knee forward. Push. A foot in front slipped, slamming into his face. He ignored the pain. An impatient hand behind clipped his heel. He ignored it. Elbow forward. Knee forward. Push.

Finally, Finbarl emerged into a wide tunnel, fingertips no longer brushing along the wall. He tried to stand. Deprived of his senses, he stumbled. His hand struck a body.

"Hold my shoulder," said a voice. "I'm in a train."

Finbarl's fingers touched the man's protruding ribs, working their way to his shoulder. A hand struck his back, climbing up him with similar intent. The human train shuffled forward.

It was a hopeless sensation: blind and led by the blind. Finbarl's mind wandered to Bartarnous. Was this how he felt? Frightened, alone, lost. A regret formed amid the fear. He had not always treated his friend with the respect he deserved. He had ignored his warnings, under-appreciating what he saw despite those useless eyes. Finbarl cursed his own arrogance.

A low rumble built behind. Finbarl's ears popped. A rush of air followed. Then came a roar.

KABOOM!

Finbarl turned. A consuming flame galloped down the narrow tunnel, escaping with a leap. As a voice cried "Down!" Finbarl flew off his feet, crashing into others. Heat tickled his throat, as his lungs fought for oxygen. A second later an eerie silence returned. No one moved. A beam creaked; a lump of soil fell. And then another. One man groaned. The creak built to a crack. Another roar, as the roof collapsed, burying all.

PART THREE

Chapter Forty-Two

"**A**h, you have the king's armour."

Aminatra turned, her arms loaded with a breastplate and helmet amid one of the countless palace passageways. "Master Klout! You surprised me. It's good to see you again."

The teenager stood upright, proud in his own armour. "I've been busy. Father needs all the support he can get now he's helping run the kingdom. It is good he gives me more responsibility. I feel more of an Adonelisian." He flicked at an armplate, listening with pleasure at the resonating clang. "Word reaches me that you too have an improved status, caring for the king himself. How is he?"

An imperceptible frown met the question. "He grows impatient locked in his room for months on end, Master."

"You've done well keeping him safe. Many enemies remained within Adonelis. Father's now defeated all. It's time for the king to lead his army and take on our enemies beyond. At last, I will earn my scars in battle."

"You're becoming like your father. He must be proud, Master." Aminatra's eye caught sight of blood still staining the wall, the attempt to wash it off half-hearted.

"I hope so," said Klout, oblivious to Aminatra's disappointment and criticism. "Adonelis has been passive for too long, while Parodis expands its control."

"Parodis! You're invading Parodis?"

"Of course. With them defeated, the river will be open, the fertile land accessible. They won't be able to hold others to ransom with their control of trade and extortionate food prices."

"What sort of army do they have?" asked Aminatra, a faint hope rising in her.

"One more interested in how it looks than how it fights," chuckled Klout, tapping his own breastplate. "In open battle there can only be one victor. But control of the river is their strength. Father has long been thinking about a strategy to defeat them."

"And the king, Master? What is his role?"

"Why, he must lead his army. The men will fight better knowing he's with them."

"But he's a child?"

"An Adonelis child: without fear or mercy."

"And should he die, Master, who will be king?"

"He won't, Athenia. You should not say such things! Father will win the battle and keep him safe. The future is bright in father's hands."

"Sorry, Master. Adonelis is lucky to possess such a powerful and benevolent ruler."

"It is," said Klout, nodding his head. "Now, I've kept you long enough. You'd better run and get the king ready. We must not keep Father waiting."

"Yes, Master," said Aminatra, bowing in deference, wondering which was the fabrication: the stereotype Adonelisian Klout now claimed to be or the insecure boy seeking a different life she used to know.

***

Two guards stood on duty before the king's chamber. Malic's men. Their facial scars were as expressive as their downturned mouths. On seeing Aminatra, one opened the door's spyhole, peering in. Satisfied, he turned the key, prising open the door for Aminatra to squeeze through. It slammed behind her.

"Ah, Athenia. Come look at this!" King Andolis, kneeling on the windowsill, stretched his neck for a view outside. An engrossed Karlmon and Coloss occupied the remaining space. "My army is mobilising. Thousands gather in the square. Perhaps they rise to rescue me from imprisonment?" He turned, seeking Aminatra's reaction. "What is that?"

"The general has instructed me to bring and dress you in your armour."

"That traitor!" exclaimed Andolis. "He wants me to play soldier while confined. Well, I won't!"

"He wants you to lead the army in battle against Parodis," explained Aminatra.

Andolis's face changed. "Lead my army? I told you they gathered for me. Quick, dress me!"

"It's dangerous," stressed Aminatra. "I don't trust General Malic. He claims they've locked you in your room for your own safety."

"Dress me, Athenia," demanded Andolis, dropping from the sill. "I'll soon have an army behind me, obeying my every word. Malic will be the one locked up."

"Hold this, Coloss," requested Aminatra, passing the bodyguard the helmet. "He wouldn't let you out to place his own freedom in jeopardy." Her fingers grappled with the ties on the breastplate.

"You put the leather jerkin on me first," stated Andolis, with a frustrated glare. "Then the armour."

"Do I get armour?" asked Karlmon, watching from the window, with Libellia in his arms.

"No!" snapped Aminatra. "You're not fighting anyone. And come away from the edge with Libellia."

"Adonelisians are the finest warriors in the world," declared Andolis. "Slaves are not worthy to fight for us."

A crestfallen Karlmon returned his gaze on the scene outside, pointing to things to stimulate Libellia's interest.

"But you will all come with me," continued the king. "An army requires more than soldiers and a king his retinue."

"Tie it tight. That's it." Andolis tugged at his armour, adjusting his body until comfortable. He glided over to his mirror. "My helmet!"

Coloss lowered the embossed helmet onto the king's head.

"It's heavy," complained Andolis.

"But it looks marvellous," opined Karlmon, admiring the delicate frills that ringed the edge as a crown.

"I do," agreed Andolis. "Father made it for me." He jutted out his jaw and spread his feet, admiring his reflection. "None dare disobey this king!"

A knock sounded on the door. All eyes turned in suspense. It swung open and General Malic stood with hands on hips and a broad smile, magnificent in his own armour. He bowed.

"Your Majesty. It is wonderful to see you after all this time."

"Malic! What is the meaning of locking me up?" cried Andolis.

"My liege, please forgive me." Malic bowed again, hands out-stretched, offered to his king. "The queen is still at large. I had evidence her spies infiltrated my household. They plotted your death. All confessed under torture."

"I see," said the king, his expression now puzzled. He tentatively held out his hands, allowing Malic to hold them. "Well, I, err, thank you for your loyal service."

"It is I who must thank you for your patience and understanding, Sire," said Malic, lifting the boy's hands to his mouth and kissing them. "I did not wish to distress you with details and so kept my distance."

"Of course. Of course." Andolis nodded, each sentence from the general disarming him further. "And how do we come to be at war with Parodis?"

"They harbour the queen and her son, Sire. While both live, your crown remains under threat."

The king waggled a finger toward Coloss. "You see. How many times have I said Parodis plots against us? Their destruction will pave the way for a world based on Sym La Panau's principles."

The giant's placid eyes acknowledged his master, then, as Andolis turned back to Malic, winced toward Aminatra.

"You look every part the warrior king, Sire," Malic eulogised. "And, if I may say, like your father. He often spent the night in this room before a campaign." Malic scanned the space, pausing on the splendour of the ornate mirror and bed. "It helped him focus and prepare."

"I am very focussed, having been here so long," remarked Andolis, earning a faint smirk from Aminatra.

"And now your army awaits you, Sire. I have selected the best men to form your bodyguard."

"Excellent. I'll inspect them now." The king skipped from the room under the spell of regal fulfilment.

An emotionless mask fell on Malic's face as he turned to those who remained. "Have the king's possessions packed in trunks. You will follow in the baggage train. Everything must be ready for him after every day's march. We leave at noon."

Chapter Forty-Three

Finbarl swung his pickaxe. A clean strike. He eased the head out and watched the soil tumble down. A twinge shot through his arm. He winced, rubbing it with his other hand.

"Quit shirking, you lazy clux." Balfour stopped for a breath.

"It's been broken, burnt and buried," said Finbarl, shaking his arm. "Just getting used to working it hard again."

"You're lucky it works at all. I was certain you were dead."

"Lucky!" Finbarl snorted. "Invalided for three months and fined three years for the pleasure! Those who died are the lucky ones. What about you? Barely a scratch."

Balfour smiled. "They don't call me the mole for nothing. You did well to spot the candle. More would have died otherwise."

"I'll know to crawl faster next time."

"You seem free of the jitters," remarked Balfour, the candlelight extenuating his gaunt features. "Returning to the tunnels after what you went through isn't easy."

Finbarl opened his mouth, a denial hanging on his lips. He paused. "No, it wasn't easy," he said instead. "The dark, the smell, the noise: they all stir up dread. Didn't eat this morning. Just no appetite."

A bell rang in the distance, infiltrating each tunnel.

"Lunch. How's that appetite now?" asked Balfour, arching his back to alleviate the aches.

"I think I could manage something," remarked Finbarl. "The morning's shot by. Could have sworn we've another hour before noon."

"That's the thing about never seeing the sun. You lose track." Balfour already trudged along the shaft, hunched and automated.

With a scratch to his head, Finbarl followed, bending to crawl through the trolley tunnel. "Oh, look out for the pool of vomit I spewed on the track this morning." A grin spread as Balfour cursed his name in the darkness.

Tired eyes winced in pain as they surfaced, daylight piercing their subterranean sensitivities. Finbarl, one hand on a ladder rung, shielded his eyes.

"Don't stop!" urged Balfour, his muscles eager for rest.

Relief accompanied the last step back to the surface. Finbarl allowed the fresher air to bathe him, the sun to stir his core. His eyes remained shut, unable to cope, but it felt good. Balfour shuffled up next to him, his nostrils sniffing, eyes squeezed tight.

"Can't smell any food," he commented. "Don't tell me they're watering down the broth."

Finbarl eased one eye open, persevering with a glowing blur. Shadowy figures mixed with the drab colours of the Flash. He opened his other eye. The world came into focus; the pain subsided. "There's no food?"

"That's not good," said Balfour, his own eyes adjusting. "Sun's not where it should be. It ain't noon."

The servenites continued emerging from a dozen shafts and channels, mingling in a confused mass, their faces and clothes loaded with grime.

"Who rang the bell?" Several asked the question.

No answer came, only an order. "Line up!" An overweight Parodisian official hurried back and forth, delicately placing his boots between the most sodden mud. His vibrant clothes looked ridiculous amid the devastation of the Flash. He waved a scroll, pointing all towards a growing row. Behind, a group of five soldiers stood, silent and watching.

"Hurry! Hurry!" cried the official, cringing at the discovery of mud on his sleeve. "I have an important announcement."

Chaos ensued as the disenfranchised miners flexed their only muscle: annoying authority with a display of time-wasting.

"What's going on?" asked Finbarl, joining the half-formed column next to Balfour.

"Don't know. Not liking the company of forping soldiers. Means they're going to persuade us to do something."

Finbarl leaned towards Balfour and whispered. "We could overpower them. Steal their weapons. Escape."

"Have you ever tried to outrun a horse?" asked Balfour. "They'd hunt us down within the hour. And look at you!"

"Not seen my reflection for a while," quipped Finbarl, but aware he now owned the typical pallor and wasted appearance of a servenite. "Anyway, better to die trying than continue like this."

"Let's hear what they have to say before committing suicide."

Overhead, a crow and buzzard tussled in a spiralling dive. Finbarl allowed his mind to wander, imagining the gift of flight. Oh, to be so free, he thought. To flap your wings and travel. A small bird flitted past the aerial engagement, exploiting the distraction. Finbarl joined him, his mind escaping into the wind.

"Silence!" cried the official, shaking Finbarl from his daydream. "Adonelis has mobilised her army. Agents report they seek conquest of the world. Their aim is to first defeat the champion of freedom, Parodis."

Finbarl snorted in derision.

"We need volunteers to join the army," continued the official, prodding his scroll towards the servenites. "Few need an incentive to protect their mother city, but our government is nothing if not generous. Each day as a soldier is worth double towards paying off your debt. Your names will be immortalised with the heroes of the past. Step forward to volunteer."

A third took a stride without hesitation. Finbarl went to join them.

"What are you doing?" hissed Balfour, grabbing him by the arm.

"Volunteering," replied Finbarl. "You heard. It will halve my debt and ..."

"Don't be a forping fool! Who do you think leads the line in battle? Who do you think they'll sacrifice for a strategic goal? Heroes of the past means the same as dead."

"But ..."

"The Adonelisians may be dumb cluxes, but they're vicious brutes and magnificent fighters. You wouldn't stand a chance."

Ignoring Balfour, Finbarl took the step. He turned. "This is my best chance to get to Aminatra and Karlmon. We defeat the Adonelisians and free them. Anyway, Parodis has the Unumverum."

"You're making a mistake, my friend," cautioned Balfour, as further servenites made the commitment. "All the Unumverum will say is hide behind the city walls, block the river, and don't risk the Kilshare cavalry. It always does."

"That's fine," said Finbarl, standing to attention as though back on parade with the Athenian guards. "Then I won't have a battle to fight."

The official walked down the line, inspecting his volunteers. Every now and again, when a victim of the Flash's vengeance stood before him, a limb missing or ribs showing, he shook his head, returning them to the line. His eyes fell on Finbarl's scarred left arm.

"I hold a sword in my right," declared Finbarl.

The man nodded, walking on to the next volunteer.

"Wait!" Balfour stepped forward with a mumble. "I'll volunteer."

"Fine," uttered the official, adding a mark to his scroll and moving on.

"What did you do that for?" whispered Finbarl.

"Better to die trying than continue like this," said Balfour with a wry smile.

Chapter Forty-Four

Aminatra scurried between rooms, grabbing at clothes, flustered and annoyed. With arms full, she returned to the palace hall, where several trunks lay open. She found a half-empty one and released her load.

"Is this going to be enough?" she asked herself. After three months in proximity to the king and his fickle demands, she suspected not. "Coloss, help me find another trunk!"

He lumbered over, awaiting further instructions.

"This isn't enough," she said, seeking Coloss's confirmation. "We haven't even packed crockery yet."

A slow nod reassured Aminatra she worried with good reason.

"I know where we can find one. Come on!"

The palace now seethed with activity. Soldiers' hurried footsteps clicked and clattered upon the marble floors, while barefoot slaves progressed with a more benign patter. Aminatra allowed Coloss to lead, his bulk clearing the way.

"Down these stairs," instructed Aminatra from behind.

A child slave, younger than Karlmon, dashed past them on the stairs carrying a small urn. Coloss reached out, patting the boy on the head. The young eyes turned to marvel at the giant while his feet continued to climb.

"Be careful," warned Aminatra with a mother's smile. "Look where you're going, or you'll drop it."

"Do you have any children?" she asked of Coloss.

Melancholy eyes answered.

"Karlmon is very fond of you." It seemed the right thing to say. "He never knew his real father. Probably for the best. Finbarl became one to him."

Coloss listened with his usual patience; Aminatra was content to muse on the past and her family.

"I think Karlmon has matured in the last year. Maddy helped. They helped each other develop. She was the big sister he craved and he the bridge to our strange world for her. The way he looks after Libellia and Andolis: he doesn't complain, knows what's going on.

"Ah, here we are. Grab a lamp from the corridor. I can't see anything." The cold, dank air confirmed they had reached the lowest depths of the building. "I remember spotting some old trunks in here when I first explored."

The light exposed cobwebs and dust everywhere. Few visited that far into the palace. Coloss waved the lamp to his left and right, delving deeper into the room. Boxes, urns and barrels lay strewn on the floor, discarded without care.

"What's that pong?" exclaimed Aminatra, holding her nose. "Ah, there they are." She pointed to a corner. "Not great, but they'll do. Might need to clear them before we try moving."

Coloss pulled the first trunk out and lifted its lid. Stagnant air wafted out, mixing with the rancid odour of the room.

"Mouldy rugs and mats," said Aminatra, lifting each out to examine against the light. "We didn't have anything like this in Athenia. Not a bad thing. They're grim. The mould's the most colourful thing on there." She peered into the empty crate. "Oh, no. The corner's disintegrated. This won't do. Let's hope the other one's okay."

"That stink's stronger." She wafted a hand before her nose. "I remember smelling something similar in Athenia. You had all sorts of aromas escaping the sewers and ditches, without knowing what was rotting."

The second trunk jammed as Coloss pulled on it, caught up in the jigsaw of discarded containers. He kicked at an adjacent box and yanked again, grunting with effort.

"Heavier, eh?"

It slid out, thumping to the floor, setting a plume of dust into the air. Coloss tapped on the edge, signalling to the coughing Aminatra.

"A lock. Cronax! Can you break it?"

He gripped the hang lock, twisting it until a loud crack.

"Well, if it's that easy to get in, can't be that precious," said Aminatra with a laugh. She held the latch and heaved it open.

"CRONAX!" Aminatra reeled back in horror, a hand covering her mouth and nose as an overwhelming stink escaped.

Even Coloss, that purveyor of palace retribution, recoiled at the sight. Two dead, putrefying bodies lay folded within.

Aminatra edged forward, fingers pinching her nostrils shut. "It's the queen and her son! The ferralax had them murdered and hidden. Parodis isn't harbouring anyone!"

Shielded by Aminatra, Coloss peeked over her head, shaking his in disgust.

"He lied to justify a war," fumed Aminatra. "I thought the Adonelisians prized honesty and integrity above all else. What do we do now?"

Coloss pointed to the trunk and then up.

"We can't," said Aminatra, brushing a cobweb from her hair. "Those are Malic's men in the palace. Just the smell will attract curiosity. We leave it here but tell the king. Malic mustn't know we know his secret." She dropped the lid, closing her eyes in relief. "I don't want to even think what Athenia's sewers held!"

***

King Andolis stood regaled in his armour before a mirror, feet apart, hands on hips. "Good. I'm glad she's dead."

"But General Malic lied," stressed Aminatra, pacing and agitated. "He murdered royalty and an infant."

"A usurper and her child who both wished me dead," countered the king, rotating to view his side profile. "I should have your tongue cut out for such talk."

"Oh, yes, punish those trying to help you with the truth!" Aminatra's hands clenched in frustration.

"I'll forgive you, as I've welcomed your conversation while I've been ... err, preparing. Anyway, it does not matter that the queen is not in Parodis. They are our enemy, and a king must have a glorious start to his reign."

"Why are they your enemy?" pressed Aminatra. "Innocent people will die."

"There are no innocent people in Parodis. All plot to destroy Adonelis."

"Your Majesty," said Aminatra, trying a different approach. "A wise king decides based on evidence, like your father. What plots do you talk about? Have you ever met someone from Parodis?"

"Athenia, you will not stop me from leading my army!" Andolis resisted a welling tantrum. He closed his eyes, regaining composure. "A king must always remain in control. Now, no more talk on the subject. You have packed all I need?"

"Yes, Sire."

"My perfumes? I expect life with my army will be hard."

"Including your perfumes." Aminatra had long ago conquered the urge to scream at the king's foolish behaviour. He was but a child, after all.

Chapter Forty-Five

"They've not even let me hold a sword yet," grumbled Finbarl, lifting another stone and placing it within the wall. They worked outside the city perimeters, exposed in the sweltering sun. He stopped to rub his shoulder.

"I guess soldiering only requires fighting on the odd day," opined Balfour, scratching at an old sore on his leg. "The rest of the time, it's preparing for the fight. Be thankful we're not repairing the bridge. They'll only destroy it again when the Adonelisians turn up.

"Your jab hurting? Ain't a pretty procedure."

"It's sore," answered Finbarl, inspecting the shoulder wound. "Otherwise, I don't feel any different."

"You're not supposed to. If you catch mencoctitus, you'll know it's worked. You'll still be alive!" Balfour's laugh carried a mournful edge.

"Amazing. I've read about inoculation but assumed it a lost art."

"Typical Parodis," snorted Balfour, kicking at a stone to force it into place. "Good enough for us once we're in the army but sod those servenites digging for metal. It's cos we're mixing with them now. Not hid away. Bless the army. Saves your life so you can die fighting."

"But if they don't train us, how we going to fight?" Finbarl stepped back, judging his repairs of the city defences. With the river wrapped along two edges of Parodis and the escarpment on another, only one sector required a wall. A structure grander and thicker than anything Athenia once had, yet neglect accompanied peace and time. Sections crumbled, while cracks worked down the stonework, a legacy of recent tremors.

"Anyway, we might not have to fight," said Balfour, inspecting his own work. "If Parodis controls the river and holds out, we're assured of victory. The navy and cavalry may undertake the odd sortie to undermine and demoralise the enemy, but time and disease will do for those cluxes in the end. No offence."

"Finbarl!" A restrained, unseen voice called out.

Finbarl looked up, the sun blinding him. "Who's that?" He shielded his eyes and squinted.

"It's Allus." A small, silhouetted head appeared at the top of the wall. "I heard you had joined the army."

"Allus! It's good to see you. Be careful up there. It's a long way to fall."

"My feet don't touch the ground," giggled Allus, her frame squeezed between the ramparts.

"Any news on finding Pet?"

"Carry on working," chided Balfour. "The punishment for slacking in the army is more severe than in the Flash."

"No," answered Allus. "And little hope, now we're at war with Adonelis."

Finbarl lugged another stone into a gap. "Well, things are looking up for me. This is my best chance at getting my family back."

"Is there anything I can do for you, Finbarl?"

The question surprised Finbarl, who was unused to kindness. He dropped another stone in place, brushing his hands free of dust as he thought. "Get word to Bartarnous that I'm here. I would like to talk with him."

"Yes, yes. Of course. Anything else?"

"Get me a sword! Sorry, no, joking. How's everyone else? You had your vaccine yet?" He showed off his raw shoulder.

"No, Lhaluma says the Adonelisians have poisoned it to weaken Parodisian defences. Prefer to take my chances without."

Balfour responded with a derisive sniff.

"But everyone's excited by the war and the upcoming reading of the Unumverum," continued an oblivious Allus. "Lhaluma wants to join the navy. Dae suggests we all should, but I'm not keen. Too short and I don't have a good record on boats."

"Yes, you stay away from the fighting. When's the reading?"

"Tomorrow."

"Ask Bartarnous to come after." Finbarl held a rock in mid-motion, his mind momentarily distracted. "I hope they don't still blame Maddy for Favo's death."

"Pet's betrayal has confused us all. They don't know what to think any more. Lies leave a stain which even the truth has trouble washing out. Sorry, Finbarl, I must go. There's lots to do to prepare for tomorrow. I'll say you asked after them."

"Thanks."

A heavy cloud obscured the sun, allowing Finbarl to see the top of the wall. Allus had gone.

"A friend?" asked Balfour with a sly wink.

"Yes, a friend and just a friend."

"Well, she likes you. Made an effort to find and help you. Though not too bright, which may explain it. Poisoned, my arse!"

"Can't a person just help as a kindness?" Finbarl slammed a stone down, hoping his colleague got the message.

"In Parodis?" laughed Balfour. "The City of Self. That's what others call us. Couldn't see it myself until they made me an outsider.

Making the individual king is fine until people become too entitled to remember their responsibilities. Fancy believing only you'd be immune to a deadly disease. If it wasn't for the Unumverum, Parodis would have eaten itself long ago."

"It is bewitching," agreed Finbarl. "I mean, I fell for it."

"We all do. Like moths to a flame. Anyway, I was wrong to say the girl fancied you."

"Thanks. That's okay."

"Yeah, why would a Parodisian fancy a clux?" Balfour's toothless grin emerged, triggering a fit of laughter.

"Stop it! You'll get us fined," pleaded Finbarl, himself consumed in a mirthful fit.

Chapter Forty-Six

Dust saturated the air, kicked up by ten thousand pairs of soldiers' boots and horses' hooves. A dry spring and long summer had left the land parched. Clouds on the horizon threatened rain but brought none.

Coloss sat clasping reins, rocking to the ungainly rhythm of his wagon, pulled by two slow but determined oxen, his mood sullen.

"It's good to be out of Adonelis," remarked Aminatra, swaying at his side, grateful for the veil keeping the dust from her nose and mouth. "There is some freedom in travel."

Coloss's silence accentuated the continual grind of wheels upon the sandy stone.

"I would be quite glad never to see the place again," continued Aminatra, her memory retrieving an image of the decapitated heads on stakes lining the road from the city. The baggage train moved at a painful, slow pace while the preceding massed army filtered along a narrow stretch. Glazed, lifeless eyes stared from every victim and Aminatra had wondered what crime each committed to deserve such a fate. Only a crow answered her, perched on a rotting head, tugging on the colourful beads entangled within the ginger hairs of a beard.

"Missing Andolis?" asked Aminatra, keen to erase the thought from her mind. "Or perhaps worried about him?"

The latter diagnosis received a near unperceivable nod.

"Me too," said Aminatra, her own feelings towards the boy an ambiguous crash of fondness and hate. "Malic has him just where he wants: surrounded by his own men, but in view of the army. Wouldn't surprise me if this entire war was part of a plan to steal the throne."

"Ando can look after himself." Karlmon's head appeared from behind a trunk on the wagon.

"You're awake. Feeling better?" asked Aminatra.

"Yes. I shouldn't have eaten before the journey. This rocks more than the boat!"

Aminatra turned with a knowing smile. "I did say."

The baggage train languished miles behind the army now, its cumbersome loads unable to match the pace of the infantry or cavalry. What they lacked in speed, they made up for in size. Hundreds of wagons and carts formed their own column, following the dust cloud and creating their own.

Karlmon fidgeted his way on top of the foremost trunk. "Will we get to see the fighting?"

"I pray not," said Aminatra. "Don't you remember how scared you were when the prisoners stormed the garrison at Athenia?"

"Not really."

"Lucky you. People do terrible things in war. The Adonelisians do terrible things in peace. I hope Finbarl and Maddy are nowhere near Parodis."

"And Captain Tarlobus and his boat," added Karlmon.

"Hopefully, they're all together on their way to Mandelaton."

Mention of the name made Coloss perk up.

"Why don't they come looking for us?" asked Karlmon.

The question tortured Aminatra throughout her time in Adonelis. "They won't know we're here." She left the most obvious answer unspoken, not willing to countenance death as their fate.

"Perhaps someone in Parodis will know where they are," said Karlmon, death having never crossed his mind.

"Maybe," concurred Aminatra, "but I doubt we'll speak to anyone from the city. They're the 'enemy', remember?"

"Not once the Adonelisians win. We'll all be friends then."

"Stay innocent," whispered Aminatra to herself before addressing her companions again. "The river provides us with an opportunity to escape. We'll find a boat and sail away. Can you sail?" She turned to Coloss.

He shook his head.

"Pity. We learnt a little with Tarlobus, but ... We may just have to risk it."

"But what about Ando?" asked Karlmon. "We can't leave him on his own."

"We don't involve him or mention it to him," urged Aminatra, looking Karlmon in the eye. "Sometimes you've no choice but to leave those you love and start over. His life is with his own kind. Only death awaits us if we stay."

"But isn't that what's awaiting him too?" said Karlmon. "Malic will only keep Ando alive for so long or lock him up again."

"My son has grown wise in your company." Aminatra patted Coloss's shoulder. She strained her neck to face Karlmon. "We still can't trust him. He doesn't understand like you do."

Karlmon grimaced, hurt by the insinuation against his friend.

"When the two cities fight each other," continued Aminatra, "they won't care about us. We'll use the chaos to slip away. It will still be dangerous, but it's our best chance. If the Parodisians win, we'll return to search for Finbarl and Maddy; if the Adonelisians ... well, we get as far away as possible. You can take us to Mandelaton. Eh, Coloss?"

The big man smiled, a cheer escaping as a hoot.

"Karlmon?"

The boy slumped back down in the depths of the wagon, arms folded under his sour face.

"We'll let him sulk," confided Aminatra in Coloss's ear. "There's little positive I can promise him." She studied the landscape. Red hills, worn and etched by run-off channels, lay to the east. The sun emphasised the shadowy recesses, while dark brewing clouds behind allowed the rich colour to glow. Such beauty and yet nullified by the pain inside. 'Where are you, Finbarl?' she mouthed.

Chapter Forty-Seven

Finbarl ran, head bent, laughing aloud, one impotent hand defending his eyes as a deluge fell from the sky. He had never known rain like it. His feet splashed through puddles, too numerous to evade.

"Rainy season!" cried Balfour, a stride behind, his voice almost lost in the clattering downpour.

Both ducked into a doorway, deep enough to offer shelter. A stream weaved down the hill, bearing the golden sand of the path.

"I'm drenched!" laughed Finbarl, squeezing the end of his sleeve.

"It's forping early," shouted Balfour, just an arm's reach from Finbarl. "At least a month early."

"Who cares?" yelled back Finbarl, flicking his sodden fringe from his eyes. "I love it!"

"You don't understand," said Balfour, his voice easing with the lighter rain, but full of emotion. "It's wonderful news. You can't campaign in the rainy season. Try moving horses and a hundred wagons through mud. The Adonelisians gambled with their timing, hoping to surprise us. Mother Nature's rescued Parodis."

Disappointment fell upon Finbarl's face. "But they will be back soon?"

"After the rainy season. But a lot can happen over three months. They won't send us back to the Flash. Too much work still to do on the defences."

"I suppose I can wait another three months," said Finbarl, his eyes staring into space as his anger and frustration were aroused, trapped within. "The Unumverum will have foreseen this, I guess?"

"We'll find out from your friend," said Balfour, sticking out a hand, checking for the last of the rain. "Move on. We have little free time before we're absento. Clouds are clearing."

With a leap over the still gushing stream, they made their way into the winding alleys of Parodis. Finbarl, unfamiliar with the area, was in Balfour's wake.

"Fic! Watch out, you clux!" swore Balfour, ducking left as a window opened, followed by the contents of a bucket. "A bonus of the rainy season," he explained for Finbarl. "Leaky roofs."

"Better than what they threw in Athenia," said Finbarl.

"All you've told me about that place sounds worse than Parodis, and that's saying something."

"It is," agreed Finbarl. "But I miss it in a funny way."

"Fic, who wouldn't miss man-eating monsters, no rain and no freedom."

"Ha, no. That's not what I mean, and they weren't man-eating. Most of my worst memories lie there, but also the best. I miss the dry heat as the chill of the night air departs, the feeling you get when you're parched and drink fresh, cold water, or you've not eaten all day and you smell dinner. A flower blossoming where before it was desert. The silence when you're ..."

"Okay, I get it. You miss it."

"And Aminatra and Karlmon," added Finbarl.

"Yeah, well, they're not there any more."

"I wouldn't miss Athenia as much if they were still with me."

"Quit brooding," said Balfour with typical dispassion. "We're almost there. Is that your friend under the pergola? Doesn't look like no normal Parodisian to me."

"That's Bartarnous," confirmed Finbarl, recognising the large, shabby scholar and his tic. His flattened hair indicated the rain had caught him too. "Bartarnous! It's Finbarl."

The old man shuffled round, his flickering eyes circling the arrivals. "Finbarl. Good to hear from you. You have a companion?"

"A friend," announced Finbarl. "Balfour, this is Master Bartarnous."

"I've heard about you," said Balfour, holding out a hand in greeting.

"You've not got a great record when it comes to making friends," remarked Bartarnous, his nose twitching in Balfour's direction, no hand offered in return.

"Balfour's all right," said Finbarl. "He's a servenite like me."

"That just means he owes money," Bartarnous stated.

"Your reputation ain't so great, old man," countered Balfour. "A nutty, blind scholar who no one listens to. And you didn't even have the decency to tell my friend here about servenites."

The recrimination caught Bartarnous by surprise. "I ... I warned him of his ways and the company he kept. One doesn't talk of such distasteful things as consequences."

"Enough!" demanded Finbarl. "It doesn't matter. You can trust Balfour." He laid a reassuring hand on Bartarnous's shoulder. "And, nutty you may be, but you know what you're talking about. He sees as well as you or me, perhaps further, just not with his eyes." A nod from Balfour met Finbarl's glance.

"You honour me with your description." Bartarnous's face, enigmatic for a second, broke into a smile and his familiar laugh.

"How are you?" asked Finbarl.

"Not the man I was, with my friends Maddy and Finbarl to entertain me. And war does not suit my disposition. I prefer rapier words to the thrust of a sword." Bartarnous's fingers ran down Finbarl's arm. "You feel … leaner."

"I'm as I was when I arrived in Parodis," answered Finbarl, self-conscious and defensive. "The city softened me."

"Make sure the Flash and the army doesn't harden you," urged Bartarnous. "You are so much more than the refugee I first met, but you must walk the right path to become that person."

"He talks funny," said Balfour.

"You just need to discover the wisdom between the nonsense." Finbarl smiled at the unseeing Bartarnous, remembering the scholar's similar words on Maddy. "Have you attended the Unumverum reading?"

"Of course. I have been in chambers all morning. All this talk of war tires an old man. I don't argue as well as once I did. Or perhaps others don't listen like they once did? It is difficult owning a lonely point of view."

"What did you disagree on?" asked Finbarl.

"It is not important. The council have made their decision. I may seek solace in solitude and hide from this war and its ripples. Yes, that is what I must do. I must seek my sanctuary."

"But the rains …" began Balfour.

"And the Unumverum," cut in Finbarl. "What has the book foretold?"

"Oh, the usual," said Bartarnous with a casual wave. "Victory will be ours, blah blah blah."

"When? How?" pressed Finbarl.

"Did it mention the early rains?" added Balfour.

"Nothing so specific. You should know the book doesn't deal in minutia. It makes mention of nature's part. Perhaps that is the early season. Yes, that will be it. As to 'when', it will be to Parodis' advantage and not before."

"That's vague," remarked Balfour.

"Is foreseeing the future not impressive enough for you? You want it to tell the time, too."

"Just helpful to know when I'm going to fight for my life and Parodis' future," said Balfour, unimpressed.

"And how?" asked Finbarl again.

"In the city is our strength," announced Bartarnous. "So says the Unumverum."

"As clear as mud," snorted Balfour.

"Perhaps to the untrained mind," retorted Bartarnous, his gesticulating hand striking the pergola's frame. "I paraphrase, of course. But the meaning was clear. Parodis is impregnable. If we control the river, a siege, no matter how long, cannot starve us out. The walls hold off all to the west: allies and time will wear down the invader. You'll have little need to venture out to battle, my brave little warriors."

"But will Parodis defeat them?" Finbarl asked. "If Adonelis still stands, how will I get Aminatra and Karlmon back?"

"Beyond the parameters of the book, dear Finbarl. It is only Parodis' fate it concerns."

"Cronax!" cursed Finbarl, before a thought struck him. "I could go to Adonelis now, while their army's away. Sneak in and find them."

"Don't be a clux!" said Balfour. "You'll have their army in your path. And the rains. They'll be retreating to Adonelis."

"But when they arrive here," persisted Finbarl.

"The city won't be undefended. Even their babies learn to hold a sword. You wouldn't stand a chance."

"They don't have a gun, though!"

"What's a gun?"

"Nothing," said Finbarl. "Just an Athenian weapon." The boast deflated as he remembered the gun went missing with his bags. "Not much use against a defended city."

"Your forthright friend is right," interjected Bartarnous. "It is a fool's errand. Parodis's victory is foretold, but not Adonelis's destruction. You can but hope for some turmoil in the wake and exploit it."

Chapter Forty-Eight

"It's not fair. I'm king!" Andolis sat curled up in the tent's corner, thumb in mouth, his cheeks burnt red with tears.

"She is pretty," said Aminatra, hoping to at least stop his crying, which had set Libellia off.

"But she's not a princess!" yelled the king, pressing his face into the musty canvas. "She's a common general's daughter."

"And you've explained this to General Malic?" asked Aminatra, rocking her baby in her arms.

This prompted another outpouring of tears.

"He threatened Ando," pointed out Karlmon as he tidied the crockery thrown at the start of the king's strop.

"So, marry Bethu or lose throne and life?" summarised Aminatra. "We warned you. This is Malic's way to control the kingdom legitimately, but he'll resort to illegitimate means if necessary."

"I hate him!" screamed Andolis, his hands searching for something to throw but finding nothing.

"So, what will you do?" asked Aminatra, allowing Libellia to grip her little finger.

"I'll have him flayed alive!"

"Not what you would like to do. What can you practically do?"

The question stopped the tears but prompted a frown. "I ... I ... What would you suggest?"

Aminatra smiled at Libellia, the baby's tears ceasing in preference of blowing bubbles. "None of the other generals want Malic to have so much power. Do you trust any of them? I mean, trust them not to do what Malic is trying to do."

A statelier manner occupied Andolis. He sat upright, considering the question. "You are right. I can play them against one another. I trust none – Father taught me that – but together they'll unite against Malic."

"Good," said Aminatra, impressed with the suggestion. "Somehow we must get them together without Malic discovering."

"But they watch the king at all times," said Karlmon. "The guards outside will have heard your shouting."

"Then they will fear a king's wrath," declared Andolis, rising to his feet. "You have proved a loyal and worthy slave, Athenia. In you, I trust the task of arranging this secret meeting."

Aminatra gave Karlmon an 'I-told-you-so' glance. "I'll do my best, Your Majesty."

At that moment, Coloss burst into the tent, stooping to fit through the flaps. He let out a pained hoot, his eyes wide with alarm, thumbing in the direction he had come.

Aminatra broke the frozen panic that greeted him. "Is it Malic?" Responding to Coloss's urgent nods, she asked a further question. "He's coming here?"

A similar response.

"Just act ..."

The general breezed into the tent, accompanied by one of his officers. "I hope those aren't tears?"

Andolis brushed his cheeks with his sleeve. "Have you come to threaten me more?"

"If you obeyed my instructions, there would be no need for threats."

Malic's quip elicited a smirk from the officer.

"Now," continued Malic, his tone lacking all reverence, "I come to inform you the army is to proceed to Parodis despite the rains. An ideal opportunity to surprise them."

"But my slaves inform me the wagons are stuck in mud," said Andolis.

With a glance at Aminatra, Malic responded. "They are. Your slaves will have to work twice as hard to get them moving. I want nothing slowing our advance."

"Is not the rain a bad omen?"

"A king never seeks to avoid battle, Sire," said Malic. "The weather is but another opponent to defeat."

"No, of ... of course not," stuttered Andolis. "You are right. We must advance on Parodis." A mumble followed. "Anything to avoid the ma ..." He couldn't bring himself to say the word.

"The marriage, Sire? Why, I can think of no better occasion to unite our two houses than in the glow of victory. Adonelis will throw the biggest parade to celebrate both. You agree the match is perfect, eh, Athenia?"

"You couldn't wish for a better one, Master," said Aminatra.

"Good. I'd hate for anyone from my household to miss it. Even the slaves." Malic leaned forward, sweeping cups off a small table with his arm. A demanding hand snatched a scroll from the officer and rolled it out on the flat surface.

"A map," stated Andolis.

"A map," echoed Malic. "I am giving you command of the baggage train, Sire." He looked up, smiling at the king. "With the able assistance of Officer Ghano here. One of my most trusted men."

"A king should be with his army, not the baggage train!" declared an indignant Andolis.

"Did I not make clear? Do as you're told!" said Malic, his eyes conveying all the threat needed. He sniffed, resetting his line of thought. "I don't want the baggage train following in the cavalry's wake. The horses churn up the land and the wagons get stuck. It will still be hard going for you, but I want you to take this route north." His finger traced a path on the map. "And join up with the army again here." He tapped a fingernail thoughtfully on a point by the river. "Our enemy lacks the nerve to leave its walls. You'll be quite safe. We'll give the Parodisians the fright of their lives while you catch up."

King Andolis opened his mouth, ready to complain once more.

"Good," cut in Malic. "I'll leave the map for you to study. To help you avoid messing up your first command, Officer Ghano will tell you what to do. His orders go further, should you disagree. Understood? Right, I'll bid you good night."

With that, the general strode from the tent without the customary bow. Ghano followed, a shallow nod some recognition of the king's status.

"I'm now to be subservient to a nobody!" wailed Andolis, before biting into a chicken leg. "Why does he treat me as a slave?"

Ignoring the king's self-pity, Aminatra peeked outside the tent, checking Malic had indeed departed. She turned back to her companions and spoke in a hushed tone. "We won't have access to the other generals if we're separated from the army. Well, not for a while anyway."

"I could persuade this Officer Gardo to support me," suggested Andolis.

"Ghano," corrected Karlmon, finding himself again tidying discarded crockery.

"He's Malic's man through and through," said Aminatra. "He'll report back on any misplaced word and has orders to kill you if you disobey him."

"Oh, I'm sure Malic didn't mean that," said Andolis, a nervous laugh escaping at the end. "Did he?"

"You're a convenience to him at present but not essential. As soon as you give him a grandson, he'll kill you. But he'll have a plan should your death occur before then."

Andolis dropped the drumstick, his face turning white. "But I'm king." His words wavered with fear.

"And how did your father obtain the throne?"

"No. No. That was different. He deposed a weak king threatening ruin to Adonelis. They were related too – of royal blood."

"Lying to yourself is not the way to prove your worth," said Aminatra with a little more force than planned.

"How dare you!" The king stamped on Aminatra's foot.

"Ouch!" She bit her lip, shaking her throbbing toes. A hand reached out, slapping the king across his face.

Staggering back, Andolis stared agog at his assailant. "I'll have you skinned! Guard! GUARD!"

Karlmon and Coloss looked on in terror, awaiting the imminent arrival of retribution.

"GUARD!" yelled the king again.

The wait went on.

"I'm sorry, Your Majesty," said Aminatra when convinced no one would come. "I had to show how powerless you are. All now owe allegiance to Malic."

"Then Coloss will do the deed," commanded Andolis, beckoning the giant.

Coloss remained still, a tortured grimace crossing his face. He slowly shook his head.

A whimper emerged from Andolis as he collapsed onto a cushion. "I am betrayed by all!"

Aminatra crouched before the boy, her voice soothing. "It is because Coloss loves you he disobeys. A glorious future awaits you, but not in Adonelis or the army. Not presently." She turned to Karlmon. "I think we can tell him now."

"Tell me what?" mumbled the king, peeking out of his huddled posture.

With a deep breath, Aminatra explained all. "We're planning to escape along the river: Karlmon, Coloss and myself. Travel to a place called Mandelaton. It's Coloss's home, did you know?"

Sodden eyes flicked between Karlmon and Coloss. "Is this true?"

"We didn't want to leave you," protested Karlmon, "but we can't go on as slaves. We want you to come with us."

Coloss nodded enthusiastically.

"But my destiny ..."

"Destiny is crafted, not delivered," said Aminatra. "Learn from the wider world and its people, become wise, and then one day you can return to shape your destiny in Adonelis, perhaps."

Andolis studied Aminatra in silence, his head tilting as he assessed her. "I will go with you," he announced at last in a pained whisper.

Chapter Forty-Nine

"They're here! They're here!" The man ran down the road from the bridge towards Parodis's main square, his arms waving, face bright red. "The Adonelisian army's approaching the riverside."

Heads turned as he rushed past; panicked conversations spread. Soon, the whole square bubbled under an anxious chain reaction. People ran off down roads and alleys, dispersing the news, lighting the fire of fear throughout the city.

"They've ignored the rain!" cried one voice.

"Nothing can stop them!" exclaimed another.

"They're crossing the river!" Lies and rumour mixed to become fact.

"What's all the commotion?" asked Finbarl when the ripple arrived on the opposite side of the city. He turned the latest concrete mix for the wall repairs with his spade.

The work party paused their labours, watching the people dart down the streets or into their homes with a slam of the door.

"Oi, boy!" called out Balfour, waving to a passing teenager. "Come here. What's going on?"

The lad slowed, his face a fusion of excitement and fear. "The Adonelisians are invading. They've already broken into the city. It's madness. They're beheading people and feeding them to monster dogs. I'm going to fight." With his message delivered, the boy ran off to seek his glory.

"Cronax," cursed Finbarl, allowing a spade full of concrete to slump to the ground. "I thought the river would hold them."

"Come on," urged Balfour, discarding his own spade. "Let's get back to the barracks. Looks like you're getting your chance to kill Adonelisians after all."

Like with most things, the barracks of Parodis bore little resemblance to their Athenian counterpart. Broad, open stretches of land hosted multiple stone buildings of varying sizes, each accommodating an element of the army and navy. An aesthetic touch embellished even the most basic building.

After the chaos of the streets, the barracks possessed a strange semblance of order. Soldiers and sailors moved with purpose, marching under the watchful eye of a commanding Terratus.

"Where have you been?" cried a voice, as Finbarl and Balfour approached the more primitive serventite quarters.

"Fic, Magor Leeanty," cursed Balfour under his breath. "We've been mending the wall, Sir."

"The enemy's marauding on the other side of the river and you're playing at builders?" growled the magor.

Finbarl and Balfour shared a look of disbelief.

"The other side? So, they've not broken into the city, Sir?" asked Finbarl, willing to ignore the magor's hypocrisy.

"Of course not, you clux. Where did you hear such nonsense?"

"It's what the people on the street believe."

"They'll believe any rubbish. I expect better from my men!"

"Yes, Sir. Sorry, Sir," said Finbarl, his respect for rank instilled from time as a guard in Athenia.

"Report to your unit!" commanded the magor. "You have a new lefteni and some regulars joining you."

"Wonder what happened to Kirkup?" asked Balfour, having given a lazy salute as the magor strolled off.

"Who cares," said Finbarl. "All commanders are the same. At least they haven't breached Parodis. Can't imagine how the Unumverum was going to fulfil its prophecy in that situation."

"The Adonelisians camped on the other side of the river, ain't exactly great," scoffed Balfour. "We're not prepared for them. Didn't even finish the wall repairs."

"If we keep them from crossing the river, who cares?"

"You've not seen a siege before, eh?"

Finbarl dismissed the question with a laugh. "Life was a siege in Athenia. The Ferrals forever tried to break in."

"This ain't no monkey with a pebble," grumbled Balfour.

Before Finbarl could respond, a member of their unit jogged past. "We've been summoned to parade. Better hurry."

Finbarl and Balfour followed, forming into the ranks of Unit 8B on the paved tiles of the parade ground. Cypress trees lined the area in their own regimented style. Within their cover, groups of soldiers ordered themselves into their units. Within 8B, new faces mixed with familiar.

Jostling shoulders separated to an arm's length as rows and columns took shape. Finbarl, poised as he once did on parade in Athenia, surveyed the amassed ranks, feeling a confidence from the scale and class of his comrades. The servenites stood out, thinner and paler than others. It allowed Finbarl to spot the newcomers among his unit.

"Eh?" spluttered Finbarl.

"What?"

"I recognise him." Finbarl nodded towards a man in the row in front.

Balfour craned his neck, inspecting the face. "Oh, yes. What's his name?"

"Parmsoli!" declared Finbarl advancing to squeeze in the next row. "Hello, Parmsoli. Remember me?"

A nervous flicker greeted Finbarl. "Why, hello. It's Finbock, isn't it?"

"Finbarl. I'm surprised to see you in the ranks. Balfour, this is Parmsoli." A questioning tone crept into Finbarl's voice. "I met him on the Medino a while back."

Balfour shook his head. "No, that's not it."

"What's not it?"

"His name. It's on the tip of my ... got it! Fordell. Jaquin Fordell. Spent a year at the Flash."

"I see," said Finbarl, his eyes piercing the man. "So, not a Terratus. Was that even your horse?"

Fordell laughed. "I don't think I ever said I was a Terratus or owned a horse. You must have mistaken some items I borrowed as belonging to me."

"You certainly mentioned something about being a magor. And your friends in the government?" asked Finbarl, knowing the answer.

"Ah, that magor thing was most likely poor translation. Language is a tricky thing when not one's native tongue. As for government friends, you may have misconstrued my meaning. I consider my representative in the Senorium as a friend. I did vote for them, after all."

"Does this man have something to do with your missing money?" asked Balfour, applying his own threatening glare.

"No," admitted Finbarl. "But only, I suspect, because I didn't have any when I met him. I've learnt a bit about people since then."

"Gentlemen, I've not wronged you," said Fordell. "You must forgive any tales I may have spun to entertain. We are comrades in Parodis's great army. Are we not friends?"

"Silence!" came an order.

A young man, dressed in the finery of a Terratus, paced in front of 8B.

"Son of Mylo Hebradon," confided Fordell.

Finbarl looked to Balfour for an explanation.

"One of the biggest landowners in Parodis," whispered Balfour from the corner of his mouth. "Spoilt brat, no doubt."

"A real Terratus," said Finbarl for Fordell's benefit.

"Quiet!" the lefteni called, clapping his hands. "I'm your new commander, Lefteni Hebradon." A pleasing smile shone as he walked along, inspecting the ranks through sunken eyes. "I'm delighted to have such a fine-looking group of men under my command." He reached out, gripping the shoulder of the man before him, looking him in the eye. "We have the future of Parodis in our hands and need all your courage and wit."

"Seems all right," whispered Finbarl.

"I don't care if you're regular army or servenite, we have a job to do," continued Hebradon, stepping to the next man in line and nodding. "Together we can teach these Adonelisians a lesson they'll never forget."

A cheer went up, interrupting the lefteni. He quietened his men with a shimmy of his fingers.

"They are barbaric scum planning to kill your families and enslave all if we let them in the city. Their heads on spikes will make them think differently." The lefteni waited for a further cheer, receiving a muted response.

"Fic, we can cut a few tongues out too," muttered Balfour. "That'll show those barbarians." He looked to Finbarl for recognition of his joke, only to find him frowning. "What's up?"

Finbarl shook his head. "Nothing. It's strange. I feel I know the lefteni but can't place him."

"Not another person you bumped into on the Medino?" quipped Balfour.

"No," pondered Finbarl, half listening, still struggling to retrieve the memory. "Never mind. It'll come to me."

"Gentlemen, your attention, please." Hebradon looked at Finbarl and Balfour, a finger to his lips and an apologetic smile.

"Far too nice to be a commander," whispered Balfour through a fake grin. "Sorry, Sir."

"As I was saying," continued Hebradon, "you will collect a weapon from the armoury and return here by elevo to commence drills. Let me know if you have experience with a bow. Our unit serves on Fendora, one of the finest ships in the fleet. We're going to be in the thick of any fighting. Our swords will soon gleam with the blood of our foe."

The men refound their voice with a hearty cheer.

"I've heard the Senorium summons our allies to support us. We'll outnumber the Adonelisians ten to one. Our Unumverum promises victory and we'll provide it. Dismissed!"

As the unit broke up chatting with excitement, Hebradon stepped into their midst, approaching the trio of Balfour, Finbarl and Fordell. He stood before them, gripping Balfour's shoulder, and leaning in. "If I catch you talking in the ranks again," his voice light and calm, "I'll rip your hearts out with my bare hands. Do I make myself clear?" He stepped back and gave his boyish smile, only his eyes projecting a darker side.

"Er, yes, Sir. Sorry Sir."

"Good. Now be obedient soldiers and get your weapons."

"Cronax!" exclaimed Finbarl, out of the range of Hebradon. "Not so nice."

"Bah," retorted Balfour. "He's all talk."

"Not how a Terratus should present himself," added Fordell, earning another glare from Finbarl.

Chapter Fifty

"I've told you already," scolded Andolis. "Don't let your horse edge in front of mine!"

Ghano pulled his reins with a grumble, slowing enough for the king to take his place at the head of the baggage train. His eyes burnt into the king's back, fantasising about burying his knife into it.

Behind, ten cavalrymen rode in tight formation, leading the wagons and their strange mix of military necessities. Further rain failed to come, allowing the ground to harden. The wagons crawled across the flat, open plain, snaking round the giant saguaro cacti, mesquite trees and occasional boulder, ploughing over the creosote bushes and cocklebur. It was Karlmon's job to remove the burs from the oxen's legs each night.

Aminatra and her wagon kept pace, close enough to witness the constant bickering between Andolis and Ghano, far enough back not to get involved. She held the reins while Coloss dozed in the back, Karlmon by her side, humming a half-recognisable tune.

"Does Coloss know the way to Mandelaton?" Karlmon addressed his mother, that source of all knowledge.

"I don't think so," replied Aminatra. "At least, not precisely. He can point us in a rough direction. I suspect he'll recognise places the closer we get."

"I'll be able to steer the boat. Captain Tarlobus taught me."

"That's good." Aminatra held back her doubts. "Keep your eyes on the lookout for moored and unmanned vessels and be ready to escape at the drop of a pinono."

"I hope we see the army in action," said Karlmon. "What a magnificent sight it must be."

"Hmmm. I'd prefer if we didn't. Are you going to grow your hair long again when we're free?"

Karlmon shrugged.

"It'll be nice to wake up when we want, eat when we want, say what we want."

"The food won't be as good as the palace," said Karlmon. "We'll have to find our own again and without Maddy's help."

"True, but freedom will taste sweet."

"It's hard work."

Aminatra's shoulders sagged in disappointment. "Yes, it is. Palace life was only easy at the expense of others. Enjoying freedom from the labours of the unfree is a life of deception. The world looks wonderful when you're brought the ripe peach on a plate, but until you've nurtured that peach yourself, it will always taste sour. Laziness is selfishness."

"I'm not selfish," protested Karlmon.

"I hope not." Aminatra let the conversation fade, hoping her lesson had filtered through.

A cry carried from the cavalry. "The river!"

Aminatra clambered to her feet, one hand gripping the wagon frame for balance. "It's true. Look!"

The silver-brown waters appeared across an expanse of reeds. Aminatra opened her nostrils, sampling the air. Something within, almost indiscernible, evoked memories of the Medino.

"I can't see," complained Karlmon, on his feet but too short.

An egret lifted in the air, further proof of water. It stretched its white wings, circling in wide arcs before gliding down to another bankside point beyond sight.

"I wonder how far we're from the army?" mused Aminatra. "We'll need to work our way upstream to locate them. This may be our best chance for escape."

"Hey, two farmers," observed Karlmon, seeking compensation for the still illusive river.

The pair, perhaps father and son, stooped by an irrigation ditch, their wooden spades clearing out a rich mud.

"They may want to be somewhere else," said Aminatra, just as Andolis's voice shrilled out.

"I gave no orders to leave the column!"

Six cavalrymen broke from the line, their horses galloping towards the farmers.

"They'll be gathering intelligence," suggested Aminatra, as the two locals realised their precarious position, dropped their spades and turned to run.

A whoop escaped from the riders as they drew swords, heels dug into mounts. They chased the farmers, circling them with impish amusement. The two men cowered together, ducking as the soldiers prodded them with swords.

"They're playing cat and mouse," said Aminatra, pulling the wagon to a standstill.

Andolis and Ghano confronted each other, arguing with a new intensity.

"He'd do well to be careful," said Aminatra, as Coloss poked his head forward, scratching at his unkempt hair. "We're at the river," she explained for Coloss's benefit. "They're questioning some locals and having fun. The king's not happy."

Coloss took it all in, eyes shifting from one drama to another.

"We can question them later ourselves about finding a boat," remarked Aminatra, her mind unable to think of anything other than escape.

"No!" Karlmon dug his head into his mother's side, whimpering in shock.

"Cronax!" exclaimed Aminatra, a sickening shiver shooting down her spine, as she tugged her boy closer. "They're murdering them."

The soldiers continued to circle, swinging their swords in elaborate patterns, no longer tormenting but cutting through flesh. Their laughter grew in volume, mixing with the screams of their victims. The raised voices of Andolis and Ghano faded, their attention drawn to the bloodbath.

"The ferralax!" cursed Aminatra under her breath as she consoled Karlmon.

Coloss released a heavy sigh, used to the barbarity of his captors.

The returning riders held themselves tall, passing the king with their blood-soaked swords raised. Andolis shrank a little, recognising the discreet threat as Ghano congratulated his warriors. The officer waved his own sword, signalling the advance. This time there was no complaint from Andolis over his usurped authority.

"The sooner we escape, the better," said Aminatra, flicking the whip to urge the oxen on.

Chapter Fifty-One

F inbarl stopped for a breath, rubbing his sore arm. Three days of drills left every muscle tired, but only his old injury worried him.

"Excellent," observed Lefteni Hebradon, moving between the man-on-man bouts dotted across the parade ground. "I've been watching. You put great passion into your training."

Finbarl glanced at his sparring partner, Fordell. "Sometimes it's easy to picture your enemy's face, Sir."

"You've fought before?" asked Hebradon.

"Not with a sword, Sir," said Finbarl, "but the principles are the same in all hand-to-hand combat."

"I've got bruises across my arms," complained Fordell.

"And killed before. I can tell." The lefteni ignored Fordell, waving his own sword, practising a lunge.

Finbarl nodded. He hadn't considered such things for a long time. Not since leaving Athenia. It had once been part of his life, bringing death. How many Ferrals had he dispatched? He couldn't remember. The thought raised an image of Maddy, and he cringed at his past ways.

"Nothing beats the thrill of a fight and the satisfaction of a kill," said Hebradon, rubbing the sweat from his forehead.

"I'm eager to defeat the Adonelisians, but it won't be a thrill, Sir. I just want my family back."

Hebradon examined Finbarl for a moment, his sunken eyes glowing. "But when the animal inside takes over, that's when you truly feel alive. Mark my words, you'll experience it in the heat of battle."

"Yes, Sir," said Finbarl, keen to escape his commander's company. "I have the afternoon off, Sir. Going to visit friends before ..."

"Before you confront death," finished Hebradon. "Of course, off you go. Find yourself a nice girl and relax."

"Mind if I join you?" asked Fordell.

"Yes, I do."

***

The streets enjoyed their usual bustle, as Parodisians acclimatised to the dormant threat across the river. They went about their daily business, seeking that luxury material to brighten their wardrobe or the latest cheese from Mossilien. Among the crowds, Finbarl wondered at the relaxed mood. Snippets of conversation floated his way, always with the word 'Unumverum' included. It was comforting to know of victory before the fight. The idea tickled Finbarl, and his step grew lighter. Yet, how strange to have the Adonelisians prowling along the south bank, content at this stage to fire their arrows at patrolling boats. It was a war of waiting: waiting for their allies; waiting for the enemy to give up; waiting for victory.

Finbarl had no friends to visit. He wandered aimless, observing the city and its people. It crossed his mind to seek Allus or Bartarnous, but a preference for solitude won out, or at least the solitude of a bustling city.

"A lucky charm, Sir?" called out a young girl, offering a sprig of lavender in her hand.

"No, thank you," said Finbarl, displaying a smile in compensation.

"Then misfortune is your curse!" spat the girl, moving on to another victim.

Finbarl blinked in disbelief. "When we have Unumverum, why do I need a charm?"

The girl ignored him, finding a sucker to pin her lavender to.

He continued to the main square, only to discover it occupied by the Kilshare and their horses. With the road to the bridge closed, Finbarl turned back, disappointed to miss a view of the enemy from the clifftop.

Passing a bar, he considered popping in for a drink, then remembered he had no money. The army owned him, provided all his needs, and sent him where they wanted. Still, it was better than the Flash.

"Halloan Park," announced Finbarl to himself, fixing on something free to keep his mind occupied. On his first day in Parodis, he walked down the same roads with Maddy.

WHOOoosh!

Finbarl ducked as the strange noise ended in a shattering bang. He stood bemused, but all appeared serene.

WHOOoosh! WHOosh!

A scream accompanied the first crash. Cries for help the second.

Running into a wide avenue, Finbarl looked skywards. Boulders soared across the blue canvas, diving into the buildings of Parodis. All came from the river. The waiting was over.

Finbarl watched as one stone after another whizzed over. Then smaller debris rained down, no less destructive or indiscriminate. Panic reclaimed the people. They dashed for cover, seeking sanctuary. But where was safe? Finbarl hesitated. An instinct to bolt west into a narrow alley fell by the wayside when a boulder ripped along the corner building, masonry tumbling to the street below.

"Help!" A man faltered before Finbarl, his forehead bleeding.

"You've been hit," remarked Finbarl, relying on the obvious in his shock.

The man wobbled, sinking to his knees. Finbarl reached out a hand. A loud bang sounded behind and a rush of air brushed his arm. Splinters of stone pelted the ground, skimming off and rolling on until stationary. Finbarl's outstretched hand remained motionless. The man slumped flat on his face, a pool of blood spreading between the paving stones.

"Get up!" urged Finbarl, clasping the man's shoulder. "Over here. There's shelter." With no response, Finbarl tried to roll the man. His listless body declared his fate, a tear to his neck its cause. "Cronax! What's going on?"

"Catapults," came the answer. A boy watched from a doorway.

Finbarl clambered to his feet, scuttling to join him. "What?"

"Catapults," repeated the boy. "The Adonelisians have a dozen lined up on the riverside. They're hitting every part of the city."

"Where did they come from?" asked Finbarl, sinking into the opposite corner of the doorway.

With bottom lip protruding, the boy shrugged.

Another hailstorm of pebbles fizzed across the square.

"At this rate, Parodis won't be standing much longer," remarked Finbarl, his words coinciding with a shop facade collapsing under a plume of dust.

"The navy will stop it," said the boy, scared but confident in his opinion. "The Unumverum says so."

"I hope so."

"My teacher told me."

"Did they say how long it will last?"

As the boy mulled over the question, Finbarl noticed the cathedral's dome in the distance. It was almost as far away from the river as possible within the city, yet already bore a wound from the bombardment. Bartarnous popped into Finbarl's mind. What must he be thinking with this unpredictable sky fall? "You going to be okay staying put?" asked Finbarl of the boy.

He nodded, hiding his fear of abandonment.

"I've got to find a friend. He needs my help."

"Can I come with you?"

"No," said Finbarl, putting a bolstering hand on the boy's head. "It's too dangerous. You've found the safest spot. Best stay here." Not wanting to argue or meet the boy's eyes, Finbarl scurried away, sprinting across the square, leaping over the rubble. He didn't glance back.

The carnage was sporadic, some streets unaffected, their residents oblivious to the threat, others in ruin. Collapsed walls, toppled columns, smashed roofs. What once seemed a strong, virulent city now appeared weak and vulnerable. The buildings, once graceful and magnificent, collapsed with ease, exposing weak foundations.

The bombardment and destruction lessened the further Finbarl got from the river. Nothing Finbarl could imagine dispensed such long-range devastation. With the streets clearer, he progressed at speed, reaching the hill leading to the cathedral. Scholars and students congregated in a mass at Halloan Park, confused and angry, looking down over the city and its fate. Finbarl weaved through them, seeking Bartarnous.

A familiar voice called out. "Finbarl?"

Finbarl spun to find a bewildered Lhaluma and Dae.

"Oh, this is terrible, Finbarl," said Lhaluma, his once immaculate beard a tangled mess.

"What are you doing out in the open?" exclaimed Finbarl. "If a stone hits, it'll plough through you all."

"Nowhere is safe," said Lhaluma, his eyes scanning the sky. "I don't want to be in a building if it collapses."

Finbarl fought the urge to respond, 'Should have built them better.' Instead opting for, "Have you seen Bartarnous?"

"No," answered Dae. "I hope he's all right."

"I'll try his house," said Finbarl. He added, "At least spread out." He turned to leave.

"Finbarl," said Lhaluma.

Finbarl stopped. "Yes."

"Allus is dead."

"What? How? I only saw her a few days back. She seemed fine."

"The mencoctitus took her."

A sickening wave washed through Finbarl. He could still see her smiling. "You told her not to have the vaccine."

Lhaluma hung his head in shame. "I fell for a stupid rumour."

"We all did," stressed Dae.

Finbarl stood motionless, allowing the silence to deliver his disgust.

"And we're sorry for accusing Maddy of being the Butcher and blaming you," said Dae.

"Another murder occurred last night," added Lhaluma.

Finbarl looked away, closing his eyes. Unwelcome news fell like the boulders. "So, someone else had to die to prove her innocence."

"I feel terrible," confessed Lhaluma.

Stepping back to face the lanky student, Finbarl prodded a finger into his ribs. "You'll have to live with that guilt. I can't absolve you."

A tear rolled down Lhaluma's cheek.

"I thought you were joining the navy?" said Finbarl, recalling his last conversation with Allus.

"Didn't want me," admitted Lhaluma, clearing his runny nose with a snort. "Too tall. An easy target, or so they said."

"Some people have all the luck." Finbarl swung around and walked away, melting into the crowd.

The terrace of houses Bartarnous lived in appeared free of damage but eerily quiet. Finbarl pushed open the ground-floor door, recognising the musty smell. He climbed the stairs, pausing at the sound of a boulder whizzing overhead.

"Bartarnous! Alusto!"

Silence greeted Finbarl's calls.

Finding the door to Bartarnous's apartment ajar, Finbarl rapped on it and stepped in. "Anyone about? It's Finbarl."

Again, no answer.

Unwashed plates lay abandoned in the kitchen, cupboards open. Finbarl clenched his fists in dread. "Bartarnous?"

A strange, wheezing noise caught Finbarl's ear. He followed it into the study.

"Bartarnous! Are you all right? Why didn't you answer me?"

The old scholar sat on his chair facing the window. His head inched a fraction left, acknowledging Finbarl's arrival, but remained transfixed on the window.

Finbarl rushed to his side, crouching before him. "Where's Alusto? Cronax! You look terrible."

Tired eyes looked down at Finbarl, their lustre gone amid a ghost-white face. "Finbarl." The name whispered through cracked lips.

"What's going on? Are you ill?"

A faint smile broke out. "I'm glad you came. Alusto left. He has family, you know."

"It's not safe here," said Finbarl, clasping the old man's hands in his. "The Adonelisians are bombarding the city with boulders."

"Who would believe such terrible weapons existed?" lamented Bartarnous. "We tried to forget the past to banish them ... from our lives and yet humanity has ... an inherent capacity to destroy." A chilling whistle accompanied every breath.

"What's wrong with you?" pressed Finbarl. "You need a doctor. Just tell me what's wrong."

"I'm dying," stated Bartarnous without fuss.

"So, let me get you a doctor!"

"I want to die."

Finbarl noticed a mug on the table with a small, brown vial beside it. "Have you taken something?" He stood in panic, grabbing the bottle, trying to interpret the writing. "What is it? Come on! I'm not letting you die!"

"It's too late," said Bartarnous, nodding his head slowly. "The poison is working. It's not as painful as I feared, though taking longer than I'd hoped."

"But why?" cried Finbarl, crouching before the scholar again. "Is it the war? I know you were worried, but Parodis will get through it. You'll get through it. The Unumverum foretold victory."

"The Unumverum," echoed Bartarnous with a spluttering laugh. "Will you forgive an old man a lie?"

"Of course," said Finbarl.

"And what about a society? Generations?"

"What are you talking about? You're scaring me."

Bartarnous gathered all his strength to straighten up. His hand reached out, searching for Finbarl's face. "I'm sorry." His fingers touched Finbarl's cheek, moving to the mouth and on to feel each feature. "Don't cry," he pleaded, sensing a tear. "I don't deserve pity."

"Why?" implored Finbarl.

"The Unumverum does not exist," stated the scholar. Relief coloured his voice as though trapped words had at last escaped. He laughed. "Well, it exists, but not as the book we claim. It doesn't foretell the future. It never has!"

"I see," said Finbarl with restraint. "So, the promised victory against Adonelis?"

"Ha, the vain, complacent Parodis has no chance against the organised brutality of our enemy. The lie will bring our destruction. I cannot live with that, nor survive what is to come. You must leave now to save yourself." Bartarnous cushioned his friend's face between both hands, squeezing with affection.

"But why? Why the lie? What purpose did it serve?"

"What purpose?" repeated the old man, releasing his hands, slumping in his chair. "A white lie they called it, but ours was a raindrop that built into a mudslide. You don't need imagination to picture an age of despair. Is not your Athenia in that pit now? What inspired you to want better, seek improvement, escape the morass? Was it not hope? That is what our ancestors sought: hope. The scholars, or whatever they were in those days, gave people a future by promising that future. Is that such a terrible thing?"

Finbarl listened, stroking Bartarnous's hand with his thumb as the old man's eyelids struggled to stay open.

"So sleepy," whispered the scholar. "But I must finish. It gave people confidence. They believed in success because success was foretold, and thus they found the strength to succeed. But every lie is cancerous. It is the survivors and victors who write history. As long as Parodis survived, who could challenge the vague prophesies of the

Unumverum? Our enemies fell for it too, feeding into the growing myth. The lies became self-fulfilling, because here was Parodis, glorious and triumphant. You don't appear shocked?"

"I believed in the Unumverum," said Finbarl, "but only because others convinced me to. Why wouldn't I? Everything the city projected reinforced the notion. In hindsight, it always sounded implausible. I mean, seeing into the future! Is Parodis anything more than a facade?"

Bartarnous responded with a groan, coughing and spluttering.

"Are you all right?" Finbarl dabbed a rag to the scholar's lips, wiping away blood-laced dribble.

"My time is coming soon. I have almost finished. Yes, a facade. Oh, yes. Hiding a complacent rot. It comes to all. Why work hard when promised riches? Why plan when the future's plotted? I've tried to warn them, but ..." He gurned in agony. "But who listens to a mad, old blind man?" The eyelids settled shut, his breathing short and ragged.

"Bartarnous?"

"Leave me, Finbarl. Please leave. I don't wish you to witness a fool's last act."

Finbarl stood, looking down upon his friend for a moment. "You're nobody's fool. Say hi to Maddy for me."

A fragile smile formed on Bartarnous's face. "Perhaps she'll talk to me on the other side." The smile faded.

Chapter Fifty-Two

U nder marching clouds and atop a low-lying hill stood the Adonelis encampment. Thousands and thousands of tents of green, red and blue dotted the ground, campfire smoke wafting skywards between them. In the shallow valley below, the serene river carved west to east. Parodis rested upon its outcrop, spreading across the plain beyond, as yet untouched by Adonelisian wrath. Only south of the river did the merciless hand of the invader show. The charred settlement leading to the dismantled bridge was a gesture of what would befall Parodis if the Adonelisians crossed.

"My hands hurt," complained Karlmon, sitting outside their tent, scouring their supply of cooking vessels.

"Palace life spoiled you," said Aminatra, cradling a playful Libellia. "Be thankful they didn't have you working down there." She used Libellia's chubby arm to point to the river.

Once more connected with the army, an industrious dance ignited within the baggage train. Those grubby souls, hunched on their transport, sprang into action. A mini town arose in enemy territory of pitched tents, ditches and defensive walls. Like ants, its populace scurried from place to place, fulfilling unspoken commands.

"They're firing again," remarked Karlmon, observing the catapults – another frightening wonder of choreographed construction.

"I hope they run out of stone soon," said Aminatra, pulling a face for Libellia.

"They're still building by the river," said Karlmon. Conversation was an excuse to stop working. "More catapults?"

"Too small. They look like boxes. A sort of boat, perhaps? There soon won't be any wood left." A stretch of woodland bordered the camp, the rhythm of saws drifting from within.

"Did you see the Parodisian ship? Much bigger than the Medino. We should escape in one of those. They fire clouds of arrows."

"I hope they hit their mark," commented Aminatra. "Have you finished? Is that a stain I can make out?"

With a playful sneer, Karlmon dunked his cloth back in the bowl.

"Here's Coloss," said Aminatra, detecting his approaching head over the rise. "No one else gets as much water delivered as we do. Every tent should have its own giant."

"Ando's with him," cried Karlmon, jumping to his feet before his enthusiasm deflated. "Oh, so is Ghano and his men."

"And they're arguing ... again!" said Aminatra, their voices carrying in the wind.

"Now, how long has that taken?" pressed Andolis, waggling a finger towards Ghano. "General Malic's slaves are on hand, mine have to trek all this way?"

"You're not orchestrating a war, Sire," stated Ghano gruffly.

"But I command the orchestrator," snapped the king. "His tent is adjacent to mine so that I might consult with him at the drop of a pinono."

Ghano sucked through his teeth, struggling to keep his temper. "Your tent is next to General Malic's as a courtesy. In fact, he complained of your whimpering disturbing him during the night. I can solve your problem by moving you out here."

"You insolent beast!" cried Andolis. "I'll make you pay. And Malic. Not today, but one day."

A satisfied smile erupted on Ghano's face. "Thank you, Sire. I've been waiting for that."

"Waiting for what?"

"A treasonable remark."

"What remark? Don't be an ass. How can the king commit treason?"

"I have explicit orders from General Malic to protect you from harm as long as you make no open threat against him." Ghano drew his sword with a slow, satisfying breath. "Were you to make one, then I have permission to kill you."

"What are you talking about? It is Malic you should punish for his treatment of me. Your king!" retorted Andolis with a disbelieving laugh that disintegrated to nervous doubt. "And ... and I did not threaten the general. Do you not recognise a joke?"

With a nod of Ghano's head, the two soldiers behind armed themselves, pushing Coloss away at the point of their swords. The giant released a forlorn moan, retreating as the tips drew blood.

"The seclusion of a tent will best suit our needs," said Ghano, grabbing Andolis by an arm.

"Let me go! Let me go!"

Ghano reached into his tunic pocket, retrieving a rag. "Something else I've been wanting to do for a long while." He stuffed the rag into Andolis's mouth. "Now, shut up!"

As the tone of the argument deteriorated, Aminatra armed herself with a pestle, still stained from the basil ground earlier. "What's going on, Your Majesty?" she asked as Ghano dragged the king towards her tent.

"Mother?" whimpered Karlmon.

"Stay clear!" ordered Aminatra. "Take Libellia. Go hide in another tent. Don't argue!"

Karlmon hurried off clutching his sister, looking over his shoulder, before disappearing into a friend's tent. The flaps twitched as he sought a view of the unfolding drama.

"Can I help you?" Aminatra blocked the entrance to her tent.

"Out of the way, slave!" Ghano lashed out, knocking Aminatra off her feet, dragging the king past.

"Mmmmm." A wide-eyed, impotent Andolis protested. With a jerk of his arm, Ghano threw him to the floor in the centre of the tent.

"Your parents should have done this at birth," snarled Ghano, standing over the boy, sword gripped tight. "You're nothing but an annoying runt. An insult to Adonelis."

Andolis sobbed, prone on the ground, his eyes unable to address his executor.

"You have royal blood, so I'll do you the courtesy of making this quick." Ghano clasped the back of Andolis's tunic, yanking him up to his knees. "Lift your head or this could get messy."

Contrary to the end, the king pressed his chin to his neck, his mumbled complaints starting up again.

"Okay, let's do it my way," said Ghano, flipping his grip from the tunic to Andolis's hair. He tugged up, almost lifting the boy off the ground, his throat now exposed. "One quick ..."

Aminatra burst through the tent flaps, a hand rubbing an already swelling cheek. As Ghano's head rotated to inspect the disturbance, she flew at him, linking her arms round his neck, legs binding his arms, clinging on with all her strength. The officer turned and twisted, struggling to dislodge his assailant. Aminatra held tight, spinning and screaming. Beneath, Andolis scuttled away on his hands and feet, avoiding the wild stamps of Ghano.

Catching Aminatra by surprise, Ghano threw himself backwards, collapsing, crushing his limpet attacker between his mass and the ground. Winded and disorientated, Aminatra kept one arm round his throat. He spun, taking Aminatra with him, gaining momentum. She flew off, her body rolling, crashing into the canvas.

"You die too," spluttered Ghano, fighting for breath, climbing to his feet. "Slow and painful." He shook his head, regaining composure.

Aminatra watched, prostrate and helpless. Blood trickled down her forehead. She blinked as diluted red coloured her vision. A breeze caught her hair, and she looked to the entrance. Between parted door flaps stood a small, silhouetted figure. "Karlmon! No, run! Get away from here."

Her son remained motionless, a strange, ambiguous smile beneath frightened eyes. "It's all right, Mother. Look who's found us?" Karlmon pulled the flap wide, allowing his companion to enter.

"Maddy?" Aminatra shook her head. "Oh, Maddy. Is that you?"

Ghano laughed as the dirt-covered waif crouched and snarled. He raised his sword to finish Aminatra.

Maddy attacked.

Chapter Fifty-Three

"This reminds me of Athenia," remarked Finbarl, staring over the fortifications at the broad vista beyond, a haze rising from the baked ground.

"Did you get all the cushy jobs there too?" joked Balfour, adjusting a leather strap digging into his shoulder.

As a distant crash of a boulder impact sounded behind, Finbarl sighed. "It was the edge of my world. This feels a little too familiar."

"You're depressed. Anyone would be, not losing one friend but two. At least your scholar lived to a ripe old age. The girl is just unfair."

"They didn't have to die."

"Fic, death isn't into justifying itself. Trust me, I had all these thoughts after my wife died. And as for Bartarnous, if we understood the suicidal mind, we'd be ... well, suicidal."

"Thank you, Master Balfour."

"Hey, come on," said Balfour. "This time tomorrow we'll be the other side of the city, onboard a ship causing merry hell with the Adonelisians. No time to be miserable. And in a couple of days, we'll raise a glass to the Unumverum, celebrating our victory. We'll toast lost friends too."

Finbarl fought the urge to shout out Bartarnous's confession: to disclose the lie, tell all Parodisians to think for themselves, take the invasion seriously, stop clinging to a false future and believing in inevitability. The deception was too powerful. "You're right," he said.

"When am I ever wrong?" laughed Balfour. "Eh, look out! Here comes your friend."

"He's not my friend," protested Finbarl as Fordell edged along the rampart.

"I've been looking for you, Finbarn," said Fordell, leaning his back against the wall. "How would you like to make a little money to buy back some time owed?"

"It's Finbarl. How much time?"

"Perhaps all you owe and more. You too, Balfour."

"And what would we have to do to get this money?" asked Balfour, making no effort to hide his suspicion.

Fordell rubbed his hands. "There are a couple of Mossilien traders in town. Stuck due to the invasion. A friend tells me their business fell through for the exact same reason."

"And?" sighed Balfour.

"Well, in my line of work we call that a ripe situation. No trader wants to return home empty-handed. I need a couple of friends to act as associates. You know, give the appearance of respectability. Help convince our Mossiliens we are trustworthy."

"You're planning to steal from them!" growled Finbarl.

"Ouch, such a strong word. More like redirect funds and educate them in the harsh realities of business. Don't you want your servenitude over?"

"You saint," said Balfour, cutting Fordell off on one side. "I say we throw you over the forping wall."

"Yeah, educate him in the harsh realities of falling," added Finbarl, blocking Fordell in the other direction.

"Now, hang on." Fordell grinned, holding up an index finger on each hand. "A simple 'no, thank you,' is all I required. I don't share my plans with just anyone."

"You've got a ..." A buzz of excitement rippling through the sentries on the wall stopped Finbarl.

One soldier pointed north, chattering to the next man. Others looked, passing on their observations.

"A dust cloud," said Finbarl.

"Wind's too light to stir that up," added Balfour. "That's an ally army approaching. About forping time!"

A sense of relief replaced the excitement among the soldiers, all except Fordell. "Fic, means we'll get used as soldiers sooner than I'd hoped."

"Who will it be?" asked Finbarl.

"No idea," confessed Balfour. "Could do with a few more. With one behind us, others will follow."

"A rider!" cried Finbarl, spotting a lone horseman leaving the city.

"Off to greet our friends," said Balfour. "Now that's a job I wouldn't mind. The hero galloping to bring two cities together. Cheered and feted by all. Living off the tale for the rest of their lives."

"You've been down the mines too long," quipped Finbarl.

"Livorians."

"Livorians!"

The name passed down the line.

"Yes, you can see red banners," observed Balfour, cupping his hands over his eyes to shield out the sun. "It's the Livorians."

"That name's familiar," said Finbarl, searching his memory.

Fordell sniffed in derision. "A miserable bunch. City's in some God-forsaken marsh to the north-west. Reluctant trading partners, but Parodis persuaded them in its usual way. Not easy to get money out of. Cynical bunch."

"Surprised they're first," added Balfour.

"That's it," declared Finbarl. "When I met the Primora. She mentioned them."

"You've met the Primora?" Balfour studied Finbarl with disbelieving eyes. "Fic, you have fallen from a height. Oh, look! That didn't take long."

The rider ploughed his own trail of dust, returning to Parodis at a gallop, hunched low into his horse.

"He has company," remarked Finbarl, spotting a small group of horsemen twenty yards behind. "What's the hurry?"

A thoughtful silence followed. The spectators of Parodis watched with curiosity.

Finbarl glanced at Balfour. "They're not accompanying him. It's a chase!"

"Fic," cursed Balfour. "What's going on? Fic! Those are arrows! They're firing arrows at the messenger!"

"Sound the alarm!" ordered a voice, triggering a bell and a rush of more men to the wall.

"The Livorians appear to have rejected our trade agreement," remarked Fordell. "You can't trust cluxes."

"The balocones!" cried Balfour. "They've betrayed us."

Lefteni Hebradon appeared, his face impassive. "Clear your position. We're returning to barracks. This isn't a job for servenites. They're bringing up the archers. If the Livorians want a fight, they can take the sharp end of a bolt. Get moving!"

Finbarl hesitated. "But, Sir, this is the weakest point of the city. Shouldn't we have as many men here as possible?"

"I know, I know," said Hebradon. "You want to fight. I understand that. But you'll get your chance."

"Come on, Finbarl," urged Balfour. "The Unumverum would say if the Livorians could breach the walls. I wonder why it didn't highlight their treachery?"

Finbarl opened his mouth to answer but didn't have the words.

"May give us time to visit the Mossiliens, if you've changed your minds," suggested Fordell.

"Don't push your luck!" With a last glimpse to the north, as the Parodisian horse stumbled, throwing its rider, Finbarl descended the stairs.

Chapter Fifty-Four

"I must have my trunk!" demanded Andolis.

"No," answered Aminatra, not for the first time. She ripped her veil off, discarding it to the ground.

"Coloss can go back to get it," pressed the king. "I only have the clothes I'm wearing."

Aminatra raised her arm, signalling silence, praying that Libellia slept swaddled to her back. She slunk behind the nearest tree, careful not to knock her child, and surveyed the route ahead. "It's clear."

"And no perfume," added Andolis.

"We can't go back. I hadn't planned on escaping during daylight. It won't be long before they discover Ghano and his goons' bodies." Aminatra smirked, recalling the joyous reunion with Maddy. She had lost none of her speed or ferocity. Or her tenderness. Perhaps she had overdone the hugging of the poor girl. An uncontrollable laugh escaped.

"What's so funny?" challenged Andolis.

"Oh, thinking about the look on those soldiers' faces when we emerged from the tent."

"Yes, that was enjoyable," said the king. "And when Coloss snapped their necks."

"Let's not dwell on that." The smile faded as Aminatra looked down at her new boots, scavenged from a dead soldier. Blisters already formed, but she could run faster and avoid thorns. She scanned their route through the cedar woods. "We've been lucky so far, but they'll suspect we'll head for the river. Our only hope is finding a boat as quickly as possible."

Maddy appeared, her scouting complete. She urged the party on with a wave.

"Where are you taking us, Maddy?" asked Aminatra, quite content not to receive an answer.

With a sniff of the air, Maddy sprinted off again.

"She's taller," said Karlmon, walking hand in hand with Coloss.

"I wish she could tell us about Finbarl," said Aminatra. "It's torture not knowing if he's dead or alive."

"Has she had her tongue cut out?" asked Andolis. "A most interesting creature."

"Maddy never learnt to talk," explained Karlmon. "But one day she will. I'll teach her."

"She would make an excellent bodyguard with Coloss," considered the king. "Yes, a fine slave."

Aminatra grabbed Andolis's ear, yanking upwards. "Now, listen to me. You've lost your kingdom, your army, your slaves. All you've left is your life and friends."

"Oooww!" cried Andolis. "But I've not given you your freedom."

"We've taken that ourselves." Aminatra released his lobe. "Either stay with us as a friend or go on your own. What's it to be?"

The king rubbed at his ear, unimpressed by the choice. "You've never treated me with respect, Athenia."

"My name's Aminatra and my son's is Karlmon."

"But I always liked you," concluded Andolis.

"Well, what's it going to be?"

"I think I prefer Amin ... Aminar ..."

"Aminatra."

"Yes, Aminatra. Much better. And Karlmon. I like that too." With that, the king strolled off, aloof and regal.

"What did he decide?" whispered a confused Karlmon.

"He's staying with his friends," answered Aminatra, brushing her son's fringe with a broad smile.

"Did you hear that, Coloss?" said Karlmon, craning his neck up. "We're free."

The giant nodded with furious delight, hooting to the heavens.

"Not so loud," cautioned Aminatra, a finger to her lips. "Or our freedom won't last long."

***

They reached the edge of the tree line. Fertile, flat farmland stretched to the river, abandoned tools littering the ground. To the south, the countryside hid all except the tips of Parodisian buildings and the city's smoky, industrial breath. A bend in the river shielded them from the main Adonelis army.

Maddy scaled a tree, balancing on the upper branches.

"Not you!" ordered Aminatra, as Karlmon attempted to follow.

"I've never climbed a tree," remarked Andolis.

"What can you see?" called up Aminatra.

Maddy remained still, absorbing all before her. A late-seasoning fruit hung half-eaten on a branch. She picked it, sniffed and swallowed whole. With a glance down, she released one hand, descending with elegant ease.

"Ando's never climbed a tree," Karlmon explained to Maddy as she landed on her feet.

"Never mind that," said Aminatra, with a nervous look. "Where to now?"

The familiar sound of her family's voices pleased the Ferral. She purred, looking content. And then she was off. Crossing the field with her low, running gait.

"Perhaps she's leading us to Finbarl?" suggested Karlmon.

"Hopefully," said Aminatra, "but why didn't he find us? I hope he's okay. Come on. We run this next bit."

"Run?" cried Andolis, aghast, as the others dashed off in pursuit of Maddy. "Wait for me!"

Mud from a ploughed field stuck to their shoes, building until it hindered. All but Maddy slowed to a walking pace.

With a flick of his boots, Karlmon sprayed Coloss with his mud. "Sorry."

A childish grin surfaced on Coloss. He swung his boot, launching a mud counter-attack. Karlmon dodged right, giggling. The wheezing figure of Andolis lacked the energy to evade.

"Argh!" The king examined his tunic in horror. "My one good top. I'll have you ..."

Aminatra turned her glare on all the children. "Enough! We don't have time for games. Ando, you can have one flick of your boot. It's more satisfying than whipping."

Andolis, still fighting his burning lungs, frowned in confusion. Slowly, his brain accepted the advice. With competitive focus, he aimed and kicked out his left boot. A splattering of mud flew off, a drop for everyone.

"Good," declared Aminatra, flicking a blob off her tunic. "Now, on we go. As fast as we can walk and no more silly games."

Karlmon and Coloss followed in her wake, giggling as they peeled the mud from their clothes. Andolis lingered behind, pondering his actions. The confused face morphed to a smile and the smile into laughter. "That was fun," he announced, skipping forward to catch up, eager to be part of the conspiratorial giggling.

They reached the river's edge, Maddy now a hundred yards ahead upstream. Every few minutes she paused, peering behind, then leading off again.

"No boats," observed Aminatra with disappointment.

The river's brown-grey surface stretched about half a mile to the other bank, swinging round in a gentle arc. A tiny, shallow island of deposited silt curtailed the sweeping currents, allowing a large reed bed to occupy the inner bend. The stalks swayed in the wind, at home amid the shallow, calm waters, as a flock of small birds harvested their plumes. Unperturbed by Maddy, the birds burst from the bed as the pursuing fugitives approached.

"Where's she going now?" exclaimed Aminatra, as Maddy fulfilled her check on them and disappeared at a right angle into the reed bed.

"I'm not going in there," said Andolis. "It's wet."

"Water's fun," remarked Karlmon. "I can almost swim. Maddy was teaching me. Can you swim?"

"I've not tried nor had the opportunity. Kings have no need," declared Andolis.

"Maddy can teach us both," said Karlmon. "And you, Coloss."

"Here's the opening," signalled Aminatra, as they arrived where Maddy had vanished. "At least we'll be out of sight of the Adonelisians. Come on." She stepped into the mud, following Maddy's footprints, prising apart the stems. "Don't dawdle, Ando."

With his all-too-familiar scowl, Andolis conceded defeat and followed into the undergrowth.

"It's cold," complained Karlmon as the water levels rose, covering their feet.

"I don't have any other shoes!" moaned Andolis.

"Quiet!" ordered Aminatra in a hushed tone, frozen to the spot, a finger to her ear. "Voices."

The others stood silent, listening against the rustle of the reeds.

"Finbarl?" suggested Karlmon, his face lighting up.

"Let's hope so," whispered Aminatra. "We'll creep closer. Maddy can't be far ahead."

The mud squelched, water splashed, reeds crackled. Each move was a loud announcement of their approach, and yet the mumbled sound of the voices continued undisturbed. As the water reached their waists, the reeds thinned out. The dark frame of a boat appeared. Those voices carried to attentive ears.

"Maddy! Where have you been?"

Aminatra frowned. The voice seemed familiar, but was not Finbarl's.

"Maddy!" A loud booming shout erupted, unmistakable.

"Captain Tarlobus," whispered Aminatra, almost in tears. She turned to Karlmon. "It's Captain Tarlobus."

"And the Medino!" Karlmon conveyed the exciting news to Andolis and Coloss, who received it with bemusement.

"Captain Tarlobus!" yelled Aminatra, ploughing through the water and reeds. "Captain Tarlobus!"

"Aminatra? Is dat my bootiful Aminatra?" The captain stood starboard on his vessel, unchanged under his tricorne hat. Above his beard, eyes glowed in wonder as the ragtag party appeared from the reeds.

Maddy crouched beside him with Gidhaert and Corelye behind, a triumphant smile greeting her family.

Chapter Fifty-Five

D espite the pleasant temperature, Finbarl shivered. He didn't enjoy waiting to fight. Stuck in a queue for the last hour, he had time to think. His destination lay in sight: the huge warship, Fendora. Its broad, flat hull rocked in the harbour's shelter. Men and women scurried up and down its ramp, loading weapons, food and material, those destined to fight waiting on the quay. Six similar ships danced to the same tune, readying themselves for battle.

"You all right?" asked Balfour.

"Better than Fordell," said Finbarl.

"Must have been that egg I had for breakfast." A grey Fordell rubbed vomit from the side of his mouth.

"Sure," said Finbarl, sharing a wink with Balfour. "Just want this over. Don't like not knowing what's happening."

Balfour leaned over the water and spat. "You know what's going on, you clux. The fleet's taking us down river. We'll harass the Adonelisians, then land on the north bank and outflank the Livorians. Give them the surprise of their lives and remove one headache."

"Not that," said Finbarl. "It's just ... Well, I'm not in control. There was a saying back in Athenia, 'never follow the fool into Ferral country'. It meant trust in yourself when your life depends on it. How many soldiers are there? Thousands! How do you manage them? It'll be chaos."

"I'd be more than happy to make it one less," groaned Fordell.

"That's what generals are for," said Balfour, ignoring Fordell. "This ain't no backwater bar brawl. The Terratus are born to lead in battle."

"They seem more interested in who has the most impressive hat," said Finbarl, nodding toward a group of Terratus conversing aboard the Fendora.

"The more splendid the hat, the more honours they've earned. Let's the Adonelisians see who they're up against."

"Gives the Adonelisians a target, more like," retorted Finbarl.

Balfour inspected the pitiful Fordell, now a pale green. "Why did you even join the army? You don't seem the type that makes a sacrifice for others."

An unconvincing smile broke with a belch. "You'd be surprised how much money floats around an army. Impending death has a wonderful habit of encouraging carefree men. Wasn't expecting they'd dump me with some broke servenites or ask me to fight!"

"Yeah, no one expects to fight in the army," laughed Balfour. "You're a pessimistic pair. No one has ships like ours. They give us speed and mobility."

"I hope you're right," said Finbarl.

"Don't worry about whether I'm right. We don't follow fools but the Unumverum, rememb ... Hang on. We're moving. This is it."

With a slow shuffle, the stream of soldiers moved up the gangway. First the archers, then the infantry, and last the cavalry.

A claustrophobic dread hung on Finbarl, the soldiers massed together on the aft deck, shoulder to shoulder. Sweat built beneath his leather jerkin. His sword, strapped to his belt, dug into his leg.

"There's not even room for a quick game of dice," complained Fordell.

The voice of Hebradon called out, bringing order. The formation eased apart and Finbarl could breathe again.

"We'll have a good view from up here," remarked Balfour, standing behind his friend.

"We're exposed," said Finbarl.

"Watch and learn. They know what they're doing."

"Silence," yelled Hebradon. "Absolute silence until we set sail."

As the soldiers fell quiet, the crew's volume increased. They pulled at the rigging, setting the sails aloft. A long line of oars appeared from either side of the hull, splashing as they met the surface.

"Those servenites who didn't volunteer to fight are powering us below," whispered Balfour.

"That's why you joined me," replied Finbarl, his wry smile unseen by his pal.

In the calm, protected waters of the harbour, the Fendora eased forward, smooth and noble. A cheer arose from the shoreline, as small boats buzzed around below.

At last, Finbarl adjusted his sword, scratching with satisfaction. He could also appreciate the vessel. How different it was to Tarlobus's boat. The Medino danced to the whims of the river, a personal relationship of mutual respect. At six times the size, the Fendora dominated the relationship: a victory of humanity over nature. 'Fate's not determined',' muttered Finbarl to himself, pushing down his doubts, dominant since Bartarnous's revelation on the Unumverum. Victory could still be theirs.

Behind, the fleet aligned itself. Parodisian power arranged in a magnificent floating column. Beyond, outside the harbour, the river's protective chain lowered with a grating clang and thud. A rhythmic stroke of the oars began, directing the ships out into the currents of the river. Along the starboard side of each vessel, the archers lined up, their basket of arrows brimming full, ready for deliverance.

As they cleared the harbour wall and crossed the submerged chain, they heard the grinding wheels lifting the latter back into its position, blocking the river. When the far bank hove into view, Finbarl gasped. There, dotted along the shallow hill, down in the valley manning their catapults and stations, lay the full extent of the enemy army. Chatter bubbled up again among the soldiers aboard the Fendora.

"There's a lot of them," gulped Fordell, his sickly pallor returning.

"Those catapults are huge," exclaimed Finbarl. "No wonder they reached the far side of Parodis."

A pulse of activity rippled across the Adonelisian camp at the sight of the emerging navy. Trumpets sounded, mixing with clanging metal and shouts of alarm. Soldiers darted from their tents, adjusting their armour, running with order. In position on the edge of the river, a troop of cavalry circled in readiness, watching the ships, yelling their insults.

"We've stirred the hornets' nest," laughed Balfour, cupping his hands to shout. "What you going to do, you stupid cluxes?"

"That showed them," said an unconvinced Fordell.

As the fleet glided to midstream, the Fendora raised a blue flag. It set the crews running, all raising their mainsails. Whoop! The wind caught the canvases, arching them forward, pushing the armada as one. A clatter of oars signalled their withdrawal.

"Here we go," declared Balfour. "Watch this."

Boards rose before the aligned archers, fashioned with a V cut-out at the top.

"Our protection," explained Balfour. "The archers fire from behind and …"

A boulder whooshed well above, landing with a harmless thump on the bank beyond.

"Ha! We're too close," crowed Balfour. "Their catapults are useless."

"Anyone want to make a bet on where they land?" asked Fordell, receiving a range of slaps and blows for his troubles.

The fleet steered to the far shore, tacking, straightening, then veering closer again. On command, each archer reached to their basket, one arrow extracted, drawn upon the bow and fired towards the bank. Phhht! Phht! Phhht!

Finbarl craned his neck, hoping to see the points of impact. Those Adonelisians working at the riverside scurried away. Some fell, others persisted with their escape, fighting through the pain of a wound. The cavalry troop veered inland, just one among them hit. A few Adonelisian archers fired back, out of range and harmless from their lower position.

"That showed them!" declared Balfour, as the fleet adjusted again, steering to the river's heart. "We'll do that a few times and soften them up."

"Hardly a knockout blow," said Finbarl. "All they have to do is stay clear of the river."

"But they can't." Balfour gripped Finbarl's shoulder and jumped, aiming for a better view. "They're up to something all along the bank."

Fordell, using his superior height, studied the scene. "What are they? Coffins?"

"Some weird Adonelisian ritual," suggested Balfour.

"I don't like it. There's a whiff of danger in the air," remarked Finbarl.

"Stop worrying. Whatever they are, they're too small to threaten us."

The fleet swung across once more; the archers released another sortie of arrows.

Hebradon appeared, a gleeful smile on his face. "Listen to the screams, lads. Metal tips sinking into soft flesh. The agony and panic. I can already smell the fumes of battle, the taste of blood."

His men cheered, pumping themselves up, ready for the fight. Only Finbarl remained unaffected, his experiences from the past too raw to allow emotion to colour his actions.

"We're going round the headland," continued Hebradon. "There we'll disembark, quick and quiet. At double-time, we then march northwards, squeezing those Livorians between ourselves and the city wall. After that, it's simple. Crush them like ants. No mercy shown. If it's not your own blood, I want to see you soaked in that traitorous Livorian gore. They'll pay for their treachery."

Another cheer greeted the commander as the fleet reached the bend. The crew adjusted the sails, turning the boat, angling towards their destination. Then a murmur spread from the bow, drawing attention forwards.

"What's going on?" asked Finbarl, his confusion shared by others. Word ebbed through the unit.

"More coffins are strung crossing the river," said Balfour, still confused. "Hundreds of them."

"Why?"

"No idea," admitted Balfour. "It ain't strong enough to hold us."

With all eyes strained to the bow, Finbarl spared a glance backwards. Among the dead on the shore, Adonelisian soldiers scampered around a hundred other coffin-like objects dotting the banks. It became apparent to Finbarl what was happening. Flaming torches accompanied each box, gripped in the hand of a soldier, an archer by their side. Another held a long pole, guiding the coffins into the currents and watching them drift out towards the fleet. Behind each tiny vessel, a black liquid seeped into the water, spreading and joining into shiny, dark pools.

"It's a trap!" cried Finbarl.

A few heads turned his way, most ignored him.

"Make for land now!" urged Finbarl, pushing towards Hebradon. "We're heading for a trap!"

The fleet maintained its line, continuing at speed, the narrow barrier to its fore.

"Back in line!" ordered Hebradon, as Finbarl reached him.

"We have to get a message to the captain, Sir," pleaded Finbarl. "We must land immediately."

"You're a sailor now, eh, servenite? What is it you know that we don't?"

"They're filling the channel with those boxes behind us too, Sir. Each full of oil!"

"So?" Hebradon flushed an angry red.

"They're going to set the river alight!"

Hebradon's anger turned to amusement. "A burning river, eh? Whatever's next? Molten rain?"

Those in earshot laughed. Then a bang. The ridicule faded, turning to astonishment. A string of explosions dominoed across the river. Flames shot into the air, clinging to congealed fuel, falling into latent pools eager to release their energy, burning with a ferocious intensity. A barrier of fire blocked their path.

Finbarl spun, scanning the rear. Adonelisian archers pushed their arrow tips into the flames of the torches. Taut strings twanged, discharging the fiery bolts through the air towards the strange, calm waters. The first hit, snuffed out in clear water. The next struck a dark pool. A dancing flame rippled out, covering the water. Across the river, the pattern repeated itself: an arrow lost to the depths, a fire ignited. Soon, a burning lake blocked the fleet's route back to the safety of the harbour.

Panic aboard the armada moved faster than the encroaching fire, as the currents tugged them towards destruction. To the fore, the Fendora tacked sharp to port, hoping to avoid the wall of fire. But there was no time. It ploughed through, the hull collecting a blazing film of oil. Men started jumping overboard, hoping to escape their fate aboard a combusting boat, only to find a worse one amid the burning water. Screams filled the air.

"What do we do?" cried Fordell, searching for a place of safety, finding none.

"I don't know," shouted Finbarl, pushing his way to the middle of the vessel.

The captain changed tack again, recognising his ship as doomed, hoping to make it to the nearest land: the south bank.

"He's taking us right into the Adonelisian's hands," yelled Balfour, gripping hold of a rope to keep his balance. "They'll massacre us."

Through the thick black smoke covering the river, Finbarl made out the other ships. One had followed the Fendora through the wall of fire, the flames creeping up its hull. The others faced in opposite directions, so far free of fire but with nowhere to go and trapped. Their fate lay with the small boats leaving shore, ladened with crackling firewood and on course to collide.

Flames licked around the side of Fendora's deck. Sparks leapt, igniting a sail. As they careered on beyond the burning water, others abandoned ship. Finbarl watched, undecided if to join them.

"I've seen odds like this before," whined Fordell. "I'm not staying on here to burn."

"He's right," cried Balfour. "Come on!" He tugged Finbarl's sleeve.

Finbarl hesitated. The shore still looked so far away.

Crack!

A burnt rope split, swinging a canvas down until its weight snapped the mast. It fell, its sail smothering those beneath. Finbarl's world darkened, the canvas engulfing him. Crushed to the deck, he pushed with his arms, trying to fight his way out. The screams and shouts from around added to his own panic. With an effort, he climbed to his feet, carrying the weight of the canvas. A beam had been pulled down in one direction; he navigated in the other. The material lightened; a ray of sun broke through. With a wave of an arm, he was free, stumbling forward into a fellow crewmate still struggling under the sail.

"Sorry," said Finbarl instinctively, helping the man free himself. He worked the canvas off, sliding it over the man's shoulder, up his chin, to his ear until one sunken eye showed. It stared at Finbarl with a bitter hatred. A shiver ran down Finbarl's spine. The itch, long plaguing his memory, was relieved. He yanked the sail one more time, revealing Hebradon. Finbarl also recognised him by another name: the Butcher!

Chapter Fifty-Six

"You've seen Finbarl?" asked Aminatra, switching to her native tongue.

"Yee," confirmed Tarlobus. "Monfs back. E searching for someone. Ffought yar Maddy was dead."

"I'm so relieved," sobbed Aminatra. "I thought they were both dead."

"If e in Parodis den not good," said the captain. "Gidhaert ope it good, bot situation bad."

Such pessimism failed to influence Aminatra. "If Finbarl's survived this long, then he'll get through it."

They stood over the familiar bags Finbarl and Aminatra carried from Athenia. Tarlobus pushed one with a toe. "Yar girl bring dem ere. Sha collects fings."

"It's incredible she sought you out," said Aminatra, crouching to examine the contents. "I thought she hated the boat."

"Tarlobus not believe too. Wen sha turn up, Captain Tarlobus confess to being frightened. E ffought sha corm for revenge."

"Revenge for what?"

"Bortell and Malto," said Tarlobus, spitting in disgust. "Dey steal ya und boy."

"I suppose so," said Aminatra, the memory of her kidnap too fuzzy. "And you let her stay?"

The captain shrugged. "Sha made decision. Captain Tarlobus not argue." He guffawed. "Sha bring food. Maddy now Captain Tarlobus's friend."

"There's an incredible brain in there." Aminatra looked across at the Ferral, consumed by a new fascination: baby Libellia. "She likes her sister. Look how tender she is with her. Hard to believe when you see her fight."

"Ya ave abit of collecting waifs und strays," said Tarlobus, with a nudge of his head towards the king and his bodyguard. "Ya bring Captain Tarlobus more trouble."

"Sorry, but I couldn't leave them."

"Dat boy complain lots," confided the captain. "Und Captain Tarlobus not like being ordered."

"Ha, you've noticed. His Royal Highness has a problem sharing or going without. You have my permission to clip his ear."

On cue, Andolis's voice carried across the deck. "She's sniffing me again! Make her stop. What's wrong with her?"

"Maddy," said Karlmon. "Leave Ando alone."

"It's the perfume," explained Aminatra to the captain. "Despite the mud and sweat, she can still smell his perfume. Anything new intrigues her. Such an enquiring mind – a true Maddy. We named her after Finbarl's mother, you know?"

Tarlobus nodded, half listening. "Und der Adonelisians look for dis annoying boy, deir king?"

"Yes, General Malic won't want him alive or beyond his control. They'll be hunting for him." Aminatra looked to the southern shoreline, enjoying the river breeze on her hair.

The captain cursed in his own tongue. "Andolisians already ruin Captain Tarlobus's trading wit deir war, now dey seek his boot. Dis bad. Very bad."

"I am sorry," repeated Aminatra. "But Maddy led us to you."

"Ya not be sorry. Wen I saw bootiful Aminatra und my boy, Karlmon, Captain Tarlobus cried tears of appiness."

Aminatra took a deep breath. "Will you help us find Finbarl? Take us close to Parodis. We'll go into the city, locate Finbarl and then come and find you again."

"Madness!" exclaimed Tarlobus. "It war zone. If der Adonelisians not sink Medino, den der Parodisians will. Captain Tarlobus not lose boot."

Corelye, the captain's mate, approached, the wind blowing his blonde locks across his face. He acknowledged Aminatra with a nod, brushed his hair back and pointed to the west.

"Somefing bad appening," said the captain, observing the thick black smoke rising in Parodis's direction.

"Cronax!" cursed Aminatra. "Is the city on fire?"

The captain shrugged. "Maybe. Another reason Tarlobus can't take ya to Parodis."

"Then at least take us to the other side of the river," pleaded Aminatra. "We can walk to the city."

"Very dangerous," tutted Tarlobus. "Let Captain Tarlobus take ya away from ere. Yar man can find ya."

"I'm not leaving Finbarl," declared Aminatra. "I thought I'd lost him. Will you help, please?"

With a slow shake of his head, Tarlobus answered. "Too dangerous. Captain Tarlobus sorry, my Aminatra."

Chapter Fifty-Seven

"What are you talking about?" said Hebradon, a smile returned to his lips.

"I recognise you from the night of Favo's murder," said Finbarl, his eyes locked on his commander's. "We bumped into each other. I saw your face. Only for a second, but it's seared into my mind. Took a while to retrieve it, but you're the Butcher."

Hebradon laughed. "You're crazy. I'm from the finest stock in Parodis. The ship's on fire, the fleet destroyed, and you're making wild accusations about a superior officer."

"Fic!" Balfour emerged from under the sail, rubbing his head. "What happened?"

Finbarl and Hebradon remained locked in their intense stare.

"Okay," said Balfour, regaining his senses. "What's forping going on? Weren't we about to save ourselves by jumping overboard?"

"Our commander's the Butcher," explained Finbarl.

Balfour laughed. "Yeah, right."

"I'm serious."

"You're mad," said Hebradon.

"I saw him," said Finbarl. "I know I did."

"Really?" Balfour studied Hebradon's features. "Is that an evil face?"

"Trust me," urged Finbarl. "Think about it. He wallows in violence, regaling the barracks with gruesome descriptions and encouragement."

"True," agreed Balfour, pressing his face closer to their commander's.

"Study those eyes, not the smile," said Finbarl. "Believe me now?"

"Oh, I believe you," said Balfour, a disturbed frown descending on his brow. "Fic! There's no soul behind them. You've been a bad boy, Sir."

"Are you trusting the word of a clux?" Hebradon lost his smile but remained calm.

"The way I see it," began Balfour, "we're going to die anyway at the hands of the Adonelisians. I'm happy to gamble on you being the Butcher and get a little satisfaction paying you back."

"It is him!" growled Finbarl.

"Gentlemen," implored Hebradon. "I can resolve this confusion." The smile returned.

"I'm listening," said Balfour.

"Balf ...!"

Before Finbarl could warn his friend, Hebradon struck. His sword slid from its sheaf and plunged into Balfour's stomach.

"Oh, yes," crooned Hebradon, withdrawing his bloodied blade. "That is living. Smell the blood!"

"You ferralax!" cried Finbarl, drawing his own sword as Balfour collapsed forward. "You sick ferralax!"

"This is glorious," declared Hebradon, weapon at the ready. "We're in the Theatre of Death. Listen to those screams of the dying; look at those floating corpses, your dying friend. We fight on our own funeral pyre. I could not have imagined it better."

"Your funeral pyre, not mine!" Finbarl lunged forward, bringing his sword down at an angle.

Hebradon parried, the clash of metal ringing out across the deck. Few remained to witness the spectacle.

"I confess to laughing when your friend got accused of being the Butcher," said Hebradon, crouched low, ready for the next attack. "How silly people are. Such a petty thing. I saw your show, don't you know? Very good. A fascinating beast, but she didn't have the intellect to be the Butcher."

"Lots of people underestimated Maddy," snarled Finbarl, making a tentative thrust.

"Oh, nice try." Hebradon side-stepped the blade, launching his own attack.

Finbarl arched his back, collapsing one knee. The sword brushed his tunic, drawing no blood. "You're going to picture Maddy, Favo and all your victims as you lie dying."

"I think about them all the time," declared Hebradon. "The images of their faces as my knife pierced their skin. Bliss!"

Their swords clashed, held together in a battle of strength. They pushed against each other, moving closer and closer, noses almost touching.

"My parents berated me for being stupid," hissed Hebradon. "My father beat me if I failed at things."

"Don't care," groaned Finbarl, gritting his teeth.

"But I proved them wrong," continued Hebradon. "They were too stupid to realise that bitter edge to their chee was poison. Left me everything in their will. I always have the last laugh."

"Not today."

"That's why I carry a spare dagger."

Finbarl's world slowed. He spied Hebradon's free hand retrieve the dagger. Instinct urged him to withdraw, but would there be time? The dagger whipped back, ready for the thrust. Finbarl's stomach muscles tightened, expectant of pain.

"What?" Hebradon looked down, distracted and alarmed.

Finbarl's eyes followed. Fordell slid from beneath the collapsed sail, one hand gripping the Butcher's ankle. With a flick of his leg, Hebradon broke free, but it gave Finbarl time. With his spare hand, he shoved Hebradon backwards. Their swords separated and, as space grew between, Finbarl thrust with all his strength. Off balance, Hebradon flapped at the approaching point. The blade drove in through the leather, deep into the flesh.

"Aaarrghh!" The cry was Finbarl's: a battle cry. He watched as realisation painted itself across Hebradon's face. "That's for Maddy!" Finbarl thrust again. "That's for Favo!" The pallor of death already coloured the Butcher's face. One more thrust. "And that's for all the rest!"

"Fire!" Balfour's weak, whispered warning broke Finbarl's bloodlust.

Flames consumed the front deck, reaching up across the sails. Finbarl noticed the intense heat for the first time. He knelt, clasping Balfour's hand. "Let's get you out of here."

"Is it bad?" asked Fordell, now on his feet, glancing around in panic at their perilous state.

Balfour shook his head. "I'm not going anywhere, you clux."

"Don't be silly. I'll carry you," said Finbarl.

"And then swim the half mile into the hands of the Adonelisians? Fic, it hurts!" Balfour's fingers, pressing down on his stomach wound, drowned in the pooling blood.

"It's not that far." But Finbarl understood his point.

"You're not Parodisian," said Balfour. "They may spare your life."

"What about me?" exclaimed Fordell.

"You can talk yourself out of anything."

"I can't leave you here!" cried Finbarl.

"The Butcher's last victim. Fic! I'm dying. I just ... I just don't want to burn."

Finbarl looked away, unable to face his friend.

"Please, Finbarl. It will be an act of mercy, my brother."

"But I'll have to live with it," said Finbarl, seeking an alternative outcome.

"Do it quick," urged Balfour, his eyes watching the flames creep closer.

"You're the only truthful person I've met from Parodis." Finbarl tightened his grip on Balfour's hand. "I'll miss you, my friend."

A faint smile appeared on the dying man. "Lying got me sent to the Flash; honesty led me he ..." Finbarl's sword slit his throat. A gurgle and hiss, then it was over.

"Fic! You killed him!"

"I saved him." Finbarl grabbed Fordell by his collar. "We don't mention this to anyone. Understand?"

Fordell nodded.

"Good. Now let's save ourselves." Finbarl dragged the fallen canvas over Balfour's body and, with a shove of his boot, rolled Hebradon's away. He inspected the encroaching flames once more and made a running leap over the side of the ship. Fordell followed one step behind.

"Cronax!" Finbarl surfaced from the water, sputtering and gasping for air. The shock of the cold caught him unaware. He swung his head in search of Fordell, fighting the currents pushing him down river. A head bobbed up surrounded by flailing arms and an eruption of white water.

"Help!"

"Calm down," urged Finbarl.

"I can't swim!" cried Fordell.

"Cronax! Of course, you can't." Finbarl bobbed stationary for a moment, considering his options, allowing Fordell to continue his battle to remain afloat. Only devastation lay upriver. The fleet still burnt despite the pools of oil exhausting themselves. A wave rode up Finbarl's face, catching him unaware. He swallowed a mouthful of water, setting off a violent coughing fit.

"Help me, you clux!" cursed Fordell, his face barely above water.

"Stop flapping!" growled Finbarl as he swam to his side. "Can't help you if you keep moving." Rotating onto his back, Finbarl clasped his arms around Fordell. "I said, stop moving!"

"I saved your life," spluttered Fordell. "You owe me!"

"What do you think I'm doing," grunted Finbarl, struggling to get into a rhythm.

"You're taking us towards the Adonelisians!"

"North bank's too far way. I don't have the strength to make it. We won't make it to land at all if you keep struggling."

"I don't want to die."

"Shut up then!"

Tiny figures patrolled the river's edge, dragging the exhausted survivors of the fleet out of the water. That was their fate, Finbarl realised.

The currents pushed them further down river, but still Finbarl heard the activity on shore. At last, they approached the bank. He turned on to his front, gripping Fordell by his collar. A man watched him intensely from the bank, a sword gripped in his hand. He looked odd and Finbarl realised a set of scars ran across his cheeks, compounding his sneer.

"Not Parodisian," called out Finbarl.

The man's expression remained unchanged.

A scream pierced the air, coming from Finbarl's right. Along the riverbank, a Parodis soldier knelt, surrounded by four Adonelisians. Above them, a man sat on a horse, his elaborate armour a designation of power. An unintelligible dialogue carried to Finbarl's ears. He squirted out a mouthful of water, completing another stroke towards land. One eye remained on the group. The kneeling prisoner wailed and struggled, but hands held him down. The rider snapped a command, waving his hand. In a blink, they pushed the man forward and cut off his head.

"What's going on?" demanded Fordell, his view restricted to the sky.

"A change of plan," said Finbarl pulling in an arm, rotating in the water, trying to change direction. "We're going to try for the north bank."

"But you said ..."

The watcher from the shore dashed forward, wading towards Finbarl. He grabbed Finbarl's left leg, struggling to keep his grip as Finbarl fought him off with a wild kick. Another Adonelisian waded in, grasping the other leg. Finbarl released Fordell. "Save yourself."

"But I can't swim!"

"Swim or die!" cried Finbarl as the soldiers pulled him to shore, dragging him across a bed of boulders. Too exhausted, Finbarl stopped struggling. Grabbed by his arms, the two soldiers lifted him to his knees, poised for punishment.

The man on the horse geed his steed, trotting the short way to inspect the next victim. He spoke to the men, and they laughed.

"I'm not Parodisian," gasped Finbarl, his drenched body hanging in their arms. "Not Parodisian." A fist punched him in the stomach. He reeled forward, fighting for breath. "Not Parodisian. I'm from Athenia."

A burst of instructions exploded from the rider's mouth. No more blows arrived. He slipped off his saddle, striding over. "Say that again!"

Finbarl lifted his head, confused to hear his native tongue. "I'm from Athenia, not Parodis. We're not enemies."

The man laughed. "Oh, we're enemies. I have a slave called Athenia – I forget her other name. From across the mountains. A dry land of savage people."

A spark reignited in Finbarl's eyes. "Aminatra! You know Aminatra?"

"I do," said General Malic. "She stole something from me. I'm half-minded to torture you, but you've no idea where she is. As it is, displaying your head will be part of her torture."

"Don't lay a hand on her!" yelled Finbarl, struggling with all his strength to break free.

"Silence him!" commanded Malic, confirming his order with a wave of his hand.

A soldier pulled Finbarl's arms behind his back and rested a knee between his shoulder blades, forcing Finbarl's head forward. The other lifted his sword, aligning it to Finbarl's neck.

Finbarl closed his eyes and whispered a prayer.

BANG!

Chapter Fifty-Eight

Aminatra lowered her shaking hand. A whiff of cordite entered her nostrils, stirring her out of a trance. She raised the gun again, her novice trigger finger squeezing hard.

"BANG!" Their last bullet released.

"Finbarl! Finbarl!" She leaned forward, clutching the boat's rail, imploring Finbarl towards them.

"That's Malic," hissed Andolis, spotting the general.

An Adonelisian soldier lay dead on the grass, his skull blown away by Aminatra's lucky shot. Malic staggered back, his arm bleeding from a bone splinter, mouth agape in surprise.

Finbarl, his arms free, rolled to his side, escaping the falling sword. Fingers dug into the sandy soil, tearing out a clump. With a swing of his arm, he hurled it into the face of his would-be executioner. Exhaustion drained the clarity. Was this reality or a dream? He heard the second bang, then his name. Aminatra's face flashed in his mind and instincts took over. Now, he turned to the river, running and diving, conscious of the boat in his line of sight, but with no time to consider it. The sounds of the world became muffled as he entered the water. Angry voices followed from behind; encouraging voices in front urged him on. His lungs burnt, but he held his breath and kicked over and over. At last, he surfaced, splashing but still kicking, gasping for oxygen. The voices appeared familiar.

"Finbarl! Swim, Finbarl! Help him, someone!" Aminatra looked to the crew.

Tarlobus kicked off his boots and dived in.

"Get to that boat!" screamed Malic. "I want that boat and that weapon!" His order set boots splashing through the shallows in pursuit of Finbarl.

Finbarl lay thirty yards from the boat. His muscles burnt and the noise of those behind grew louder. He willed himself on. One arm forward, then the next. A plop sounded in his ear, but he didn't have the energy to turn and notice the arrows descending upon him.

"Hide beneath deck!" cried Aminatra, as the arrows reached the boat. She ignored her own advice, preferring to compel her husband on with encouragement. "You can do it Finbarl!"

Maddy joined her, orders still not part of her lexicon. Around her head she rotated her sling, building up speed, then releasing. An archer slumped to the sand: one less to worry about.

Malic continued to shout on the shore, encouraging more soldiers to his side. "A gold bar for the man who brings me their weapon." A gift from Maddy skimmed his forehead, rattling his helmet. Blood trickled down. "Kill them!"

Splash. Finbarl's stroke deteriorated with his energy levels. His arm flopped into the water. It was so hard to gain traction. The river pulled, tugging him away from the voices. The voices? They didn't make sense to his addled mind. He recognised Aminatra, but that defied logic. Then something rubbed his leg. He tried to kick it away, but the sharp stab of cramp entered his muscle. The leg seized. His arms had nothing left either. He accepted his fate and closed his eyes, sinking beneath the waves.

Chapter Fifty-Nine

Finbarl awoke with a groan. An enormous nose came into focus, big eyes peering back. "Cronax!" Finbarl sprang upright, pushing himself backwards in fear. "Where am I?"

"Finbarl! You're awake." Karlmon appeared to his side.

"Is this a dream?" Finbarl blinked, trying to clear his mind.

"Welcome back. We've missed you. I've missed you."

Finbarl turned his head, confusion and wonder on his face. "Is that you, my darling?"

Falling by his side, Aminatra smothered him in a hug. "We're together again."

"I heard you calling," cried Finbarl, fighting back tears. "I didn't know what to believe any more. The truth has become harder to discern of late." He furrowed his brow. "I remember a boat."

"We're on the boat," declared Karlmon, smothering Finbarl with his own hug.

"And I remember ... I remember giving up." Finbarl's head drooped into Aminatra's lap. "Is this heaven?"

"Don't be foolish," chided Aminatra, stroking his hair.

"I thought the same." A sodden Fordell appeared behind Aminatra, sporting a black eye.

"You learnt to swim!" declared Finbarl, trying not to laugh.

"Not quite," said Aminatra. "Tarlobus saved you both. He risked all to come and rescue you. I couldn't believe it when we saw you on the bank and bumped into your friend. The captain dived in to drag you aboard. He swims like a fish."

"Better dan fish!" boomed the captain, appearing to Karlmon's side, a sling on one arm. "Dey spear Captain Tarlobus like fish, bot still Tarlobus bring ya ome. Even der Terratus!" The captain spared Fordell an accusatory glare, rubbing his knuckles.

"I understand they've met before," said Aminatra with a wink.

"We're on the Medino!" The revelation charged Finbarl's exhausted body. "Thank you, Tarlobus. That's twice you've saved us. Are we safe now?" He tried to climb to his feet but conceded defeat.

"Let's get you fed and better before you try that again," said Aminatra. She looked to the growing group which had come to meet the person they'd risked their lives for. "We're safe, but we're homeless again."

"I'm not homeless," Andolis pushed his way forward. "I have a kingdom."

"This is Andolis," introduced Aminatra. "He's a king, and Karlmon has been teaching him to speak our language."

Finbarl's eyebrows rose. "I've never met a king."

"My full title is Supreme Highness King Andolis, son of Gordian II, grandson of ..."

"E also as dishes to wash!" growled Tarlobus, stopping Andolis in his tracks, threatening the boy with his hand.

"And this is Coloss," said Aminatra. "He has no tongue."

"I see," said Finbarl, recognising the enormous nose from a moment ago. "You gave me a scare there."

Coloss smiled.

"He's from Mandelaton." Aminatra delivered the news with a casual air.

"Mandelaton!" Finbarl straightened, his tired eyes expanding. "Can he take us there?"

"That's where we're heading. We think," said Aminatra. "The captain kindly agreed to this small diversion to save you. But if anyone can get us there, it's Captain Tarlobus."

The captain stroked his beard. "Captain's boot for riufer, not sea. Bot ya right, Captain Tarlobus is der best."

They laughed.

Finbarl's face darkened. He hung his head. "I have bad news."

"Oh?"

"About Maddy. She ..." Words failed Finbarl.

Karlmon stood back, creating a space, waving the Ferral forward.

"Someone else to say 'hello'," said Aminatra, encouraging Maddy forward.

"I ... I ... Oh, Maddy!" sobbed Finbarl. "I watched you die." The Ferral snuggled into his chest, and he squeezed her tight. "I should have known you could cheat death." Finbarl held Maddy by the shoulders, inspecting her through his welling eyes. "How did you find ...? Oh, never mind. You've grown so beautiful."

"What's happening in Parodis?" Gidhaert squeezed his head into a gap, desperate for news of home.

Finbarl shook his head, wiping his nose with a sleeve. "The fleet's destroyed, their allies have turned against them, and buildings are in ruin. I fear it's only a matter of time before the city falls."

"Impossible!" cried Gidhaert. "The Unumverum?"

"I feel betrayed," said Fordell.

"The what?" questioned Aminatra.

Finbarl took a deep breath. "Sorry, Gidhaert. The book foretold Parodis's collapse."

A chuckle escaped Fordell's mouth, a connoisseur of a good lie.

"I don't believe you."

"It imparts the future, not good news. Parodis hadn't prepared itself. It's best to plan and build towards a better future, rather than drift on the currents of fate."

A pale Gidhaert stood dumbfounded.

"The future?" asked Aminatra. "What does that mean?"

"I'll tell you later," said Finbarl, a finger caressing Aminatra's cheek. "What have you been up to? You're thinner, yet still radiant."

Aminatra blushed and laughed. "Cronax! Where to start? There's someone else I want you to meet. Maddy, bring Libellia."

The teenager ducked away, returning with the infant in her arms.

"A baby," exclaimed Finbarl.

"Your daughter," said Aminatra. "Libellia."

Maddy tilted her head, watching the tears trickle down Finbarl's cheeks as he took his daughter, cradling Libellia in his arms.

"She's beautiful. Thank you, Maddy." Finbarl looked at the gathered faces, smiles adorning everyone but Gidhaert. "Are we all going in search of Mandelaton?"

"Captain Tarlobus not making land before sea, so no choice," chortled Tarlobus.

"I am keen to see this land from which Coloss came," added Andolis. "They can help me reclaim my throne."

"Do they have lots of money?" asked Fordell.

"Looks like our family has grown by more than one then," declared Aminatra.

"I guess it does," said Finbarl, a discerning eyebrow raised to question Fordell's inclusion. "What do you make of that Maddy?"

The Ferral's lips parted. "M ... M ... Mmmaaddeee."

The End

ABOUT THE
AUTHOR

A graduate of Reading University and civil servant by trade, Wrey published his first novel, *Liberty Bound,* in 2020. It achieved critical success, winning a Readers' Favorite Award 2021 in the Dystopian category, a finalist placing in the Wishing Shelf Book Awards 2020, a long-listed placing in the Millennium Book Awards 2021 and a semi-final placing in the Indies Today Awards 2021. *Where Liberty Lies* is the long-awaited sequel and second book in the Liberty Trilogy.

In 2021, Wrey published a novella, *Triumphant Where it Dares Defy*, a prisoner of war thriller from the Second World War. His collection of short stories, *The Dividends of Love and other stories*, is also available via Amazon.

As well as writing adult fiction, Wrey has also published a children's book, *Mooge – The Prehistoric Genius,* under the name Nate Wrey. With illustrations by artist Helen Cochrane, Mooge is an hilarious rhyming tale exploring the key inventions and discoveries by early humans. Aimed at 7 to 11 year olds, it also has supporting learning resources on its unique website: www.moogeprehistoricgenius.com.

Wrey lives in Kent, England.

A message from the author:

Thank you for reading *Where Liberty Lies*. I hope you enjoyed. It was good to bring Finbarl and Aminatra back to the page again.

As an Indie Author, I don't have the marketing clout of a traditional publisher behind me or the profile, or hair, of a celebrity, while most bookshops only stock traditional publishing house books. So, it is tougher to get the message out to potential readers. If you want to help, a review is always welcome and easy to do via Amazon or GoodReads. If that is not your cup of tea, a simple recommendation to a friend or family member is always welcome.

To keep informed on my future publications you can subscribe via my website www.nathanielmwrey.com

Many thanks,

Nathaniel

PRAISE FOR LIBERTY BOUND

"Great book, and highly recommended for all fans of dystopia and those looking for something that little bit different to read." Readers' Favorite winner of a bronze medal in Dystopian category 2021.

"Liberty Bound checks all the boxes of an intensely satisfying dystopian thriller!" Indies Today, 5 Star Review.

"A superbly plotted post-apocalyptic novel populated with memorable characters. A FINALIST and highly recommended!' Wishing Shelf Book Awards Finalist 2020

"The sophistication in the setting and the social and political norms of this society qualifies the author's work as one of pure genius." The Book Commentary, 5 Star Review

"Intelligent and compelling, and thought-provoking. Much more than a futuristic fantasy." AuthorsReading.com

"A storyteller who does more than spin a highly entertaining narrative, to cleverly explore human nature as he questions what it really means to be free." Book Viral Reviews 5 Stars

"Liberty Bound is an addictive page-turner that's not afraid to ask weighty questions." International Review of Books - Gold Star Award

Also By Nathaniel M Wrey

Fiction for adults

Liberty Bound (Part one in the Liberty Trilogy)

Triumphant Where it Dares Defy (A novella)

The Dividends of Love and Other Stories

Children's fiction as Nate Wrey

Mooge: The Prehistoric Genius

Printed in Great Britain
by Amazon